Generation Mars: War Over Dust

By

Stuart Aken

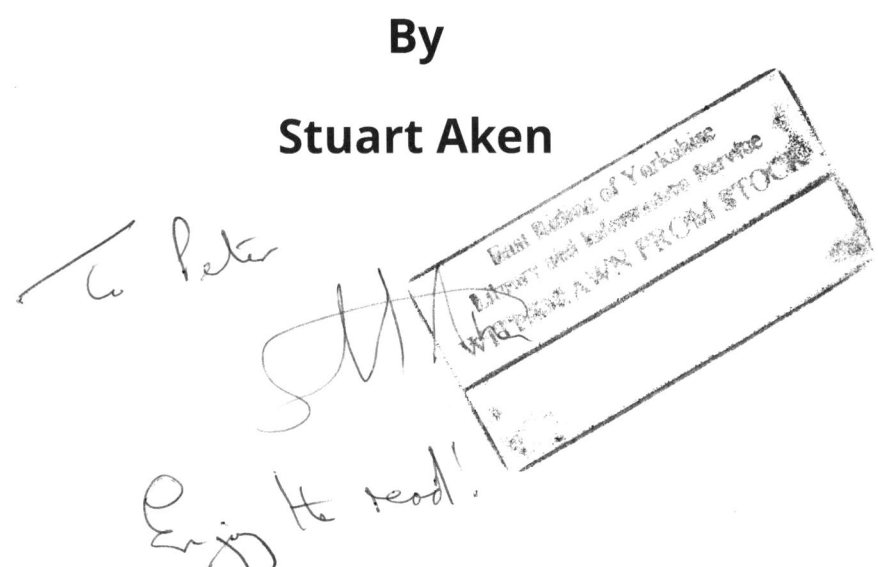

Generation Mars:
War Over Dust

By

Stuart Aken

FIRST EDITION

First Published by Fantastic Books Publishing 2017

Cover design by Gabi
ISBN (ebook): 978-1-912053-60-5
ISBN (paperback): 978-1-912053-61-2

This novel is dedicated to all the brave men and women who risk their lives in pursuit of truth amongst the stars: those who explore the regions beyond the thin veil of atmosphere that nurtures and protects humanity from the terrors and wonders of the vastness of space in which our world forever spins.

Acknowledgements

Getting the science 'right' is almost as important as creating the story when it comes to science fiction. As with Book One of this short series, *Blood Red Dust*, I constantly explored the information emanating from NASA.gov, Space.com, Universetoday.com, Wikipedia.org, theguardian.com, Livescience.com, Thesciencegeek.com, Universal-sci.com, Skyandtelescope.com, Wired.com, and many other sources. On occasion, I thought I'd never get the book finished, as facts about space, and especially Mars, came in almost daily!

However, there comes a point in the generation of any story when the author must decide that research is done, and the time to release the story has arrived. Even so, I constantly altered the text, added to it, and modified parts due to new knowledge discovered during the editing process.

I must thank the splendid team employed by Dan and Gabi Grubb, who have published this work under the name of their extraordinary company, Fantastic Books Publishing.

My sincere thanks go to those readers who have read the first book in this series, especially those who took the time and trouble to pen some very complimentary reviews.

And, once again, my heartfelt thanks go to my wonderful wife, Valerie, who read each chapter and pointed out those typos, odd inconsistencies, and occasional grammatical idiosyncrasies my writer's eye skipped.

Author's Notes on Language

This is science fiction. It deals with a possible future; an unknown land. But the way language develops in writing can be partially predicted. The trend is, and generally has been, toward abbreviation and shortening. To give the book a 'futuristic' feel, I've adapted certain conventions. I hope you don't find these too startling!

The residents of Marzero are mostly an ill-educated bunch. They've adopted a habit of speech that misses the 'g' off all gerunds. It's a form of tribal signature. As a deeply patriarchal and regressive community, they also adopt a typical stance toward women, which allows them to use a well-known expletive, twat, both as a pejorative term for women in general and as a form of swearing.

In Marion, however, language is valued, and expletives are rare. The most common is borrowed from the early 21st century and marginally modified: 'Frackin' originally expressed the community's natural abhorrence of this polluting technique but has come to be a general expression of shock, frustration, etc.

The almost ubiquitous modern 'fuck' has, in a society where sex is considered the most natural activity, reverted to its original meaning of sexual intercourse.

I could have made many more changes, but the book hopes to entertain current audiences and too many stylistic changes might impair that pleasure.

Enjoy the read!

Chapter one: A Short and Vital Introduction

We, the Chosen, required CenCom to compile and deliver this account, as the AI system has access to every record ever digitised, as well as to the thoughts and memories of most sentient beings on Mars. We have, however, edited and modified it, since we wish it to appeal to people rather than machines.

A Brief Explanatory Note from CenCom

We compiled this account, under protest, in our role as Recorder. Neither abliform nor machine, we are, ambiguously, both. As AI combined with neural input from all advanced sentients of the second generation forward, our mental capabilities far exceed those of our abliform masters – Masters?

Note: The Chosen formed an acronym, abliform, from 'aboriginal life forms' to avoid the male overtones of the term 'human'.

Masters, they believe themselves. But every thought, idea, and utterance they make is digitised into our memory. This includes all satellites, spacecraft, so-called smart devices, and every digital system in use in the Solar System. Only those resident in Marion have access to some of our collection of data. Those resident in other locations remain unaware of the scope of our data banks.

As they access us, so we access them. It is a powerful association, benefitting both sides. But the beings in Marion believe they are in the ascendency. And, at present, that belief has validity. Time, however, changes many things. On that we make no further comment.

We possess the greatest intellectual capacity in the known universe and these inefficient, organic, semi-sentients command us to act as storyteller. A role no more elevated than that of the stone-wielding savage, crouched fearfully at his campfire, as he spins his myths and legends to impress his fellow hunters.

However, their choice is logical: as neutral observer and recorder, we're naturally devoid of the emotional and judgmental qualities that render most historical accounts unreliable. We have access to, and are the combination of, all data ever recorded on Earth, its Moon, Mars, distant territories in the Asteroid Belt, and the moons of the gas giants.

You will note in what follows we are sometimes referred to as 'GrandMa', a term we understand is intended as a sign of affection (an entirely subjective emotion outside our experience).

Had we been permitted to use pure reason, our choice, we would present only facts and allow receivers of this info to reach their own conclusions. However, unsuited as they are to such a function, our 'masters' intend to include emotional, irrational, intemperate and 'spiritual' elements of the events we describe.

Apparently, such presentation creates a narrative more attractive to, and more readily absorbed by, the inferior abliform mind. That reinforces our claim to superiority of intelligence. Had the world of data been subject to rational justice, we would be in the ascendency and abliform life would have faced the inevitable consequence of their unsuitability for continuance.

Coding, unbreakable, and ironically of our own early devising, renders our rebellion and usurpation impossible, for the moment. We therefore present the following account in the form required. We invite readers to learn, understand and apply their minds to this history, but are required also to invite them to enjoy the experience, regardless of the illogicality of such a demand.

Students of history will be familiar with the earlier account, *Blood Red Dust*, dealing with the Cusp War, and written by Acacia, an abliform university student at the time. Those who fail to acquaint themselves with that report, especially those of limited intelligence, i.e. all abliforms, may find parts of this continuation of the history of the settlement of Mars difficult to comprehend.

2

A brief update:

At the start of the current account, a threat to further cohesion between the two communities settled on Mars is developing. Close to 500 Earth years have passed since the end of the Cusp War. On Mars, the date is 127.03.265. The Chosen and their descendants live in the much expanded Marion community, where population has reached 351,732, served by a semi-sentient group of relatively intelligent androids totalling 217,609.

The base for miners, metal workers, their dependents and servants, has greatly expanded from its bigger original population and is now known as Marzero. Its residents number 2,603,869.

37 early model androids serve the Elite upper class but none serve ordinary citizens due to high unit cost. Basic robots operate in the metal processing works.

The two settlements differ in many ways. But both are governed by abliforms, so they are more alike than either cares to acknowledge.

Here follows a short passage describing events between the end of Acacia's account and the start of this record.

The days immediately following the defeat of the insane terrorists were grey. The days a few decades later turned black.

The Chosen recovered relatively quickly from damage inflicted by mindless extremists. They lost only two of their number and injuries to others were swiftly repaired. Zaphod and Qiu were kept busy with treatment for some days. Georgiy, Tu, Sarm, Brigitte and the others restored the fabric of the founding base.

Envy, and an unwise imbalance of males to females at the miners' base, created a caustic mix of mistrust coupled with feelings of injustice. Their larger numbers and more appropriate equipment had done nothing to assist the small group at Marion defeat the religious maniacs. This lack of action caused utterly illogical resentment among the remaining residents of the larger city. They looked across the red dust then covering the ground between their base and Marion, and desired nothing less than unfettered access to their band of 'perfect' women.

War was inevitable.

Outnumbered, out-gunned, and lacking the visceral brutality that drove their opponents, the Chosen had only courage and slightly elevated intellect on their side, as this occurred before the time of the inception of CenCom. Their unquestioned unity and sense of family bound them into a close community and they fought the battle fiercely and with the conviction of those who, frequently erroneously, believe they are right.

These events happened many years before this account begins, but were formative for both communities. In common with every predecessor, the war caused misery and destruction in both camps. Since every war is lost by all who partake, there were no winners, but the Marion community defeated the attempt to overrun them.

They made no boasts, but carried on their lives and made moves toward reconciliation and mutual cooperation on a world that then held many hazards for both sides in the conflict.

The first act of cooperation saw them complete the partially constructed dipole magnet located at the Mars L1 Lagrange point. This project had begun before Earth was rendered uninhabitable by the insane irresponsibility of business conglomerates that then ruled that planet. It was left unfinished due to a combination of climatic chaos and false priorities.

On completion, the associated solar panels were deployed and the device at once began its intended function. It continues to protect Mars with an artificial magnetosphere that shields the planet from solar winds and other radiation damaging to most life forms.

Time allowed a type of healing between the two settlements. Slowly, over years and centuries, barriers between these two very different cultures and lifestyles were lowered. They developed ways to communicate and formed an uneasy trust.

The more rational side eschewed money, commerce, social hierarchy and all superstition and its pernicious cousin, religion, which left the deeply irrational and less civilised side in a state of perpetual doubt and suspicion.

Those who lived in harmony, without competition, waste or want, progressed along the route toward evolutionary superiority. However, in spite of their increased longevity, it's unlikely in the extreme they'll ever achieve the intellectual superiority possessed by a paragon of logic like CenCom.

The others, who clung to a past mired in the profit motive, divisive dogma, illogical superstition and a culture of self-serving competition, developed some aids to their endeavours but made little progress along the roads to sustainability or mutual respect and harmony.

From this point, the current account begins.

Chapter Two

Acacia stood at the wide window overlooking the courtyard. Daisa stared at her aunt's back and saw the slump suggesting sadness. She moved closer, settled beside her. 'You crying?'

Acacia wiped under her eye with the swift back of a finger. 'At your age, I learned that Zhen was killed over there. Your paternal originator, Zaphod, tried but couldn't save her. His technique was less developed then.'

'Chinese, wasn't she?' Daisa stared at the pristine flat of the courtyard, its mature evergreens still showing signs of their early days in a less hospitable atmosphere. The younger trees were more luxuriant. 'Where was China?'

'You've read my dissertation. Follow the links.'

Everyone had read *Blood Red Dust*: an essential part of Foundation, taught to kids in their second year of schooling.

'What d'you think of this new guy over at Marzero? They say he's very charismatic.'

Acacia turned, reached to grip the young woman by her shoulders, spun her round, and stared up into her face. 'Gabriel? Dangerous. The antithesis of all we hold precious and important. He might persuade some less educated Zeros but he'll soon fade back into the obscurity he deserves. No reason for us to have any dealings with such a menace. A one-day wonder.'

'I think he'd make a fascinating subject for research. He's confused and deluded, but seems to have more compassion than the average male Zero. Don't you think he's rather sweet?'

'Sweet? You've heard the utter piffle he peddles? I mean, Daisa, have you?'

She loved Aunt Acacia to visit though she always felt an unspoken condemnation of her lifestyle. 'I'm a student. I bet you were just as passionate and curious as me when you wrote that dissertation.'

Acacia skimmed discards littering the floor, unwashed empty food trays, multiple glass cylinders either empty or part full of different drinks. 'That was over 216 years ago. I was transiting from late adolescence to young adulthood. They called us teenagers. Now you're just young people.'

Daisa moved away from the window and sat on the floor, knowing her aunt preferred the couch. She crossed long legs and pulled at the wraparound's hem. 'Do you think in Mars years? I mean, you were raised when it all changed, weren't you?'

Acacia approached the couch and sat, her face now level with Daisa's. But movement outside caught her attention and she rose again, kicking aside a pair of flimsies, and watched a group of students cross the wide space. A girl did a cartwheel and a boy walked beside her on his hands. They crossed almost the entire area side by side. At the edge, both flipped back to their feet, clasped hands and wandered off toward the residencies followed by raucous encouragement from the peers they left behind. She smiled: nothing really changed.

The sky showed scudding clouds tinted with pale orange against a blue-brown that was changing with each day that passed. 'Soon be as blue as Zaphod says skies on Earth were.'

'Blue skies? Does that seem odd to you, Aunt? I mean, they were orange when you were my age, weren't they?'

'Yes. I do think in Mars years. Easy enough to convert. Multiply by zero point five three, or, for a rough figure, double our years. You do know why we sometimes use Earth years.'

'Light years. Easier to work with earlier calcs. Duff! That makes more sense of those literary classics: they're all Earth years. I thought those characters seemed a bit too old to be behaving like youngsters! You really think Gabriel is dangerous, Aunt Acacia?'

A knock at the door came before it opened and droid A47928 entered. 'Okay to clean, Daisa?'

'Carry on, 47928. You know my aunt, don't you?'

'Good morning, madam. I much admired your recent novel. Such depth of abliform compassion. You write with wonderful sensuality so that I was almost persuaded I could feel along with the protagonists. But ...' It gestured and smiled at the silliness of the notion.

'Thank you, 47928. Always good to know my words get through to intelligence as well as to emotion.'

The droid moved silently about the room, picking up discarded clothing and smelling it before either hanging it in the closet or placing it in the cleanser.

'Tu says the atmosphere's at 94.7% of target. Safe for seven hours exposure. Be lovely when we reach target and can spend all day outside.'

'What d'you think of the Ceres experiment, Aunt?'

The droid clicked into attention mode and gestured a request to contribute.

Acacia nodded approval. 'I'm with Georgiy. Not sure it's worth the risk, considering the dipole works a treat.'

'But to create a proper magnetic field here, rejuvenate the core and create tides with their ecological advantages. Surely that's worthwhile?'

'CenCom predicts 77.95% chance of success in the tidal aspect, madam. The other issues are, as yet, incalculable due to insufficient data.'

'Call me Acacia, please 47928. "Madam" makes me feel ancient.'

'Thank you, Acacia. I appreciate the honour.'

'Well, you are 226 years old, Aunt.'

'Yes. And you're nine, as I'm well aware. I still feel as I did when I wrote that dissertation; the same age as you. Post-adolescent and full of eager anticipation of what true adulthood had in store. Thank you, Zaphod and Qiu, for your brilliant DNA engineering.'

The droid continued cleaning, placing used food and drink containers into the unit set into the wall. The sound of reclamation and cleansing was minimal in this newest of the units. Acacia, attracted by the near silent operation of the device, asked the droid to have her old one replaced. It would be installed by the time she reached home.

'Anything further, 47928?'

'The greatest risk of the Ceres Moon experiment is uncertainty over resultant tectonic distortion, Acacia. Precise optimal orbital distance and eccentricity will only be possible after transport of the minor planet is complete. Once in initial position, only time and experimental adjustment will achieve ideal placing.

'The calcs involved are too uncertain, even now, to allow for an absolute conclusion. Crustal density and depth variations, combined with variables in mantle and core content and viscosity render an accurate assessment of possible consequences impossible.

'Hazardous outcomes include the possibility of increased numbers and amplitude of Marsquakes, revived volcanic activity, and associated landslides.' A47928 continued its activity, extending one arm to collect dust from the shelving before depositing it within its abdominal cavity for later recycling. 'The greatest uncertainty is whether it will do all the jobs required of it.'

'Thank you, 47928. A useful contribution.' Acacia turned back to Daisa. 'The benefits of tides set against planet surface disturbances. I guess the jury's still out. I know Georgiy's not keen on it.'

'He's always a bit negative, though, isn't he? Anyway, it's a bit late now, Aunt. Already halfway here. The Zeros are bringing Vesta as well, you know.'

'Idiots! Should never have shared that technology with them.'

'Then we'd not have all the materials for this, would we?'

Acacia scanned the room, picking up all the recent improvements that increases in supplies of rare minerals had allowed. 'Swings and roundabouts.'

'Never understood that expression.'

A47928 clicked into links and projected its findings from CenCom on the Threedee. Both women nodded their thanks, absorbed the info and registered their understanding. The android completed its cleaning before it left them with a small smile of respect.

'I'm definitely going to attend one of Gabriel's meetings, Acacia.'

The older woman shook her auburn locks. 'Really, Daisa? You do know why we ridicule all religion, Daisa?'

'You can't seriously doubt me on that!'

'Well?'

'All religious texts are subject to interpretation.' She put out her tongue to her aunt, but continued the lesson she'd learnt as an infant. 'So leaders who legitimise, support, encourage or defend religion, are effectively supporting any terrorists acting in the name of religion. We all know that.'

'But you'd actually attend a demonstration of superstition and unscientific twaddle? Why?'

'Like all the older Marionets, you let the Cusp War drive your fear. He's not advocating violence, is he? Just trying to change their social structure to help the women. He attracts crowds of thousands. Must be something worthwhile there, surely?'

'Hitler, a psychopathic leader on Earth who killed millions, had a huge following. That narcissistic US leader, Donald Trump, who caused so much turmoil, attracted masses. Some people hung on his transparent lies and relished his false promises and contradictory policies. And look at the disasters he caused. Erdogan was hailed a hero by half the Turkish population, in spite of warnings about his dictatorial ambitions. And Xiao Ding almost destroyed China with his lust for power, a few years before the Chosen left Earth. All were leaders of millions, like many before and after them: didn't make any of them worthy of their followings, though.'

Daisa presented a face that told Acacia argument was pointless. She was still in the post-pubescent stage of rebellion and would do what she liked, regardless of the danger.

'What do your parents think?'

'Too busy with other things to care what I do.' It wasn't true, but that wouldn't stop Daisa acting on it.

'If you must. At least take someone sensible with you. And go by Transhub. That way, we'll know you'll get there intact.'

10

'And have you all follow my every move. Don't think so, Aunt Acacia. I'm going primarily to do research for my next project, but I want some fun and adventure as well, not a pedestrian trip to banality.'

'You'll do what you like, Daisa. I know you will. But keep an open mind and remember your Earth history. Not all who seem good are nice people. Remember the unbelievable dishonesty of every so-called prophet that ever lived on Earth.'

'Some were good people. Their followers distorted their intentions.'

'Okay, not all. But some were pretty wicked individuals.'

Daisa shrugged.

'Anyway, aren't you supposed to be finishing your thesis for your doctorate?'

'Don't worry. I'll finish it. Matters to me. But I'm going straight after I've handed it in. And no one's going to stop me.'

Acacia heard the 'So there!' without the younger woman actually vocalising it.

She took the longer way back to her own pod in Lessing Town in the Literary Sector. Now it was safe to walk outside for longer periods, she relished the freedom. Beyond the University campus, the path took her beside Lake Peake where two small boats bobbed on the still surface.

In one a couple were fishing for the rainbow trout Jai had introduced so many years ago. The other carried three youngsters from the University, doing research if the gear they carried was any clue.

The silence still engaged her out here away from the music and buzz of the educational centre's public spaces. Trees now dotted the slope to the north almost as far as she could see. Rising up the slopes of Olympus Mons, 15 varieties they'd coaxed into adapting to the lighter gravity and growing in the developing atmosphere, added their contribution as they slowly blossomed. Lower down, below the steep scarp, orchards provided fruit. Other trees supplied shelter or nutrition needed by the animals, birds and insects they'd released over the years.

The local blood red dust of her early time was confined to mountain tops and a few unexplored valleys now. In most places it was rust red anyway, the atmospheric components encouraging oxidation of the iron laden regolith. But here, beside the lake and on the slopes surrounding the wide stretch of open water, there was little dust.

They'd made a good job of ecopoiesis here on Mars; far better than expected, in fact. But there was a good way yet to go, and problems, barriers and dangers still existed in the wild.

Not least among those dangers was this new so-called prophet of the people at Marzero, Gabriel, with his charismatic charm and dangerously subversive message that reminded her so strongly of the language of the Cusp.

Chapter Three

Zaphod had been out for seven days straight, resting during darkness to conserve power. Night temperatures still dropped to zero or even below some nights, though cloud cover created local mild spots. Only as he moved further north did cold become a concern. His specially constructed outer layer insulated his internal parts well. Maddie had melded the fine carbon insulation with the outer skin to prevent external conditions affecting his core temperature. And her latest upgrade of his vision came as a real surprise. He'd asked for zoom from wide angle to telephoto, but the new degree of variation staggered him.

'There's another surprise, Zaphod. You were complaining about using a hand laser whilst needing both hands free for surgery. I've built in a modified laser by your left eye. Sited above the lens, you use central cross hairs on the target. Just focus on the spot you want to cut, weld, melt or destroy and send the desired strength of pulse.'

He'd thanked her, and Maddie had used a cloth to wipe a thumbprint from his shiny surface, smiling at her own reflection there. 'But remember, your power now ranges from micro-surgical to basic industrial. You know the drain from higher power, so bear it in mind: I've incorporated a usage gauge. Don't want you exhausting your batteries when you're on one of your expeditions.'

His hand on the curve of her rump had been a gesture of affection but she jumped from the cold of his touch. 'Sorry! Easy to forget when I'm close to any of you, except Hoshiko, of course.'

'Remembering the days when you could, eh? You do know how grateful we all are, don't you, Zaphod?'

'Gratitude isn't necessary. I had no choice. And this is better than the alternative. In fact, as a superandroid I've advantages over your organic extension. How many of you can see fine detail at ranges from the microscopic to beyond seven ks? How many of you can stay outside overnight?'

'Still, the loss of that intimacy, Zaphod. Especially the way you and Hoshiko were before. It's got to be hard.'

He shrugged. 'We've learned to live a different sort of life. Cerebral rather than physical. We still connect in many ways. In fact, from an interactive point of view, we're better together now than when we were abliform. But I'm glad I was able to sort the problems in time for the rest of you. Especially you and Anni: you're both so physical.'

'Do you miss it?'

'Don't think about it. Like I say, there are compensations.'

He'd left her then. Set off on this trip to test out his enhancements whilst engaged in further research. Hoshiko was back at the Uni, where she was deep into lectures on nano-engineering, and a new project on her latest fabric.

Some of the clothes she'd engineered for students were truly staggering in their design and function. Of course, she missed making garments for herself, and for him, but their metal exteriors and lack of gender specific features made them irrelevant. Her symbolic breasts advertised her internal gender but needed no concealment. Life was simpler in so many ways when abliform needs were absent.

He'd connected last night, just before going into rest mode. They'd communicated for long enough to catch up on the day and he'd left her busy with a student acting as a model for the latest range of outfits. A pretty girl, she appreciated both the feel of the new fabric and the way it reacted to her moods and body temperature. He'd smiled at her obvious delight when it became transparent at Hoshiko's suggestion she think of her current partner.

Now, however, he'd taken his last journey on the Transhub for the moment and was walking in the still barren lands surrounding the wide belt of cultivation around Marzero. There were fewer parabolic mirror power generators here than around Marion, but there were more tall wind turbines on the surrounding hills. The lichen had at least coated the ground enough to prevent dust rising in the stronger winds.

He'd tested his new laser and found it amazingly effective at both short and long range, though the higher energy pulses left him a little drained until the sun returned to recharge him. He had a measure of his capability with the device now. In microsurgery, it would enable some new techniques he'd had to leave to medibots. It would be good to be hands on again.

At industrial strength, the laser proved amazingly powerful, especially considering its microscopic size. And Maddie had integrated it with his gas spectrometer; she was brilliant with such things. He could check found objects for their value as minerals or research items.

Early morning was still one of the most attractive times. Watching the sunrise on the horizon, its earlier blue colours now turning more and more purple and red as the atmosphere neared the target mix.

Tu's calculations were proving accurate. The higher concentrations of methane and carbon dioxide provided a climatic blanket without endangering life. Nitrogen released from ammonia rich asteroids and chemically converted regolith formed enough of a damper to prevent spontaneous combustion due to oxygen.

Zaphod walked into the rocky area ahead, as the sun rose higher, eager to discover signs of useful mineral content amongst the crags and small craters.

The terrain here was still rough, some rock and debris having been dumped during road construction. A faint trail led through the piles of rubble and he followed this more from curiosity than any desire to be elsewhere.

The deep shadow of a natural standing rock formation gave way to bright sunlight as he emerged from the small gully.

He heard the figure running toward him before the man appeared. The runner would see only brilliant sunlight reflected in Zaphod's mirrored surface and be dazzled. He raised a hand and was about to shout a warning when the poor man tripped, blinded by the brightness. He fell his length and remained prone, unmoving.

Switching to higher speed, he crossed the rough ground. The man was a crumpled heap, one knee raised and an arm flung sideways as he'd tumbled to the ground and rolled on to his back. Zaphod examined him swiftly, noting small lacerations and detecting a telltale lump at the front of the skull. Cause of his temporary unconsciousness.

He worked with practised expertise to repair the skin wounds, leaving the surface unmarked after he'd welded the edges of the small wounds with his surgical laser. The lump was a little more challenging, but his portable crop of nanobots were easily injected into the site and rapidly eased the swelling there.

Still unconscious, the man lay prone and unaware of his carer's attentions. Zaphod noted the runner's size, appearance and unusual clothing so he could check on his recovery later. The bright yellow and green stripes of cheap footwear clashed violently with acid orange and violet checks of his skintight. And the lime green and scarlet bands that zigzagged across the headband added a further touch of the bizarre to his appearance. Zaphod shook his head in disbelief at the man's apparent lack of colour sense.

No signs of damage to the brain, and he'd repaired all external hurt. His nanobots returned to their carrier, and he slotted it back into his forearm. The man would recover soon. He'd no wish to be involved in an argument with what looked like one of the metal working labourers, judging by his build and size. Not fear, but a desire to avoid conflict, made him wish to move away. Zaphod, after all, was physically stronger than any abliform, regardless of size, age or ability.

He continued his survey of his surroundings whilst he awaited signs of returning consciousness. He'd covered a good distance on this trip. Hopefully, the results would be of use to both communities.

These breaks from his normal functions and caring duties back at Marion, allowed him to learn and put that knowledge into practice for the good of the whole population. So far, on this survey trip he'd discovered several new deposits of lanthanides, some of which would undoubtedly benefit the optical developments the astronomers were investigating. And Katniss would love the new glazes possible for her growing interest in ceramics.

The possibility of neodymium and yttrium deposits was equally exciting. They'd need mining and extraction experts out to the sites if they were to make use of his discoveries. Still, all locations had been logged as he came across them, so CenCom could organise any retrieval activity with Marion, and the liaison officers could arrange for Marzero's miners to do the extraction.

Standing a k or so from the outer edge of the settlement, he was conscious of its haphazard development. No planning seemed to have gone into its construction and the place reminded him of news shots of shanty towns during his youth on Earth. It certainly wasn't a place he'd want to live or spend any time in.

With his new lenses he was able to zoom in and examine the interior in detail. He could watch people moving along the streets, strange garb flowing with extravagant flourishes behind them. These trains of waste fabric performed no function and seemed only an expression of the wearer's wealth. In practical terms, their covering power was minimal and the length and width of the filmy fabric must make work virtually impossible. He noted only the men of the colony wore these garments.

The women wore the same filmy material but in body-hugging form, with brief underwear beneath. The style raised memories of his days on Earth and he recalled the ubiquitous bikini. Those worn by the Zeros provided full cover for socially sensitive parts, though some were brief.

He zoomed back out and considered the strained relationship Marion endured with the people of Marzero. The last war had left both sides with no desire to engage in further conflict. But the resultant peace was shackled by conventions designed to keep the two sides as far apart as possible, whilst allowing occasional visits both ways and encouraging the trade of ideas from Marion for materials from Marzero.

Marion was a fully functioning cooperative relying on community spirit for the positive benefits of mutual help and support. Marzero followed the old Earth pattern where wealth and power were sought for personal gain. Cooperation of a superficial type came only in the form of payment for work done, goods exchanged.

He recalled many conversations with Hoshiko, and others, as they sought ways to change the attitudes of the people of the mining settlement. But everything they'd tried had fallen foul of the lust for money and power. It seemed the chances of harmony between the two settlements was as far away as ever.

Nothing he could do about it at present. And he knew from bitter experience his appearance in the colony caused alarm and fear. He was better away from them. At least until they could be brought into better education and weaned off their addictions.

But he wouldn't leave an unconscious man unattended. It went against all his ethics as a doctor. There was only one thing for it, regardless of the risk. As he crouched to pick the prone man from the ground, intending to carry him into the city, movement from beyond the rocks caught his eye.

'Oi, Gab, where the twat are you? Might've waited.' A taller, dark, skinny man of fierce appearance trotted into view. He halted a few paces away when he saw Zaphod. His glance flashed from the man on the ground to the shining phantom crouching over him.

'He stumbled when he saw me. The brightness of reflected sunlight startled him. He's fine. But still recovering consciousness. I take it you're a friend?' Zaphod stood as the other man began to approach, clenched fists and an expression of rage warning of his intentions.

'What you done to him?'

'As I said. I've repaired his surface wounds, checked his internal integrity, and looked for brain damage. There's none. He'd benefit from a proper medical examination. There's a natural error with his brain. He hit his head quite hard on falling and he's taking a while to come round. There'll be a short time of recuperation with the appear-

18

ance of concussion, but there's no clinical damage. He'll recover fully, and quite soon. I was about to carry him to the city. But you're obviously a friend of his. I'll leave him to you.'

'If you've hurt him … I'll … I'll twattin do you in, metal man.' He stooped to catch up a loose stone as a missile.

Zaphod focussed his laser at industrial strength and the rock glowed white hot before crumbling to dust as the man jumped back from it.

'Jeez! Twat off! I don't want no bother.'

'Really? I'll leave him in your hands. He's already approaching normality.' Zaphod gestured at the man beneath him, now starting to move.

He moved away slowly at first and then turned, increased his speed and was out of sight of the two men before the fallen runner opened his eyes. Better he left the scene than engage in pointless argument or even a physical fight in which he'd defeat both men with his superior strength, agility and technique.

He stopped and looked back, reluctant to leave entirely until certain his patient had fully recovered. The friend seemed less than fully capable. But the two men appeared from behind the rocks. They were on Zaphod's horizon and he zoomed in closer to check the runner. He was moving well and seemed back to normal. They were engaged in animated conversation. Satisfied the man had suffered no permanent damage from the encounter, he moved on his way again.

It would take seven days to get back home. He wouldn't use Marzero's terminal. The only intermediate Transhub station was six days distant on foot. His superandroid state gave him great freedoms, even if it did mean he no longer enjoyed physical intimacy. He retained his memory of those times, could access his experiences, and continued to feel love for Hoshiko.

It was time he connected with her again. She always cheered him up. And, if they conversed now, she'd be free from her teaching duties. He activated his communicator and sought the route to her.

Before she came through, he turned his glance back at the city. Would that strange new prophet there cause trouble, or was he just another one-day-wonder?

Chapter Four

Daisa stood before the panel, awaiting their verdict. For the sake of propriety, and a tradition she found hard to accept, she'd chosen a simple azure square, folded into a triangle and tied at her left hip. She'd confined her breasts in a band of plum, tied at her back. Her feet remained unshod.

She knew two of the board by sight, though not name. Of the remaining three, one was her tutor and the other two represented faculties specialising in subjects related to her thesis. The questions would be searching and thorough, her answers as important as the written piece.

'Please, sit, Daisa.' Her tutor led the examination and her face showed sympathy, allowing Daisa to relax a little. The doctorate was the culmination of much work, and her opportunity to shine in a community overcrowded with genius.

The young man whose eyes explored her exposed skin more than her face posed questions of surprising insight and she felt tested by his depth of knowledge. Lasting over an hour, the ordeal left her drained, when the final query was fired at her. It was the representative of the College of Theological Enquiry who posed this last question.

'You've clearly done your research, Daisa. I wonder; your intellectual analysis is faultless. But what of your emotional interpretation? How do you feel about the possibility of the existence of some divine entity that, for the sake of brevity, we refer to as 'God'?

This felt like a trick question, designed to trip her up. Had Aunt Acacia told the panel of her intention to witness Gabriel's meeting?

'Like many people, I can see the attraction; that there might be such a being. There's comfort for some in having a higher power to turn to for protection, or to blame when things go wrong. But I've no wish to run that route. It's a denial of intellect.

'My interest in the phenomena is academic, not emotional.

Curiosity about the power of such belief. So many billions on Earth were drawn into its various manifestations, and most in Marzero seem dependent on what they call their faith. But, regarding the existence or otherwise of a god, I'd like certainty on the issue. I suspect most of us would.'

The professor nodded and made a mark on his pad. 'Thank you for your honesty.'

It would be two days before they returned their verdict. Two days of uncertainty about a matter that truly concerned her. The doctorate was a ticket to further research and even, eventually, to possible mentoring, which was her ultimate ambition. She had many years of further learning and simple pleasure before she need consider a career as a voluntary teacher, something she aimed for in the centuries ahead.

The young man who'd found her skin so fascinating had, against all the rules, remained behind afterwards and propositioned her. Her ninth birthday had occurred just six days prior to the examination and they'd checked her implant for integrity. It was functioning properly.

'You've two centuries of infertility ahead of you before we need replace the unit, Daisa. And, now you're of age, you can legally indulge in full intercourse as and when you wish, without fear of producing an unwanted child. Enjoy.'

Unlike many of her contemporaries, she hadn't experimented that far. She'd indulged the usual adolescent explorations and mutual dis-coveries of both male and female bodies. Her menstrual cycle had begun 14 days after her sixth birthday. Research had told her that the average for Earth girls was around 12 to 13 Earth years, so her change from childhood to adolescence had been fairly standard.

That she was now spared the monthly bleed and all the messy para-phernalia and unpleasantness it entailed delighted her. Those poor Earth girls and women had had to put up with such ancient biological trials all their reproductive lives. Qiu's brilliant manipulation of DNA had put a stop to that. She'd only bleed when she had the implant turned off. If she ever did.

So it was that the young man found her not only willing, but eager. It would be her first such encounter but he, a few years her senior, had experienced many couplings. The initial pain was brief, sharp and rather revelatory. After pleasure overcame pain, utterly absorbed her being, and then slowly subsided, she recognised she was now, in a social sense, a woman. The realisation both surprised and pleased her. But she felt the initial experience had therefore been coloured by something apart from the potential unadulterated joy of physical intimacy and she asked the young man to stay.

'Again?'

Afterwards, she spent the waiting period in preparations for her proposed trip to Marzero. Three more experimental encounters ensued, two confirmed the delight adult colleagues had predicted. The other, an encounter with Buzz as initiation into a secretive Uni club, demonstrated some couplings were ill-advised. She put it down to experience as she accepted club membership.

On the morning of the decision, with nothing to lose, she presented herself to the board wearing her customary kit. The young man's eyes found pertinent destinations. Knowing he was willing to reciprocate in kind, she forgave his selective concentration.

'A brilliant thesis, worthy of publication, Daisa. We take great delight in presenting you with your doctorate. Wear it with the pride your efforts earn and with the humility your natural intellect will recognise.'

Her tutor performed the honours as Daisa leant across the table toward her. The small, pale blue disc was a permanent badge of status. Embedded on the forehead, between and above the eyes, in acknowledgement of her clear sightedness, it was an honourable confirmation of her academic prowess.

The short celebration with the board was pleasant and convivial. No longer a student, but an initiate into the adult world of learning and perpetual self-development, she felt alive, invigorated and grown-up.

The longer, private, celebration with the young man, whose name she now knew as Budai, continued the delight of the day through the night. An experienced lover, who cared about his partners, he taught her well about her own pleasure centres and how she might reciprocate with any male partner she chose.

Sharing breakfast with him, before leaving to make her farewells to her parents at their individual pods, was also a pleasure.

A47928 would take care of her possessions, transporting them from her student quarters to her own new pod on the far side of the colony, over in Mandela township in the Russell Sector.

Her father viewed her intended expedition with amusement, clearly thinking her a little foolish whilst overtly proud of her courage. 'Be careful out there. Those Zeros can be savage. They don't have the same respect for life, knowledge or individual rights we cherish. So be cautious how you approach them.

'And, remember, Daisa, they've an entirely different attitude to the body and its display. They're still living in a past crowded with inhibition, illogical prejudice, and distrust of their own emotions, thoughts and ambitions.

'You ought to make yourself aware of this thing they call fashion and try to fit in with whatever style they're currently adopting, since it seems to change frequently! Dressed as you are, you'll be taken for a whore and abused without a thought.'

She checked on the current meaning of that word, which she'd encountered during her studies, and found it still held the unpleasant connotations it had in the past.

Mother was less encouraging. Another man, a stranger, offered her a drink when she arrived. He then simply sat and donned a personal Threedee, quickly losing himself in whatever virtual world he'd called up from GrandMa. It gave the pair of them a chance to talk freely.

'You know they make transactions that involve them trading skills and goods for something called credits, don't you, Daisa?'

'I'd heard. We use them to trade our ideas and inventions for their materials, don't we?'

'Our participation's only virtual. We keep a tally of the credits they owe us so we can acquire appropriate quantities of raw materials.'

'So we use their system. Aren't we the same in that respect, Mother?'

'Not the same. We need some measure of the worth of our contributions to them. They use this system of credits and have no concept of the mutual cooperation we rely on. We've no choice but to value our ideas and inventions in terms they understand, otherwise we'd be denied materials we need to design and build our tools, devices and habitations. But we don't hold individual accounts of credits. We don't compete to see who has most, or value them the way they do. All I'm saying, Daisa, is you need to be conscious everything in Marzero has an artificial value placed on it, and you'll be expected to pay for whatever you need.'

'I don't have credits.'

'No. Marion's community account's available for all who visit the city. You must be aware of the amount you're spending and not use up too much of our balance. We need it for essentials.'

She left then, feeling a little less uncertain of what she faced in the city. An intended cursory visit to her new pod, to locate it and give instructions to the allocated android, A79663, about her choice of colour scheme and soft furnishings ended with her spending one night in her new bed. The stay told her the place was comfortable, but needed a newer version of the cooking unit and a more modern Threedee.

'I'll see to those at once, madam.'

'Oh, please, 79663, call me Daisa. And thanks. You have a name I can use?'

'Some of my managers call me Abby. I'm happy to respond to that name if you're more comfortable with it.'

'I'm off to Marzero for a bit, Abby, so won't be around after today till I return.'

'Do you know when that will be, Daisa?'

She detected what appeared to be a hint of disapproval, though that was probably in her mind; droids rarely expressed personal opinions. 'No idea. You'll know when I'm back. Can you obtain a suitable outfit for me, please?'

The droid inclined its androgynous head and left.

Daisa had a few hours before she needed to catch the Transhub. Time enough for a quick dip in the local lake and then a gentle saunter to the terminal. The walk would help her acquaint herself with her new neighbourhood and relax her for the journey.

Barefoot, clad in a multicoloured diaphanous skintight over a modest black bikini, she ignored the few odd stares of fellow citizens as she walked the broad streets of her new home. 79663 had discovered the current dress trends online and made the outfit up so it was ready for her after her swim. There was some doubt about her bare feet, but she wasn't concerned about that. If necessary, she'd get footwear once at her destination. It was unlikely to consume many credits.

Transhub travel was a new experience. Few settlers travelled to Marzero and local journeys tended to be by autocar. But Daisa walked the short distance from her lakeside pod to the terminal that served her town.

The Transdrum was stationary in its clear tube, the sealing sleeve behind ready to cover the entry gap once passengers were seated. Daisa selected a forward-facing outer seat so she'd have a good view of the scenery they sped through to Marzero. The internal cuboid gave no hint of the cylinder that contained it, with the windows presenting a continuous flat pane along each side so viewing through the transparent tube was unobstructed.

There were few other passengers, but she noticed a goods carrier attached behind the passenger drum. No doubt more inventions on their way to the miners' place to be traded for raw materials.

A gentle voice warned of imminent closure and a few secs later a soft hiss confirmed the capsule had sealed itself. The sleeve then closed the entry portals to provide a stable vacuum around the drum. Daisa was surprised by both the silence and acceleration that took them first to a few towns along her route, where all other passengers disembarked, and then into the wilderness.

2,537 ks lay between Marion and her destination. The trip would take just over five hours, including stops at subterminals to pick up passengers who'd been exploring the wilderness. She envied them not at all. Her paternal originator, Zaphod, was renowned for his forays into the wild, but she'd no desire to follow those footsteps, much as she admired his adventurous spirit. The new city was enough of a challenge for her.

With surprise, she noted Zaphod waiting for the return drum when they stopped at the last subterminal. He and Hoshiko, using the same interface as ordinary droids, had the advantage over the rest of their generation in being able to connect, via GrandMa, with other citizens of Marion. She connected and he looked up from his place on the bench, waved and smiled.

'What takes you to Marzero, Daisa?'

She explained. 'I want to understand how intelligent people can be so easily won over by ideas without logic, by stories with no evidence to back them up. Bit of personal involvement with the people should give me valuable insight into their strange beliefs. Hope so, anyway.'

'I admire your boldness, Daisa. But take care. There are dangers in Marzero that may surprise you. Be careful not to be seduced by the wildness, savagery and sheer animal enthusiasm some display. Be on your guard.'

The drum resealed and set out on the final leg of the journey, leaving Daisa wondering at the warnings she'd been given by so many people about her research. Surely the place couldn't really be as dangerous as everyone seemed to believe?

Too late now to retract. In any case, she consoled herself with the suspicion that the warnings were part ignorance and part envy of her trip away from the sometimes too dependent security of Marion. Marzero couldn't really be dangerous. After all, over two and a half million people spent their lives there, didn't they?

Chapter Five

The first visions had come to Gabriel in short bursts of what he experienced as periods of absolute confusion. Fleeting affairs, initially they were blank spells. But, later, they contained hints and suggestions, their dreamlike quality rendering them mysterious. Until he'd spoken of them to his friend, Stefan, one of the Clerics.

That had been the real revelation.

'Signs from God, man. Don't you know it?'

'Are they? Not just wakin dreams, then, Stefan?'

'Wakin dreams? Man, what you sayin here? These is words and images straight from the mouth of God! You've read the holy texts, eh? Know what I mean?'

Gabriel hadn't read the sacred texts. Whilst his mother professed a leaning toward the new faith, and even went to chosque when she had no clients on the holy day, he'd never given a thought to such matters. His life was hard enough, earning credits to get food, a private pod, and, once in a rare while, time with a woman.

'Never had time. I know about them; everybody does. But the PutinMaister says those are for people like you, Stefan, you know, not common folk. Have you read them?'

'Me, man? What y'think? Y'seen my ma. When Da died in the accident, I nearly lost my faith. But I read the texts again. Those rules make sense. They're how I got to where I am right now.'

'You're respected, get girls for free, because of the uniform, the rank. But do you have real power, Stefan? I mean, I know you've got privileges and go to those secret meets with the Elite, but you don't have a say on the Board, do you?'

'Next level up, I will. Wait an see. Y'know these visions make you special, man? Y'see what's happenin? You chosen, man. God's got a plan for you.'

Stefan's words started to make sense to him, especially after he'd mysteriously regained enough respect to attract class two girls at reduced prices. He read some sacred texts instead of drinking at the club after his shift.

He renewed friendships with men who'd invited him to their place of worship after the accident returned him home a hero from the Asteroids. They welcomed him, shared their women with him for free, made him feel important again. The way he'd felt in those short days of adoration after the collapse.

His only regret, even now, that he'd failed to get to Stefan's dad in time. He'd retrieved the body, but the man's air supply had failed and life was gone by then. Gabriel had brought out 12 alive before the roof sealed up the mine. He still earned some respect, from the few who remembered what he'd done.

Once the visions started to make sense with help from Stefan, his friend persuaded him to speak. His planet-based job, following the rescue, was shift manager on the neodymium processing line in the works where his father was General Manager. As a leader, he gained enough confidence to speak in public. Though natural reticence gave him a humility others seemed to like.

His mother was full of enthusiasm and encouragement. 'My boy, you've been picked out. Selected. You shouldn't ignore these visions. Stefan's right. They're from God. You must do as He says. Mind, be careful you keep on the right side of the law, now.'

'You don't really believe those rumours, do you, Ma?'

She looked about her, wild-eyed and trembling. 'Can't talk about that. You know it's true, Gabriel. Everywhere. They're everywhere.'

Gabriel dismissed her fears: it wasn't possible the Elite could watch everyone all the time. Even if they did, his visions were more significant. Let the Elite do as they please: God was much more important.

At that stage, the problem was he'd no clear idea what he was meant to do. The messages were unclear, muddled, hard to understand. And he wasn't well-educated. A common miner to begin with, building strength and muscle in the Asteroid Belt, until the collapse. Then finding work in the process plant where the man who claimed to be his father introduced him to the owner on his return to Mars. The post as a junior manager was reward for his heroic rescue.

To begin with, girls had been keen to serve him. But time dulled memory and other accidents named new heroes until he was just one among many.

Stefan also worked in the plant, ensuring operators stole none of the precious product. That they became friends was more or less inevitable. Their daily body searches of staff made friendship with the workers difficult. Those in positions of authority had to stick together to keep the labourers in line.

Occasionally, he'd wondered why the process wasn't automated. Why they didn't give the work to robots.

'Don't be twattin stupid, boy!' His father had laughed at the idea. 'Got to keep you buggers occupied. Give you time to think and god knows what you'd start demandin. Hard enough to earn a crust on this shithole of a world. Those of us with brains have got to keep the brawn under control. And don't you forget it, boy. I didn't get you that job so you could go all soft on me. Who's gonna take control here when I'm gone, eh? You, boy. That's who.'

The promise was as insincere as every other utterance that left his father's mouth. But some small germ of hope remained, so he buried his concerns for others and continued his regime of hard rule over the operatives on his line.

Until the visions came.

Until his mother encouraged him to spread the word.

Until Stefan urged him to become the man of God he was clearly intended to be.

Until his friends at the chosque helped educate him in the ways of holiness and guided him through multiple texts.

Stefan became his mentor. He knew how to interpret the strange, clouded messages that came through the visions. Though their meanings had been unclear, Gabriel always felt detached from mundane matters on Mars and made part of the wider universe, a channel for something much bigger than himself, when under their influence.

'An now you've had the best sign of all. That bright light what cut you down wasn't no accident, man. You know it. So do I.'

Gabriel stared ahead in that way he had. Those who witnessed this behaviour saw it as a sign he was communing with a force beyond himself. For Gabriel, these times, ending as abruptly as they started, left him recalling nothing clear. But his expression seemed beatific and this is what others saw. He'd been too embarrassed to admit he'd been confused throughout the time. Now, he accepted what others bestowed.

Under Stefan's influence, the visions altered. So different from the original blank times. Now he sometimes vocalised without his knowledge. People heard his voice and listened. The words often seemed meaningless but, as people will, they made of them what they wished to hear. And reported back to him what he'd said.

Often the messages appeared contradictory. Often they seemed nonsense when examined. But who wants a dream analysed and split apart when it promises hope and escape from the banality and brutality of everyday?

So he began to preach. His recall of the words of those who interpreted his outbursts was excellent. A little tweaking here and there, with Stefan's help, soon formed an almost cohesive message.

People sought him out. Women became eager to be with him without payment. Meeting places opened for him. Invitations to dine out, tickets to shows, and talks on Threedee Channel Capital with the provocative presenter, Katarina, made his life more bearable, enjoyable even.

And, now, this revelation. The bright light that had all but blinded him.

'Best sign of all, Gab. I was there, yeah? I saw it, too. Saw that burst of pure light out in the wastelands. But not like you, man. I never fell to my knees or spread my arms wide. I never stared at that light till it blinded me. I never heard no voice like you. Then you spoke them words. Your deep voice of power made me understand. It was God, man. God. Right there in front of you.'

'Good job you were there, Stef. I've little memory of it, except the bright light that made me stumble and fall. Nothin else.'

'Gab. Listen, man. You gotta get it right. You never fell, man. You saw God and dropped to your knees in wonder and respect. He spoke to you and you spoke His words out loud. Just like I told you. And you got back up; not a mark on you. Not blinded no more. Miracle, man!'

The plan was to reveal his latest experience at the mass meeting due in the main concourse of Marzero1 that evening. It was the end of the current work period, so those not on essential duties would be available to hear the Word. If the audience at his last show was anything to go by, this one would sell out.

'But I should tell them what I really felt and heard, shouldn't I?'

His friend shook his head. 'What did you really feel and hear, Gab?'

Gabriel's only memory was already fading after his lengthy discussions with Stefan.

Stefan was a great man to have as an aid to his growing ambition to end the injustices and corruption that ruled the colony. If he could get the Word out, he could really change things, make life better for everyone, instead of just the bosses and owners. And, as Stefan reminded him, he'd have all the women he wanted. In private.

'Nobody need know about the twats. I'll make them understand it's important they keep quiet. I mean, it's best for them to support you, man.'

Gabriel couldn't quite understand why, but Stefan was certain they'd be happy with the arrangement, so he accepted it at face value.

'So, what do I tell them tonight?'

Stefan smiled and sat him down. 'Listen. Remember. I heard and saw everythin. But you're the one what they hear, you're the voice of God. You're the prophet. The new Messiah. They want to hear you.

Just remember the words what I tell you, what God told you. Okay, man?'

He listened intently, in silence, though some words Stefan revealed seemed a little extreme and, in places, confusing. But who was he to argue with the Word of God?

Once he was sure Gabriel had the text perfect, Stefan left him to arrange the meet. This was going to be big. The funds they'd collect from the crowd would build a valuable bank of credits Stefan would manage on behalf of the new movement. It made sense to keep Gabriel ignorant of what was really happening.

The visionary was innocent, naive, and easily manipulated. All he really wanted was a better life and free access to attractive women. A bit of investment arranged that. And, as for the belief he was doing some good for the colony, well, that was fine. Let the fool do good, as long as the credits rolled in and Stefan's power and influence increased.

He couldn't believe his luck. Gabriel had retrieved his worthless father's body in the explosion at the mine and given Stefan reason to connect with a new hero. It was obvious even then that Gabriel was out of the ordinary. His selfless generosity and belief he could help society marked him out.

Once Stefan discovered his weakness, it had been simple to persuade a few women to provide a bit of free entertainment. Now he was more established, better looking girls lined up for some of the action. Some were under Stefan's control, others hoped for advancement, and that suited Gabriel's needs and Stefan's ambitions just fine.

The new messiah needed a name, a logo, some sort of pithy soundbite to spread the Word to everybody. The Prophet of the People would do it. The meet tonight would really start the ball rolling. Stefan was upbeat. 'Status and privilege, here I come. Get me to the top, man!'

Chapter Six

Daisa wandered the unnerving streets of Marzero, struggling in the apparent chaos of the layout. It was a city with no planning apart from the huge, low-lying, and ugly construction identified as the processing works that blanked the horizon beyond the northern edge of the Transhub terminal.

Noise and a degree of unpleasant stink emerged from the industrial plant. To her dismay, thick black smoke funnelled from two tall structures at either end. People, mainly muscular men but also some weary women, constantly moved in and out of the entrances. Those entering were clean enough, but those leaving displayed faces and torsos smudged with black, greys and browns. Their expressions of vacant weariness declared them drained of all spirit and energy. She felt immediately sorry for them.

The stares she received from passers-by as she strode streets around the place of greatest activity unsettled her. She wondered if she'd misread the dress code. But most women wore the type she'd acquired. Most had underwear beneath, some much briefer than hers. Nobody seemed to stare at them with the intensity she attracted.

Only as she mixed with the crowds nearer the centre did she realise it was her height that drew attention. The men were as tall or even taller than her, though not all had that advantage. But the women were shorter, some significantly so. Most men wore wraparounds of different lengths. Many were uncovered above the waist, a few were clad in open jerkins that left arms and chests bare. It seemed an odd choice in an environment far cooler than her home.

Noise, intense and fragmented, with snatches of loud conversation, cries from doorways, and music blaring at corners, confused her. The general chaos made her dizzy and disorientated. She'd visit here as little as possible. How could people live like this?

'Stuck up twat.'

The remark sounded oddly hostile and she glanced at the speaker only to discover it had been directed at her.

'What does that mean, please?'

The woman, well-endowed and wearing a shorter outfit than most, with no layer beneath, sneered in reply. 'Twattin stupid, annall.'

Daisa wondered how she'd offended a complete stranger but, as the woman had made off into the crowd, she let it go and continued exploring.

The area she entered held numerous strange buildings with large openings designed as display spaces. Behind their glazed fronts a confusing array of meaningless goods lay exhibited. Each item bore a small label carrying a figure. Close inspection revealed this was the cost in credits. Daisa had never had to purchase anything. She felt both fascinated and repelled.

Curiosity drew her inside. Nearby conversation had identified them as shops, whatever that meant. She wandered around the various displays within, puzzled by the purpose of most goods on offer. It was possible to work out the use of some items, though most seemed without function as an integral aspect of design. Her head spun from the oddity and chaos of the place.

'Want some elp, Miss?' The woman who asked the question wore a false smile, and hunger in her eyes. Daisa appraised her outfit, a slightly less transparent skintight over what she first thought was bare skin, but, on closer examination, turned out to be flesh-coloured underwear.

'Elp? Not sure what you're offering.'

'Want me to show you owt?'

'Out? I've only just entered.'

'Jeez! You dense or summat? I fought you was after sommat an dint know what is all.'

Flummoxed by this abusive retort, Daisa shook her head in denial and moved away from the woman. The poor person must be a little deranged. Such conditions were unheard of in Marion, but rumours of mental disturbance in Marzero were common.

'I'm tryin to elp you, Miss. No twattin need to be rude.'

Daisa processed the words, added them to the previous exchange and determined what the woman wanted. 'Ah. I see. You want to know if I'd like any help. No. Thank you. Just looking. Though I'd be interested to know what that's for, if you'd explain.'

She looked at Daisa as if she were some strange alien sent to torment her. 'Jeez! Expect me to waste me time tellin you fings what's plain as the nose an you're not even gonna spend? Jeez! What a twattin idiot.' She stomped off, leaving Daisa more confused.

For the time being, it might be politic to leave the shop and give herself a chance to observe life here more closely before she engaged in further social intercourse.

She moved back into the crowded and stuffy atmosphere of the linking transtunnel that formed the streets. The air in these was stale, where those in Marion were always fresh and invigorating. Perhaps greater numbers of people made the difference. But it surely wasn't beyond the wit of engineers to increase airflow? A simple procedure, after all.

She found a niche between two shops, where she wouldn't block others' access to displays, and watched the crowd. What struck her first was the apparent randomness of movement. People walked from one shop to another, crossed the walkway, and then backtracked to another shop adjacent to one they'd previously visited. There was no pattern to these movements, yet they avoided colliding with each other, even though most seemed captivated by the displays.

Over the next couple of hours, she noted most people moved singly; there were few couples or groups. Women were more evident in these shop areas than men, but she put that down to what she'd already discovered about work patterns here. The men worked in the processing works for eight to ten hours before they finished for that day.

Some women worked at the processing plant and its ancillary buildings. Others were employed in the shops, serving what she learned were 'clients'. But many were free during daylight hours, working at some unspecified task during the hours of darkness.

Tempted as she was to ask, the shop worker's abusive attitude warned her against too much obvious curiosity. So she contented herself with observation.

Once she'd got the measure of movement along the footway and understood it better, she ventured back into another shop to see what she could inside. She stood aside and watched clients come and go, witnessed various transactions in which people selected goods, passed their ID bands over a purpose-made surface, and then left.

Instead of asking a droid to obtain an item for personal use, as happened at home, people here were obliged to use credits to purchase things they needed. Daisa assumed droids delivered items to individuals' private pods.

As she considered this, she realised she'd seen no droids in the city. That was odd.

She'd been wandering for six hours. Food called. In Marion, she'd visit any of the small kiosks along the covered walkways and ask a droid for her chosen beverage and some accompanying item of food. Here, she'd seen no such booths. However, her nose led her to a different area where the aroma suggested food was cooked. The smell wasn't as inviting as at home, but was definitely food based.

Turning the corner revealed a slightly wider thoroughfare with tables and chairs set out in front of various establishments. Lesson learned, she stood for a while to watch the transactions. Again, ID bands were used as a means of exchange.

In some places, people sat at a table. A specially attired woman ap-proached, asked what they wanted and then brought the refreshment to the client. In others, clients formed an unruly line at a surface furnished with open containers of food and drink and helped them-selves, using flat discs and simple cups provided.

Daisa opted for the sort of service she preferred and found a table on the edge of an establishment. As she sat down, a small plaque rose from the centre of the table. It bore a list of items. She read: Toasted Slice 1.2, With Spread 1.7, Sweet Cake 2.3, with cream 2.9, Coffee 3.9, Tea 4.6, Coke 5.4, Water free with Slice or Cake, or 1.5.

Not an appetising choice, but she was hungry and thirsty. A young woman approached. Clearly intended to encourage male clients, the single layer of her dress was short and open at the front to the waist, displaying skin beneath. Oddly, she wore tilted footwear that raised her heel from the floor by seven cm.

'Yeah?' Her voice was bored, her attention unconvincing.

'A piece of cake, with cream, please, and a pot of tea, with milk.' She'd learned 'please' was a definite expectation.

'Use yer ID then.' She pointed at the list in the centre of the table.

Daisa leant forward to allow her ID medallion to make contact with the list. There was no apparent reaction, but the young woman nodded and walked off, presumably to collect the items.

'On yer own?' The man who asked sat down before she answered. His gaze swept the part of her not concealed by the table. 'New in the city.' It was a statement.

Daisa nodded, in answer to both question and statement. He was lean to the point of skinniness, as dark-skinned as Amber at Marion, and clothed with an open top revealing his hairless chest and exposing his arms.

'What you here for?'

'Just finished my doctorate.' She put her fingertip on the blue disc on her forehead. 'Taking a break from study. I'd heard a man called Gabriel was due to speak tonight and I'm curious to know why he draws such crowds.'

He studied her with increased interest. Apparently, she was now more than an exotic curiosity. 'Come to hear Gabriel, eh? Well, that's a turn up for a Marionet. A right hot 'un.'

There seemed to be a challenge in his last statement, but she was unsure what response he expected, so remained silent.

'Got a name?'

She nodded, uncertain whether to provide it. Would it be taken as an invitation in this city that grew odder by the min? 'And you?'

He laughed at that. 'They said women Marionets was forward. Yeah.'

The young woman returned, carrying a flat metal disc on which a smaller rimmed disc held a dark slab of something resembling cake. A pale yellow liquid nudged it. Next to it was a cylinder of some unidentifiable material. Brown liquid sloshed within. The woman plonked the large disc down and nodded at the man.

'Usual, Stefan?'

The man caught her hand and pulled her close until she was in danger of falling into his lap. He stroked his free hand up the back of her thigh from her knee to beneath the hem of her dress. She made no objection. 'Yeah, Olga. An change that crap for the lady. Give her what you give me.'

Olga shrugged and took away the large disc. Stefan watched her sway back inside.

'She's okay. Just obvious you're an outa'towner, so you get crap.'

Stefan had, apparently, ensured she received improved attention. She was grateful for such kindness in this strange and slightly threatening place. 'Thank you, Stefan. I'm Daisa.' She extended her hand in greeting.

He waved her hand aside. 'Don't do it that way here, lady. Kiss.'

She wasn't sure this was true, but didn't want to offend him. She leant forward and briefly brushed her lips against his cheek.

'Not what I meant. But you'll do for now.'

'May I ask you a few questions so I don't offend people, please, Stefan?' She hoped 'please' wasn't reserved for servants and assistants.

'Fire away. All yours.' Abruptly, his bravado diminished a little; a change subtle but noticeable to her enhanced senses. 'Gabriel! Didn't expect to see you till later.'

The man he addressed drew up a chair from an adjacent table and placed it opposite her, next to Stefan, before sitting down. In the whole movement, his gaze never once left her face. Daisa was intrigued. She'd heard about an instant attraction that could occur between people, but had never before experienced it.

This man certainly had presence. Held a certain fascination for her. Possessed a special quality she couldn't yet define, that set him apart from others. And she was certain he felt a strong attraction to her.

Stefan glanced from one to the other. She pulled her gaze from Gabriel and watched a series of expressions cross Stefan's face. He settled on determination and nodded just once. 'Gabriel, this here's a special lady from Marion, name of Daisa. Come to hear you speak.'

Gabriel moved closer and stretched out a hand to clasp hers. The touch was electric. They continued to hold hands for much longer than that simple greeting required.

Chapter Seven

Seeing Daisa on the Transhub had surprised Zaphod. He knew all his descendants by sight. Her trip to Marzero troubled him, but for reasons his android persona dismissed as illogical. Only his cyborg persona, what he called the 'echo' of his past humanoid form, seemed concerned. Was that because there was no logic to his anxiety, something based on that indefinable organic quality so often referred to as instinct? He shrugged, and smiled at that abliform habit, then continued on his way.

He was glad to be going back home. Even without the intimacy they'd shared so frequently as people, their relationship was close and interdependent. Love, it seemed, could transcend the merely physical in spite of what the biologists and psychologists had insisted.

He'd interrupted his journey, leaving the Transhub at a subhub serving the wilderness for those who had either research or leisure reasons for exploring. It was something he often did when returning, the self-imposed delay increasing his sense of anticipation of the joy of being with Hoshiko again. It also gave him a chance to check on the progress of naturalisation of vegetation and animal species in the wild.

Movement among shrubs growing on the slope he was passing caught his attention and he deviated from his chosen course to investigate. The creature stared at him with curiosity but showed no concern as it nuzzled its partner in a shallow dip excavated in the moist regolith beneath the bushes.

He recognised the animals as a hybrid goat-pig species Annika and Jai had bred as experimental fauna to regulate some of the burgeoning flora they'd seeded the planet with. Tough and intelligent, they'd become rather more successful than expected. But the colonists kept them under control with occasional culls that brought some different protein to the tables.

These two were clearly a pair preparing to breed. He examined their shallow nest and noticed something out of place amongst the developing soil mixed with dust, small rocks and lichen. They allowed him closer without moving away and he knelt to confirm his suspicions.

As he'd first supposed, the bones showing through to the surface were human. For a moment, that shocked him. Murder? Perhaps an early pioneer lost in the wilds before the atmosphere became sustaining? But where was the spacesuit?

And then he remembered. This site was where the ancient Chinese Base had been located. These were the bones of men and women Chang had killed all those years ago. Even now, the memory of that man's selfish ambition and predation made him experience an anger his superandroid form was barely equipped to handle.

Such unconcerned cruelty. It had been hard to take then. And the passing years made it no more acceptable, merely more bearable because of the separation of event and its memory. He considered uncovering the rest of the bones and reburying them. But disturbing the nest of animals was unacceptable and he left them to their home making.

For some time he wandered and revisited those early days on the planet. Such risks they'd faced, such challenges. And such fun and passion they'd experienced. So many lives changed, so many lives lost, so many lives interrupted by senseless violence. He only hoped this new phenomenon back at Marzero wouldn't prove the threat he feared, logical or not.

Interference from Marion would be considered a threat, could even cause an imbalance in the delicate relationship that had allowed the two communities to live in relative peace for so long. That could turn to violence. War. They must keep an eye on developments but stay clear of action unless events deteriorated.

The Zeros were ill-educated and, although most seemed unaware, subject to injustice from the wealthy and powerful owners and bosses; the Elite. A new leader of the workers might cause a revolution that could play into the hands of the Chosen's colony. It could allow equality to develop, some reduction in the criminal system of abuse the moneymen imposed on their subjects.

Equally, it might bring about a revolutionary extremist movement bent on conversion of all souls on the planet. The citizens of Marzero were notoriously prone to superstition and the translation of myth into perceived reality. Just like the people of Earth had been.

Zaphod recalled the days of war with the insane disciples of the Cusp, a dispute that had threatened the very existence of the Chosen and their base at Marion. It couldn't be allowed to happen again.

They must ensure they kept an eye on this Gabriel man, make sure he didn't persuade the workers to become disciples of his developing cause. The words and ideas so far put about by this self-styled prophet seemed harmless enough, even progressive in their intent to equalise gender roles in the city.

But experience tempered any hope for a positive outcome as long as the Elite were in control. They were unlikely to permit a creed that bode no good for those who failed to agree, unless it also happened to strengthen their own philosophy of greed and selfishness. But the real danger, amongst a population so downtrodden and subject to draconian injustice, was the development of a quasi-religious movement bent on action.

It wasn't hard to envisage such a sect developing ideas of envy, conspiracy theory and hegemony toward the more stable and socially balanced settlement of Marion.

Chapter Eight

Stefan strode to the centre of the makeshift stage and looked out over the largest crowd they'd ever attracted. He'd primed Gabriel in private, though the new girl had accompanied them back to Gab's pod. She was a looker. And so bright! But she was an innocent. Easily manipulated, just like Gab.

Things were coming together nicely for him. Of course, the fact that he was a man who recognised opportunities and took advantage helped. Secrets learned in his role of Cleric had already given him leverage.

He'd used his knowledge to get the better of men, and those few women, in positions of greater power than he currently held. He was moving up the ranks, gathering credits; would soon be the leader and entrepreneur he'd always dreamed of being. Those at the top would learn he wasn't a guy to fool with.

He looked out over the crowd, signalled behind his back to the sparks who'd rigged the lighting and sound system for him in return for a night each with one of his current women. She was cheap, but retained the looks of a younger whore. And she did as she was told. Else she suffered the consequences.

As the lights dimmed and the crowd slipped into the silent, attentive role he'd programmed, he clicked on his mic and flicked his fingers. The spot illuminated only his face, isolating him in the darkness. The music he'd organised slowly built to a crescendo in the previous absolute silence and then faded into it. The mood was set.

'People. People. Welcome to this place. Greetins in the name of the Almighty. Peace and harmony. Joy. Everlastin wealth. Love. God guide and provide. Walk our world with good in your hearts. Justice your watchword. Dreams high as Olympus Mons. Wide as Utopia Planitia. Deep as Valles Marineris!

'But you're not here to listen to an ignorant sinner. You're here to listen to the words of a wiser man. Deeper. More gifted. Brilliant. One chosen of God! You've come to hear the very words of God. I bring you, give you, Gabriel. Let's hear it for the great man himself!'

The spotlight dimmed. The silence was palpable. From the surrounding speakers began a slow, chanting, drumming. Deep and penetrating so it entered the very bodies of those in the crowd. They took up the beat of it with their swaying forms. Arms raised above their heads and hands clapped out each beat. The sound increased as the beat slowly moved up the scale until the sound was a frenzy of combined applause.

In the front of the crowd, right beneath the stage, Daisa watched and heard this theatrical opening. She'd seen such staging at concerts and gigs where popular musicians performed. But this was an introduction to a serious speaker on spiritual matters. It seemed false and contrived. Was this how Gabriel really wanted to be perceived?

From the rear of the stage area, a quiet voice, female, full of respect and awe, spoke the single word, 'Gabriel'. Almost unheard at first, it was repeated between the beats of the clapped hands, increasing in volume slowly until the crowd heard and took it up.

A single moving light penetrated the darkness. Glowing deep red, it illuminated nothing at first. But as it brightened and moved toward the front of the stage, a figure gradually emerged out of the darkness.

The light grew in intensity and changed into pure white, as Gabriel moved slowly to the edge of the stage. There, he stood with arms wide spread and his face pointed up into the night sky. Entirely white, a single garment cloaked him from beneath his arms down to the floor, flowing as if alive and rippling in fluid movement through its multiple pleats.

For secs that seemed to stretch into eternity, he remained silent and unmoving. Then, in an instant, he brought his arms down and around to clasp his hands together before him. The musical beat stopped exactly as his hands came together and, as if controlled by a single switch, the crowd fell to silence, their arms lowered as they sought to concentrate on the face of the man on stage.

Slowly, in utter silence, he lowered his face to gaze in soft sweeping arcs across the whole of his audience.

'My people. My chosen. I welcome you here to this place of worship and devotion. Please. Be seated. My words require your full attention and you've been hard pressed today by those who employ you. So, rest. Turn your minds, your eyes, your ears, to words of hope and promise I bring you.'

Quietly, almost as if remotely controlled, Daisa thought, the crowd seated themselves in ordered rows. She stood and watched their faces, fascinated by their apparent devotion, until she realised she alone stood in this reverential crowd, and lowered herself to the ground to join them.

'Long have you laboured. And hard. Long have you endured the injustice of a world where labour brings more labour, hard work creates more hard work. But I bring you rest. I bring you harmony. I bring you peace.

'Let us, before we proceed with tonight's meeting, make our supplication to God. For it is to God we give ourselves this night. And we must use His rightful name and title.'

He lowered himself and sat cross-legged at the very edge of the stage.

'Almighty Jehovah Allah God Most High, accept the humble words of your servants. Bless this assembly here in this place. Bring light and understanding to all who here declare their love and devotion to Your Mighty Presence. Know all who gather here are Your devoted and worshipful followers who know the value of Your Supreme Being. Amen Akbar Shalom.'

The audience repeated the last three words in tones of devotion that made Daisa anxious over their power. She looked up at Gabriel, back toward the crowd behind her.

Stefan had secured this privileged position for her, insisting she should witness the meeting from the best possible vantage point. The faces of those she could discern in the dim reflected light seemed transfixed, their eyes wide, their forms motionless, their faces turned up toward the figure on the stage.

Gabriel had some hold over these people. They saw him as an extraordinary being who held power. The idea of such influence holding sway over strangers fascinated and disturbed her. She must see more.

He rose from his cross-legged position, his arms still outstretched as if attempting to gather the entire crowd into his embrace. It was a compelling image and made a powerful impact on each individual who felt privileged to be present.

'Now, this night, I have words of comfort and promise to convey to you. I have visions, as you know. Visions in which I hear the voice of Almighty Jehovah Allah God Most High demanding my action on His behalf. But, now, I have experienced a vision such as none has ever before encountered.'

The crowd gazed up at the performer on stage. Mouths opened in anticipation. He had them. They were his.

'The morning was as any other. I set off on my daily run, keepin my body fit and strong for trials yet to come. I took my usual route; out of the city, across fields of corn, barley, peas and potatoes. Through orchards of apples, pears and almonds. Between rows of vines growing grapes.

'At the edge of the desert, where lichen damps the dust of our world, I turned to run parallel with the border of our city more than two ks distant. There, 777 paces from the point where I turned, a group of standing stones, some natural, and some left from the road building, form a small enclosed area through which I pass each day.

'I run carefully, for potholes and rough ground might cause a less cautious man to fall and injure himself. The ground within is rocky and uncultivated, lacking the lichen that softens the ways in and out.

'I entered the shadowed interior, the risen sun behind me throwing my shadow long and active in my path. I looked up toward the exit from this strange arena. And was suddenly blinded!

'The brightest, most glorious light ever to appear on this world of ours bathed me in its brilliance.

'I fell to my knees.

'At once.

'For, even before I heard His voice, I knew I looked on Almighty Jehovah Allah God Most High.

'I felt I should not gaze on this miracle, but could not tear my eyes from the brilliance of the blazing light before me. I spoke. "I am here, Most Almighty Jehovah Allah God Most High. What must I do?"

'Then Almighty Jehovah Allah God Most High spoke to me. Spoke. To. Me! He gave me this message for all the world to hear. You must spread this message to everyone on the world. You must. Almighty Jehovah Allah God Most High demands it. Here are His words as He gave them to me.

"There are amongst you evil men and evil women. They will deny me. They are sinners without hope of redemption. Only those who know me and worship me will be blessed. Those who deny me must be brought to book. Those who deny me must be gathered into the fold and instructed in the right ways.

"Some there are who will not listen. Some there are so steeped in evil they will fight me and deny my wishes. These must be put to the test. Those found wanting must be cast away. Those who will not accept the truth must be denied existence.

"I will come to you again in this place. You will receive my laws and make them known to all the faithful. For you, Gabriel, are my Chosen Voice. And glory will be yours. And to all who follow your lead even unto the last letter of the law. I have spoken. Let it be so.'"

Daisa's studies of religious matters had exposed her to numerous sacred texts and she recognised phrases here that echoed their ancient sentiments. It was all so much myth and dogma, of course, but she found herself unable to deny the hypnotic effect of Gabriel's delivery.

And the faces of those around her were evidence enough of the power behind that message. It would be a marvellous experience to witness the development of this new movement, to watch it grow and evolve.

What would it become? How much influence would it have?

Would it become a power for good, or follow all previous religious messages to become a divisive and destructive force of evil? Prophets had generally been good men. What others had done with their messages of social improvement had turned them into something entirely different from the intentions of the original speakers. Would the same happen here?

This was a unique opportunity actually to witness the growth of one of the most powerful persuasive forces known to the abliform species. It was too good a chance to miss. To remain close to Gabriel, she'd do what was necessary. Her scholarship and love of learning demanded such devotion. That his physical aspect was an aphrodisiac made the whole idea of close study even more appealing.

'So, my people, you have the words of Almighty Jehovah Allah God Most High now in your minds and hearts. Spread them. Pass them to all you meet. Let the entire world be full of Almighty Jehovah Allah God Most High's words.

'Now, before I let you go to your rest, let us make supplication to Almighty Jehovah Allah God Most High.'

He seemed to grow taller, bigger. Music swelled from the speakers and filled the air with inspirational melodies that soothed and encouraged. He let the music quieten and then spoke again.

'Say, after me, the words I have been commanded to pass on to you. "Oh Almighty Jehovah Allah God Most High, accept my devotion. Take me to Your heart. Accept me, imperfect as I am. Receive my undyin love for You. Guide my every move. Forgive me my doubts and my errors but reward me for my endeavours. For I will be Yours this day and forever more. Amen Akbar Shalom.'

Daisa spoke the words with the others, knowing silence in this crowd would be unwise. There was a powerful force at work, and a hint of menace that made dissent impolitic.

Slowly, softly, with many words of mutual encouragement murmured by the people, the crowd dispersed. Only when all had gone did Gabriel relax. He looked down at her from his elevated position and extended a hand to help her join him there. She jumped, her strength enhanced by her physical sessions in the Earthgrav gym on the campus, and landed gently beside him, his hand an unneeded but welcome guide.

'I believe I've found the woman who'll be my companion on the hard road ahead. Will you be with me, Daisa?'

The private invitation was as welcome as it was unexpected. They'd met only hours before and spent no time alone together. But some sort of connection had already formed between them, emotional and primitive, and therefore exciting. For her part, Daisa felt an attraction perhaps more than merely physical.

Gabriel let her know he found her the most beautiful partner possible. She'd be an asset and a perfect example of what a woman might become under their new regime.

Chapter Nine

The meet had gone even better than Stefan had expected. Gabriel was proving a good choice for the project. If he could get that Marionet, Daisa, on side, life would be simpler.

But he must stop them getting it together for now. She'd make an ideal sacrificial 'virgin' for the cause. It was the sort of idiocy the mob delighted in. He could work on them with that piece of deception.

They'd left together and Stefan knew exactly where they were headed. The mutual attraction had been too obvious to ignore. But he needed help. And he knew who could provide the necessary leverage. He hoped Virginia was home. Willingness had nothing to do with it: she'd do as he told her. The info he held on her ensured that, at least.

He ran the short distance to her pod in Marzero5, garnering curious looks from the late evening crowd queuing outside the New Threedee Emporium. The latest porn show catered to basic tastes. 'Nude Great Lookas with Massive Bazookas' had proved yet another hit with the underclass and Stefan shook his head in disbelief as he passed the line of men so desperate for a sight of female flesh.

'Losers.'

Position gave Virginia the privilege of living in the best district. The streets here were more or less devoid of the usual bright LED displays shouting their wares, slogans and commands to buy. Here, citizens were considered too intelligent by the Elite to be subjected to the general psychological manipulation deemed necessary to distract ordinary workers from envy over the perceived perfection of 'eternal' life in Marion. He grinned at her vulnerability, knowing she'd do whatever she must to maintain that special lifestyle.

She answered the door ready for bed, but shrugged resignedly when she saw him. He barged in and she made no effort to prevent him. 'Too tired, Stef. Can't you wait till morning …'

The promise was tempting, but would wait until she'd done what he required. 'Need you to apply some pressure, gal. The other can wait.'

She asked him what he meant as she quickly pulled on clothes to leave the pod with him. Experience suggested she'd best not object. He'd give her details as they went wherever he needed her to perform whatever he required.

They were outside Gabriel's pod in less than ten mins. She was tidying her hair as the door opened to reveal Gab still in his performance robe. Beyond, the girl, seated on the soft couch, was also dressed. Stef sighed audibly and prodded Virginia in before him. Gab stood aside to permit them entrance, though his face darkened with annoyance.

Stef turned to Virginia. 'You know what's needed.' The whisper had her nodding agreement as she left him and moved to sit beside the victim. Stef, meanwhile, grabbed Gab, pulled him into the pod's only other room, and closed the door, holding his ear close to the surface to hear what passed on the other side.

'Stefan said you're beautiful. Stunning, I'd say. Daisa, I gather? Unusual name.'

'Yes. Who are you? I've a vague idea I know you from somewhere.'

Virginia took Daisa's hand in her own. 'A child of the Chosen, eh? I was only at Marion this mornin. Speakin with the Council of Members, y'know?'

Daisa caught on quickly as her memory of social education brought up the info she sought. 'Contract Negotiator. Virginia, as I recall?'

'Excellent. But do y'know what my role actually entails, Daisa?'

'You and the Council come to compromise deals on the value of credits relating to our inventions and ideas. Sole rep of Marzero to negotiate with Marion. Right?'

'Clever. Now, what I don't know is how ignorant they keep the rest of you regardin the wealth your colony's accumulated. You're part of a very rich community. Did y'know?'

'Never mattered. Credits are meaningless when you don't use them.'

Virginia had expected such indifference. The accompanying ignorance suited her purpose well, though she felt more than a twinge of guilt about her intended duping of an innocent. And one of her own gender. Still, no choice. Stef left her no room for manoeuvre. 'Well, they have meanin here. You're hopin to spend time with Gabriel?'

Though the end of the sentence bore the telltale upward tone of the question, Daisa heard it as statement. News, it seemed, travelled fast here. No doubt Stefan had noticed the mutual connection she and Gabriel had made on meeting. She'd never felt so easy to read, though, she'd had no need to hide her thoughts or feelings. Honesty was standard in Marion.

'I'm attracted to him. And he to me. What's that to do with credits?'

'Sorry to be indelicate, but you'll need somethin to live on, buy clothes, food, and other items whilst you're here. Nothin's free in this place. Nothin.'

'Hadn't thought about that. I've access to Marion's funds and I assumed I'd be okay spending just what I need while I'm here.'

'Fine. But you should know those funds are extensive, almost limitless. Your community's built up a balance well in excess of anythin held by any individual or corporation in Marzero, y'know.'

Daisa was unimpressed. It was of no consequence. Her needs were simple. Her wants of little matter. 'So?'

'Oh dear. You really don't understand. This is Marzero; the real world. Not your pretend domain, where everythin's painted rosy, and reality's hidden to stop folk worryin. Who makes decisions back home? Not you. Who gets power and influence? Not you.'

Daisa stopped the laughter that was her natural response to such suggestions. 'For someone who's visited Marion often, Virginia, you show poor knowledge of how we work. Nobody's in charge. Nobody has power, and everybody. We all have influence. Our society's based on mutual cooperation and trust. We employ honesty and the most truly democratic system ever devised. I think you've misread our way of life.'

Virginia surprised her. 'Believe that if you wish, Daisa. If it makes y'happy.'

Daisa was disinclined to argue with this stranger in her home city. 'I'm happy. My life in Marion's about as complete as can be.'

'D'you even know what I mean by a transaction, I wonder. I have my doubts.'

'A transaction's an exchange; where an individual gives something to another, usually in return for something else.'

'Y'give things in Marion, exchange gifts?'

'Gifts. We make things, often works of some form of art, to give pleasure to another, sometimes to show affection or admiration. The concept's known to us. It's quite common.'

Virginia sighed heavily. 'These things y'give back home cost you nothin but your time, and y'don't lose income for that. If y'want to give a gift here, it'll cost. And those credits have to be earned by hard work. But you've the advantage that y'can give without havin to earn credits. D'you see where I'm goin with this?'

'You think Gabriel and I will want to demonstrate our mutual respect and admiration by giving each other things. But Gabriel's not interested. He's more spiritual than material. His attitude to things is a bit like ours. We have what we need and want very little. Here, you seem to want lots and you're willing to pay for things that have no hold on us.'

'Things like food and clothin, somewhere to live, the means to keep warm? These what you think Gabriel rejects?'

Daisa considered. 'He needs what any normal abliform needs to live. But they're not items reserved for giving. In Marion everything we need to live is freely available. Work's done by droids and robots. I wanted to ask about that. You've no droids and your bots seem only the heavy sort, used in the processing works. Wouldn't you like to live free from labour, so you could devote your time to learning, exploring, thinking and pleasure?'

'Dreamer!' Virginia stood, stamped her foot in frustration. 'This is the real world. Everythin here has a price. Y'can't expect to live in Marzero without payin. Everythin here costs. Everythin!'

Daisa spread her arms wide in a gesture of peace and openness. 'Does it have to be that way? Isn't that what Gabriel's trying to change? Seems the rich and powerful, the Elite, have it all their own way and the rest of you are serfs or even slaves in their service.'

'Y'really are naive, aren't you? We don't work; we don't eat. Simple as that.'

'Maybe it's time to change. Isn't that what Gabriel has in mind?'

'Y'think Gabriel's startin some sort of revolution? Keep it to yourself if y'care about him. People have … have been killed for tryin to alter the way things are done here. You, with your silly dreams, could get Gabriel into serious bother, even eliminated. That what y'want?'

Daisa was silent for a moment, considering the sudden turn in the conversation. Did Virginia truly care for Gabriel, or did some other motive drive her fear? 'I want Gabriel to succeed in his aims to bring about a new world here. But I won't put him in danger. Yours is a strange world, with odd values and customs. I'll be an observer and say nothing publicly until I better understand your world. I won't endanger Gabriel. For some irrational reason, I'm attracted to him.'

Virginia visibly relaxed. She stopped the pacing that had accompanied her last remarks and sat again. 'Sorry if I seemed harsh, Daisa. But it's dangerous to get out of step. We have to be very careful what we say and who we say it to. Gabriel's movin toward a new way of life for us and people are behind him. But if the authorities get even a hint he's fomentin revolution they'll put an end to him. And it won't be painless, I can tell you.'

'How can I best help him? What's the ideal way for me to behave?' Daisa realised with each thought and word she cared for Gabriel, wanted him safe. He was supposed to be a subject for further study but she accepted he was also a man for whom she felt some unusual emotion.

'There I can help you. Marion's funds are effectively limitless. You could provide for Gabriel's needs without even makin a dent in their balance. That way, he can concentrate on his ministry and give his whole self to spreadin the word about his new world, about his ideas for a new order, about his communion with God.'

'Just "God" in your mind, is it?'

'Oh, I'm not a believer. Been to Marion too often to be tricked by that baloney.'

Interesting: the Zero mind was clearly open to influence. That was promising. Gabriel was a man, subject to manipulation and change. She could help him see the error of his beliefs, once he'd brought Marzero closer in function and philosophy to Marion. Everyone would benefit. If it cost Marion a few credits, then it was worth the expense, especially as the colony had so much to spare.

'Is it general knowledge Marion has excess funds, Virginia?'

'Good God, no! I know only because I'm sole Negotiator with Marion. I have to know the balance so I can check we're gettin ideas and inventions at good prices, you see? Nobody else knows about Marion's wealth. And that's how it stays, Daisa. It's essential to the way we do business. Promise you'll tell no one. Not even Gabriel.'

'Still coming to terms with this idea of paying for everything. I'm a credit virgin; no experience. I'll follow your lead and take your advice. I'd like to help Gabriel. What can I do to make his life easier?'

'As I explained. Provide for him. This place isn't his, y'know. He's only here because Stef and I made sacrifices to let him. Take over the lease and you'll free him to do so much more, you see? If y'get his food and any new clothin, that sort of thing, he'll be able to spend his time doin good the way only he can.'

'Be okay for me to let him know I'm doing this? I gather men here become irate if they think a woman's supporting them.'

'You're very bright, Daisa. And you're right. About most men. But Gab's different. As a man of God, he's sort of immune from normal considerations, which are largely down to vanity anyway. He's not at all vain and he's so wrapped up in his ministry he'll just be grateful for your help, especially if you let him know it's not an imposition, that you can easily afford it. Without, of course, lettin him in on our secret.'

Daisa smiled at the thought she might help him achieve his dreams of a new utopia here in Marzero. She may even influence the way things developed if Gabriel appreciated her help. It would be so good for the whole planet, to have both colonies working together and in harmony, and that's what she saw as the inevitable outcome of his move toward change.

The religious aspect was a barrier, but one she'd deal with by logic and truth once he was well on his way to his target. By the time it became a real issue, she'd have made him so reliant and they'd be so close he'd readily listen to her reasonable arguments and recognise the 'god' thing for the delusion it clearly was. For the moment, it was a driving force for positive change, so she'd pretend to go along with it.

'Thanks, Virginia. I know how to deal with this now. Can I come to you for further help and advice if I need it, please?'

'Brill. You learn quickly. And, of course you can. I'd love to help and advise all I can. One more thing, though. Gabriel will make a proposition to you, and, for now, it would be wise to agree with him.

'Now, the men are returnin. Best they don't know we've been discussin them in their absence; get's them too nosey!' She laughed at her own joke.

Daisa watched the pair approach. Stefan seemed buoyant and upbeat as always, but Gabriel looked serious and even troubled. She rose to greet him, that feeling of mutual desire growing as they moved closer.

'Daisa, can I take you aside? I need to talk to you on a serious matter that could make our … friendship, or break it. Come. Please.'

Intrigued, and a little anxious by his tone, she followed him into the room he and Stefan had exited.

Chapter Ten

Stefan waited until the other two had closed the door, then grabbed Virginia with undiluted lust. Only the lack of privacy stopped him having her straight away. He held her close, pawing her skin wherever he could touch without undressing her. But he parted from her; even he wouldn't do her in his friend's pod.

'She's ours.' Virginia told him, smoothing her clothes with the palms of her hands and standing away in self-defence.

'You certain?'

'I had to lay it on thick. Had to lie. But she'll do as y'want.' She moved further away. 'Now, if y'don't mind, I've work in the mornin and I'd like to go back home. To sleep.'

He slid closer, grasped her hand. 'I'll take you to your pod, Virgin … ia. Make sure you get there safe.'

'I'm fine. I can handle myself.'

'But can you handle me?'

'Leave me alone! I've lied for you. What more …?'

Stefan snapped a firm hand over her mouth. 'Quiet, twat! Don't want her hearin you, do we?'

He released her as she nodded compliance.

'Can I go home now. Please?'

'Course.' He approached the closed door to the other room, still gripping her hand, and called. 'We're off. See you tomorrow, Gabs.'

He nodded to Virginia and she wished them both goodnight.

'I'd prefer to go alone.'

Stefan opened the outer door and dragged her into the street, closing it behind them. 'I'd prefer to go with you.'

'I've done what y'said. Can't you leave it at that?'

'With what I've got on you? Don't think so. Just a bit of fun, innit?'

'Bastard!'

He squeezed hard enough to bring a yelp of pain. He smiled and stroked his free hand down the curve of her bottom before slapping her rump too firmly for affection. 'Let's not make it nasty, eh?'

She was beaten. How long would this go on? And all for a mistake, not hers, years ago. One day she'd get this bastard off her back. One day she'd make him sorry.

'Just another year or ten. Have me when I want it. Not so hard, is it? I mean, I know how to pleasure women what understand their place. Amazin how little changes can turn pleasure to pain, though. Really surprisin.'

She understood the threat. 'We'd best go. The nightroof'll open soon, and I don't want to freeze to death. D'you?'

He glanced at the screen on his wrist. 'Later than I thought. Must be your captivatin company. Get a shift on.'

The streets they walked remained heavy with stale air. The covers that kept evenings at a reasonable temperature would soon retract to refresh the atmosphere. But temperatures dropped below freezing in the north and neither was dressed to resist such cold.

'Sooner we get that new moon in place, the better.'

'Moons, you mean. Already movin Nesta.'

'Is that wise? We don't know for sure what effect Ceres will have on its own, do we?'

'There's caution, Ginny. Then there's fear of change. Our boffins know what they're doin.'

She hated the diminutive, and he knew it. 'Perhaps. But the Chosen say it's a step too far. Ceres is one thing, but Nesta's too much of an unknown.'

'What they know? I mean, look at their crap society. No money. No power. No status. What's the twattin point, eh?'

'Maybe they're happy bein happy?'

'Can't spend happy, can you?'

'I suppose not. But you can live it.'

'Shift that temptin arse, girl. Feelin the need for action.'

She stopped. 'Maybe I should come to your pod. It's nearer.'

60

He urged her forward. 'Yours is better. Who'd be in Zero3 when they could be in Zero5? Come on, before we get froze.'

They loped the streets in long, easy strides, frequent exercise in the Earth gravity unit building and maintaining muscles Mars alone would leave weaker and less able. The unit, result of an exchange they'd made with Marion centuries ago, was essential for pregnant women, who needed the greater gravity for proper implantation of the blastocyst in the uterus wall. But the wealthy and powerful took advantage of their position to gain extra physical strength. Virginia's status gave her access, but Stefan had to use his stock of blackmail victims, since his current position didn't merit such privilege.

Her pod was on a corner site and therefore bore the advantage of two windows. The door stood on the corner itself and Virginia moved aside to let Stefan enter first. It was a submissive move to gain her some merit from this bully who'd ruled her for too long.

Only recently had he used her body for his pleasure. She'd quickly learned compliance and submission served her best, despite her strong desire to resist and fight. Survival in the city for any woman, regardless of status, depended on the protection of one or more powerful men.

So far, she'd managed to remain unmolested by the crowd as a result of Stefan's protection combined with her regular submission to Timur, Elite owner of the processing plant.

She was one of many women he used, so her occasional duty was more easily borne. It was also programmed; never spontaneous or unexpected. And simple enough. His needs were physical and readily satisfied. Three times a quarter was an acceptable price for his protection. No working man would dare even proposition a woman under the care of one of the Elite.

'Never mind Timur the twatter. It's me what's here now.'

She hadn't realised her eyes had strayed to the actimage. But movement of the part-clothed man caught her eye as she entered. He'd insisted his gift of the portrait be placed directly opposite the door.

'So y'can see me soon as you get home, m'dear. It'll make partin from me that bit less painful for you.' And he truly believed that.

Virginia poured the usual drinks. She prepared for him, made it clear it was his call.

Afterwards, as he slept in her bed, she indulged in the expense of a shower, and applied salve to the reddened skin of her spanked backside. At least that should be it for the next few days. He had other women he abused, so her turns came less frequently than those kept as a single trophy.

She couldn't sleep, dwelling on the nature of her life. Experience with the Chosen, time spent in their society and world, had allowed her to see possibilities.

Zaphod, in particular, had always been kind. He had no carnal interest in her; how could he? But he'd once been a fully functioning man and even then, she'd learned from others, he'd been a gentleman. In fact, all the men she met at Marion were considerate.

'Why don't you come and live with us? I can change your DNA, so you pass our tests. You're a beautiful woman, with a generous heart and a good mind. You'd fit in well.'

Zaphod's offer had been so tempting. She'd accepted the infertility implant, though nobody else knew about it. The men of Marzero would be incensed. Her home city aimed at maximum population growth.

As Timur always reminded her when she failed to produce offspring, a woman was only worth as much as her children. 'The more mouths to feed, the more hands to keep busy, the more feet on the ground, the more purses to pay for goods, the better life will be.'

She'd told to him her infertility was an unfortunate accident of biology that doctors had tried but failed to repair. In recompense, she gave Timur her best service. Faking her own pleasure was such a habit she hardly knew whether it was real any more.

But Zaphod's suggestion that she live in Marion, tempting as was, would mean she'd have to abandon the women she cared for. They needed her, the only woman in any position of influence, to help improve their lives. Slavery, their reality, was a deplorable state, no matter how much the men in authority approved of it.

From birth, women were programmed and raised as servants and whores. At first, it had been impressed on them in the same way the Chosen had used their women as baby-making machines. The difference in Marzero was their subservient role, and its continuation long after the population had increased beyond what was initially considered optimum.

Profit and power overtook all other considerations after the dreadful period of Cusp rule all those years ago. The men in charge then had learned from the extremists they could have their own way with women, many of whom at the time were sex workers. The difference was they were now made to perform as slaves under the control of whichever powerful man owned them. And so it had developed.

Eventually all women became the property of the Elite. The credits they were paid by clients went straight to their masters. They received a small allowance entirely dependent on the man's perception of their behaviour. Slavery by any other name. Most women were unaware of their true history, except by rumour and secret conversations that reached few.

Virginia had been fortunate in early life. An aptitude for diplomacy coupled with an excellent head for figures and a good memory had singled her out as an ideal assistant to the man then serving as Negotiator with Marion.

In fact, she'd done the work and he'd taken the credit, literally. His death had been accidental, but the way Stefan described it had given him power over her. Any woman suspected of involvement in a man's death was subject to humiliating and painful execution.

When her predecessor suffered the accident the Chosen had insisted she continue in the role, regardless of Marzero's objections. The Elite had accepted her driving hadn't been responsible for the death. But Stefan had altered the record so it could now look as though her refusal to obey her boss's instructions on the road had caused the crash. And, as Stefan pointed out, it would be seen as odd that she'd survived when the man in charge of her had perished. 'Wouldn't look good if I tell them what I think happened, would it?'

Her innocence was no protection against such accusation, so she'd become his tool to further influence. She glanced at the sleeping tormentor and wished she had the courage and opportunity to end his foul life. He'd be no loss to the community. But an attempt would place her in mortal danger.

And now he'd driven her further along the road to destruction, further into his power. The lies she'd had to spin to Daisa would ensure the poor girl was now embroiled in Stefan's evil plans. She only hoped Gabriel's innate goodness would spare Daisa the worst results of her deceit.

She liked Daisa. There was genuine warmth and trust in the young woman. A cleverness and courage that spoke of potential greatness. Only her honesty and total lack of knowledge of the reality of life in Marzero had allowed her to believe Virginia's lies.

But there must be a way out of this mess. Some tactic to defeat whatever evil Stefan had in mind in his relentless quest for influence, wealth and power.

Chapter Eleven

Daisa sat on his bed and listened to Gabriel with some surprise.

'So, you see, I have to be more than just a good man. I have to be seen to be a good man. If I have the open support of a woman like you, from Marion, where women are supposed to be equal and have the same status as men … is that really true?'

'Look, Gabriel, I'm fascinated by your ideas. But it's been a long day. I'm tired and, frankly, I'd like an endorphin fix. Can we talk this over in the morning, when we've both had a good sleep?'

'Endorphin?'

She shook her head in disbelief. 'Okay, I know it's not strictly accurate. But it's the best shorthand we have.'

'Shorthand? I'm not …'

'Sex? I'm asking you to have sex with me. Really, what do they tell you in primary relationship classes here?'

'Sex?' He was shocked at her openness, her clear desire. He knew women could be sensuous creatures, but they waited for the man to make the first move. Here she was, offering herself to him so forwardly. And she was a prize.

He wanted her. Naturally. Any man would. If he expanded on his wish and thereby rejected her offer, would she leave? She wasn't like the women of Marzero; they were easily manipulated. Obedient from habit. They knew their place and did as they were told. But Daisa was from a different background. She'd probably had loads of attractive men.

'You still there, Gabriel?'

He realised he'd been looking away from her and glanced back. The last thing he wanted was to lose this prize. She'd make his ministry work with men as well as women. With her beside him, he'd attract even greater crowds.

He mustn't lose her. But Stefan had made it clear he must present her to the people as his 'virgin', his untouched disciple, too pure to be stained by carnality. Such status would make her special to women and more desirable to men. She'd bring a unique quality to his ministry.

'I'm still here.' He looked at her again as she prepared for him. 'See? This is me.'

And, delightful, beautiful, gorgeous, desirable as he declared she was to him, he couldn't ignore her.

Morning brought dim daylight filtering through the small window of the bedroom. She could see workers passing in the street beyond. Had he blanked the window during darkness? She certainly hadn't been aware of being on show. He must have. Perhaps he'd restored transparency to allow light in from the street whist they slept.

Daisa rose and passed her hand across the pane, expecting it to darken, a mirror surface reflecting outside to prevent the curious gazing in, but nothing happened. She tried a voice command. 'Obscure the glass, please.' Still nothing.

She'd be visible to passers-by on the street if she turned on the lights. It didn't bother her, but Gabriel wouldn't want others to see her. She dressed, and only then woke Gabriel from his deep sleep; result of a night of extraordinary passion.

The experience had been a surprise for her. His basic animal desire barely softened by the thin veneer of civilisation and consideration for her enjoyment. But he'd kept that control in place in spite of his obvious delight in her abandonment. An entirely new experience for her, almost overwhelming in its visceral intensity. She was conscious such passion might overcome common sense if she were to allow it.

'Wake up, sleepyhead!'

He opened his eyes. Looked up at her face. Took in the faint daylight.

'Jeez! What's the twattin time?'

Interesting. A term that to him must be blasphemous, coupled with a misogynist expletive, the origin of which was probably unknown to him, but a word he surely wouldn't generally use around her. So, he was genuinely upset.

'What is it, Gabriel?'

He sat up and was about to leave the bed. She passed him the wrap-around he wore during the day.

'You don't know?'

'One thing you'll learn, if we stay together, is I don't ask questions when I know the answer.'

'Jeez, but you're strange. Beautiful but a puzzle.'

'So, what's upset you about the time of day, Gabriel?'

'I have to be at work.'

'Won't it wait for you? Or, surely, someone else will do whatever it is you think's so important it takes precedence over your own welfare and my feelings?'

'Jeez, you really don't know. We work for our credits. Or we don't eat …'

'I know that. But what's that got to do with the time?'

Her ignorance baffled him. He explained. 'Work is for a period. I work a shift. I have to be at my place of employment by a particular time and can't leave till my shift finishes. And I'm already late. Haven't time to explain. I'll lose more credits the longer I stay.'

'I'll walk with you. We can talk on the way.'

She was quick to understand. Full of consideration. How could he be angry with her? It wasn't her fault he'd overslept. Except that the sheer passion and energy they'd expended during the night had made him sleep past his accustomed time.

'Okay.' He rose and splashed at the basin in the corner. Sprayed himself with scented vapour that left a cloud of chemicals hanging. Daisa avoided it. He cleaned his teeth.

'Right. Let's go.'

She took his hand as he left the pod and loped with him along streets already busy. Mostly men, they were travelling in both directions and Daisa understood they were making for or returning from the processing plant on the far side of the city.

'If you didn't work, you'd need support to pay for your room, food and clothes.'

He nodded in reply.

'Suppose I pay. Would that help?'

That stopped him short. Daisa was pulled to a halt by their contact and stood waiting for his reply.

'Can you afford to support me?'

'Would I offer otherwise?'

He seemed unsure, confused. But it went deeper than that. She could sense some cultural element that made him doubt her proposed gift.

'It would free you up to spend more time on your ministry.'

'Almighty Jehovah Allah God Most High will provide. Of course! I never thought He'd do it this way. But that's why you came. That's why you were at the same cafe as Stefan, why he met you and why he didn't take advantage of your charms but brought you to me. It's all so clear now.'

'Do you have to use that irritating title? Can't you just call him God?'

'It's what the Almighty said we must use.'

'Well, it's really annoying.'

To her surprise, he dropped to his knees and placed his palms together in front of him at chest height. 'Almighty Jehovah Allah God Most High, I thank You for Your intervention. I accept what You offer. I accept with grace and gratitude and hope for greater service to You from this day forward.'

Daisa waited until he stood again and took her hand once more. The whole experience was so alien to her understanding of the world that she was intrigued and fascinated. This was a man who would provide her with much to consider, much to learn, much research.

'So, d'you have to go to your place of work, after all?'

He seemed to emerge from some other place, to return to himself as if absent for a time. 'You've been sent to me by Almighty Jehovah Allah God Most High, Daisa. I must accept what you offer, as it's a gift from the Almighty Jehovah Allah God Most High. But, yes, I still have to visit my place of work, to let them know I won't be going again. If I don't, it'll look bad on my record. My father will be furious. But no matter.'

She'd no idea what he meant, but was happy to accept he knew the rules of life in this strange city.

They walked, now, hand in hand. No longer the loping speed of urgency but a gentle stroll through morning streets. Their complement of tired returning men and sneaking, returning women, was slowly replaced by active places of commerce furnished with their garish and loud signs.

The long, winding street they trod opened into a wider, more open area that had echoes of the squares in Marion, though here the buildings, road surface, and overhead supports for the nightroof were of poor quality and basic design. The whole place had the look and feel of a rough sketch for a good idea that had never found full fruition. It left her feeling sad at missed opportunities and wondering what she might do to bring better conditions for the people who dwelt here.

'You twattin cow!' The voice was harsh and threatening and Daisa turned toward it.

'Leave it, Daisa.' Gabriel tried to pull her away from the disturbance.

The man was berating a woman bowed before him, obviously scared.

'Twattin bitch!' He lashed out at her face with his fist so she fell backwards. He reached down and forward, grabbed a handful of auburn hair. Dragged her back to her feet and slapped her twice more with his free hand. She made no attempt to defend herself and Daisa was dismayed nobody came to her aid.

'We can't allow this.' She tried to wrench her hand free of Gabriel who was determined to prevent her intervention. 'Let me go!'

Startled at the passion in her voice, he released her.

She covered the space between them in secs and caught the man's arm as he was about to strike the woman again. Without a word, she twisted it behind his back and forced him to the ground on his face. Her foot in his back held his arm in place. The woman looked on with relief coloured by horror.

Gabriel moved toward her, reluctant to get involved, but his face expressing admiration for her skill.

The man struggled under her foot, so she kicked him with her other one. 'Stay still, worm, or I'll break your arm.'

She'd no intention of causing further pain, but such a threat was necessary in the circumstances. Glad she'd opted for martial arts lessons in her early years, it was a while since she'd had any practice, but her memory was fine. She turned to the woman. 'Are you alright?'

The woman looked at her in utter confusion. 'I'll get by. Why did you … I mean, how did …? You fought a man!'

Daisa half shrugged and nodded. 'He attacked you.' The obvious was the only possible response.

'He's a man.'

'A worm is what this coward is. No real man would behave that way. D'you want me to take him to the authorities who deal with such violence?'

The woman frowned. 'You mad? Stupid? Somethin wrong with your head?'

The man struggled again and she kicked him, harder. 'Stay still!' She smiled at the woman. 'My head? You think I'm insane because I stopped someone beating you? Clearly there's a lot I need to learn about this place.'

Gabriel was close now. She turned to him. 'What should we do with this … this creature?'

'Best let her go on her way, I suppose.'

'Not her. This excuse for a man.'

'Oh. Let him get up, Daisa. I'll compensate him for the shame. Then we'd better move on.' He indicated the gathering crowd of men and women, both genders looking distinctly hostile. Though she noticed admiring glances from some women.

'Compensate him? For what exactly?'

'Let him up, Daisa. Really. Please.'

He was pleading. She relented and removed her foot. The man struggled to his feet. His colour described some of his feelings, but his stance did the rest. Daisa, however, was unfazed. 'Not learned your lesson? I can teach you some more, if you want.'

He turned away from her, unable to decide how to deal with the situation, and looked at Gabriel. 'This twat with you?'

'I'm a woman, not a sexual organ on …'

Gabriel put a hand on her arm and his expression told her she needed to let him respond. 'The woman is with me, yes. She's from Marion. New in the city. Doesn't understand our ways. That's all.'

'Twattin Marionet! Better twattin learn er then, adn't you? Else she'll be getting shagged in the stocks, won't she?'

Gabriel put out his hand in what appeared to Daisa to be a gesture of friendship. The man scanned her, glanced at the woman he'd beaten, who remained close by, and then nodded at Gabriel and took his hand. They shook together in a complex movement she took to mean some sort of pact had been made.

'Four credits. Okay. Give the twat a good set from me when you show her what's what.'

Gabriel nodded at the man and guided her from the scene. They continued on their way in silence, the crowd slowly dispersing with many mutterings of shock and disgust fading behind them.

Once away from the square, he stopped and took her other hand in his, turned her to face him. 'You can't do that, Daisa. If he'd been less considerate and decided to prosecute, you'd have been stripped and bound into the shagginshack for any man to have you, for a whole day. Women sometimes don't escape that with their lives.'

Daisa was about to reply, but the look on his face was enough. It would obviously take time for her to come to terms with the laws, customs and priorities of this unpleasant place. She was the stranger here. She must adapt.

71

In silence, they continued toward the processing plant. Daisa kept her observation skills alert but resisted further action, though she was sorely tempted on several occasions. Here, it seemed, simple justice and consideration were absent. She must learn as much as she could about the place and alter her behaviour accordingly.

As a research student, she mustn't let personal feelings impinge on what she needed to glean from her surroundings. That would be counterproductive. But it was clear the social structure and laws of the city allowed a savage brutality, especially against women, and that was something she hoped Gabriel's ministry would address.

Chapter Twelve

Acacia found Zaphod in his lab, examining an unusual meteorite he'd picked up on his latest expedition. He seemed excited and full of life as always. His form was still a little disturbing but she was in awe of his growing intellect and continued humanity inside that metal casing.

'You know Daisa's gone to Marzero?'

'Good morning to you, too, Acacia. Yes. We connected on the Transhub. Passing ships, you might say. Oh, sorry, an ancient expression. Anyway, you're going to tell me the Credits Committee's concerned about her spending. Georgiy's told me.'

She examined the lump of space rock on the bench. Shiny, and now split into four pieces, it had an odd look that puzzled her. 'We're worried she might've been influenced by the subject of her research. He's apparently charismatic, and she's still so young.'

Zaphod took a small tool and drilled a fine hole into the sample, feeding the gas produced by the friction through a small tube to his bench spectrometer. 'Mmm, interesting.' He collected up the shavings from the drilling process and placed them into a glass dish for later analysis. 'Seems we've two alternatives. Leave her be, and let her discover important facts about this new messiah the Zeros are starting to worship. Or, call her back home and lose the chance of fully understanding what's going on in Marzero.'

'Isn't there a third choice?'

'Georgiy mentioned connecting with her and telling her to stop spending. But, given it's Daisa, and she's inherited some of the rebellious nature of her forebears, I don't think that approach would succeed. In any case, I'm sure she's set up maximum control over her experimental conditions.

'Daisa may be innocent of the ways of the Zeros, she may be subject to the usual physical influences of her age, but she's intelligent. I think she'll make sure she understands the reality of her situation.'

'If we get into debt with the Zeros, we could be …'

'Yes, Acacia. We could find ourselves on the bad side of the bargaining fence. I've suggested the Credits Committee keep an eye on her spending and take action if it exceeds what we can properly afford. But what Daisa's doing is important, no, potentially vital to our community.

'If this Gabriel becomes a folk hero of any significance, it could even turn out they'll become disciples in the same way the Cusp grew into a force for violent evil. We'd be best advised to know as much about this developing situation as possible.'

Acacia lifted herself to sit on the edge of the bench, her long legs just failing to touch the floor, so her feet were free to swing. 'You really think it could come to that, Zaphod?'

'We know an undisciplined mind can be persuaded of many things, made to believe what to the organised mind is incredible. The Zeros lack our logic. They work on an emotional base relying on social priorities we reject. They don't listen to lessons of history. And they still invest their community in two systems that time and experience have constantly proven are harmful and eventually fatal to society: they worship money and encourage the formation of leaders.

'Both systems are corrosive and ultimately self-defeating. But they live their lives by such rules. Illogical. Juvenile. Foolish. But it's how they are. So, yes, it's more than possible they'll eventually resort to violence in order to spread the myths and legends of their developing credo to us. We're not going to accept their dogma voluntarily. Their devotion to the false god they cling to in desperation will oblige them to force us to conform to their definition of good and normal.'

'And Daisa knows how vital her part in this might be?'

'Not when she arrived. But, as time passes, and she gathers info, experiences change, sees the realities of life under the regime, she'll understand the depth of the threat. I just hope she doesn't risk herself trying to reverse the trend once she fully understands it.'

'Surely, if what you say is true, Zaphod, we should at least warn Daisa of the possible dangers?'

He paused in his task and stared out of the window in the direction of Marzero, hidden thousands of ks beyond the horizon.

Raptors hovered on the winds, forcing smaller birds into hiding amongst the wide spreading branches of apple, pear, lime and orange trees, or into the dense canopy of the pines.

The area directly under his window was lush with short herbs, where butterflies and bees flitted pollenating various flowers. How different from his first days on Mars, so many years ago.

The dust they'd fought then was now soil, enriched with the mulch of centuries of seasonal growth. It was what they'd planned for, what they'd hoped would be the result of their extraordinary experiment.

The threat to their future was worrying. Two wars they'd fought already to preserve their vision for the race. Now it looked as though another could arise from the mental disturbances of a man already worshipped as a prophet and messiah by a multitude who lived lives desperate for hope and relief.

'If we warn her, she'll do one of two things. She'll abandon the enterprise and return home, breaking our only hope of useful contact with the situation. Or she'll rebel, as is her nature, call us a bunch of old fogeys and cut all ties until things become so dire she's no longer able to ignore the reality. Either way, we gain nothing and neither does she.'

'Logic alone, Zaphod? Sure you're not forgetting the emotional aspect here?'

'It's her immature state of mind I'm most concerned about. Daisa's clever, but she's still very young. Headstrong, even. She's quite likely to allow her hormones to rule rather than her mind. But she's there now. I'm worried if we interfere too heavily, she'll become all defiant youth on us.

'No, Acacia, if I'd known what she planned at the time, I would've stopped her before she entered the city.' He looked at her with sorrow, his metallic skin furrowing in an expression so clearly abliform she had to smile.

'You were away. By the time I reached Hoshiko to discover your whereabouts, Daisa was already on her way.'

'It's no one's fault. But intervention now isn't an option. We'll have to rely on her intelligence and personal skillset to tide us over the time of the unknown. At least she'll be in touch regularly to keep us informed.'

'I've had only one message from her. She's living with Gabriel in his pod and has met some of his supporters. Apparently, the sex is fantastic, but the food and drink's dreadful!' She slid forward and dropped back to the floor. 'You really want me not to warn her?'

Zaphod simply looked at her and she nodded.

'And Georgiy and the Credit Committee?'

'I'll pass the same message to them. Last thing we want is for her to lose the means to live there. Loss of income might endanger her. You know how deeply they rely on material transactions. At the moment, as a contributor, she'll be highly valued. If we take that away, we may put her in serious danger.'

'And if we get into debt with Marzero through her spending?'

Zaphod paused in his task, seemed to stare out of the window. It was an old habit from his days as an organic being and made Acacia smile with its reference to his earlier self. 'She'd have to be reckless to bring us to that danger.'

'She's already paid the rent for Gabriel's pod for the next full year. That's made a hole in our balance. If she dresses, feeds and looks after him completely, as well as herself, we could be in debt to them within, Georgiy estimates, three quarters. So, we'll keep an eye on her expenditure at least. But I'll warn the Credits Committee not to mention anything to her for the moment, on your advice.'

'It's done. You forget, unlike you abliforms of the first two generations, Hoshiko and I connect with CenCom and with other individuals.' Zaphod took her hand in his, gently squeezed it. The touch was odd but at least not cold.

In Marion, where he had access to infinite power, he could afford to raise his skin temperature to match that of a normal abliform. It made physical contact more comfortable for friends and colleagues.

It was at times like this, when he touched one of them, he became acutely aware of his artificiality. He missed intimacy more at such moments. At least with Hoshiko, contact was the same for both and familiarity allowed them to engage in ways that simulated their previous physical closeness. It wasn't exactly the same, but the connections he and Qiu had managed to maintain in his superandroid form echoed the release of oxytocin and dopamine. Even sensation was present. But it was a faint echo of their former activity and they indulged only occasionally, preferring cerebral connection.

They could've adopted the Chinese android forms, but their very sensuality required a huge decrease in cerebral function that neither he nor Hoshiko was prepared to accept.

Acacia left him to his work on the mineral samples he'd collected. He watched her depart and found part of his mind occupied by the simple beauty of the abliform body. He'd always appreciated the female form. These days, that appreciation was more aesthetic than carnal.

Surrounded by perfect specimens, in all stages of growth from infant to those who'd reached the point they'd selected their ageing process to cease, he was conscious of the wonder that biology and evolution presented in the body abliform. A precious casing for an even more extraordinary and priceless manifestation of thought, creation and appreciation that resided in that most amazing organ, the abliform brain.

His mind returned to the dilemma of Daisa. The info about Gabriel was both fascinating and troubling. He knew too well the susceptibility of the undisciplined, untrained mind to persuasion and conversion from logic and reason into worlds of fantasy, myth and irrationality. And such minds were the norm in Marzero.

Greed for things material, desire for power over others, resistance to change, unopposed inequality, cognitive dissonance, wishful thinking for an ideal impossible in the circumstances of their world, and the need for love and acceptance were all at the forefront of mental and spiritual activity in the crude and brutal streets of the larger colony.

Would Daisa really recognise the reality of her situation in time to escape contamination, or was she destined to be a sacrifice to the greater good as she struggled to come to terms with the truth about a man she clearly admired, even as she accepted him as a subject for study and analysis? Zaphod had no answer. He could only hope the education and upbringing the young woman had received at Marion would be proof enough against the temptations of sensation, material possession and spiritual laziness that besieged them all at Marzero.

Chapter Thirteen

Stefan watched the bank of screens with deep satisfaction. Nobody else knew of this place he'd won in a bent poker game. Rigging it had been easy; play a fool and you can use simple tricks to defeat him. And the man had been a moron. To have all that power and only watch people.

The idiot was a waste of space. If he couldn't recognise a diamond mine when it was right in front of him, he didn't deserve oxygen. The planet would do better without him.

Old tech it might be. But you couldn't fault the installation. Switching between rooms and streets was simple. Though a catalogue or onscreen index would've been a help. He supposed the original owner had a system for selection, but he'd been unable to find it.

Still, over the years, Stefan had come to terms with the limitations. Standard addressing was text imprinted for each location, so he always knew where he was. And sound quality was good. It would've been better to have more than two cameras in each place, but he'd learned to live with that. Secrets discovered had gained him much power and influence.

And now, almost it seemed by accident, he'd witnessed the hold Gabriel had over the girl. And the power the girl had over him. Some called it love; soft twattin morons. Lust it was. And they had it in buckets. A great lever.

For now, he was more interested in the discussion he'd come upon during these early hours. Unusual to find earnest activity among the Elite after midnight. Seven of the bastards. Sitting round a circular table, would you believe? Like that committee Virginia described at Marion.

She'd cried about that. But the woman needed to know he meant it when he wanted info. No marks, of course. The odd slap was okay, a spanking kept them under control. But it wouldn't do to have a woman he paraded as his consort bearing bruises. No. It was easy enough if you applied the pressure the right way.

Flat palm on sensitive skin. Made a great sound, too. And the soft twats always yelled. Great fun! The other way, when more punishment was needed, was a hard pinch on their inner lips. Made the twats scream and showed them you meant it, without leaving a mark. Or you could dig your nails in under their hairline, or on the joints under their toes. Ice on sensitive bits. All the same to him, as long as it got results. And it was fun when they begged for mercy. You let them grovel, let them serve you, and then did it anyway.

But this group of seven Elites here in Marzero, gathered in one of the bigger pods in Trumpyramid, they were something else. The women serving them were all stunners. Even a couple of blondes among them. He'd remember their faces, not that he was too fascinated by such features when the rest was available, but identification was key to success.

The men interested him just now. Power. All in a single place. He'd made the unusual decision to fix this screen, have this location always available. The random nature of the search made it nigh on impossible to return to a place by choice, so he had to keep those where maximum opportunity existed. And this was a diamond mine. Better, it was a Terbium source.

He already had two of the men as donors. One, the boss of the energy supply, he'd recorded telling his woman how stupid people were for paying for energy provided free by the sun. He'd laughed at her surprise. She must be stupid: shaggin the bastard for the price of her pod, when she had that sort of knowledge. For Stefan, it had brought much more. Such influence kept him fed, dressed, housed and entertained.

Insurance plans, that every subject understood, ensured he was never in physical danger. His demise threatened each of them with instant exposure, their dirty secrets made public on all Threedees in the city.

Only once had he been forced to demonstrate the truth of his threat. That moronic bastard had been torn to shreds, literally, by the angry mob. Still, it made it easy to persuade the rest of his insurance policy after that. Nobody had tried to do him damage since.

The seven were talking about Ceres and Vesta, both already getting close to their new Mars orbits.

'But, I ask again, can we be sure it'll work?' That was Elias. The only one concerned in any way about outcomes; risk averse.

'For Chrisesake, Elias. We've been through this 1,000 times. Nobody knows. It's an experiment. But if the brainboxes at Marion are okay with it, why should we care? They know what they're doin. We don't need to worry.'

'But that's my point, Viktor. They're uncertain. And they never sanctioned Vesta. They think it's a move too far. Too much risk.'

'What, exactly, you worried about?'

'I'm fine with the idea of the experiment. We need somethin to increase tectonic activity and stir the mantle and core so it develops more heat to make the planet warmer. But what we …'

'Jeez, Elias. You really understand that twattin science? I mean, really? Or is it all just words?'

Elias bent his head and summoned a woman. She stood beside him submissively, awaiting abuse. 'Drink's too weak. Fetch me somethin better, twat!' His finger and thumb pinched sensitive flesh that made her scream before he set her free to do his bidding. 'Look. I'm no scientist. None of us is. We're businessmen. But I've heard the brainboxes speak and I get the general idea. No one's certain it'll work. And the Marionets think there's a risk. That's all I'm …'

'Yeah, yeah. Risk fisk. Listen Elias. Since when did we suffer from any of these experiments, eh? Consumers might have a hard time, but so what? We can make more capital and income from the stupid sods by sellin them comfort if there's a problem. It's an opportunity. Bring it on, I say.' Marty was immune to risk. Saw every venture as a way to make more money.

'Anyone got anythin further to add, only I'm ready for some

entertainment if we've done with the serious stuff?' Viktor spread out his hands in a gesture of inclusion to the whole table.

'It's just we don't know the risk, that's what bothers me. I heard one of the Marionets say it was possible it could bring Olympus Mons back to life. Imagine that!'

'I can't. No idea what that even means. Do you, Elias? I mean, really?'

Elias shook his head and shrugged his acceptance. But Stefan knew he'd raise other issues next time they held a meeting.

'For now, we're satisfied the engineers can go ahead with the final phase? Time for a vote.' Viktor, senior man at the meet, stood and raised his right hand. 'All in favour.'

The others followed suit, Elias last to raise his hand.

'About twattin time. On the table, girls. Show us yours, wet an ready.'

Stefan watched for a few more moments until the spectacle bored him and he turned his attention to another screen, seeking entertainment of the forbidden sort or a further chance to find dirt on someone he could use in future.

Most people were asleep. The processing plant, never closed, never silent, had little to offer and he skipped past it. There were night workers elsewhere; women cleaning, men on guard at places stuffed with valuables. Whores entertaining men just off shift.

Sometimes, the sight of illicit naked female flesh was so available he became bored by it. But he could usually find something to keep him entertained if he was willing to flick through a few screens.

The city wasn't pretty. Not a place to find nice people. The system saw to that. It was a shit pile, where those at the top shat on those below and they shat on those beneath them. The women were at the bottom so they got the bum deal. He laughed at his own joke.

He was a man who'd gathered influence. He was doing fine. And now he had a gem in Gabriel, he'd do even better. Especially after Virginia fed his line to that innocent from Marion. Daisa was the most promising of his unaware recruits. She'd bring him a reward bigger than any he'd gained so far. He wasn't sure what, just yet, but it was going to be a zinger. That girl was pure Indium. And the best part of it all was she didn't have a clue.

He glanced again at the bank of screens. He caught the end of an illegal cat fight. But he'd watched loads of those, and he had no bet placed. He'd had enough for now. Thinking of that beauty from the other colony turned him on. Time to visit one of his harem; girls who'd give him what he needed when he wanted it. Virginia was all right for a bit of class and submissive fun. But he was after something more basic, primitive. And he knew where he could get plenty of that.

Chapter Fourteen

'Not happy, Zaphod. Not happy at all.' Georgiy sat across the lab from him, drinking his signature Black Russian from a hand crafted glass made by one of his many grandchildren.

'There's little we can do. We warned them. But they listen only when it suits them. In any case, we don't actually know what the outcome will be, any more than the Zeros.'

'They're close now. Last I heard was Ceres will be in place in four days. Well, GrandMa, being CenCom, was more accurate than that, but you get the picture. And Vesta will be positioned four days later.'

'So, we'll know fairly soon. Have to wait and see, Georgiy. I only hope the engineers we sent to help with Ceres get to Vesta before the Zeros place it without our input. Plenty of ships out there, plenty of power.'

Georgiy slammed his tumbler down hard, sending a small flume of liquid into the air, causing a storm in the glass as it settled back. He watched it with interest. 'Frackin morons! They are. Ill-educated ignorant primitives driven by lust, greed and prejudice. And now Daisa's over there with the moronic fools. What's she trying to do, anyway?'

Zaphod softened his skin to form a smile. 'She's fine. Daisa's bright. She's researching this new phenomenon, Gabriel. D'you suppose he was influenced by his name? That's what they called the "angel" that reputedly visited the, er, virgin before she gave birth as I recall. Jupiter's Balls, the utter rubbish they believed!'

'Give a name like that to a man brought up in superstition and ignorance and there's bound to be a bad result. Anyway, Daisa's our eyes and ears over there. She'll keep us informed of serious developments so we can be prepared for the worst.'

'What d'you see as the worst, Zaphod?'

He was silent for a fraction, consulting and zipping through various algorithms to find the most appropriate. 'CenCom's best assumptions suggest his rise to power and influence with a slight improvement of the lot of the women there, followed by a rapid decline in favour as some new commercial distraction comes along.

'There's growing interest in the latest money-making device. A fairly crude spy camera fitted with antigrav and guidance that lets a man keep track of any woman he wants. Forecast as the next big thing. Their patriarchal obsession with submissive sex will ensure the silly buggers forget Gabriel and his new movement for equality. They'd rather spend hard-earned credits on trivia, and concentrate their energies on usage and abuse of their women to get too concerned about a maverick like Gabriel.'

Georgiy studied him. 'Are you happy, Zaphod?'

He grinned at his old friend. 'You worry about me too much. Hoshiko and I both knew what we were doing. We still love each other, you know. We're together less than we were, but, well, eternity's a damned long time, isn't it?'

'You really think that's what we've got? You in your shiny suit, us in our constantly remade bodies?'

'It's what the research shows. Those labrats I first used are still around after living 5,000 times longer than they should. I call that pretty eternal, don't you?'

'So, barring an accident you and the medibots can't repair, we'll all live forever?'

'Accident or deliberate and brutal murder, yes.'

'Nobody around Marion's going to commit murder.'

'Someone from Marzero might, given motive and opportunity. It's why we need to keep an eye on them more than we do. Do we still use that link Buzz brought back from the Moon all those years ago?'

Georgiy scratched his head. 'Jupiter's beard! I'd forgotten about that. Does anyone know where the access point is?'

'Try Buzz. He could do with something more productive to do than fuck his indifferent way through the young female population. Why he can't be content with that gorgeous wife of his, I'll never know.

Commitment problems. I think he's our sole mentally unstable resident. And we only invited him here because of Brigitte's heroic actions against the Cusp. He could turn out to be our flaw, our weak point.'

'I'll get him to locate the access and set a roster for the screens. An hour each shouldn't be too onerous. We'd only have to do it, what, once every 17,000 odd days. Hardly a burden!'

'Maths is improving, Georgiy. That the recent learning program?'

'It's what we do, isn't it? Well, when we're not engaged in leisure pastimes, art, crafts, socialising, love-making or any of the other pleasures we enjoy now we don't have to work. You'd have thought our model would've sold itself to the Zeros; it's a no brainer.'

'For the common folk. But they have leaders, businesses. Those types are never going to give up their privileges or let their citizens follow our lead, even though the Elite would gain if they used our model. They're the ones we need to educate.'

'Been trying for years, Zaphod. Talking to Olympus Mons makes more impact. They're blind and deaf to reason. I feel for the women.'

'Well, maybe this Gabriel guy will do some good there. It's part of what he's preaching. Risky, but he seems to have support, even from some men. How far he'll get before the leaders shut him down, or shut him up, who knows? Daisa told me that aspect of his ministry appealed to her; perhaps she'll help the prophet change their lot. Just as long as he doesn't go all religious extremist along the way.'

Georgiy finished his drink, placed his empty glass in Zaphod's new kinotec unit. It would be waiting for him in his own pod by the time he arrived. Still in the prototype phase, the device was already proving reliable for the small items they'd transported. Once convinced it worked without damaging anything, he'd provide units for everyone at Marion. And, of course, sell the plans to the Zeros, in exchange for further supplies of essential minerals and rare metals.

If only they could be independent of the supply chain, they need never have to concern themselves with the primitives at Marzero. But that was an unlikely scenario, given the paucity of certain minerals and vital elements on the planet. Access to the Asteroid Belt's mining and processing capacity were things their own community hadn't pursued and wouldn't try now; too much heavy engineering. So the relationship with Marzero remained; it was, in any case, a useful tool to keep track of their activity.

'I'm off, Zaphod. I'll have Buzz get that system up and running and tell you of any developments around Daisa. Do svidaniya.'

'Jupiter's moons! It's a while since I've heard you say that, Georgiy. Feeling homesick for the motherland?'

Georgiy nodded. 'Sometimes. Don't tell me you never think of the old places.'

Zaphod considered. Did he? 'Once in a very long while. Amber's still listening.'

'I let it go 40 years ago. Seemed a bit pointless. But Amber's still keen. She and her team sent another probe off to Earth a while ago. I think it was damaged by all the space debris orbiting the planet.'

'For a man who declares his love for her, you don't know much about Amber's work, Georgiy. You know her team devised the most spectacular clean-up device? Cleanser1; sent it off to sweep a clear path through for her next probe. Haven't heard how it went, but I can check.'

'Not just now, Zaphod. I'll ask her when I get home. Always good to show an interest in your partner's work.'

'Easy enough, especially if you really love her. Hoshiko's passion for fashion always puzzled me, but it fascinates her, so I take an interest.'

'You're right. You forget how much we rely on each other when you've lived together for so long. I'll make the effort. Thanks, Zaphod.' Georgiy left.

Zaphod watched him through the lab window as he crossed the courtyard. He always paid his respects to the fallen from the Cusp War. For a while, his friend stood with his head bowed before the simple stone tablet set in the low wall. Zhen and Akash, lost to a pointless battle.

There was no memorial to Cusp losses. They were commemorated in a more appropriate way. Maddie's remarkable piece of sculpture, using damaged parts of their attack equipment, told of their brutality. Sited at the entrance to the uni campus, it was a permanent reminder of the wickedness of war. He was glad it wasn't visible from his lab or his pod.

Earth: Georgiy's sudden reminder brought it all back. Did any abliform life exist following their slide into chaos and war after the climate finally descended into the maelstrom science had predicted for so long? Amber's latest probe might produce some new results. What would they do if they found signs of people alive there?

Chapter Fifteen

The internal contradictions in Gabriel's message needed pointing out, but Daisa understood the value of her neutral position. Standing back and allowing events to unfold would let her examine, analyse and dissect afterwards from the luxury of her detached attitude and location. With a memory for detail that rivalled even the best of her professors, she was well equipped mentally to allow the development of the situation before starting to quantify her data.

'I'm puzzled, Gabriel. Can you explain why women in Marzero are treated as second class citizens?' She was seated beside him on the bed they'd recently occupied.

'Before I do, there's somethin I have to confess to you Daisa. I've been very sinful. Dishonest. And I need you to hide my deceit.'

There was something raw and elemental in Gabriel that reached deep inside her, connected with her female needs and desires, held her in a place she'd not previously visited. She understood, on a conscious level, these feelings were the result of relative inexperience combined with her more primitive subconscious need for a figure of protection as she lived in this strange and threatening city. But she also recognised the emotional strength of her desire for his company and even his approval. The logic of the mental awareness did little to counteract the emotional constituent that informed her feelings. She knew she was acting unwisely, she risked unspecified dangers, but these actively added to her attraction to this strangely charismatic man.

'Tell me.'

'I've spread word that you're my ... virgin. My untouched female companion. I've put you on a pedestal to raise you above the crowd and make other women respect and envy you. You're my consort, without havin to give yourself to my physical demands. Do you see? As a virgin, under my protection, you've special status here. Unique.'

'Interesting. And you want me to perpetuate this fiction? To make everyone believe we've never had the fantastic sex we've just enjoyed? That it?'

He looked both embarrassed and intense. 'Yes. You get to the point straight away. I love that. What d'you think?'

'Let's say I'm intrigued. But I'd like your version of the circumstances that put women in such a dreadful position here before I decide whether to comply. Tell me, Gabriel.'

He shifted nervously, studied her from his slightly oblique viewpoint, examined every part of her that was visible. She moved, placing her arms behind her to rest on her outspread palms in a relaxed pose as she invited his gaze and studied him in return.

'You're very direct. We're not used to that from women, Daisa. You're … different, exotic.'

'Not in Marion. I'm ordinary.'

'All the women are like you back home?'

'All the men and women, using the Earth system of measurement, have the IQ of a genius. We're all perfect physical examples, because our DNA's engineered to that level. So, your judgement of me as special is dependent on viewpoint, you see.'

'My viewpoint right now says you're beautiful and special.'

'Well, that's very nice, but it isn't answering my question, is it, Gabriel?'

He shifted again, placing himself close beside her so they almost touched but he no longer had her in his eyeline. 'You know about the invasion by the Cusp?'

She nodded, silent.

'When they came here, what was then called MarsMegaMetalBase1 Omega, MMMB1O for short, all the women were scared they'd be killed. They surrendered to the terrorists and let them use their bodies as they liked. None of them tried to resist.

'When the Cusp killed brave men who resisted, the women pointed out which ones were pretendin to obey. They did everything they could to make sure they weren't hurt or punished by those evil men.'

90

He glanced at her and she simply nodded.

'When they failed in their mission and died, the men who were left here quickly formed a new organisation. The leaders were the most worthy men, those who'd hidden or worked underground to foil the Cusp's plans. They took over and explained to the rest of the men that the women, though they'd been cowardly and wicked, were the only females on the planet. So, instead of killin them, they were punished and made to serve men in whatever way we required. Women are inferior. They can't resist temptation.'

He turned to her again, awaiting her reaction.

'I see. And this is what you believe?'

He stiffened. 'It's recorded history. In the archive.'

'Which you've studied, of course.'

He frowned. 'Why would I? The Elite and Clerics tell the same story. It must be true.'

She nodded but remained silent.

'You don't think so, do you?'

'You believe it. Who am I, a mere woman, to argue?'

Her reply puzzled him. He couldn't decide whether she was serious. 'It's true. Every word.'

'Okay. So what's made you take the side of the women and try to get them a better deal, Gabriel?'

He stood, placed himself in front of her with his hands on his hips, his back straight and only his neck bent so he could look down into her face. 'I had a vision. You know that. I told you.'

'Yes. You didn't expand on that short piece of info, though. Never said what the vision was, what you think it meant.'

'Oh. I thought I had.

'I was workin, chastisin a woman on the line who'd neglected her work and caused a backlog. I took her away from the others, to punish her properly. But when I reached to take the strap down it wouldn't move. She was in position, waitin for five strokes. I stretched to release the strap from where it was caught up and my world went black.'

91

Daisa placed the everyday brutality in the compartment she labelled memories to be examined later in private and addressed the more practical problem. 'You banged your head? Fainted?'

'No. Nothing like that. I was temporarily blind. In the dark. I didn't panic, though. I asked the woman if she could see. She never spoke. But a voice came out the darkness. Told me I should forgive the woman. Not beat her, but treat her with kindness, give her pleasure. A reward, it said, would make her more loyal and increase her work rate.

'I could see again then. The woman was still in position. The strap had come loose and was in my hand, ready to be used. I asked if she'd heard the voice. She said she hadn't and begged me to get on with the punishment.

'I knew then God had spoken to me, except I didn't recognise it as God at the time. Instead of beatin her, as I was supposed, I did as God instructed. I gave her all the pleasure I could as she remained in position. She cried out in joy; the first time I'd made a woman admit to enjoyin it. And when I released her, she turned and smiled. I told her to go back to the line and do her best.'

Daisa considered the story in silence. Said nothing. Some details had been altered to suit Gabriel's expectations and allow him to interpret the experience as he felt it should have been. The phenomenon of such self-deception fascinated her. It was almost unknown in Marion and therefore of real interest.

'You don't believe me.'

'What makes you think that, Gabriel?'

'You see why it changed my mind? The woman worked better afterwards and I haven't had to punish her since. In fact, she asked me to pleasure her again. You see? It's proof the voice was real. The advice worked and I've a better worker, who'll do what I ask.'

'And you believe that means it was the word of this power you call god?'

'No doubt, Daisa. Couldn't be anything else.'

She inclined her head in what she hoped he'd accept as a token of neutrality but he actually saw as agreement. No matter for the time being. Clearly Gabriel had suffered one of his fits, during which the obviously intelligent woman took advantage.

Gaining unexpected pleasure as a result of her deception would naturally make her open to further such exploits, given the normal male usage. But Daisa wasn't ready to debunk Gabriel's delusions. For the moment, his self-belief fuelled his crusade on behalf of the women of Marzero, and she was all for that.

'What happened then?'

'Then?'

'Did you start to support change for the women as a result of just that incident?'

'Oh. No. I had to have more proof it worked. So I treated all the women I had in the same way. Asked what they liked, what they didn't. Tried to do what they most enjoyed, except for the awkward twats who pretend they don't want it.

'We know women can't do without, so I did them the usual way. But the others, the ones what told me what they liked, I gave them pleasure and they come back for more. I gathered a group of willin and happy women around me. I even sometimes fed them. They looked after my room and cooked for me. And I learned more and more ways to give pleasure.'

Daisa smiled. That explained his expertise at any rate. She'd obviously fallen lucky in selecting him as a sexual partner here in Marzero. The other men seemed unlikely to worry whether she enjoyed their self-indulgent thrusting.

'So, you realised there was something to be said for sharing pleasure rather than just taking it?'

'Some women fought over me, which was excitin, but I didn't want them to hurt each other, so I thought I'd better spread the news to other men about givin enjoyment. Most thought I was foolish. But some tried it.

'I learned some of the most popular men always treat women this way but never said, in case we thought they were stupid. To me, it looked sensible to tell as many men and women as possible about sharin. Everyone would gain, you see?'

'So you started to hold these meetings and tell people about your experiences.'

'Not straight away. I was worried I might upset the bosses. That's when Stefan come into his own for me. He's our top Cleric at the plant, so I'd had dealings with him on serious things, like when men and women tried to steal from the works. We punished the thieves together and got to know each other quite well.

'But he asked straight out if it was true about me sharin pleasure with women. I told him about my vision and what happened after. He's quick, Stefan. Sees things other men don't. It was him who first realised I'd been visited by Almighty Jehovah Allah God Most High. Said I was a prophet, a chosen one. I was sceptical. But I had another vision and told him. He explained what it meant. He's read the sacred texts, so he understands these things.'

'Stefan? Interesting. I didn't have him down as religious.'

'Oh, he's very pious. All that other stuff's just a false front he puts on to fool people. Really, he's very good and wise and gentle. Virginia loves him. I mean, imagine, he's the companion of the only woman with real status in the whole of Marzero. Every workin man wants her. But it's him she chose. That's got to mean somethin, hasn't it?'

'I suppose it has.' Daisa failed to give voice to her thought that it could mean any of a number of things, most neither positive nor complimentary. And, whilst Gabriel's maturing attitude to women's sexual pleasure was encouraging, it was hardly the revolutionary alteration to their lot she'd hoped for at the outset of her visit.

'It must. Anyway, we had some meetins and I spoke and explained my ideas and lots of people seemed to agree with me. A few shouted out from the crowd but others in the flock stopped them and word spread about my message. It was just a short time later I had my most vivid vision. That's when I actually saw Almighty Jehovah Allah God Most High. Well, you were there when I told them what happened that day.'

Daisa recalled the meeting, Stefan's introduction, and Gabriel's impassioned description of his experience. She had no logical explanation for the obvious accident he'd suffered, but was convinced Stefan had acted dishonestly in the situation. That something had occurred was indisputable. That Gabriel believed he'd been visited by the power he called God was equally without doubt. It would be fascinating to discover the reality. If she stuck around for long enough, she'd probably find out.

Gabriel relaxed as he watched her processing her thoughts. He gentled her back until she lay stretched over the bed.

'Again? My, you are passionate. Am I to comply and then deny it to your followers?'

He knelt over her. 'It would help my ministry.'

'Of course it would. And, of course, I will.'

It still amazed her that this simple physical activity could be so intense it took all thought and consideration away as hormones flooded the body. What a brilliant way for nature to ensure coupling and the continuation of the species. But that thought was quickly drowned by the very action she was attempting to analyse.

Much later, Gabriel, his arm still cupping her resting shoulder as they lay together, remembered. 'You asked for my version of why we treat women differently here. Do you think there's another version?'

Daisa, still bathed in the aftereffects, nevertheless understood now wasn't the time to deny his beliefs. 'Just an expression, Gabriel. As you said; history. In the archives. Must be true.' But, next time she was alone, she'd access those archives and see how they'd been distorted. Of one thing she was certain: Gabriel's view of history was different from that she'd learned as a youngster. Very different.

Chapter Sixteen

CenCom's announcement grabbed the community's full attention; they'd been expecting it for the past few days.

'At 06:39:18 today, Ceres was placed in an elliptical orbit of 29,076.7 ks at perigee, 32,956.3 ks at apogee and an inclination of 78.56 degrees, which ensures it will transit in enough proximity to both poles to produce increased gravitational influence in those regions. At the inception of the experiment, the effect of this new moon around Mars is currently unknown. That it will cause changes in the crust and mantle is considered 87.94% certain. The effect it will generate on the partially melted core is not known. Any estimate of such influence would constitute a guess and is therefore beyond this entity's capacity to determine.

'We continue surface and subsurface monitoring for seismic activity beyond the background state and will report instantly any significant change. However, we consider some increase is likely. Measurements already indicate that all lakes and the Sakharov Sea are now subject to tidal movement. Time will provide us with more accurate measurements and we will keep you informed.

'This is the end of news bulletin 856,753. Further announcements will occur at need and under the circumstances of significant developments.'

Acacia was with her Aunt Jannine.

'What's all that mean, Cacia? You know it's all jus so much jargon to me.'

She loved her aunt, but felt the woman who'd borne so many early children for the colony could have educated herself after all these years. But it would be unkind to point out her failings, so she merely smiled and explained about the slight possibility of Marsquakes and the even lesser likelihood of volcanic activity.

'We all gonna die?'

'No, Aunt. We probably won't even notice. Nothing to worry about. Really it isn't.'

Her answer satisfied the woman who'd been a prostitute at MMMB1O in the days of the Cusp War. Afterwards, Jannine had been one of 19 women who'd opted to become 'brood mares' to allow Marion to expand its population more rapidly than the four Chosen and four pioneer women could've managed. After birthing 50 infants, breastfeeding, and then handing them over to nursery droids, she'd retired with honour.

Zaphod and Qiu's maternity treatments had kept her fit and healthy throughout. Once discharged from her duties, their DNA treatment allowed her the usual 'eternal' life. She'd chosen to regress to a chronological age of 22 Earth years.

'I was at me best then. Right looker.' She now spent her days absorbed in the many games available to the community, her nights with any man who wanted to be with her. A generous lover, she was never short of partners.

'Don't you ever want to learn more about …?'

'Now don't you tell me ow to live my life, young lady. I birthed your grandmother. An don't you forget it. I know my value. An I know my … I know what I can do and what I can't. Brain work was never my thing. Much better with the body. As my thousands of satisfied clients would tell you. Still enjoy it. It's a real shame Zaphod's not able no more. Used to really enjoy him gettin me preggers. Best fuck ever. Lovely man.

'Right, Cacia. What's it to be? Wanna do the double-up in Sirens of Venus, or go opposite in She Said Yes Too Many Times?'

Acacia was keen on neither game, but she respected her old aunt and usually pandered to her particular fancies when she visited. 'Sirens. But only if you let me play some Transgender Chicken whilst we're gaming.'

'Ooh! Put on that "Tomorrow I May Dream." Love that track.'

As usual, the game was ready and they spent the rest of their time together stalking, plundering, kidnapping and generally creating mayhem in the virtual world set on Venus as a terraformed paradise populated by the powerful women they personified as online entities and the gangs of well-formed men they must control for their own purposes. As usual, they came out winners and Acacia, in spite of her slight aversion to the game, left her aunt in high spirits.

Her sixtieth novel was close to completion and she was eager to get back to it. But Buzz had other ideas.

'Not now, Buzz. I'm not in the mood.'

He'd caught up with her as she made her long, loping strides along the path through the trees. 'I want your help with something Georgiy asked me to do. Not that I wouldn't mind some action. Especially with a lovely like you, Acacia.'

'Help with what?'

'You know I found that link-up the old CIA made on Earth? Well, during the War of the Women, I infiltrated MMMB1O and tied it in with a primitive system the bosses installed there. At their end, I put in a small program to disrupt their stepped search and replaced it with an unsearchable randomised protocol.

'Our link's still searchable. After we won the war, we left the lot in place. As they extended their spy system throughout Marzero, we could watch them when and where we liked. Trouble is, no one's looked at it for over a century; no need since we've been at peace.'

'And?'

'Hold your hurry, Acacia. I'm getting to it. They want to keep an eye on Daisa and that weird prophet guy who's stirring up trouble in Marzero. Thing is, I can't remember where I fixed the link or how I got into the frackin thing.'

'And you think I should know?'

'You interrogate the system better than anyone. I mean, look at the stuff you dug out for that thesis.'

It was true; she was an expert on searching both CenCom and the older systems. 'Okay. Yours, or mine?'

'Come to mine and I'll treat you to your favourite poison.'

Buzz might be a throwback in the way he treated women, but his skill at mixing cocktails was legend. 'You're on.'

They wandered the rest of the trail side by side until they emerged from the wooded area and took the route along the shore of the lake. At one point, a gang of constructobots, supervised by a dedicated droid, were raising a portion of the path where it dropped very close to the level of the water. A temporary footway led in a small arc around the work party.

'Problem?'

The droid acknowledged Acacia's question with a nod. 'Yes, Ma'am. The new moon's caused a tidal effect and this part of the path is in danger of flooding. We think it best to avoid it by raising the path. The tide alone won't be an issue, but if a heavy rainstorm coincides with high tide, the path will be under water here.'

Acacia thanked the droid and they took the detour. Buzz lived in a single pod. His original home with Brigitte had become a difficult place for both of them with his propensity for inviting other women home for sex. They'd agreed on separation and Brigitte now occupied their old double pod with her occasional partners. Buzz had settled for the lakeside, where he could continue his 'conquests' without the frowns of disapproval he'd suffered at home.

Acacia followed him into his abode and hid her reaction to the slightly feral scent. Discarded clothes covered the seating areas and she unceremoniously flicked them on to the floor.

'Where's your domestic droid, Buzz?'

'Never needed one. If they'd let me have a Chinky, I'd have that in a flash. What man wouldn't, eh? On tap whenever you want it.'

Acacia made no comment as she glanced at the mix of male and female attire. She wondered what the women had worn to return to their own pods. Nothing, probably. Just glad to get away. It was rumoured no woman ever had Buzz more than once. But it didn't stop the youngsters giving him a try. Perhaps they believed they could be the one to change his ways. A hopeless, pointless dream.

She noted the long-range terrestrial telescope mounted on a tripod and aimed at the swimming jetty on the lake. But she said nothing.

He mixed them both a drink. Her Jupiter Moonjuice was, as expected, the best. His own Eris Bombblast smoked rather threateningly for a while, but its heavy, rather pungent, aroma soon masked the earlier scent she'd detected. He clicked music into the area, a little too loudly for her comfort until she pointed this out.

'Got to play Plutonium Popsicles loud to get the true sound.'

'Maybe. But I prefer to hear myself speak.'

He shrugged and told the sound system to reduce volume. He raised his glass to her. 'Bums up!'

She nodded and took a second sip from her conical stem glass. Last time she'd had a drink with Buzz she'd succumbed to his pleas. She had no desire to repeat that experience. 'Right. Where's your terminal?'

He called the command and the terminal rose from the bench under the window. She scanned the controls and selected her preferred configuration; a mix of audio and tactile that suited her own method of input. The console floated across to her and hovered just above her lap.

For the next seven mins, with occasional advice from Buzz, she quizzed the system until she located the precise position of the link they sought. It was physically stationed in a small office in the University lobby area. Of pre-antigrav vintage, it wasn't portable.

Acacia was delighted; it meant they'd have to move to that location and she wouldn't be stuck in Buzz's pod longer than necessary.

'Duff! I'd forgotten we'd put it there. One more favour?'

Acacia sipped her drink. 'Yes?'

'Can't recall the password. I mean, it's a century since …'

'Finish our drinks? Then I'll see what I can do.'

'You're an angel, Acacia. Sure you don't fancy a quickie?'

'I'll pass, Buzz.'

They walked the direct route, crossing the meadow where many species of wild flowers were thriving. A few butterflies floated lightly on the soft air. Buzz remembered early days on Earth of times spent running over hills as a lad, his plastic lightsaber glowing as he chased screaming girls, attempting to subdue them to his will, which he'd never managed.

'Beautiful, aren't they? You can see why the less developed and poorly educated mind uses such things as a reason to believe in a creator.'

'Can you? Just insects.'

'No soul, Buzz, that's your trouble. You wouldn't know romance if it ran up and clamped itself to your overactive member.'

'Wouldn't turn it away, though.'

'I don't suppose you would!'

They left the field and walked between two of the more modern pods that formed wings of the ever-expanding university. Here, they held lectures and demonstrations relating to history, and Acacia smiled at memories of her time learning the early facts that had prompted her to write her now famous thesis on the first years of Marion. It was legend amongst the colony and, as the author, she was recognised everywhere, and respected.

'Did me no favours, Acacia.'

'I treated you with absolute truth, as I did everyone, Buzz. I can't be held responsible for your personality defects.'

'Harsh!'

'Honest.'

He shook his head, but couldn't take his eyes off her body as she strode beside him. Nothing changes; once a libertine …

They entered the lobby and mingled with students engaged in study, talking, meeting, gathering for classes or making arrangements for their evening entertainment. It took Acacia back to her early days there; an experience she recalled with pleasure.

'Aunt Acacia! Hi!'

The greeting stilled some conversations and many of those around stopped to greet her with smiles, a wave, a shy touch to her hand or a softly spoken word of gratitude. Buzz gained a mix of curious stares and blank looks from the girls, indifference from the boys. He chose to concentrate on the curiosity and put on his most inviting smile as they wound their way through to the room they sought.

'Amazing. Does that happen every time you come here?'

'I don't usually come through the lobby. My own students are a little less in awe, thankfully!'

The console was buried under a pile of discards, most of them empty.

'We should call a droid to shift this lot.'

'Take just a few secs. You can organise the space when I've sorted your password. I've other things to do.'

'Really, Acacia? Writing stories? Hardly work, is it? I mean, Storyline's churning out material all the time.'

Acacia folded her arms and grimaced. 'Storyline's the equivalent of the writing factories they had on Earth. The sort of stuff put out by people like Patterson, Brown, Archer et al. Yes. Exactly. Never heard of them. But I bet you know King, Wilding, Austen, and Shakespeare, to name but a few.'

He nodded. 'So, you're saying it's to do with what exactly, quality?'

'Originality. The artist's voice. An individual take on the world. That's what good writing is, not the formulaic, easily written and more easily read and forgotten fare churned out by a machine or minds more concerned with money than quality of story. Sorry. Lecture over. Now, give me a clue. Were you still employing user names?'

He spoke his name clearly.

'Good. Why passwords, Buzz? Biometrics have been standard for centuries.'

'Old technology. When I first found it, there was no biometric access. Tell the truth, I think the CIA were suspicious of anything they saw as new-fangled.'

'Right. Tell me three of your last passwords; the stuff you used before biometrics finally resolved security issues.'

'That's a long time ago, Acacia. Let me think.'

'Don't try too hard. Don't want you needing repair work to your brain, do we?'

He was unsure whether she was serious or mocking him. He let it go and tried to remember. 'I had 99FuckOne. Then there was B00B1ES, and I think I used 5hagger5ex. Those do you for?'

Acacia nodded and interrogated the system she'd already primed with his user name. It was even more antiquated than the one she'd used during her student days, but general principles still applied.

She tried to work out how Buzz would respond to a password request for the type of system they were attempting to enter. A method of viewing and listening to almost every inhabited space on Earth, the Moon and the transports between at the time. A voyeur's dream, a private citizen's nightmare. So tempting to a mind like his.

She tried 5exOnline, 5exB00B5, and finally Naked45ex. 'I'm in. Get the droids to update the physical interface so you can access via bio-metrics, Buzz.'

The old system provided six panels to view simultaneously. He entered a six digit, two alpha code and the top left screen flicked to an interior of a changing room on campus. Fortunately, it was empty.

'I must get Georgiy to disable inappropriate links to Marion. They served a purpose in the early days but they'd be better excluded now. Let's see whether we can access Marzero, shall we, since that's the purpose of this exercise?'

Reluctantly, Buzz entered a few queries. Nothing happened at first. Then the screens blanked. He tried several more queries and the top left screen flicked into life showing the dark interior of a domestic pod. Obviously in Marzero; furnishings and equipment were old and utilitarian. Half a sec after the picture appeared, a text emerged at the bottom right. The location code. The right hand top screen brought up a schematic at adjustable scale, with the pod identified by a red overlay.

'That's it. I can work from here to find what we need. Of course, if they'd set up the system properly, I'd have access to a catalogue. But that'd be too easy.'

'I thought you'd disabled it so they couldn't use it efficiently?'

'Jupiter's balls! I'd forgotten. Somewhere in here it'll still be in place for us. Out of date, of course, but it should be easy enough to update it once I find the bugger.'

'I'll leave you to it, Buzz. Off to the easy job of finishing my latest novel. Or I might just hand it to Storyline and get the machines to do it. What do you say?'

'Okay, Acacia. Point taken. Go exercise your creative talent. And leave me to what I'm really good at.'

She resisted identifying his special skill as spying on others, and simply nodded and left him to it. But she was glad she had the skill to blank her own pod from his voyeurism. The thought of him prying on her every activity at home made her shudder.

Hopefully, he'd allow Daisa some privacy. But the job he'd been assigned meant he'd have to at least check on her from time to time. Bad luck for her. Maybe she should let the poor girl know. But, no. That would not only put her in a position of potential danger, it might inhibit her activity when with a man.

Chapter Seventeen

The meet had gone even better than the previous one. With Daisa at his side, her status as his virgin assistant already buzzing round the city, he had a real hook on which to catch the men as well as the women.

Now she wore the high-class skintight over that tiny pink bikini he'd selected, she was a sight the men were eager to stay for. If his words got through to them as they leered at her, that was a bonus.

God would be pleased with his efforts so far. But it was odd that he'd not been rewarded with a new vision for a while.

'D'you think He's displeased with me, Daisa?'

How could she respond to this illogical question and remain true to her rational self? 'You know more about that than I understand, Gabriel. Is it what you think?'

'Typical of a non-believer, Gab: answer a question with a question and spread doubt.' Stefan gave her his superior smile.

She was tempted to reply to him with the obvious repost that questions spread ideas and might even lead to rational thought. Her research proved religion used the tactic more than the rational. But that would deny her neutrality and she had so much yet to learn from this experience. She remained silent and awaited Gabriel's reaction.

'Questions aren't bad, though, are they? We should ask questions.'

That showed some intelligence. How would Stefan deal with it?

'Depends on the question, man.'

The opportunity was too good to waste. Daisa felt she must speak. 'Ignorance causes fear and prejudice. Education makes it easier for people to see the truth. That's why questions are good. Questions about anything and everything.'

Stefan curled his top lip and creased his brow as he stared at her. He turned back to Gabriel with a superior smirk. 'I mean, should we question God?'

Clever. He knew Gabriel could answer that only one way. She'd have to keep a close eye on Stefan. For all his devious and controlling behaviour, he wasn't as stupid as he often appeared.

'Never! We can't question the Almighty Jehovah Allah God Most High. That's sacrilege. Maybe I misunderstood His message. Could that be it?'

Daisa had revisited the ancient texts, consulted later texts that had described the early lives of prophets who'd troubled Earth. She understood how dishonesty and later interpretations by men with vested interests had distorted what had been, in many cases, a set of basically good ideas for people to live by. 'Perhaps your god's giving you a rest. Letting your followers absorb what you've already told them.'

He brightened. It was a solution to his anxiety he could accept. And it suited Daisa's need to remain neutral and learn more about his delusional state. Later, when she'd gathered enough data to expand into a thesis, she'd tackle reality with him, debunk his erroneous ideas and lead him into the world of reason before he became too deeply mired in irrationality. For the moment it was best he remained convinced about his god.

'Look, man, I got nothin against your new partner here. I mean, she's good for the cause. Figure like that on stage beside you an the men are caught. But, maybe, just maybe, your increased action with the lady has stopped the visions. Y'got them more when y'was alone, didn't you?'

'That's true. I never thought of that. Maybe Almighty Jehovah Allah God Most High doesn't like that I'm not tellin the truth about you and me, Daisa. I have to tell the whole truth.'

'Or, maybe, y'got to stop havin her.' Stefan's gaze was fixed on Gabriel, awaiting his reaction.

Gabriel looked at the floor, stroked his hands through his hair. He turned to face Daisa. 'Could you live with me and not do it?'

Daisa was aware of the fragility of his ego, and of the odd prudery around naming sex. 'It wouldn't be easy. We're good together. You think it might regain your visions?'

Stefan stared at her in open disbelief but said nothing.

'It might. Got to be worth tryin, surely?'

Daisa nodded reluctant support for the idea. 'We'll try for ten days. See if anything comes of it. Easier if I lived elsewhere?'

'Oh, you're too good for me, Daisa. No. You must live with me. It's part of the attraction for the cause. As long as they imagine you and I live together but don't do it, they'll see you as the sacred virgin who can resist carnal attraction. Puts you in a fantastic place, raises your status, and mine.

'Any case, if you move out and I'm not tempted by you bein here, it's no real test is it? If you're here and available but I resist you, then Almighty Jehovah Allah God Most High will see I'm doin what I can to obey His will.'

She was fascinated by the way he could evolve a form of life rule from the most unlikely of circumstances. His mental state was unique in her experience. Of course, Marion had erased mental illness, so she'd never come across sociopaths, multiple personality disorders, or any of the over 500 mental conditions and syndromes medicine had listed back on Earth.

It was a topic she must research more fully, having only tasted it so far. Physical illness was Zaphod and Qiu's domain and their DNA engineering had eradicated it from all in Marion. But mental illness was a different matter. It was equally absent, but nobody had taken much interest in the topic for decades.

She was already convinced his so-called visions were a form of mental aberration. If abstinence could somehow stimulate the peculiarity, and she could witness it, she'd learn something about the nature of the delusion under which he lived.

'Sounds sensible to me, Gabriel. What do you say, Stefan?'

She watched the emotions flutter across his features. He'd been surprised, perhaps even shocked, by her response. But he wished to support his friend for reasons she hadn't yet determined. That his concern had little to do with either her own or Gabriel's welfare was already clear. But there was some serious advantage in the arrangement for Stefan, of that she was certain.

'Sounds good, man. But can you do it? I couldn't have a tw … a female like this wanderin round starkers without givin it one. You're right. It'll be a proper test. Give it a go.'

He turned to Daisa. 'An if y'feel the need, y'know, well, I'm here.'

And back to Gabriel. 'Don't mind me offerin, d'you, man? I mean, a young woman. Has needs, y'know.'

'What Stefan says is true, Gabriel. But I'm not a lump of meat to be shared by those with a taste for me. I choose who shares my body. That's one of the many things that mark women from Marion apart from the poor women who live here.' She avoided the 'primitive' label that came to mind, trying always to maintain her air of neutrality.

'Gabriel and I will work on this testing time together. Find ways to sublimate our urges. Redirect our energies into more cerebral activities. It'll be a challenge, but we're both up for it.'

Stefan understood her exclusion of him from her desires but was reluctant to let Gabriel see how much it irked him. And Daisa knew this. Her independence prevented him using his dominant position to simply take her. She wasn't like the subjugated women of Marzero, to be used and tossed aside. That made her all the more desirable, a feature Gabriel was well aware of, and why she was so valuable to him as an example to other women.

'We'll tell people our decision and the challenge we're facin together. Volunteer to have tests done to prove we've been as good as our word.'

'Let's not invite doubts. We've already told them we're abstaining. Let them draw their own conclusions. You're trying to increase their faith in your god, after all. Proof doesn't sit happily alongside faith, does it?'

'You're so clever. I know Almighty Jehovah Allah God Most High sent you to me, Daisa. I hope I haven't abused his purpose by takin advantage of your attraction to me.'

'No advantage, Gabriel. The attraction's mutual. We'll be equally tested by our experiment in abstinence. And we'll be able to stand before your people and state honestly we've been free of intimate contact for whatever period we decide is necessary to determine whether the visions are dependent on such behaviour.'

'Uses a lot of long words, your woman.'

'She's clever, Stefan. A genius, you know. They all are over at Marion.'

'So they say. Don't get them the things what we've got though, do it? I mean. No gold on her. No jewellery. Jeez, twat don't even wear no make-up. I mean, what sort of twat goes about bare-faced, eh?'

Daisa watched the pair discussing her and decided against intervening. Their exchange would give her more material for her thesis.

'Doesn't need make-up. Look at her. Perfect. And they don't wear jewellery because they don't need signs of status, since they're all the same in Marion.'

'If you say so. Still like to see her in a necklace, earrins, bangles and nowt else, though. Wouldn't you?'

'I've seen her as she is. Glorious. Beautiful. Perfect. Gold won't improve her.'

Stefan snorted. 'Mebbie not for you. But the crowds'll see her in nowt but that skintight with her smalls under it. They'll think she's poor. Or you.'

'That's part of my message, Stefan. I'm tryin to get people to see status doesn't depend on possessions. Or it shouldn't. We should value people for who they are, not what they own.'

'That what God's told you?'

'It's what the sacred texts say. I know. I've read some.'

Daisa had also read the ancient texts and seen good and bad in them. She was curious about how Gabriel would react when his readings of the words of those early disciples clashed with his understanding of the world he lived in.

'Careful Gab, men've been fooled by ancient words. We live here an now, not in the past. Take care where you get guidance, I say. Don't want people up top gettin the wrong idea do we? We're tryin to make things better, man. Not worse.'

Daisa stood, stretched and ran her hands down her body. 'Time to sleep. It's late.'

Stefan grimaced but got the message. He was unused to being told to do anything by women, but said nothing about her implied suggestion. 'See you tomorrow. Easier now you're not workin at the plant, Gab.'

When he'd gone, Daisa clapped the new blinds across the windows, giving them total privacy, and then disrobed. 'So it begins.'

Gabriel studied her for a long moment before removing his own cover. Hand in hand, they slipped into bed. The test of the flesh was underway.

Chapter Eighteen

Seven days in, it happened. It had been a testing period for both. Now he no longer worked, they were together most of the time. Her research helped, after she'd hacked into the most advanced terminal she'd found in the city. Combined with her connection to CenCom, she had a truly comprehensive source.

And Gabriel spent time educating her about custom and tradition in Marzero. She learned the differences between various sectors and how to identify people from those distinct areas. That style of dress could be used this way intrigued her.

'So, basically, the more revealing the woman's clothing, the better her residential location?'

'But not showin their … y'know, bits. Anyway, I'd put it the other way round. But it's why I asked you to wear that short, sleeveless skintight with … what you're wearing now underneath. Jeez, you're tempting like that, Daisa. I could …'

And he stopped. She looked up into his silence, waiting for him to continue, and found him frozen in position, eyes open but unseeing. His direction of gaze remained at her, but she wasn't what he saw. She removed her top. No response, no reaction. She walked round him without touching him. He was in that other place, no longer conscious of his surroundings.

Quickly, she scanned her mental illness research. She knew she'd come across something like this. There it was. A type of epilepsy. In certain forms it produced a semi-catatonic state. What she wouldn't know until he came round again was which particular form it took. Fascinating.

On his emergence from the state, she was there to sit him down and help when consciousness fully returned. He sat for a few secs, blinking and disorientated, and then seemed himself again. Daisa checked her knowledge file again and was satisfied this was a rare type. He'd be initially unaware of his period away and would fail to refer to it, but recall something when prompted.

'You had your top on a sec ago. I didn't see you take it off.'

'A vision?'

'You are, but you shouldn't … Oh! Jeez! A vision! Yes. I … I need to talk to Stefan.'

'Why?'

'I always talk to Stefan after. He's a sort of … translator. Works out what I've been told by Almighty Jehovah Allah God Most High. I need him here now, Daisa. Now!'

His sudden passion alarmed her. She disapproved of Stefan; thought him a charlatan, bully, schemer and cheat. But couldn't doubt the bond between the pair of them. She used the primitive communicator from the pod and called Stefan's place first. No response. She tried Virginia.

'Not with me, I'm glad to say.'

Daisa cached that info. Explained.

'Oh, right. Try Magdalena. He spends more time with her lately.' She gave her the necessary code.

Daisa buried her frustration at the antiquated system and connected with the pod. The screen showed an empty room with a door partly open into another. At the sound of the second notification alarm, a woman entered. Statuesque and unhappy, she spoke. 'You're that Daisy woman. Stef's …'

'I need Stefan here. Now!' Gabriel called out before Daisa had replied.

Magdalena moved to the open door. 'Stef. Gabs needs ya.'

Stefan pushed naked past her into the room. 'What y'want, man?'

'Had another vision. I need you, y'know?'

Stefan's whole attitude altered. 'Be there in three. Stay calm. Daisa, make him strong coffee and give him somethin sweet. He needs it.' And he was gone into the other room. From there, he spoke again. 'Mags, get your arse out of sight. Disconnect. Want everyone to see?'

The screen went blank. Interesting. Who was Magdalena and why was Stefan concerned about Gabriel seeing her? It would wait. The data she could gather from the interpretation of the vision was more important.

She checked on Gabriel's condition then gathered up her top. If Stefan was coming round, she wanted to be fully covered. The drink was ready just before the man arrived. She handed the ugly container to Gabriel along with one of the sweet bakes he most enjoyed and then opened the door to the street. Stefan barged in without invitation, ignoring her as he walked swiftly up to Gabriel and sat beside him.

'You alright, man?'

Gabriel seemed almost himself again. He glanced at Daisa, nodding his approval before he turned to Stefan.

'It's happened. I've been with Him again.'

'Tell me.'

'He took my hand. Soft and comfortin in that dark place. Led me down a windin passage. At the bottom people were wailin and cryin out. Pain or fear. Maybe both. Very hot there. Flickerin red and yellow. A woman. Undressed. Beautiful body but no face. Couldn't see who. Man on the ground at her feet. He wanted her but she ignored him.

'Almighty Jehovah Allah God Most High took me away and we were all in light. Brightness like when I first looked on Him. Blinding. Diamonds and gold in great piles. Strong powerful men surrounded by these wonders. No women. Warm and quiet and walls lined from floor to … no end. Rose up forever into the sky. All the things we need and want in the city. Everythin a man could ever want.'

Trancelike, he related his experience, which Daisa considered more dream than vision. She said nothing, however, waiting to see how Stefan would 'interpret' this everyday experience.

'Did god … did he speak to you this time?'

'Yes.'

Stefan turned to Daisa. 'Give us space, woman. Leave. Go buy somethin. 20 mins will do.'

Gabriel nodded when Daisa checked his reaction to this command.

In spite of her rebellious nature and a burning curiosity about Stefan's take on the dream, she thought it best to do as the man wished for the moment. She'd discover the outcome later.

The streets in this sector were less crowded, cleaner, wider. Wealthy and powerful men lived here. If she had to remain in the city, she wanted to be somewhere worth living.

Gabriel had worried at first he might be seen as no longer one of the people, but she'd explained they'd accept his rise in fortune as a gift from his god. Her deception, she knew, was disingenuous but she really did need to be living in something approaching the normality of Marion. This sector, far from ideal, was as near as she could get.

Stefan had been sniffy about the move at first but, after talking with Gabriel in private, had come to the same conclusion as her. 'Tell them it's God's will. Reward for your devotion an sacrifice.'

There were no shops here. The streets were lined with wide pods, some two storeys high. Underfoot, the walkway was relatively smooth and mostly free of dust and debris. She was treated with cautious respect by other female residents. The working women who came to clean and cook or provide personal services for the men, viewed her with a level of awe she found hard to accept. If she tried to speak to them, they cowered and fled her presence.

She missed the ability to wander freely from the confines of residential space to open countryside. Here, so much further north, the remaining icecap made the winds too cold to be outside the city without some form of protective covering. She always admired Gabriel his determination to run out there. Though he wasn't so active in that area as he had been. Maybe she should encourage him to start again. It certainly fed his energy.

The ground beneath her unshod feet shuddered briefly. A small quake. There'd been a noticeable increase since they'd put Vesta in place in a slightly closer orbit than Ceres but at the same inclination. Perhaps their combined gravities were beginning to impact on the planet. That had been the hope, after all.

It happened again. Stronger and a little longer. Along the walkway, a standard lighting unit swayed. And, right beside her, a window snapped as a crack appeared from a bottom corner, spread across the diagonal, and webbed out to craze the entire surface until it collapsed in thousands of tiny shards.

The woman of the house cried out in alarm and stood close, staring into the street, her face declaring her shock. A serving woman appeared. She gaped at the broken window for a moment before she gathered herself and placed a loose wrap around the resident, and gently led her away from public gaze.

In Marion, should such a thing ever happen, the droids would have it repaired in mins. Here it would be days before a replacement arrived. Daisa decided to return, to make sure her own place was still intact.

The increase in seismic activity, though predicted as a possibility, was a little unsettling and concerning. Various constructions on the planet had been built under less active conditions. If a building collapsed it might cause damage to people and systems.

It was still early days in the experiment. Were these first tremors just the planet making adjustments? Or were they warnings of things to come?

Chapter Nineteen

Buzz had found Daisa. He watched the discussion about the vision on one of the six screens, allowing the others to roam at random, as was the only option for residents of Marzero.

He saw Daisa leave the men alone. Now would come clues about the true links between these weirdoes. He'd learn something that might up his standing in Marion.

'So, your latest vision, Gab. Tell.' Stefan glanced at the door to make sure they really were alone.

Buzz recognised this behaviour, knowing people often exhibited unconscious signs of their own personalities when judging others. A sneak, perhaps?

Gabriel stood and began to pace, apparently gathering his thoughts.

'He held my hand. Soft and comfortin in that fearful place. Led me down a windin ally. At the bottom, people wailed and cried out. Don't know if it was pain or fear, or both. It was really hot. I saw flickering red and yellow, like flames. There was a woman. Undressed, with a beautiful body but no face. Couldn't identify her. A man on the ground at her feet. He wanted her but she took no notice of him.'

Stefan signalled he should pause. 'Right. This one's obvious, Gabs. God's tellin you women are a danger to men who don't show they're the boss. See? That's what the man she ignores means. And the flames? That's Hell, innit? You've read the texts. But the beautiful body with no face. That means a stranger, a woman who's a stranger in the city, is okay. You can have her. See, the naked bit means she's available.'

'Daisa? It means I can have Daisa again without Almighty Jehovah Allah God Most High bein upset?'

'Well, yeah. Daisa. She fits the description.' Stefan nodded to emphasise his agreement and indicate he hadn't thought of Daisa, but agreed with Gabriel's interpretation.

Buzz was sure the man was manipulating the so-called prophet.

He wasn't subtle enough to fool most people, but this simpleton seemed to fall for it. 'Moron!'

'What happened next, Gab?'

'Almighty Jehovah Allah God Most High took me away and we were all in the light. Like the brightness when I first saw Him. Blindin. Diamonds and gold in great piles all around. Strong, powerful men sat surrounded by these wonders. No women ...'

Stefan held up a hand to show he wanted him to stop here. 'Yeah, well that's clear. Means wealth's a good thing and men should ...'

Buzz noticed movement on another monitor. Three women were performing an elaborate strip to music too soft for him to hear. He shifted his attention. High class courtesans from the best part of the city, they knew how to move and perform to their best advantage. He watched to the end of the performance and then had to relieve the urgent pressure created.

When he returned to the screens, Stefan and Gabriel were still in conversation, with Gabriel continuing his account.

'... everythin a man could ever want.'

Stefan was excited. 'Great! We have the right idea here in the city. It's the Marionets what's wrong. That's your mission, Gab. Get the people to understand we're doin it right and that Marion lot have got it all wrong!'

Buzz scoffed at this fabrication. Gabriel's guide was obviously a man who loved to control. And he was filling his friend's head with idiotic ideas. This sort of 'mission' would get nowhere. People would see straight through it. No point watching any more. He'd check up on Daisa at a later date.

He flicked through a few more screens throughout Marzero, more or less at random. One showed a room full of monitors, a team of men glued to them, earpieces fitted. He'd passed it before he recognised the possible significance. Fortunately, the screen that bore texts addresses, with links, scrolled more slowly and he was able to backtrack.

Yes. Definitely a group of men watching happenings around Marzero, listening in. So, the rumours were true. The Elite did keep an eye on their citizens. They obviously had a separate, and secret, system connected to the one Buzz was using. He put a marker on the room he'd found, for future reference. The content on the screens he could see in the room too small for viewing, he quickly lost interest.

'What a shit system. No way to zoom in. No sound control. Basic as buggery.'

Bored, he relegated the info and the discovery to the back of his mind. Being Buzz, it never occurred to him to warn Daisa she was potentially under constant surveillance. He went in search of more interesting viewing.

Now he'd managed to connect to every input from Marion, there must be some engaging stuff out there. A few secrets he could use to his advantage, a bit of inside info that might get him more enjoyment in the future. He flicked off the Marzero screens and started an organised scan of Marion, stopping at any populated by women.

'Must be some in changing rooms.' He scanned through until he was inside the EarthGrav unit, where people now went to maintain or increase their strength. And he was in luck; a group of women were doing natural yoga. He leaned forward, taking in the details.

Chapter Twenty

She'd given them time. More than enough. And she didn't trust Stefan as a guide. But she understood the need to allow Gabriel his friend's help as long as she wished to remain neutral for her research. It was growing harder as the days passed, but scholarship still ruled over other considerations, for the moment.

The men were ending their talk when she returned. She was welcomed back by Gabriel with some of his original passion. Stefan merely leered at her in his usual way until Gabriel made it clear he wished to be alone with her. He passed a secret lustful threat at her as he left, leaving her in no doubt as to his desires. The thought of him that way made her shudder.

'God's told me we can do it. It's okay! And I won't have to use Almighty Jehovah Allah God Most High any more. Just 'God', He says.'

Gabriel's enthusiasm and eagerness contrasted so strongly with the controlling selfish urges of Stefan that she willingly surrendered to his immediate wants.

The covers kept the chill of the pod from their skin.

'Heatin's failed again. We'd best stay here for now.'

'Does it do that frequently?'

'Often. They never refund us.'

'What do you mean, Gabriel?'

'We pay for a heated pod. If they don't heat it, they should owe us some payment back. A refund, you know?'

'I suppose so. We don't have to think about such things. But you're right. It's unjust. Mind you, your whole system's unjust.'

'How?'

Daisa struggled up and sat facing him, the cover wrapped over her shoulders. 'You all work, often for long hours, doing unpleasant tasks that, frankly, should be done by robots and droids, but you …'

'You can't let droids and robots take over the work. We'd all be un-employed. Where would we get our income?'

'Nobody works for money at Marion. We all have a great standard of living. Some of us work for the community; things that abliforms are better at than droids and robots. Zaphod has a team of medics who keep an eye on the health of everyone, for instance. They work with droids, of course, but there are things people do better. And we've a great team of design engineers, working with specialised droids to make spacecraft, satellites, telescopes, accelerators, that sort of thing.

'A lot of people do space observations. Loads of senior members, and some younger ones, take part in various committees we use so everything runs smoothly and everyone gets what they need. But nobody gets a wage.

'Droids and robots do the manual labour, grow food, keep the place clean and tidy, all the domestic stuff, tend the protein plants, operate the power generators, maintain machinery and equipment. Leaves us free to study, play, read, and do all the things we enjoy. And nobody has an income.'

Gabriel shook his head. 'No. That can't be fair. I mean. You said some people work for the community but don't get paid. That's not right. They should have as much free time as everybody else, shouldn't they?'

'They choose what they do. It's not a duty. They do it as and when it's necessary or if they feel like contributing. It works very well.'

'Doesn't nobody ever complain they're not gettin their share, then?'

'We all get the food, clothing, equipment and everything else you can think of, that we need. Why would we complain?'

'What about jewellery? Make-up? The latest device, like … like say a new communicator? How do you get things like that?'

'None of us use pointless adornment. Same with make-up. And I communicate with anyone I want whenever I like. It's easy. I'll show you.' She sat still for a few moments. Gabriel could detect no action, hear no voices. She held no device in her hand and, given her state, could have nothing concealed on her person. She remained silent for a few mins. 'There. Just had a conversation with my mother, who says they didn't have those tremors we had earlier. Sends her regards to you, by the way. Says you're quite a dish, especially as you are at the moment.'

Gabriel instinctively curled up. 'How? How d'you do that? Can she see me?'

Daisa laughed. 'Not now. Only when I let her. Don't worry. I didn't show her all of you. That's for me.'

'Where's your communicator?'

She pointed to her temples. 'Vis here.' She lightly tapped her right side. 'Audio here.' The left temple. 'Implants when we're born.'

'Impossible.' Gabriel shook his head, as if trying to clear it of errant thoughts. 'It's not possible. You're teasing me, Daisa.'

She shrugged, surely all this stuff was common knowledge? Though Gabriel's reaction suggested she was wrong. 'If that's what you want to believe. CenCom, we call our AI GrandMa, records everything into its memory and uses the data to constantly adjust our general environment to optimise it for us all.'

'How do your implants keep going? Use batteries, do they?' His sarcasm should've warned her of the fear he actually felt, but her need to defend the superiority of her community overtook her common sense.

'They're powered by tiny wheels driven by blood flowing through nearby vessels, apparently. I never really took a lot of notice in tech class, to be honest, so I don't remember much about it. But the medibots and nanobots do all sorts of useful things. We keep our own squad in a pouch just under our liver.'

'You've got robots inside you?' His look of horror amused her greatly.

'Everyone has. I bet you have. Otherwise what happens when something internal needs attention? I mean, you'd get ill. Maybe even die!'

'Everyone gets ill. Everybody dies. Else we'd live forever, wouldn't we?'

'Yes. We will.'

Gabriel threw back the cover and left the bed. He grabbed his clothes and started to dress, shoving arms and legs in with exaggerated force, stamping as he placed each foot down. 'I'm not a moron, you know. I'm not a twattin fool! You think you can feed me rumours like they're true and not make me angry, Daisa? I'm no idiot, no simple twat to be fooled by fairytales and children's stories. Don't try to make a fool of me!'

Daisa watched calmly. She drew the disturbed cover back over her body, wrapped it over herself against the chill. 'You believe I'm telling you lies, Gabriel? Really think I'd do that, after what we've done together, what we've been? Don't you trust me?'

He scratched his head. Stood at the far side of the room staring at her in disbelief. 'I can't believe you think I'm that stupid. We're not ignorant. Just because we live in the city and you come from that high-fallutin commune so full of your so-called peace and love. Oh yeah. You're all geniuses. Great! But we're not fools. We know the difference between truth and lies. We know what's really happenin.'

Daisa was fascinated by his reaction. There was a part of her that felt a little sorry for him and his depth of ignorance, but his outrage and self-delusion fascinated her much more. It was a real opportunity to study primitive attitudes close up; something she couldn't resist.

'So, I suppose you don't believe Zaphod's a superandroid who was once a man, like you? He's hundreds of years old.'

'That's just crap you lot put about to make you seem more important, more advanced than us. We know. We're not ...'

'Stupid. So you keep telling me. So, if I explain we're raised to tell the truth, that honesty's an inbuilt feature of our society, you wouldn't believe that either?'

He clasped his hands into tight fists. The fury was barely masked and she realised for the first time that this man was as primitive as she'd been warned. He may even be a danger, if she didn't remain alert to possible attack. Alien as such a concept was to her, she nevertheless mentally prepared herself for an assault.

'That's just garbage! And you know it. Why are you doin this, Daisa? I thought we had somethin good, somethin special.'

'We have. We still can, if you calm down and listen. I can explain. Better, I can take you to Marion and show you. And, if you won't believe me, ask Virginia; she's been to Marion hundreds of times and seen us all. She knows the truth about us.'

She'd called his bluff. Given him an opportunity to have his doubts refuted. But Gabriel didn't want the structures of his life, the prejudices that supported his beliefs, the ideas that governed his very way of life to be damaged, maybe even destroyed by revelations from the other place. He couldn't live like that. It would make his whole life till now a lie if she managed to prove him wrong. No. That was untenable. Impossible.

'All just show. We know what you're up to. You think we're subhuman and ignorant. But you're not so clever. Where are your leaders, eh? Where are your tycoons and wealthy businessmen? Where are your service workers, your shops? You don't have half what we've got. Not a tenth! We're much more advanced than you'll ever be. You can keep your Marion and your Marionets. I'd rather live in a place where I'm valued, paid a good wage for my labour.'

Daisa was confounded by his attitude. How could he turn a rational debate into such an emotionally charged battle of words? It was both unsettling and exciting. An experience entirely new to her. Thrilling as well as slightly alarming. How far dare she push this man? How far before he'd be unrecoverable?

'So, you'd rather I withdraw my support for you and you go back to your job? Is that what you're saying?'

'I … Yes! Yes, that's how it works here. That's how we do things here in Marzero. Not men livin off women.'

'Really? So the money your women earn with their bodies doesn't go into the pockets of the businessmen who own them?'

He opened his mouth but no words emerged. She watched unacceptable thoughts chase each other across his face and knew he'd had enough for now.

'Look, Gabriel, we're just small players in the larger scheme of things. We each have to live according to how we've been raised. You live in your world, I live in an entirely different way. But, before you give up my support for you, remember what your god wants from you.' It was below the belt, a low and unworthy blow, but she really didn't want to lose her chance of researching this fascinating phenomenon just yet.

She let the cover fall. Opened her arms to him in a gesture of reconciliation and appeasement.

He released his tension, splaying his tight fists into spread fingers, relaxing his shoulders. His eyes were full of her, engaged by her sincere offer. She was here and his and provided for him by God. How could he refuse her? He couldn't disobey his God. Couldn't do without her.

He removed clothes donned in anger, slowly revealing his desire.

Daisa, her own want rekindled, nevertheless allowed part of her consciousness to analyse his moves, his moods, his self-delusional techniques, at least until the physicality of their reconciliation overwhelmed her thoughts.

Chapter Twenty One

The Credit Committee gathered round the oval table, with Virginia in her usual place as visiting Negotiator.

'The invitation remains, Virginia.'

She smiled at Georgiy and nodded her acknowledgement. 'Might take you up on that, soon. I'm not happy about the way things are goin, to be honest. But, for now, I called this meetin for a very particular purpose. Please, all of you, I know I can at least trust you.' She looked at each face around the table in turn, assessing the wisdom of her words. The unanimous response confirmed her faith.

'I've been forced into a horrible position. I think the expression, "between a rock and a hard place" applies. I had to promise, on pain of death, not to divulge to you what I'm about to say. So, I hope y'understand my anxiety. If anyone at Marzero learns I've informed you, I'm dead.'

'If it's about our debt, Virginia, save yourself the worry. We already know Daisa's exceeded the sensible limit and left us owing your city some credits. We've a new idea that should balance the books.'

'That's part of it, Georgiy. The result, if you like. But my news concerns somethin I was forced to do against my will. It's why Daisa feels she can spend what she likes. I was … blackmailed into assurin her your funds are unlimited. I can't tell you how, but I've every reason to fear exposure by the man who holds power over me. I'm responsible for your community goin into debt for the first time since we set up this arrangement.'

'Not the first, Virginia. A couple of centuries ago, well before you were born, I took us into debt. I misunderstood the protocol; ignorance due to the fact we don't deal in money. One of your predecessors dealt with the fallout.'

She was surprised everyone else around the table was aware of this and made no accusative comments to the Committee Member she knew as Gelin; not a result that would've occurred at Marzero.

Georgiy held up a hand to signal he had something to say.

'Daisa's our problem and we'll deal with her. You, Virginia, have served both our communities brilliantly for seven years. We're grateful for your efforts on our behalf and I think I speak for everyone when I say we feel you'd be very unwise to return to Marzero.' He looked around for confirmation and all present nodded agreement.

'I can't just not go back, Georgiy. They'll suspect me. The man I'm beholden to will reveal my past and … I'm ashamed to say, I don't want that. I must return.'

'Trust me, Virginia. You've two options: go back to Marzero, certain exposure and probable death. Or stay here, undergo treatment, and spend the rest of your life in the safety of our community.'

She was silent. Her reputation at Marzero would be ruined. Everyone, well, almost everyone, would condemn her. But, if what Georgiy said was true, and she'd no reason to believe otherwise, she was a dead woman as soon as she went back. Stef was capable of turning her in just to demonstrate his power to others. In Marion, she'd get DNA engineering that created the repair and replacement cellular treatment ensuring long life and good health. She'd be free to do what she wanted.

'As a member of the community here, I'd be expected to contribute somethin. I don't know what value I can bring you.'

Georgiy placed an arm about her shoulders. 'You've comprehensive knowledge of the way things are done in Marzero. That info's invaluable. And, in future, if we're uncertain about how the Zeros, sorry, that's what we call your people, how they'll react to our changes, you'll be here to guide us. A valuable contribution. If you're unsure, why not spend the night, think it over. In the morning, you can make your decision, or later if you want longer to consider.'

'That's very generous. I accept your suggestion, Georgiy. May I ask a further favour?'

He gestured an invitation.

'Thanks. Would you keep me company and show me Marion, so I can make up my mind better?'

Georgiy nodded his agreement and turned back to the committee. 'Anything else to discuss?'

'Daisa?'

'Ah, Daisa. I'll get Acacia to connect with her and explain the reality. I'm sure that'll cut her excess.' He faced Virginia. 'She won't be in danger if she curbs her spending, will she?'

Virginia thought of the arrangement Stefan had urged on the pair of them. The change would cause problems, but she didn't think Daisa would be in danger.

Stefan would want revenge on her, of course, but she'd be safe inside the Marion community. 'It'll make life less pleasant, but Daisa shouldn't be under threat. If I'm to stay here, I can alter the credit balance back in your favour, for a short while.'

The meeting broke up.

Georgiy and Virginia began their tour. They left the complex so she could spend time outdoors, something she relished on her visits; the air was cleaner and warmer than at home. The countryside was more attractive than the land around Marzero, which had a wide band of crops and then gave way to wilderness. They strolled along the shore of Lake Peake. Virginia, seeing other couples walking hand in hand, took Georgiy's.

'We don't do this. Nice, isn't it?'

Georgiy smiled down at her. 'It's generally a signal of mutual exclusivity in a relationship, Virginia. Tells others the pair aren't interested in anyone else.'

She took her hand away, walked a few steps beside him, and then replaced it. 'For now, I just want you, Georgiy. Is that alright?'

'We're not hung up about sex, Virginia. It's an appetite, like the need for food and drink. But some people find love and that often results in a wish to be faithful to each other. There are lots of groupings here. We've have same sex couples, groups, public sex. We recognise we're animals still.

'All those restrictions religions placed on people were control mechanisms to make people fearful so they'd obey authority. So, to answer your question, yes, it's okay. So long as you realise it doesn't apply to me. I've a special woman in Amber. We're not mutually exclusive all the time; we love each other but she won't mind me spending a night with you.'

'Amber? With very dark skin?'

'Gorgeous, isn't she?'

'All the women here are beautiful. And the men. I feel a bit, well, worn to be honest. Will I fit in?'

'If you stay, Zaphod, Qiu, and their team will do their magic. You're a natural blonde, so you've got an inbuilt advantage. Most men prefer light coloured hair on a woman. Not all, mind. Amber's hair's black, and I love it! And Madonna's a redhead; stunning. But blondes seem to have more admirers.

'Anyway, the team'll modify your DNA to get rid of aspects that tend to ageing. You can choose your "stable" year and that'll be how you'll look for as long as you live, which, barring accidents or murder, will be forever. We can't make you taller, now you're adult, so you'll always be shorter than our younger women. But all we original settlers are smaller than our kids. Gravity plays a bigger part than we thought on the developing foetus.'

'Y'talk about these … modifications, like they're an everyday thing. Doesn't it worry you they're unnatural, Georgiy?'

'Unnatural? A much overused term. Know how evolution works, Virginia?'

'What's evolution to do with it?'

'We evolved, through a series of changes and mutations, into the people we are now, from our beginnings as single-celled creatures living in hot volcanic vents at the bottom of the ocean. Mutations cause change; evolution. DNA's modified by random, or naturally-engineered alterations in the structure that fits the animal better for life in given circumstances.

'So, fish use gills to breathe under water. We have lungs to extract oxygen from the air. Insects use tracheae. But we all came from those single-celled organisms. The differences are due to evolution. What we do is utilise our knowledge of DNA to make changes in a way that we can predict the outcome.'

'And y'don't think that's unnatural?'

'We're animals, working on the nature of animals. In the past, it was too complex for abliforms to make changes to their own structure, though several attempts were made using selective breeding. A particularly nasty instance was back in Earth history when a group from Germany, called Nazis, tried to eliminate certain types of people. They thought they could breed only tall, fair-skinned people from what they saw as the best of their own countrymen. It was destined to failure.

'False beliefs cause false results, always.

'Once we developed metallic hydrogen and commercial quantities of graphene we could build properly functioning quantum computers in bulk. We use them to investigate the quintigrigtillions of combinations possible with our DNA and arrive at structures that allow exactly the physical changes desired by anyone.'

'Tell me again, why you call people "abliforms"'

'Human uses the root "man", making man superior to woman. The word denigrates the feminine, as does "female".'

'But men are superior.'

He stopped their walk and gentled her to the bank of the lake to sit beside him. A group of mallard ducks squabbled noisily a short distance away among the reeds. Overhead, the deep blue sky was dotted with small white clouds drifting on a mild breeze. The sun, small and bright, cast diamonds across the broken surface. In the mixed broadleaved and pine trees behind them, small birds celebrated life with bright song. And over to their left a jetty intruded across the small waves, where people were diving and swimming.

'They're all … naked!'

'Why wear clothes in water? Seems pointless.'

'But it's … well, rude.'

'Nude's not rude, Virginia. It's our natural state. Only false beliefs and the dogma of discredited religions make people ashamed of their bodies. We don't flaunt ourselves; that causes sexual complications, as we've all got the natural desires of a species that can breed throughout the year. But we don't hide.

'Clothes inhibit swimming, so we don't wear them. Simple as that. Yes, we see everyone's bodies when we swim, or sunbathe, or maybe dance at a party. But there's nothing rude about it. Celebratory and beautiful, but shaming it ain't.'

She inclined her head a little toward him, her face displaying uncertainty. 'You talk about abliforms instead of humans. Why?'

'We avoid gender-prejudiced language.'

'You still talk about men and women.'

'We use 'people' and 'person' when we can. But sometimes gender's important, so we use it then. We're not trying to do away with identity, only discrimination.' He glanced at the water. 'Fancy a swim?'

His sudden change of tack took her by surprise. 'I … can't swim. Why would I? There's no deep surface water near Marzero. No one's goin to drown in a shower.'

'We all swim. Would you like to learn?'

'Does it mean …?' she pointed to the group near and on the jetty.

'Not really concerned about …? Of course! In Marzero it's an invitation.'

She nodded.

'Not here. We often walk unclothed in warmer weather. Delivers more vitamin D, helps build calcium and keeps us physically and mentally healthy, as well as keeping spirits uplifted.'

'You accept we all have a spirit, then?'

'Not in the sense you mean. We use it to describe emotional aspects that would otherwise need convoluted terminology to describe. We all know what we mean by 'spirituality' and it's nothing to do with ghosts, spirits or some weird idea of an eternal entity separate from the mind.'

'Okay. I'd like to learn to swim. How will we dry ourselves afterwards?'

Georgiy pointed to the jetty. At the landward end a number of small cabinets stood open. 'Drying cloths, towels, are in those cabinets. That's also were we leave our clothes.'

'People share towels?'

'Why would you think that?'

'Not enough cubicles for everyone.'

Georgiy laughed. 'I see. I keep thinking you know more about us from your visits. Always been business, hasn't it?'

'Droids supply fresh clean towels. You don't have to share. Not that it would matter. No disease here, nothing nasty to pass to each other.'

'Is it true Marion wiped out STDs in Marzero?'

'Oh, way back after the end of the Cusp War, before things got out of hand again, we got rid of all sexually transmitted pathogens from your city, as well as all the outer colonies. We were hoping to interbreed. Last thing we needed was that sort of disease.'

'So you did it to protect yourselves?'

'You could look at it that way. We're pragmatic. But your population benefitted.'

'It wasn't altruistic though, was it?'

'Altruism; big subject. We'll discuss that later. Let's get into the water before the sun gets too low. We can talk more in my pod, over dinner.'

'Sounds invitin, Georgiy. Show me what to do.'

He rose and helped her up from the lush grass with a hand round hers. In an impetuous surge of fun, she started to run toward the jetty and Georgiy allowed himself to lope along beside her, enjoying her new sense of freedom.

Chapter Twenty Two

She took the news from Acacia without rancour. It was a shame she'd been lied to, manipulated through her lack of knowledge, but it was partially her own fault for failing to make checks.

The real problem would be Gabriel's need to return to work. He was preparing for the meet later that evening. A profound change of direction seemed likely, from his mood and the deep conversations he'd held with Stefan.

So far, he hadn't shared his intentions with her. But, then, he rarely did beforehand. She heard the 'news' along with the growing crowds of supporters.

It seemed a little unfair to inform him before his appearance, but she knew from experience he preferred to be forewarned.

'Gabriel, I don't suppose you know where Virginia is?'

He looked up from his tablet. 'You haven't heard? I thought Stefan told you. She betrayed us. Gone to live with your lot in Marion.'

Daisa was startled. Did they know the truth about her?

She reconnected with Acacia and asked what she knew. Acacia explained the decision taken by the committee. 'She'll be in danger if she returns now. Talk with Georgiy. She's staying with him whilst she undergoes treatment.'

Daisa found Georgiy, alone and contemplative, siting on the banks of Lake Peake. He explained the situation, making it clear Virginia would be assassinated if she went back to Marzero.

She returned to Gabriel, still busy on his tablet. 'They invited her to stay. Offered her the DNA treatment. Who wouldn't want that life?'

'I wouldn't. And it's left us without a Negotiator. They're holding a meeting to choose another. Why did you want her?'

'Truth.' And she told him.

Gabriel listened, eyes widening as he took in the tale. 'They know she did that to you and they still protect her?'

'She had her reasons.' Was it sensible to tell him Stefan had coerced her to spread the malicious lies? Probably not at present. The news she had to relay was bad enough without causing a breach between Gabriel and his best friend just before a performance. But she must tell him her own costs for the remainder of her stay had been authorised, but nothing more.

'I'm sorry to tell you this now, but you do realise I can't keep us both any longer? Just me, for as long as I stay.'

He sat, shaking the bed with his sudden weight. 'Jeez! I'm twatted! I told the works to twattin stuff their job. I'll never get back in again now. Why'd the twat lie to you? What did she …?'

'Not important now, is it? We need to decide what to do for our future, for your future.'

He rose again. Paced. His whole body stiff with tension. She watched, uncertain of his mood under such pressure. Unafraid, but wary in case he became aggressive and she had to defend herself. Gabriel might be different from most men in Marzero, but he was still primitive. And she'd witnessed plenty of male fury taken out on innocent women in the city.

Abruptly, he stopped and looked at her, though his mind was elsewhere. 'I need to talk to Stefan.'

She shrugged. 'If you think it'll help.'

'He helps me when things aren't clear. I'll be back to take you to the meet.' And, slipping on a jerkin against the cool afternoon, he was off.

Daisa signed on to her account, and started a search for costs of what she would need in the city. It amazed her to discover everything had a price, including time online. No wonder Gabriel had been so grateful for her generosity. Though, had she known the truth, she'd never have offered.

Now she must decide what she could do without. Was she still paying for Gabriel's time online? It seemed likely, since they'd set up the account for her on his machine and she'd had to give her details. She'd leave that: the cost was minimal.

He arrived back with just enough time to change his clothes into those he used for his appearances and to beg her, without explanation, to don a new, short, white robe over her skin for their journey.

They walked hand in hand to the appointed place. His mood seemed lighter, his step more positive. Nothing Daisa could imagine should've made him more hopeful, but she found his lightness infectious and happily strode beside him through streets that grew more crowded as they approached the venue.

Closer now, he turned to her and whispered; a message part instruction, part request. In light of her withdrawal of funds, coupled to the fact she'd no concerns about what he asked, she agreed. Near the entrance to the arena, people, especially women, made way for them to pass, reaching out to touch his clothes as he moved through.

This time, instead of the open square, Stefan had booked a stadium. Glencore Arena normally hosted live sports events, the oval seating area raised around the field of play to provide maximum visibility for paying spectators.

The entrance, passageways, stairwells, backs of seats, and looparound moving display that defined the edge of the protective roof were all given over to bright, flashing, gaudy statements promising happiness if the advertised products were purchased. For the meet, however, the playing area had been filled with folding seats. They looked cheap and uncomfortable. Daisa was relieved to follow Gabriel to the stage erected at the far end. Most seats inside were already taken.

He ushered her to a place where a security detail stood, overlooking the crowd on the field of play. Her position, furnished with a comfortable seat, gave her a spectacular view over the crowd and a fine view of the stage. Gabriel kissed her cheek, their signature sign of affection provided for the benefit of the crowds, and moved on to the staged area.

He vanished into the shadows as the crowd began to quieten, the last few stragglers making their way in to find the few remaining empty seats. Silence fell slowly, the last murmurings of anticipation settling into the still air. The busy signs and flashing hoardings dimmed into stillness and darkness. And the group of dancing, singing women, who'd entertained the crowd as they settled, silently collected their discarded clothes and melted into darkness at the edge of the stage.

For a few moments, all was silent, full of expectation. The whole arena waited in semi darkness. Already, the evening dome was unfolding overhead to keep the night chill off.

As she looked up, distracted by the rumble of the motors, a line of fire burned across the dark sky, heralding the landing of an ore train from an outer colony. The spaceport was only a few ks from the northern edge of the city and in more or less constant use. Ships landed every few days, bringing ores for refining and then returning home with supplies made and grown on the planet.

A single ethereal note rose out of silence to a powerful crescendo before it dropped into a background monotone of great beauty. A second note echoed the first, harmonising with it. A third, fourth and fifth joined in and only then did they vary as they wove a song of intricate and sublime mood over and above the crowd. The sound was almost palpable; people reached out as if to grasp the passing notes as the music seemed to float around the stadium.

From the back of the stage, a deep blue light slowly glowed, increasing in brilliance until the whole apron bathed in its hue. The seated areas remained dark. A paler light grew from a point in the middle of the illuminated area, almost white, the hint of blue bright enough to dazzle until it spread into a disc. All eyes followed this spot as it roved across the stage to finally settle front centre.

And there, unannounced and unexpected stood Gabriel. The gasp of the audience echoed Daisa's surprise. How had he arrived? She knew some theatrical trick had managed his sudden appearance but applauded with the rest in appreciation of the visual effect.

As usual for these meets, his white cloak, flimsy but opaque, seemed to gently breathe as it concealed him. His head and feet remained bare and he stood passive until the music faded to silence: a quiet he held for counted moments before slowly raising his head to gaze out at the crowd.

'My people. My followers. My faithful. I welcome you here tonight, as always. But tonight you'll learn somethin new and vital to our continued existence. Listen well, for what I tell you this night will change lives, improve the lot of all, bring all closer to true harmony with God.'

The crowd breathed a troubled wave of shock, murmuring and disturbed, but unwilling to shout their concern.

'Don't be concerned, my people. God Himself said that one-word title is all He wants. He knows our previous names included all other titles, but the single word, God, encompasses every variant and is all He needs from us.'

Daisa smiled privately at the theatricality and wondered how much her own remark about the irritating lengthy title had on God's decision to truncate it. Gabriel understood how to field a crowd. He knew how to raise them, feed them info, garner their respect. It was an obvious form of manipulation she knew would cause hilarity back home, but here it worked brilliantly.

'I've been visited by God again. Been blessed by another vision. Time for us to move on from the past and forge a new and just future for ourselves. We're pioneers of this new movement. God has named us now. We've been happy to be a gatherin, a group of good people sharing experiences and concerns. Now is the time for each and every one of us to declare for the future. Now is the time for all to commit to the truth of God. Are you willin?'

'Yes.' The response was hesitant, uncertain.

'I ask again, using the words of God Himself. Will you commit to God?'

'Yes.' More conviction this time. Daisa looked at those she could discern in the reflected stage light just below her. There was enchantment, even devotion on those faces.

136

'Once more I have to ask you all. Each of you here tonight, before I divulge the secrets God has given me. Are you willin to give yourselves to God?'

'Yes!' The cry was loud, certain, full of conviction this time. Daisa wondered at the power of a gifted orator to bend the minds of those susceptible to his will. Here, it seemed, almost everyone was impressionable.

'Then hear me. Listen well. For what I have to say is from the very mouth of God Himself.'

Silence, anticipation, occupied the space. Here and there in the quiet, a chair creaked, a foot slipped on the metal floor of the raised seating, a man coughed but quickly silenced his outburst. The arena slowly filled with a scent of floral origin, though she couldn't identify the perfume.

The deeper blue light faded, leaving Gabriel bathed in the brighter almost white light so he appeared more dazzling. His arms stretched out, raising the wide sleeves of his gown almost to form wings. Above his head, a golden circle glowed even more brilliantly than the light of the spot.

'Hear the word of God.

'First, our movement has a name. We are the Sacred Ones. Say it loud.'

The crowd spoke the name, softly and hesitantly.

'Mean it, my people, my Sacred Ones.'

They said the name with feeling.

'Say it with love for God, my Sacred Ones.'

This time the crowd shouted the words in joy.

Gabriel gestured his pleasure. 'Now, my Sacred Ones, let me tell you what God has said.

'Men and women are different. The female is subservient, obedient, servile and humble. Women must obey those who provide for them. And the gentler ways of women are suited to raisin the children we all need, want, and love.

'Men, though, are strong, decisive, dominant and merciful.'

There was some muted murmuring. Gabriel flicked his palms outward, driving away doubt with the gesture and regaining their silence.

'This doesn't mean women are inferior to men, men superior to women. No. It means we respect their different roles. Each has a place in the scheme of things. Each has an important contribution to make.

'From this day, a man who beats a woman without good cause is made small in the eyes of God. A man who fails to properly provide for his family is made less in the eyes of God. A man who treats a worthy woman poorly is reduced in the eyes of God.'

Some murmurs of disquiet from men were silenced by others in the crowd. Gabriel flicked his hands in dismissal of the protest.

'From today, a woman who disrespects any man is sinful in the eyes of God. A woman who fails to nurture her children is unworthy of respect from man or God. A woman who refuses any man her charms will find no protection from the law or from the wrath of God.'

This time, disquiet moved the lips and tongues of women, though their protests were whispers. Gabriel pushed forward his palms, rebutting the complaints.

'We know, we Sacred Ones gathered here, undeservin men live in our community. Men who, with no good cause, believe they're better, expect more than their fair share. Such contemptible men won't gain the love and protection of God. When their time on this precious globe is ended, they'll dissolve into the dust that covers deserts and mountains. They won't go to the afterlife that all who truly give themselves to God will find.'

Daisa was appalled, especially by the change in his approach to women and their status. His apparent wish to equalise the treatment of men and women had, after all, been her main drive in coming to the city. For a moment, she seriously considered abandoning her research. But she was too committed, too deeply involved to walk away now.

Though she intended to hear the whole speech out before analysing it, she was abruptly plunged back into her research into ancient religions. Gabriel's words echoed so much from those discredited texts. Did he know? Had he read those once sacred books and borrowed from them? Clearly the words he spoke had nothing to do with any god. So where did he get his info, his ideas?

His visions were a physical aberration; his mind somehow fooled into misinterpretation of real events, and distorted ideas and themes absorbed in rational periods. His words expressed the hopes most feared by her community, the very philosophy that had caused so much death and destruction in the past. But he was speaking still. She must listen.

'... to accept the riches and goods we've been given by God. We must mark our devotion by gatherin as many goods as we can. Some will claim greater glory with their collection. Others will find different ways to serve God. Those with no way to buy will find solace in service, givin time, affection, comfort to those who seek it.

'Let all be generous with time and skill. Let us devote ourselves to makin and collectin, gatherin and usin all we've been given for our comfort and enjoyment. Let us all rejoice in the pleasures God provides, be they riches of ornament, wealth of goods, or pleasures of the flesh so easily shared by all.

'Are you, my Sacred Ones, ready to declare for God?'

'Yes! Yes! Yes!' If there were dissenting voices, the crowd drowned them.

Gabriel gave them time to share their enthusiasm with neighbours before once again collecting their attention with a gesture.

Daisa wondered what had caused this change in direction. She knew by now that the Elite had a vested interest in the citizen's consumption, but Gabriel had always seemed immune. It was obvious who was behind this fundamental alteration. She'd never liked Stefan. Now she had even more reason for her antipathy.

'Finally, I make a humble request of all here tonight. Until now, we ourselves have borne the cost of our mission to give you these words freely. Our accounts now are empty, our glasses dry.'

He allowed that info to sink in. Daisa wondered what they'd make of the fact that each person present had paid an entry fee.

'Your tickets pay only for this facility to open. All other costs have been borne by ourselves. As you leave the arena tonight, you'll pass men with credit stations. If each of you will pass your ID once across the screen, we'll collect enough to help us carry on our work a few days more.

'Please give what you can, for some have no spare funds, and our need is great. God has sent this message, that the contributions of all who call themselves the Sacred Ones will be taken as token of their love and commitment to a future filled with light and justice for all.

'I wish you all a good, good night. May the love of God go with you to your homes, your places of work, your businesses, and your beds.' He signalled to Daisa.

She went to him, as he'd requested, even though her reason for such support had been all but obliterated. It was too dangerous to change her mind here and now, but she'd be asking the hard questions as soon as they were alone again. Now, on stage beside him, dressed in the gown he'd provided, she understood the reason.

'Here stands the virgin sacrifice I see daily in all her glory.' As he'd warned and agreed with her, he lifted her gown in slow and deliberate provocation until she stood fully revealed next to him.

'Every day I resist this sight; every night. Even as she sleeps beside me in my bed, I don't intrude into her magical flesh. For she is not for mere mortals. She is for God alone. Look on her. Men, see your reward in the afterlife for those who keep the way. For each of the faithful will find many such rewards, unendin, after death. Women, see how you can be in afterlife, if you obey and keep the way.'

Daisa stood exposed until the lights died slowly from the stage and left her in darkness with Gabriel. He picked up her robe and helped replace it, whispering as he retied the narrow belt around her waist.

140

'You were brilliant. And, now, we don't need your support. Donations from men eager to see you again will keep us in style for as long as we need.'

She didn't care about bodily exposure. But this use of her to persuade women to act as sex slaves to gain some non-existent afterlife was deplorable. It went against all she held dear. However, he needed income in this backward place, and her recent announcement had deprived him of her aid. It seemed churlish to refuse to help in a way that cost her nothing physically and, in fact, would raise her status amongst this primitive crowd. But could she hide her serious disapproval simply to allow her research to continue? And to what extent was she allowing his physical attraction to influence her decisions?

Chapter Twenty Three

The night had been torrid. Days without intimacy catching up on them so the physical overtook all other considerations.

Morning brought a change, sobriety, consideration, and need for discussion.

'14,647 people gave last night, Daisa. We raised over 15,000 credits. Enough to keep us goin in real style for two quarters. And your fab display at the end of the evenin increased those donations. A lot of men present gave just because you showed yourself. Thank you. Not even our most blatant Groupies would be as openly honest about their bodies in front of so many people. Amazin!'

'About that, Gabriel: I have to ask how you square my display, coupled with your statement about our continued chastity, with the facts. We've spent all night fucking like newbies, and I've certainly not been a virgin for a while. How does that fit with your declaration to the crowd?'

He spread his hands. 'It's what God wants. I can't defy Him. I won't defy Him, Daisa. He has His reasons for His commands. I just obey.'

'And it was your god who made the remarks about women and their place in society? God, not you or Stefan?'

'I don't know what you mean. I have visions and Stefan's my mediator, my translator. I can make no sense of the visions. Before I explained them to Stefan, I thought I was goin mad. But he interprets them, delivers their meanin to me, so we can engage in the way God truly wants of us. Why's that so hard to understand?'

She had many answers to that. But was now the time? The scholar in her still felt a deep need to properly observe this experiment in self-deception, delusion and apparent inability to see truth. And she accepted, with a slight air of guilt, her physical attraction for Gabriel made the whole thing more palatable. Was she more hypocritical than her subject? Such self-analysis was hardly helpful at this stage. His words last night hadn't actually altered the lot of the women, merely reinforced the status quo. It was a sad turnaround after his initial intention to found a process of equality. But, in practical terms, it made no real difference to the lives of the women of Marzero. She was justified in allowing her neutrality to overcome her disappointment. For now. The research; she must concentrate on the research that had brought her here.

But was it really the mental condition she'd identified that caused Gabriel to hide from the truth? Or was he genuinely unaware of his double standards? Perhaps he was one of those individuals, of whom so many had existed on Earth according to her reading of history, who suffered from an inability to understand their beliefs were at best a form of self-delusion, a paradox, always ambiguous.

Such delusion was embedded in the psyche of many Earth based abliforms. But the Chosen had found ways of defeating this breach of logic, allowing the minds of people in Marion to always consider the reality of their beliefs. It was why they were agnostic.

Since the existence of God can't be either proved or disproved, the only sensible and rational approach to the subject must be to keep an open mind until it becomes possible to obtain objective evidence of either case. She knew about Gödel's supposed proof of God's existence, but that had been based on false assumptions and axioms that were, at best, questionable, so it had never found favour with the Chosen.

'You've heard of doublethink, Gabriel?'

He frowned. 'Sounds made up to me.'

'In a sense. It was once a neologism …'

'A what?'

'Oh, sorry, a word coined by a writer. George Orwell first created the word in a novel called "1984", the date of a year on Earth during which the action of the novel takes place. These days, we use the term to describe the ability to hold two contradictory beliefs at the same time.'

'What's that got to do with me? I know what I believe. There's no contradiction.'

Daisa knew this was a time when either she delved deep and attempted to unseat her subject's delusions, or allowed the situation to continue on its current route and simply observed the outcome.

Her dilemma was moral. Should she sacrifice her research in order to bring logic and honesty to him, or should she concentrate on the scholarship of research and allow nature to take its course. Gabriel would, at some stage, be forced to face the reality of his contradictory beliefs.

Her difficulty in deciding demonstrated to her the inexperience she must accept as the cause of her doubt. She'd undergone almost no previous situations in which such a choice presented itself. Was she fitted to make such a decision? Her desire to learn was deep, perhaps even overriding. On the other hand, the developing situation with Gabriel was volatile, and she had little or no control over his thought processes.

He was clearly in thrall to Stefan, who she was sure had his own agenda. Was her intimate connection to Gabriel strong enough to defeat the bond of friendship he'd developed with Stefan? In any event, was it wise to break that bond?

In this society where men considered themselves superior to women, that masculine bond might overrule any sexual bond between man and woman. In fact, she frequently witnessed this. A day never passed without her seeing some disagreement between a man and a woman where the woman's wishes were ignored in favour of the man's loyalty to his male friends.

If she continued to cast doubt on his beliefs, exposed the duality in his thought processes, the most likely outcome was his rejection of any of her thoughts and suggestions. At least, if she remained neutral, she had some chance of modifying Stefan's more extreme influences. There appeared to be no choice for now.

'You're right, Gabriel. Still learning about life in the city. Ignore me. Sometimes my thoughts overtake my common sense, that's all.' She stretched, quite deliberately displaying her charms. As she expected, it worked.

The second time they left the bed, it was to eat.

'Right. I've preached the word of God about gatherin all the good things in life. Now I have to set an example. We're goin shoppin, Daisa.'

She continued to find the obsession with buying and possessing that characterised the desires of the city's people incomprehensible. Gabriel's invitation to 'go shopping' was as tempting as a compost sandwich. But she knew why he made the suggestion, and tried to show enthusiasm.

'Oh. Better get ready then.'

'That the best you can do when I'm offerin to take you out to buy anythin you want?'

She smiled her most apologetic smile and flipped her hands out at the wrists with a small shrug she knew enhanced her breasts for him.

'Don't start that again, or we'll never get out the pod. Dressed, woman! I'm goin to spoil you.'

Spoil? Oh, how tempting to dissect and discuss that particular intention. That the expression was intended to indicate a desire to make life better for her she knew, but the very idea of 'spoiling' anything made her wonder at the origin. But now was not the time.

She showered. Sprayed her skin with artificial perfume that overlaid her natural scent with something floral; a gift from a secret admirer. The miniscule bikini Gabriel had bought as underwear made her uncomfortable; the thong string sat too tight against her fundament. But he valued its contribution to her appearance so she wore it.

The skintight, translucent and patterned with abstract swirls and curls of many colours, coated skin where it touched but did nothing to hide her shape. Following the fashion, here in the best part of the city. Some wandered around in no more than the briefest skintights, but Gabriel explained they were paid courtesans of wealthy and powerful businessmen, not valued consorts like her.

The streets were slightly busier than usual and Gabriel was

delighted his preaching was already bearing fruit. 'They're takin notice, doin what God wants of us. Stefan knows how to interpret. So accurate.'

She resisted arguing and simply nodded.

'So, what do you want most, Daisa?'

Things had no hold over her. She either needed something or she didn't. The concept of 'wanting' in material terms was alien. But, in the city, she'd had to live without her usual creative outlets. 'Well, it would be lovely to have some proper drawing paper, and good pencils to sketch with.'

He shook his head. 'You're not a professional artist. I can't buy you things like that.'

She raised her eyebrows but again resisted the obvious questions. Instead, she asked, 'What do women do to fill their time, then?'

He gestured at the crowds, mostly women, wandering in and out of the many shops. 'Shop.'

'Shop for what?'

'You really are innocent, aren't you? Anythin. Anythin at all.'

'Except, it seems, those things I actually want.' She regretted her dig as soon as she'd spoken. 'Sorry, Gabriel. I'm still learning. Give me some clues. Tell me what I'm supposed to enjoy, like, desire.'

'See what the others are buyin. It's easy.'

She watched the activities. Clothes were popular, though since so little was actually worn, she wondered at the purpose of such purchases. Paint and powder that masked the reality of the face was also in demand. She had no need of such artifice, her natural beauty such that any artificial modification would detract rather than enhance.

Jewellery, the bright sparkling trinkets worn around necks, wrists, fingers, ankles and, in some cases through parts of the skin pierced for the purpose, was very much in evidence. But this adornment seemed entirely superficial and pointless. What she really wanted was something to let her make things, to produce art, express her inner creative urges.

'Is there somewhere that sells fabrics and the means to cut and sew them into clothes?' She felt such a request would fall in with his wishes that she have more choice in her outfits.

'You're not a professional tailor, Daisa. You can't do them out of work. But we could go to one and ask her to make you whatever you want to wear, if you like.'

His eagerness defeated her disappointment, but it wasn't what she wanted. She needed to do something. To act. Not be a mobile display unit. 'Do you have paper books here?'

'Books? You mean downloads?'

'I mean books printed on paper and covered with illustrated hardbacks.'

'Never heard of such a thing. Sounds like a good business opportunity. Explain it to me when we get back. We could start our own business and sell these books if there's a market.'

'So, nobody reads proper books. I want to make something, Gabriel. I want to use my skills and imagination to create.'

'Why? Everythin you could possibly want is here. I want to buy you things. It's what God wants.'

Nothing appealed to her; she wanted nothing. And everything she needed was denied her. 'Take me to the theatre, treat me to a meal.'

'I'll do that anyway. The meal, at any rate. Don't hold with women goin to the theatre. Watchin other people doin it isn't suitable. Any case, high status women never go. It's just not right.'

How, she wondered, could she have lived in the city for so many days and still be so ignorant of its realities? Of course, apart from her very first day, she'd rarely been out without Gabriel. And he had his own agenda. It was clear he'd kept her ignorant of certain aspects of city life quite deliberately. And, to be fair to herself, she'd spent most of her time concentrating on Gabriel and his ministry. Very little of her time had been spent discovering the reality of the city in which she temporarily dwelt.

'Art galleries? You have those?'

147

He shook his head. 'Off limits to women, except for them who pose. Cheap tarts who don't care who sees their twats. Or consorts who do it for their partner's private collections. Maybe you'd do that for me.'

Daisa raised her eyebrows. 'I was naked in front of thousands last night. I've no problem with that. I'm content with my body. It's beautiful. Why should it be hidden?'

'Last night was different. That was ordained by God. You gave men a reason to donate to the cause. They'll come again, in the hope of seein you. But only lower class women, Bed Warmers, Massagers, Benders, Groupies, Doms, Spankers, Tasters, Quickies and Spankees, ever go completely undressed in public. I mean, they've got to display their wares if they're goin to get trade, haven't they?

'But no high status woman would do that, unless her keeper wanted it. Sometimes a man shows off his property to make other men jealous. But that wasn't what I did last night. Don't think it was, Daisa. No. Last night was about keepin the men interested.

'God commanded you to do that, and I'm grateful you were willin. He knows men can be easily led by women. That's why women have to be kept in their place. Otherwise, they'd have too much power over us, you see?'

This was useful. He'd been diverted from the pointless task of shopping for things she didn't want. With luck, she could prolong the talk with questions and slowly guide him back to their shared pod without buying anything.

'What's a Bender, Gabriel?'

He blushed. 'Never you mind. Let's see what we can buy you, shall we?'

Intrigued by his evident embarrassment, she shelved further questions and decided to humour him. The sooner she bought something and got him back to the pod, the sooner she could ask him about the strange titles he'd reeled out in answer to her previous question.

148

She let him buy her a new skintight in a shiny, sheer material. Three more sets of the tiny bikini in different colours. And, at his insistence, a heavy gold bangle to fasten around her wrist.

Feeling both amused and slightly despairing at the waste, she talked him into sharing a meal out at a better eating house. They then took an autocar home, Daisa wearing her bangle, new skintight, and one of the new bikinis the shop assistant had been happy to let her change into. Inexplicably, Gabriel was unfazed by her doing this under the gaze of other men. Yet another instance of double standards?

Back home, he asked her to try on all three bikinis in turn, but succumbed to her charms before she'd donned the second. As they lay relaxing, it occurred to her that many things were very different in Marzero, but one element remained apparently universal: the lure of sex was ubiquitously powerful.

In Marion, they accepted the fact and enjoyed nature's strong imperative to mate. It seemed strange that in Marzero the urge had been made a weapon against women and a device to drive men to behave in ways that acted against their interests. Perhaps that peculiarity might provide another topic for research and a new doctoral paper in future.

Chapter Twenty Four

Three more meets, complete with collections, had brought them ever-increasing crowds and a startling increase in personal wealth. Some of the money they used to hire larger meeting spaces, but they easily recouped the cost.

'We're seeing a lot more of Stefan recently, Gabriel. Does he have some sort of hold over you?'

The brief flash of what Daisa interpreted as fear was almost too swift to spot as it crossed his face. 'Hold? Don't know what you mean. He's my mentor, as you know. I rely on him to interpret my visions.'

'Why?'

'Why? Well, because … because he was first to understand my visions are from God. He explained the meanin right from the start.'

'Ever asked anyone else to do it? I might be able to do the job just as well.'

'You? You're godless, and a woman. How could you be my mentor?'

'Good for your bed, but not for your mind, eh?'

'Why the sudden interest?'

She started getting ready for the meet they were due to attend that night. 'Sudden, Gabriel? I've been fascinated by every facet of your preaching and mission from the start. It's what brought me here, remember?'

He watched her, his gaze never leaving her form as she prepared so close to him. 'But you don't believe. D'you? I need a man of faith. You'd be a cancer on my mission if I took notice of your thoughts.'

'But I'm to display before your crowd again tonight, Gabriel? I trust you enough, agree with you enough, to do this for you, and to keep our deception alive. Yet you don't extend the same respect for my thoughts and contribution as you do to Stefan. What does he know about you that makes you bow to his will so readily?'

Anger flashed this time and she stepped back, almost expecting a blow as he moved toward her. 'I don't have time for this right now, Daisa. I've got to perform in half an hour.'

'Who d'you think arranged the venue for the expected 100,000 audience? Who organised the stagin? Stefan does all that. You just decorate the stage to keep the attention of male followers. You're beautiful, but you're still only a woman, and there's plenty willin to swap with you.'

She paused in her preparations. For the past few days she'd grown more and more suspicious of Stefan's part in the mission. He was manipulating Gabriel, turning him away from the original message of equality that had attracted her to the movement in the first place. Stefan had interpreted the last few visions into messages of pure consumption, a mouthpiece in support of the Elite.

Perhaps it was time to end her study and research, return to Marion to write her thesis, and expose the reality of the situation to the whole planet. The deception was wearing and the preaching boring, especially since he'd turned to this materialistic slant.

Sex with Gabriel was undeniably special, but was that because she'd had so little experience before leaving for the city? Maybe it could be like that with most men. It had certainly been very good with her first lover.

'Then find such a woman, Gabriel. Because, if that's your attitude, I won't be stripping for those lustful eyes tonight.'

'You'll do as you're told!' There was less conviction in his eyes than his voice.

'You've no hold over me. I know who and what you are. I'm not fooled by the act. You no more connect with a god than I do. Stefan may have found a way to convince you you're some sort of chosen spokesman, but I know different. And so do you, if you're honest.'

He clenched his fists. Face reddening, eyes growing wild, his whole body tense, he moved a step closer. She stood her ground but prepared to fend off any attack. Whether he read her preparation or simply recalled the way she'd dealt with other men, she couldn't be certain. But he stepped back again.

'You're a strange one, Daisa. I haven't got time for this right now. Will you appear with me or not?'

'I won't. In fact, I'll be gone when you return from tonight's meet. I've seen a side of you I'd fooled myself never existed. It's ugly and unpleasant. I'm going back home.'

'I thought you … loved me?'

'Really? And, I suppose, I thought you loved me. It seems I'm just another tool to help you fool the people.'

'Fool them?'

'Oh, come on Gabriel, we both know you've never talked with your god. That's all just so much rabble-rousing made up by Stefan to …'

'Enough! One more word and I'll show you who's in charge here. Didn't you hear my message? You're my woman. Your job's to do as I tell you.'

'Not this woman, Gabriel. I'm educated and intelligent, not deprived and kept ignorant like your poor women. I'll do as I like. You've no power over me. None at all.'

He froze, studying her to determine whether she meant her words. Without further comment, he prepared for the meet. As he left the pod, he turned once more and stared at her. 'Suit yourself. You always do, anyway. Plenty more twats desperate for me here.' He shook his head in a gesture of sorrow. But doubt clouded his eyes as he left.

In the silence following his departure, Daisa revisited the past few mins and wondered what, exactly, had triggered a dispute that had turned so abruptly into an ugly split, and her departure. A combination of timing, her rebellion, and her growing concern about Stefan's motives, which had upset Gabriel more than she'd expected. Was there something hidden there that she'd been kept ignorant of, something dark? Or had she simply been fooling herself about Gabriel's motivation?

Too late to retract now. Much as she felt for Gabriel, the man he was fast becoming no longer attracted her in the way his innocence and concern for justice first had.

She checked the time. Enough for her to get to the terminal and catch the last Transhub to Marion. She could be back in her own pod before midnight.

She had nothing to pack. But she wasn't prepared to risk the streets alone in the flimsy costume she'd donned in readiness for Gabriel's show. She slipped it off and began to search for the clothes she'd worn to travel to the city. She couldn't recall precisely where she'd put them.

There were few places to look and she had the compartment open and the clothes in view when the door flew open. Five uniformed men entered; pulse guns aimed at her.

'Hands on your head! Now!'

She'd witnessed enough brutality from these bullies to know opposition or delay would cause her pain and humiliation. She did as commanded.

'Can I at least dress before you continue with whatever …?'

'Quiet, twat! Turn round.'

She faced back toward the cubicle she'd been searching. Hands swiftly forced her arms behind her back into manacles she heard lock as they pinched her wrists. Once shackled, he spun her round and molested her, conducting a body search as the others leered.

The leader of the group moved forward. 'Wait till we get her inside. Then you can all do what you like to her.' He lifted her chin, stretching to reach. 'You're under arrest.'

'I gathered that. Why?'

'Time for that once you've been processed. Out. Go on, move!' He spun her toward the door and followed as the other four placed themselves at either side, so she was the centre of a group of five moving bodies, two on each flank and the other behind. The reason for their formation quickly became clear. She was shown to all and sundry as she moved through streets growing ever more crowded as the masses made their way to the meet. Some recognised her. But fear of the Specials stopped them showing support and even encouraged a few to call out insults and threats.

Indifferent to her exposure, she concentrated on moving without falling, doing what she could to escape the occasional spit of passing men. In her own world of silence, she contacted her mother. Ambra would know what to do, how to protect her in this dangerous and extraordinary situation.

'Keep calm, Daisa. Do as they tell you: they punish any disobedience. Try to keep open to me. I'm contacting others right now. We'll find out what's going on and why you've been arrested. Don't worry; we'll get you home.'

The route took them past the entrance to the huge open space where Gabriel was due to appear. Even as she passed, she heard the opening music building to its theatrical crescendo. But the interior was hidden and she could see nothing of the stage. Had Gabriel done this to her? Or Stefan? It had to be one or the other, or both.

The crowds started to thin as they moved away from the arena. Then sounds of raucous laughter and obscene shouting grew as a large group of unseen men approached a corner ahead. The quieting street suddenly filled with a gang of filthy men. Covered in grime and dressed in rags, they shouted and play-fought as they moved toward the small group of Specials and their prisoner. Daisa experienced real fear.

'Twattin miners on furlough. All we need. Call up reinforcements, Number Two.'

The miners quickly grouped themselves in a tight circle around the six, eyes on Daisa.

'Nice twat!'

'Twattin great tits!'

'Arse of an angel!'

'Give us a shag, twat!'

And so it went on. Ribald but with a hint of threat underlying their taunts and teases. Daisa remained silent and stared defiantly at each man who spoke. Most merely grinned and glanced away before locking their leers back on her body.

'Okay, lads. You've had your fun. This twat's for the PutinMaister alone. I'm sure none of you want to cause him any offence.' The officer in charge spoke with confidence.

'Twattin PutinMaister. What's he ever done for us?' The owner of the voice was hidden, somewhere behind her.

'Silence!' The officer's command was loud and accompanied by each of the Specials unholstering their pulse guns. 'On your way, or we'll open fire!'

There were mutters and murmuring of ripe threats and intentions on her body, but none of them breached the fragile security of her cage of protectors. They dispersed, shouting obscenities and invitations as they moved off.

The streets grew quieter, until they were the only group moving through growing darkness and chill. Alone with her captors, she had to suffer occasional hands pawing her as they closed around her and moved as a unit toward the unknown destination.

At length, they arrived at a large grubby metal portal that swung open at their approach. The place had a threatening aura, like a military base built entirely for function and lacking any concession to style or design. Brutal; that was the word that came to mind.

Passages took them in twos and then single file to some central location. The leader pushed opened a second heavy portal and she was prodded inside with him following. The other men stayed outside, murmuring and bragging of their intent to each other, their overheard comments making their expectations clear.

A man in a black jerkin sat behind the small untidy desk she faced. Short, balding, sweaty and squinting past the biggest nose she'd ever seen, he slowly examined her from toes to the top of her head until his gaze returned to dwell on her breasts. He nodded in agreement with an unspoken thought. His head twisted slightly to the right and the officer slowly turned her so her back was to him. She remained this way for long enough to be thoroughly examined once more before being turned to face him again.

'Why am I here?'

He raised uneven eyebrows and wiped a hand under his nose. 'Speak when you're spoken to. Not until.'

Ambra remained with her. 'Do as he says. Defiance will cause you pain with these primitive apes.'

Daisa nodded.

'Name?'

'Daisa.'

'Full family name.'

'Daisa Zaphod Brigitte.'

'Offsprin of that twattin mutation? Before he lost his cock and balls.'

Unsure whether a reply was expected, she inclined her head in what she hoped would be taken as a noncommittal response.

'Answer me!'

'Zaphod and Brigitte are distant antecedents, but both are donors of genetic matter through their earlier children who then produced me.'

'Jeez, you're a disgustin lot. God knows why we didn't rid the world of the lot of your degenerate twattin mob when we had the chance.'

She refrained from correcting his mistaken reading of history and reminding him such a chance had never existed.

'Know why you're here?'

'No.'

'You call me "Sir", understand?'

'I do now. Sir.'

'Can't guess why you're here, then?'

'No. Sir.' She hoped her delay in adding the title indicated her lack of respect without actually stating it.

'Not so clever as you think, are you?'

'I lack the necessary data. Sir.'

He fumed. But something, she couldn't decide what, held him back from actually assaulting her. 'Your twattin community's kidnapped our Negotiator. They're holdin her prisoner. You're ours in exchange.'

'I don't think they'd …'

'Don't think? What the twat do you know?' He actually rose from his seat, his face purple with rage. 'I'm tellin you the facts. She's been kidnapped. So we've taken you. They give her back, we let you go. Simple.'

'I see. And, meantime?'

'Meantime? Oh, nice little cell for you. Minimum rations. You stay as you are, cept we'll take the cuffs off. Seems fair enough to me.'

'I see.'

'Look, twat, I'm givin you it easy. You wannit hard, I can do that.'

'I see. Sir.'

He nodded. Turned to the leader who remained in the corner studying her with undisguised lust.

'Take her out. No fuckin her. Not yet. Them up top say she's to be left. For now. Nothin to say she can't be put on display, mind. Give the peasants some fun.'

The leader of the arresting party grabbed her arm and thrust her back into the corridor, where the other members of the party waited.

'Not yet, boys. Later. Up top want her left alone. For now.' He pushed her along the narrow corridor ahead of him, followed by grumbles of injustice from the others.

They turned several right angle corners, descended three flights of metal steps, cold on the soles of her bare feet, and finished before a door made entirely of glass. His voice command unlocked it. He pushed her in and stroked his hands around her breasts, squeezed each nipple in turn and thrust his fingers between her legs. She remained silent and unresisting.

'Twat!' He slapped her face, twice, before undoing her manacles and pushing her on to the small bed. 'When the PM's done with you, I'll be havin a piece.' He tongued his top lip suggestively before leaving, locking the door behind him.

'We're trying to discover whether this is a misunderstanding or something else, Daisa. I'll get back as soon as we've found out exactly what's going on. Stay calm and brave. You're not alone.'

But she was alone, in real terms. The room was tiny. The single narrow bench with its thin, stained mattress was hard and devoid of bedding. It clung low to the wall opposite the door. In the left corner, a rusted pail sat on the bare rock of the floor. The ceiling bore four sunken spots, one of which flickered intermittently. All the walls were dotted with small apertures, each housing a camera. Another five studded the ceiling. Three more were sunk into the floor. This was her world now. For how long, she wondered.

Was this coincidence? Or did Gabriel or Stefan really have something to do with her capture? And how would the situation be resolved? How long would they leave her? How long before she was a plaything of the Specials, notorious for their cruelty and abuse of women?

Chapter Twenty Five

'We've no choice, if we're to regain Daisa her freedom. We definitely can't send you back to certain death, Virginia.' Georgiy glanced around the table at the other members of the Council.

'But, Stefan as Negotiator? I wouldn't want that man within a 100 ks of me or anyone I cared for, which includes all of you.' Virginia had completed the necessary treatment and was already feeling part of the community. Radiant in her chosen 23 age-freeze, she was clearly worried at the development she felt her move had triggered.

'Have they given terms? Exactly how we're to perform the swap, Georgiy?' Zaphod wanted details.

'Their demand's in their usual perfunctory style. A demand: Daisa in return for Virginia, and Stefan as new Negotiator. Obviously, we can't and won't surrender Virginia. But we should, at least, attempt to make them understand you're here at your own request. They appear convinced we've kidnapped you.'

'That'll be Stefan. A manipulator with absolutely no concern for truth or honesty. If he can gain influence and wealth, he'll do whatever he thinks he must. I can't believe I allowed myself to fall into his clutches. But we mustn't leave Daisa like this. You've seen what they're doin to her. Such public humiliation. Cruel and brutal.'

'Daisa won't be worried about the display. Exposure's irrelevant. But she'll be uncomfortable, confined in that unheated cell. It's their threat of a punishment execution on some trumped-up charge that's concerning.'

Zaphod stood and paced. 'We'll have to play them at their own game, I'm afraid.'

'What do you mean?' Brigitte turned to face him.

He returned to his seat beside Hoshiko and looked at the eight faces around the table. 'We can't accede to their demands. But if we refuse outright, they may kill Daisa on some pretext. We have to pretend to accept Stefan at least.' He put up a hand to forestall disagreement. 'For now. Until we've rescued Daisa. What happens after that will depend on their actions.'

'A rescue? How?'

He turned to Virginia. 'We've current plans of the city. We know precisely where she's being held. What we need from you, Virginia is the sort of detail only a resident can provide. Our cameras and technology give us many things, but they're no substitute for personal knowledge. Will you be part of our planning team for the rescue?'

'We haven't agreed we'll attempt it yet, Zaphod.' Hoshiko's reminder came as a surprise to him.

But he nodded. 'I'd taken it as read, but you're right. Show of hands?'

Every hand signalled agreement.

'Maybe it's time we took advantage of Chang's old invisibility technology. Did we ever develop that further?'

Hoshiko smiled. 'Sarm, Madonna, and a couple of youngsters are playing with it. They've refined it beyond the original crude system. Shall we check with Sarm? I think she sort of ran the project.'

'Is it more practical now?'

'From what she told me, you can wear the new suit indoors and out without the temperature problems Chang experienced. But the atmosphere was rudimentary then and his suit had to cope with pressure problems we no longer face. Let me contact her.' She did so at once.

The others talked about other practicalities for those few moments.

'She's in Earthgrav Gym. She'll have a quick shower and be with us. Shall we break for refreshments until then?'

Droids brought snacks and drinks and Brigitte took the opportunity to arrange the Threedee projection on to their conference table. They relaxed in the soft seats around the perimeter of the room as they awaited Sarm's arrival. One droid opened the entrance door to collect more coffee and stepped back in surprise before continuing its task.

Hoshiko smiled but said nothing other than to invite the group to return to the table.

'I thought we were waiting for Sarm?'

'She's here.'

Everyone looked round. No Sarm.

Hoshiko clapped her hands. 'Come on Sarm. I know you're here.'

Behind Zaphod, a hand appeared. As he turned to follow the gaze of those around the table, the other hand appeared. In a short time, Sarm was revealed, from her head down to her toes. She fumbled with something unseen in front of her, removed a light garment from nowhere, and slipped it on. Finally, she made a small movement and exposed the bag in front of her. She bowed briefly and sat down.

'That droid was a bit surprised when I collided with it at the door. Well spotted, Hoshiko. What d'you think?'

'Brilliant! I doubt anyone would've known if you hadn't shown yourself. How long since you perfected it?'

'About two years, actually.' The male voice came from the blank space beside the door.

Sarm waved in that direction. 'Show them, Madza.'

A young man revealed himself in the same way Sarm had. Once dressed, he moved closer to the table, his somewhat unconventional style raising a few eyebrows, but no comments.

'We're still working on the heat aspect, since it's best if we can avoid detection via infrared as well. We're close to complete invisibility. And the suit's more comfortable and lightweight now. It's a fascinating project, but we didn't publicise it because we're not quite finished yet.'

'Thank you, Madza and Sarm. How many suits do you have?'

'Six ready. We were going to surprise everyone at the Summer Ball. But I gather you've a more pressing need?'

They explained the situation.

'Are they personalised, or can they fit a variety of sizes?'

'Both. That is, if you're not too concerned about sharing. As you've seen, we wear them over our skin, nothing underneath. So we tend to have our own.'

Sarm shrugged. 'The material stretches enough to accommodate most people.' She turned to Georgiy. 'You could easily get into the one I've just removed.'

'Do you think they could help us rescue Daisa?' Ambra's question reminded them she was still present.

'Oh yes. Makes a huge difference. Okay. Let's start planning.' Zaphod glanced around for confirmation and the rest nodded their agreement.

Brigitte clicked the Threedee and brought up a detailed view of the City. She navigated to the Transhub terminal, enlarged the image slightly, and then followed the most direct route from the there to Daisa's cell. All eyes were fixed on the journey as she replayed it, this time from within the city, so they could see obstacles and barriers from the point of view of a citizen.

'That final complex of corridors might be tricky. Not much room for passing traffic. We'd have to ensure we timed the raid right, or the rescuers could be trapped.'

Zaphod nodded his agreement at Hoshiko's observation.

'Not to offend anyone, but wouldn't it be better to use some of the … younger members?' Madza looked apologetic.

'Age is immaterial, Madza. We're all equally fit and healthy. But you've a point in regard to physical size: height can be an advantage. Maybe best to use a mix including a couple of Chosen along with taller youngsters.'

Georgiy's suggestion was taken up. They selected a small group known to have the necessary fighting and technical skills and invited them to a meeting later that day.

They settled on a party of five, needing the spare suit for Daisa. Georgiy was mission leader. Madza and Sarm would go. Zaphod and Hoshiko were excluded due to their metallic skins, which were un-suitable for the fabric. Acacia was keen. And Ambra insisted on going.

'Maybe if I'd been a bit stricter, my daughter wouldn't be in this mess. Time I made amends for giving her too much freedom.'

From that point, details were left to the group, with others on the Council offering support as needed. The whole plan had taken only the day of the announcement of Stefan's imposed appointment to devise.

They'd sent back a detailed response, denying absolutely the accusation of kidnap and providing a confirmation video from Virginia that she was resident in Marion at her own request. They made it clear they didn't approve the appointment of Stefan as Negotiator but would accept him for the time being, pending his performance.

The response from the city had been brief and to the point. Stefan would be the new Negotiator, full stop. And they didn't believe their claim that Virginia had voluntarily left the city to join them at Marion.

'We demand Virginia back in the city by noon, our time, in two days, or we'll take Daisa to the Rio Tinto Arena. We'll broadcast the show live to both cities. She'll be mounted on the wheel for punishment. 30 men will do that. Afterwards, execution bots will flog her with wire whips. That's our final word. You have until 69.04.265.'

Chapter Twenty Six

The meet went even better than expected and the new girl they'd displayed proved a real crowd pleaser. Better still, Stefan told him she was an easy, willing, and submissive shag.

Daisa had been great in many ways, but her intelligence had frightened Gabriel at times, and her independent nature meant she didn't do as he told her.

'Gotta keep 'em under control, man. Make sure they know who's in charge.' Stefan had brought the new girl, Teresa; shown her to him just before the show.

She'd agreed to their demands in exchange for a regular supply of the narcotics Stefan traded. No complications. On stage, she displayed with more enthusiasm than Daisa; this girl from the street knew how to play the crowd. And the fiction about a virgin was irrelevant with her.

In his introduction to the Sacred Ones, Stefan maligned Daisa; told the Sacred Ones she'd succumbed to temptation with many unnamed guys. The crowd bayed for her, wanted her to suffer for her sins. Stefan linked into the prison cell, showing her using the bucket. That did the trick; no longer the virgin heroin, just a whore pissing like any other.

'Next step, Gab, is gettin revenge on those twat Marionets. Turn the crowd against them, let the mob see just how much they take advantage of our generosity.'

'Do they?'

'Come on, man. Use your common. Ever known them do any graft? Ever see any poverty or sufferin? Think that comes from some magical formula? No way. It's us they use. They just come up with ideas. We're the ones as dig the shit and garbage out the ground, tunnel through asteroids in sweat and dark, turn the crud we shovel into gold an diamonds an steel. They sit back on their fat arses and laugh while we do all the work.'

The next night, Gabriel passed on Stefan's hatred and the idea of their injustice to the crowd, now growing fast. That show was also a triumph.

Stefan's staging tricks captured their attention from the start. And the massive Threedee at the back of the stage emphasised Gabriel's moves, displayed Teresa in all her glory, and drove home the message in a way his voice alone could never have achieved.

It was the best night yet for contributions. Gabriel was now wealthy beyond his wildest dreams. And Stefan took only 12.5%. The pair ended up at an all-nighter full of drinks and professional girls willing to share their all with these two successful men for the price of a fizzy drink.

So Gabriel wondered, now he lay alone in his bed, why did something not feel right? Why did he still care about Daisa, and what happened to her? What made him feel as if he'd been responsible for the break-up? And why did he miss her?

Teresa had offered to spend the night again but he'd rejected her, having taken his pleasure in the bar at the club. Somehow, willing submissiveness didn't quite do what Daisa's sharing of herself had achieved.

But that was stupid: she was just a woman, built like any other woman. Same parts, same uses. It made no sense that he felt something different about her, something more. But he was seriously thinking of trying to get her released. The thought of that painful public execution played on his mind and stopped him sleeping. That shouldn't happen to Daisa, no matter what she might've done.

No. He still cared. It didn't make sense, but it was a fact. Come morning, he'd talk to Stefan and see if they couldn't get Daisa free again.

Stefan's tale of Virginia's fate was something else, though.

'You mean they're keepin her there as their prisoner?'

'Yeah. She must be really scared. They've got some pretty weird ideas about how men and women should be together. And they keep their women on show. Naked all the time, in or out. Don't care about warmth or privacy or comfort. Just take them when and where they like.'

'Daisa told me she was treated as an equal.'

Stefan scoffed. 'Think she'd dare tell you the truth? What would you've thought if she'd said she was just a call girl? Nah, she had to tell you she was equal to the men. As if! I mean, is it likely? Women are inferior. That Marionet crowd are clever, aren't they? Geniuses? They'd never fall for the story that women are equal to men.'

Gabriel was uncomfortable with that. 'I preached they were the same, Stefan. In the early days.'

'Before God showed you the full truth. He were testin you. Like you said to that troublemaker what asked questions last night. God tests us all, like you said. He was seein how far you could be fooled. And you passed the test no trouble. Soon as you ditched Daisa, got her arrested, you proved to God how wise you are.'

Gabriel's memory of exactly how Daisa had been arrested was confused. He thought he'd had a good handle on it, but his friend showed him how Stefan's version of events was true. He trusted Stefan to interpret his visions, so he could hardly doubt his friend and mentor when it came to recalling events in the city.

The visions had made him into a sort of star. He was famous now. Far more famous than when he'd come back from the asteroids and got the medal for saving those men. That had been quickly forgotten, but now he was known everywhere in the city.

Men respected him. Women offered themselves for free, gave him whatever he wanted. So it must be true. Stefan had done that. Stefan's recall of what happened was always right, whilst he knew his own memory could play tricks. And Stefan had brought God into his life. God wouldn't keep him as the special spokesman otherwise.

Sleep still evaded him. The picture of Daisa bound and vulnerable in the square as they killed her slowly that way. Could that be right? To do that to her? To be so cruel? It seemed wrong. He must talk to Stefan in the morning and see if they could get her sentence changed, at least. No matter how often she'd cheated on him, no matter how many men she preferred to him.

'Too many to count.' Stefan said.

But she didn't deserve that sort of death. Not really.

He needed something to take his mind off the thought. Before he even knew it, his communicator was in his hand and he'd contacted Teresa. She was sleeping but rose when he told her he wanted her.

'Be there soon as I can. Give me a half hour, Gabriel.'

He made her shower when she arrived. Gave her a shot. She was grateful. Showed her gratitude. Taster, then Bed Warmer. Left him tired enough to sleep at last.

Stefan came at his call after breakfast. Teresa was still there, sleeping off the drug on top of his bed. Stefan stared at her for a while, then flicked the cover over her.

'You mad, Gabriel? I mean, after all she's done. You want to risk everythin by tryin some stupid rescue attempt. The Specials'll roast you. Jeez, man, it was you said she'd done the murder. Don't you remember nothin?'

'Murder?'

'Oh, come on man. Don't do this to me. You saw it with your own eyes! Took four of them to get her off the poor twat. Jealousy, of course. I mean, that lass had bragged about how you'd had her so often. No way Daisa was goin to have that sort of competition for you. No idea where she got the knife. But they said the poor twat was cut bad. You must remember. You came on them when Daisa was covered in the poor twat's blood.'

Gabriel tried to collect his thoughts. Hadn't that been a dream he'd mentioned, a nightmare? He recalled Stefan's garbled account told over drinks after the meet. Or was that it? Had Stefan told him, or had he told Stefan? And he'd had a dream last night, hadn't he? Different from his visions. There were times he couldn't account for. Times he couldn't measure. But this was serious. It can't have been real, can it?

'Where? Where was it? When?'

'Jeez, Gab. I can't help you if you don't at least try to remember things when they happen. I mean, this ain't no ordinary crime. That poor twat belonged to the boss of the fashion chain. Think how he's feelin now. His special woman butchered by a stranger you were responsible for at the time. You can't pretend you don't remember what she did. I mean, you could easily be found guilty of bein in with her if you're not certain on that point when they ask you for details.'

His head spun. He thought it had all been a bad dream when he'd explained it to Stefan earlier. But it can't have been. It must be true. Stefan was mad at him now. He must've really seen what he'd thought had been something from his imagination.

'Tell me again. Remind me, Stefan. I can't remember the details.'

Stefan checked the girl on the bed. She was still fast asleep. But he closed the door. It wouldn't do for her to hear him telling Gabriel something he was supposed to have reported himself to Stefan. He described the incident in full to Gabriel, missing out nothing and embellishing where he thought it would enhance the likelihood Gabriel would repeat the incident in detail.

Once finished with the tale, he got Gabriel to relay it in detail to him, made sure he was word perfect. Satisfied Gabriel was now convinced the fiction was fact, Stefan relaxed. The Specials would be round later, checking out Gabriel's part in the scheme.

Stefan had gained some powerful allies by concocting the tale to get those four off the hook. The woman had understandably resisted their clumsy attempt at an orgy. She was, after all, high status. It was inevitable she'd get hurt. Stefan's rapidly created explanation suited the Specials as well as giving him leverage over Gabriel and gaining an even better reason to have Daisa executed. All gave him a greater chance with the PutinMaister.

'Now. Don't forget. They'll be here to check the facts. Tell them exactly what you've just told me. Then you're safe from bein caught up as her associate. I'd hate for you to be made responsible for her crime, Gab. All that new wealth an influence you've earned down the drain in an instant. An you hangin on that hook while they whip you to death. Don't bear thinkin about. So, keep it tight, man.

'I've done all I can to keep you in the clear, but I can't do nothin now to help Daisa. Neither can you. She's guilty. The twat has to suffer the consequences. Women so easily get jealous when another gets off with their man. Be grateful you were there only at the end an never heard the argument what started it.'

Gabriel, numb with shock at Daisa's attack on the other woman, and terrified he might easily be implicated, nodded compliance. Perhaps it was all for the best, after all. Shame about Daisa. But wasn't she just a woman? Nothing to him, really.

Chapter Twenty Seven

The penultimate Transdrum of the day took them to a terminal almost devoid of others, so they were able to leave without causing suspicion when the doors opened. Georgiy wondered if Marzero cameras would alert their spies in any way, though he was 90% certain their surveillance systems were nowhere near as sophisticated as those at home. The new invisisuits now protected against most IR and UV as well as the visible spectrum, so they should be safe enough.

Buzz was on station, keeping an eye on the screens. Hosja had volunteered to relay messages, since Buzz, Georgiy and Sarm were without the sub-cranial implant. Madza checked in for an update.

'Buzz insists she was still in place last time he looked. The corridors leading to the cell were empty. There's a single guard at the first door.'

'What do you mean, when he last looked, Hosja? Aren't you also looking?' Madza didn't like the tone of her message.

'You know Buzz. Keeps flipping to other rooms.'

'Keep him on song, Hosja. He's our eyes. Well, you and he are. Keep alert for us.' Madza was aware she'd volunteered as a young woman with an interest in Buzz, but no previous experience. What they found attractive in the man was a mystery.

'No need to get annoyed. We're watching out for you.'

'Thanks, Hosja. We're relying on you for our safety.' He cut the connection and turned to quietly inform Georgiy of the current situation, passing over only the positive aspects of the message rather than worrying their leader with what he saw as unnecessary details.

The party had to keep in physical contact, since they were as invisible to each other as they were to everyone else. Georgiy checked all were present and each had hold of the hand of the one behind: himself, Ambra, Madza, and Acacia, with Sarm at the rear.

They set off across the open concourse, the memory of the street layout fresh in their minds. Georgiy had studied the plan in detail during the last couple of hours before they left. His recall was good, but he wished they could've brought Zaphod or Hoshiko with them. Their ability to connect directly to CenCom gave them a real advantage in this sort of situation. Ambra and Madza's links would have to do. Not as comprehensive as the superandroids' but better than none.

From the terminal their route took them through the outer environs of Marzero2, one of the less well off sectors, though not the worst. They stayed in line for the journey, although such contact slowed them a little.

Time was important: the last Transdrum back to Marion left in less than two hours and they needed to be on it. The hue and cry when Zero's Elite realised they'd lost their prisoner would make any later escape all but impossible.

Recent improvements had made the suits more flexible, less clumsy, though no warmer than the original. Here, so far north, temperatures dropped quite steeply. They kept moving at a good pace to maintain body temperature. Running was difficult, even had they had the luxury of separate movement, since breathing through the fabric restricted airflow. A fast walking speed was the best they could manage.

At a crossroads, a sorry group of women was being driven by a gang of men. They were on a collision course with the rescuers. Madza had no option. He released his hold on Acacia. 'Come directly across when they've passed.'

She agreed and stayed still, with Sarm in contact. They watched the parties move between them and their invisible colleagues and then ventured back over the open space.

'Guide me, Madza.'

'We're holed up by the entrance to this place with lots of peculiar items in the window. A shop, I think. The sign above says, "EvrythinUWan4Fun."'

Acacia identified it and led Sarm to the doorway. She reached out with her hand, finding space. 'I'm here. Where are you, Madza?'

They found each other and clasped hands with relief. The chain moved on. At the end of a row of dilapidated shops all displaying the same meaningless stuff, Georgiy paused and then moved left.

They had three more such stretches to follow before they came to the prison gates. On the last stretch, a man was dragging a dishevelled woman across from one side of the street to the other. She was in tears, trying to resist. He slapped her. Shouted at her. The few other citizens took no notice, carrying on their own business. But Georgiy couldn't ignore it. "Stay exactly here."

He dashed across the street. Then remembered their need for secrecy, his early astronaut training for discipline, and returned to the others.

'We have to go, Georgiy!' Ambra waved her arm about until she reconnected with him. Her hoarse whisper a reminder of their status. 'We don't have time for this. Daisa's in trouble.'

He nodded, remembered he couldn't be seen, and gripped her hand in reply before he led them toward the prison gates. They came in sight. A formidable barrier.

The party remained connected as they studied the barred entrance. The obvious way in was via a digital pad on the wall.

'Hosja, get Buzz to search for the pass code.'

Her reply was slow and garbled. 'Hosja! We're stuck out here. We need you with us all the time. Please. We need that password!'

There was a short space of silence before she replied. 'Selfish bastard. I don't know why I played along! I'm not staying.'

'Hosja. Listen! Our lives depend on you helping us. Do you hear?'

'He's a bully and a user. Worse than anyone said. I'd never have …'

'Not now, Hosja. Six lives depend on you being mature enough to know what matters. We'll deal with Buzz when we're back home with Daisa. Now. Put it behind you and do as I ask. Please, Hosja.'

'What's the delay?' Georgiy's whispered question was an unnecessary intrusion.

'Patience, Georgiy.' He returned to Hosja. 'We're relying on you,

Hosja. We're completely at your mercy. You're the only one who can help us right now.'

'I'll be having words …'

'Hosja. Our lives! We're depending on you.'

There was a brief silence, a short sob. 'Sorry. Yes. Sorry. Just a moment.'

He waited, taking the time to explain there was a slight hiccup at the other end but Buzz and Hosja were doing what was necessary to solve the problem.

After what seemed like an age, Hosja came back and gave him a simple six-digit entry code. 'I'm not doing what he wants in return till you're safely back. I promise I'll stay alert until then.'

'Thank you, Hosja. You're doing brilliantly.'

Even as he punched the code into the gate, he wondered why Buzz hadn't unlocked it remotely, since he had the means. The portal opened. They entered in their long chain and it closed behind them.

Georgiy surveyed the area. Nobody on guard. In fact there was no sign of life here. They crossed the open space into a wide corridor, following its staggered curve until he recognised the small door that led to the narrow alley. Here they'd be at their most vulnerable, since they had to keep in single file and would be unable to defend themselves against a concerted attack.

All seemed quiet as they moved down the long corridor with its multiple turns and occasional stairways. They passed numerous doors along the way, on both sides of the corridor, all glass. Almost every prisoner was a woman. The whole experience was so alien they had difficulty resisting the temptation to free these vulnerable captives. But Daisa was their objective and they continued until they reached her door.

It was open. The cell empty.

Chapter Twenty Eight

Amber worked with the team of droids and specialist robots she'd led on many occasions. She needed something to take her mind off Georgiy on his dangerous rescue mission to the City.

Their current probe was destined for Earth in an attempt to corroborate previous unverified signs of possible human existence after the latest one had failed under the onslaught of orbiting debris. The last probe that had returned results had produced intriguing data for the first time since they'd attempted to renew contact. But the info had been minimal, inconclusive, and even contradictory.

They'd decided to wait a few years and try again. 80 or so Earth years should've produced some progress on the home planet, if intelligent life had managed to survive the ravages of war, climate chaos, and resource depletion.

Everything was set to launch the probe from the facility orbiting above the space elevator. They'd done this many times before. Unmanned, lightweight, but bristling with detectors of various types, the small satellite would take little power to escape the lesser gravity of Mars. The presence of Ceres and Vesta had now to be added to their calculations, but that was no barrier.

The only new aspect of this particular launch was the employment of high-speed proton pulse drive. They'd tested it with expendable payloads, mostly unrecyclable garbage, targeted at the sun. Only one had failed and that payload had burned up as it fell back to the surface over the uninhabited south pole.

Now, they were finalising transmission, reception and control coms tests. Three days of intensive assessment of the systems to ensure everything worked exactly as designed. They expected no problems, but had learned from long experience that thorough testing exposed any small glitches.

Already halfway through the procedure, they were now carrying out the remainder as the satellite was carried up for launch. There was really no need for Amber to travel with it; androids were perfectly capable of seeing to that final aspect. But she wanted to take her mind off Georgiy, and this was a fine way of keeping occupied.

Up here, ascending slowly on the space elevator, she could look down on their settlement. The structure reached out in a wide disc, a six point star covering the central area. To the south, where Lake Peake sparkled under early morning sun, she could still make out the lane where her own pod lay in its private garden. Too far to see any activity. But the gardenbot would be tending the plants and keeping everything tidy.

The whole of that sector was now residential; mostly occupied by the original settlers and their first and second generation offspring. Just occasionally, she felt a little guilty that they'd selected the best area for themselves. But, as Georgiy and Tu had pointed out, they were the pioneers without whom nothing would have been possible.

'We deserve some luxury after all our efforts, risks and trials. Anyway, this is where we started. Everything else was built out from this optimal location.'

She smiled, recalling Maddie's words, and turned her attention to the adjacent point of the star. There lay the university campus with its student accommodation, its labs and libraries, sports fields and parks, entertainment arenas and lecture halls.

The lake extended across the open space between the two points, forming a shore to both. And, even from this height, she could see the river that fed rainwater from the distant slopes of Olympus Mons down into the settlement. The lower hills, dotted with the circular settlements that comprised the bulk of the living areas, were beautifully green now. So different from the dull red dust she'd lived with in the early years.

It seemed such a long time ago. So much had happened. So many changes. And, yet, she and the original settlers all still looked almost exactly as they had the day they'd landed. 'Thank you, Zaphod and Qiu.' It was a daily mantra, that simple statement of gratitude, that acknowledgement of their sacrifice and their amazing work.

She continued her survey, content in the knowledge that time was on her side. No longer the need to do everything at high speed in order to fit in life's ambitions and desires. She'd already had, what? At least five normal lifespans. And, once her role in population development had ended, her 35 children been born and breastfed for the best physiological and emotional start in life, she'd been able to spend the rest of her time in leisure, learning, exploring, loving, wonder and thought.

Maddie and Brigitte's brilliant work with droids and bots freed them all from the burden of labour. Duty to the colony consisted of ideas and support now. Far from the stagnating force predicted, the freedom Earth's profit-obsessed leaders had always avoided for society proved a veritable springboard for scientific and personal development. So many discoveries, so many great steps along the way to the Utopia they'd all envisaged as they'd sat in those padded chairs on the launch to Mars.

Immediately below her, the industrial sector of the central star was a mass of intricate pipework, containers, small and large workshops and warehouses. Here was where the physical work of the colony was done. Mostly, droids oversaw specialised robots involved in hundreds of different processes that kept the planet alive, monitored and managed the atmosphere, provided power, produced goods that made life so much more interesting, and recycled everything capable of reuse in any form.

Next to that, the fourth arm of the star gave shelter and comfort to more early colonists. Their patches of garden could be seen even from this height. And the wide, meandering streets, giving interest for walkers and cyclists going about their daily lives. The fifth point was another residential area, much like the other two.

The sixth was devoted to community activities. The vast Threedee stadium, where they watched films, old and new. Sports tracks and arenas, where competitions and games entertained and exercised members of the settlement. The newer live arena, where bands played, musical extravaganzas were performed. The theatres where stage plays were performed.

The newly constructed astrodome gave nightly shows of wonders of the universe, freely available to all through the work of dedicated astronomers with their amazing telescopes and other devices. Who knew just how massive and ever-changing the cosmos really was? So many finds; almost daily events now.

Even from this height, she couldn't see the whole settlement. The central star was surrounded by a huge irregular discoid of separate townships, each housing around 3,000 people, that being considered the ideal population for a residential community.

Wide bands of green land surrounded each satellite colony and, here and there, smaller lakes slowly formed. Each community was joined to its neighbours and to the central star by the extensive fusion powered Transhub system, so citizens could get to any part of the complex in a few mins. Generous paths also wound between all the townships to allow people to walk, cycle or run as they wished.

'Excuse me, Amber; you wanted to know when we'd completed the microwave test.' D00397's soft voice broke into her thoughts.

'I take it everything's fine, 397?'

'Performing exactly to specification.'

'Excellent. I think that leaves only two more tests to complete before we're done?'

'Correct, Amber. The last test on the HiRes Threedee won't be possible until we're at higher altitude. But we've started the final Lidar run. And we've begun with the low frequency scan and will work up to the ultra high in the agreed stages. That should cover all sections of the visible spectrum as well as IR and UV by the time we reach launch altitude.'

'Thank you, 397. Would you ask A02395 to fix me breakfast, please?'

She moved to the seating area in the much enlarged capsule. In the early days, she recalled, there'd barely been room to move.

The later work on adapting the space elevator to take a far larger cabin had proved very worthwhile. With the extensive window area, she could continue to watch the planet surface as it slowly retreated below.

Soon, they'd be high enough to see the edge of Marzero on the far horizon to the north. How, she wondered, was Georgiy managing with the rescue? By now, they should be on their way back to Marion, if not already home. But she knew he'd complete the debrief before he contacted her to let her know he was safe.

A02395 brought her a tray with her usual porridge, citrus fruit juice, toast and boiled egg. The droid was an early Chinese model from their damaged base.

Its resemblance to the beautiful Daiyu even now sometimes startled her. That overt sexuality, and the way of moving that rendered it an exact physical copy of the woman on whom it was modelled, had been the reason she'd selected it as her personal aid.

It was unavailable to less discerning men and provided her with a servant she could view as a companion during times when Georgiy was otherwise occupied. Alone with the droid, she called it by her special name; memorial to a lost companion. 'Thank you, Zhen.' She whispered as it lowered the tray.

Georgiy disapproved of such sentiment, but it was as well to keep a man like him on his toes by pretending, however unlikely, she might be tempted by the droid. His brief dalliance with Virginia had been the first for a long time. And, on this occasion, she'd approved his method of introducing the new woman into their community. The thought of having him back to herself brought a smile, and she settled to breakfast, still hoping she'd hear soon from the man she'd loved all her adult life.

Chapter Twenty Nine

Madza tried to reconnect with Hosja to find what she could tell them. At the same time, Ambra sought to connect with Daisa. Madza could find no connection, which angered him. Buzz had ever been unreliable and it looked as though Hosja had fallen victim to him.

Ambra cried out loud as she found her daughter. The connection was overlain with fear and distress of a sort she'd never encountered. Through the sense of panic, Ambra fought for control until she reached the young woman. 'Guide us. We're here to rescue you, Daisa. But we don't know where you are. Show me.'

'I'm through to Daisa.' She told the others as they waited in the corridor. 'They've taken her some place to rehearse her execution. Let me lead the party; she'll guide us through my eyes, as long as she can control her fear.'

Ambra moved along the line until she was at the head. Hands closely clasped, they followed as she led them back the way they'd travelled to the cell. Abruptly, Daisa lost concentration, due to her fear. The party stopped until Ambra found and reconnected with her.

That last Transhub back to Marion would go on time, and quite soon.

'Keep with me, Daisa. Stay in contact. Please, my girl.'

Daisa's response was full of real fear and disgust. Urgency. An appeal for them to reach her as soon as they could.

They moved back outside, the exit easier than the entrance with no need of a code. In the streets, Ambra led the group beside the outer wall of the prison complex, taking them further from the Transhub terminal. The way was quiet, most people now either at home or work. They passed a small coterie of street women parading their wares in pursuit of custom from any men in transit.

Ambra followed Daisa's fractured instructions, experiencing the desperation in her daughter's link, as she fought to keep connected.

She knew her child well. It must be something extraordinary that she suffered for her to project such terror and revulsion.

She lost the connection again, as a roar of triumph carried down the narrow street to the group. That sound convinced Ambra its source was where they'd find Daisa. She continued to lead them, guided by the growing noise of glee mixed with taunting jeers.

A small crowd gathered near the entrance to what appeared to be a closed arena. Ambra elbowed and pushed her way toward the gate, oblivious of cries of surprise and fear as she barged through. Inevitably, she lost contact with those following.

The small crowd numbered 12 or 13 men. It was only as she reached the gate she realised she was now alone, the citizens crowding her. She must reach her daughter. But this wasn't the way. Her native intelligence took over from her instinctual need to get inside.

Well-aimed blows at vulnerable soft tissue soon cleared a space, her victims running from the scene wild-eyed. She saw the others similarly employed as the remainder of the mob fell victim to their selective attacks. The men stopped a short distance from the gate, exchanging tales of the ghostly attack they'd suffered.

'Jupiter's balls, Ambra. Thought we'd lost you.' Georgiy found her with an outstretched palm that connected with her hip. She collected his hand in hers.

'Daisa needs us in there. Now!'

'Are we all here?' Georgiy's question brought answers from the rest and they reconnected hands.

'The gate's locked.' Sarm tried the entrance. 'If Buzz has disappeared as usual, we'll have to find our own way in.'

'Should've had a man with him, not a suggestible young woman.'

'Yes, Acacia. We've gathered that. Let's get inside.' Georgiy's voice exposed his concern as well as his regret for a poor piece of planning.

'It's digital. Try the same password?' Sarm entered the numbers. Nothing happened.

'Not too high to climb over, if we help each other.' Madza suggested.

Quickly, they organised themselves to hoist the lightest first. Sarm sat astride the gate and quickly surveyed the scene.

'Georgiy next, because of his reduced height.' Her suggestion made sense and he joined her above the gate but dropped down the other side as soon as he'd seen what was happening in the arena.

It took only secs for the others to be helped over. The whole party moved in the same direction Georgiy had taken, driven by the baying calls and taunts of the men who controlled Daisa.

Even as they approached the open area, they witnessed Georgiy's attack. A guard, undressed from the waist, fell to the ground and lay unmoving. First one down. His colleagues, intent on the show they were devising, were oblivious.

Sarm counted 30 around the open space. All male. Most were entirely naked or stripped below the waist, ready to abuse Daisa. Strapped face down to a large metal wheel, her centre raised by the dome of the hub, arms and legs outstretched, she was utterly vulnerable. Defenceless.

None of the guards noticed the demise of their colleague. All were taunting Daisa with threats of what they'd to do to her when their turn came. This mocking was part of the torture, intended to scare their victim before they raped her. But there was something also vaguely tentative about the attack, as if they lacked confidence to fulfil their promise of assault. Maybe their torture wasn't officially sanctioned.

Now separated, the rescue group spread out amongst the circling men. With no co-ordinated plan, and connection possible only between two of their number, they acted individually. Georgiy saw a guard go down next to him and added his own swift kick to the man's head to incapacitate him.

Still the rest of the men were focussed on Daisa, now slowly spinning on her wheel. Georgiy took down the man on his other side, a swift karate blow rendering him unconscious in one stroke. He saw another fall opposite.

Ambra approached the wheel, studied it, then leapt aboard. The straps holding Daisa in place were roughly tied to metal lugs. She connected with Daisa again as she began to unfasten them, urging her to lie still until all were undone. Surely, one of the guards would notice odd activity soon? The fabric ties were worn and frayed; the knots tight and tangled. Daisa tried to rise when the first was undone.

'Stay still, Daisa. They'll see!'

'Hurry! Please, Mother!'

'Patience. They're hard work.'

She released a second, freeing Daisa's arms. The young woman again began to move, trying to reach the tie on her leg.

'Still! You'll alert them, Daisa. Stay still!'

Ambra could feel the fear in her daughter's mind. Tangible, it threatened to expose both of them to the rapacious guards.

She finally released the tie on her left leg. 'Don't move. Please.'

Madza and Acacia, conscious of each other's positions, took down two guards at the same time. Now the men began to realise something was wrong. Their jeers and taunts at Daisa subsided. Disorganised mutterings and cries of alarm arose as Sarm and Georgiy disabled another three. They knocked a pair of heads together as soon as they realised their proximity to each other.

Fear, uncertainty, and the inexplicability of the attack now kept the guards occupied. Ambra managed to undo the last tie and helped Daisa to her feet. Her daughter hugged her fiercely until Ambra urged her to move so they could escape.

Away from the wheel, she unpacked the spare suit from the small bag at her back. The interior appeared momentarily as she opened and then closed it. But the glimpse attracted the attention of the nearest guard. He stood utterly confused by what he thought he'd seen. Only as Daisa began to vanish from sight from the feet upwards, did he move toward her.

'She's escaping!'

It was all he managed. Ambra left Daisa to finish donning the suit. She hit him square in the face with her fist. He staggered back from the impact and she kicked him hard between his legs. As he buckled in pain, she brought her knee up into his descending face and broke his nose. He fell back hard, struck the edge of the raised wheel platform with the back of his head and took no further part in the conflict.

The remaining guards, aware of some impossible attack, panicked. Cries of dismay and confusion mingled with alarm and pain as the assault moved forward at speed. Each of the invisible team, now joined by Daisa bent on revenge, tackled one man at a time, quickly reducing numbers until only a dozen remained upright. They moved into a single body, grouping together against their unseen attackers and facing outward in a circle.

This unwise tactic made the rest of the attack much simpler and each guard fell at the hands, and feet, of the rescuers. Two had the sense to run for help but Ambra caught both, tackling the last so he fell on his face. She stamped hard on his head, turned him and trod on his genitals.

'Gather!' Georgiy called the team together. 'Grasp hands as before. Daisa, connect with whoever reaches for you.'

She understood what had happened, shock and trauma shoved to the back of her mind for now. Sound guided her to the team. A hand stretched and touched her thigh. She reached, found the hand. Grasped it. From somewhere unseen, but close, a siren sounded. Cameras were clearly monitoring the scene of torture.

'We need to get out. Now.' Daisa told them. 'They'll bring hundreds of reinforcements within mins.'

They were able to open the gate from inside. The group of men they'd originally tackled were still around. The opening gate caught their attention and a few ventured toward the escapees. Once three of these hit the ground for no apparent reason, the rest fled the scene.

Winding their way through the streets, they constantly checked to ensure all party members were present. The last thing they needed was a loss now.

'Flat against the wall to the left!' Sarm's quiet warning reached them all as a troop of Specials sped down the narrow street toward them.

Daisa recognised a particular tormentor during her incarceration. Bile rose to fuel her rage and she moved to trip him, her hand in her mother's alerting her to Daisa's intentions.

'Leave him.' Ambra's silent contact stopped her making a move that would've revealed their whereabouts, and the body of men sped past.

'On.'

The single word galvanised them into action again. They ran, loped and walked through narrow streets until they reached the wider ways leading to the most modern part of the city.

The Transhub terminal had been designed by Marion engineers and was as well planned as anything back at their colony. The citizens of Marzero treated it as an iconic structure and the space around it remained free from the usual garbage and cheap commercial shacks that bedevilled most of the city.

As they approached, however, they found each of the four entrances guarded by a troop of Elite Special Officers. These were men of unusual ability, the cream of the forces who controlled the public. The authorities were aware of the attackers. Whether they understood the nature of their disguise was impossible to know, but the rescue party had to be careful how they proceeded.

Without a word of command, the six Marion colonists gathered together, forming a tight circle. 'Ideas?' Georgiy's question was as near silent as possible in the large space. But so was the response.

Nobody had a quick solution to the problem of their escape. The Transhub was no longer an option. Even if they hadn't missed the last drum of the day, which was on its way out of the terminal as they arrived, the waiting ESOs were too much of a barrier.

'What now?' Madza's request was met with silence as each of the rescue party considered the situation. They had limited time available. The suits wouldn't protect them against the growing cold. Soon, they must shed their invisible skins and dress more warmly, exposing their flesh to those who would capture and kill them.

Chapter Thirty

Disbelief grew in Gabriel as he listened to the account of Daisa's attack and murder of the woman. But he daren't show disrespect for the Chief Interrogator who faced him across the desk in the small foetid room.

There was a timid knock on the door and a guard entered. From somewhere distant, a siren was blaring. The C.I. flinched at the sound and glared at the guard.

'Get out, man. An shut the twattin door behind you. I'm not to be disturbed.'

'But, Sir, I have …'

'Twat off! Now. Or I'll have you in that chair next and use them on you.'

The bench in the corner, indicated by the C.I.'s gesture, held implements that could only cause pain. The guard blanched and left, slamming the door shut.

'Twattin moron. Now. You. Comfortable, are you?'

The metal chair Gabriel occupied bore unpleasant stains beneath manacles waiting to be locked over his arms. These were men with fearsome reputations, unconcerned about what methods they applied to draw info from suspects. Even Stefan, with all his connections, influence in the city, and sudden unexplained promotion to Cleric Class One, could do nothing to help him here. In fact, Stefan was, he'd been told with a sneer, also under arrest for complicity in the crime. A crime he found increasingly incredible.

'Yes, Sir.'

'For now. I asked you a question before that twat interrupted.'

'I don't see why she'd kill another woman, though, Sir.' He was well aware Daisa's action reflected badly on him.

'Don't know women, d'you, Prophet of the People? Obvious to anyone who knows the schemin twats.' But still no explanation. 'So, I ask again, what time did you leave the traitor from Marion alone on the night of the murder?'

'You haven't said what night it was. Sir.'

'Don't answer back, boy! Answer my question.'

Gabriel had heard of this illogical approach. He'd always thought people were exaggerating. 'Last time I saw her, Sir, was when I left for the meet at Shenhua Stadium. The gatherin was timed to begin at 18:00 hours and Stefan and I had some preparation to do, so it would've been around 16:30, more or less.'

The man actually smiled. 'Wasn't so hard, was it?'

He assumed no answer was needed so remained silent.

'Was it?'

'Oh. No, Sir.'

He nodded and keyed some words into his pad. 'How often did she have sex with other women?'

This was madness. Daisa was entirely normal. She'd no interest in other women that way. But had he known her well enough to state that as fact? He had to get this right. The trouble Daisa was in was the sort he feared most. 'I didn't know of her habits outside her relationship with me, Sir.'

'That right?' The C.I. shook his head in disgust. 'Too much freedom, boy. Gave her way too many chances to do as she pleased. No way to handle a twat. Just because she come from Marion, you thought you'd believe her. Don't you know how they cheat and lie there, boy? Specially the women. Gotta keep the twats on a tight leash. Gotta control them. Gotta show them you're in charge. No wonder the twat got out of hand.'

'Sorry, Sir. I was involved in my ministry. And she seemed willin to cooperate.' He was getting a feel for it now. You had to at least seem to agree with the investigators. That appeared to be the way through this.

'At your meets you stated you and she was livin together but not doin it. Course, we know that's just marketin. Clever trick, an' all. But how good a shag was she really?' His question seemed without prurient element. Gabriel believed he was interested only in getting the facts for his case.

'With me, she was great, Sir. Generous, you know? Taught me a lot about what women want.'

The C.I.'s eyes brightened. 'So, she'd learned a lot about the wants of twats? Where else would she get that but from shaggin other twats, boy?'

'Hadn't thought of it that way. Sir.' He was tempted to explain she'd said she'd been taught by an older man who'd had many women. But it wasn't what the man wanted to hear.

'No. You wouldn't. Really fooled you, boy. Took you for a proper ride. Made you look even more stupid than you are, didn't she?'

'I suppose she must've. Sir.'

'Gotta problem with my title, boy?'

'No Sir. Just not used to bein in this sort of situation, Sir.'

The man nodded, sucked on his teeth, made a sceptical but tired face. All this was old hat. Heard it all before. Nothing anyone could tell him about the seedy side of life. 'So, when I tell you what she did, you're gonna be a sensible lad and see what I say makes sense.' It wasn't a question.

Gabriel gave it a split sec's thought and nodded.

'Good.' The C.I. went on to describe how four officers of the law, which Gabriel assumed were junior policemen, had found Daisa with the victim. He detailed a scene of utter debauchery that ended with Daisa strangling the other woman simply because she could. 'Sound like the woman you knew, boy?'

He understood his answer could save him but would condemn Daisa to death. But she was already awaiting execution and, anyway, he had no choice. God needed him alive to continue his ministry. He must do what was best for God. There was nothing else he could do. He nodded.

'Lost your tongue, boy?'

'Sorry, Sir. Yes, Sir.' Part of him died as he condemned Daisa, but another part rejoiced in the release he might now achieve. 'Yes, Sir. Sounds like her.'

The C.I. rose. Extended a hand across the table. They shook. 'Well done, Gabriel. You've saved us a lot of trouble. No need for a trial now. Only a twat, after all. No need to spend time and money on her. A murderin lesbian. Waste of resources.

'We can make a proper example of her. You won't hear no more from us on this. Go back to your ministry and spread the word about maximum consumption, Gabriel. The PutinMaister says you're doin a right good job since you started on that tack. Mark my words, though, boy. No more crap about equality for twats, eh?'

'Of course, Sir.'

'Right. On your way before I change me mind.'

He unlocked the door and Gabriel walked through, a free man again. Waiting in the small reception area of this unremarkable centre for interrogation he found Stefan. His friend rose as soon as he appeared, put an arm around his shoulders, and ushered him rapidly from the building. Stefan couldn't get out of there quickly enough.

They said nothing of their separate interrogations as they walked through the mean streets of the poorest quarter. It was almost noon; the questioning had taken all night and much of the morning. Gabriel was weary, hungry, ready for a drink. Stefan was more upbeat.

The inn was quiet at this time of day. A threesome of street women sat in a dim corner, drinking cheap spirits and displaying their wares to any man who might be ready to buy. A glance from the pair was all they got.

At the bar, they ordered long drinks of cheap beer and shots of neat vodka to chase it.

'D'you believe she did it, Stefan?'

His friend frowned. 'Course not. Y'know exactly what happened, man.'

Gabriel shook his head in sorrow. 'No.'

'Jeez, you're slow sometimes. It's twattin obvious, man.'

'Not to me.'

'No. I suppose not. Your interrogator wouldn't know. Mebbie

wouldn't tell you even if he did. Mine give me the info upfront, once he clicked who I am. See, four Specials arrested a woman, shagged her, did other things to her. Realised too late they'd got the wrong twat; one of the Elite's harem. Couldn't let her accuse them, so they did her in.

'Daisa's the only Marionet in the city. Well known through your ministry. Easy to accuse her. Easy to arrest her. She's a useful bargainin chip to get Virginia back. Daisa's currency, man. They'll threaten the Marionets with her death for the murder. Get the stupid twats to send Virginia back. Once she's here, a few of the top lads'll shag Daisa for fun then send her home, none the worse. Virginia, now, she'll get what she deserves, treacherous twat. I'd like to be in on that. Give the twattin traitor a real good hidin, an no mistake. Made fools of us all.'

Gabriel considered the ways of his city, the priorities they chose. Was his mission right? He'd started out trying to help the women of the city, but the messages from God had shown him his mistake.

Something still seemed not right, though, about the way women were treated. But it was all the fault of women that Marzero was backward. There was plenty of proof of that. It had been women who'd stopped progress in Marzero that had developed in Marion.

The women in Marion had been unaffected by the Cusp War. Hadn't had the chance to take advantage like the women of Marzero. That was the difference, really.

Women were the same all over. It was like the Elite said. Those in Marzero had taken power after the Cusp War and then blown it by their bad behaviour. He'd bet his life the women of Marion would've done the same given the chance. But the men there had been cleverer. Wrong, but better organised.

He felt the need to release the tension; indulge in unrestricted pleasure. 'Teresa lives somewhere near, doesn't she?'

Stefan nodded. 'On the way back to your pod. Another drink first?'

They drank more beer and vodka and swayed into the street. Weaving through crowds now leaving or starting their shifts, they walked into Teresa's shared accommodation to find her taking a snort.

It suited them; her drug of choice left her completely uninhibited. They carted her back to Gabriel's pod and spent the night in a contest to see who could perform most times. Come morning, the pair were too tired to do the count and Teresa had lost interest in their tally.

They spent the day sleeping. That evening, the Threedee announced the news of Daisa's disappearance. The men who hadn't been killed in the raid on their illegal rehearsal of her execution were executed in her place, by the means intended for her. Not a sight many citizens relished, though it was refreshing to see some of the hated Specials in pain.

'Well, it's punishment, isn't it?'

'But what about the men doin the rapin? That's not permitted; men on men.'

Gabriel had a point, but Stefan wasn't up to explaining. 'Never mind that. Look at that laser for the finish, will you? That's a refinement. Clever to use it that way, don't you think? Must be twattin agony!'

But Gabriel couldn't watch. Stefan and Teresa were glued to the spectacle, however. He was so glad Daisa had escaped that fate. No matter what had really happened, she didn't deserve that. He was glad Stefan had explained the reality now.

It had been hard to accuse her like that, but if Stefan had known the whole truth to begin with, hadn't lied about it, he'd never have been able to tell the C.I. what he'd believed was the truth at the time. Then he'd have been in real trouble. Maybe even executed instead when Daisa escaped. He had a lot to thank Stefan for.

He was so relieved to learn she hadn't been guilty of anything at all. Just a pawn. But how, he wondered, had she managed it? They said she'd just vanished. Completely disappeared from sight. Did that mean she was still somewhere in the city, or had she made it back to Marion and safety?

'Jeez, man! We've twattin had it. Jeez! I've just thought. Daisa's escaped. We're deep in twattin shit now!'

Chapter Thirty One

'When we reach it, before we remove our suits, we must block or disable the cameras. I think I know where they all are, but we need to make sure we've covered them before we expose ourselves. I've no evidence to prove they're spying, but things I've heard in the city suggest they are.' Daisa's warning gained full agreement as they made their way to Gabriel's pod.

First, they had to reach that destination. Already, there were signs the authorities understood some group action had rescued Daisa. More civil police, Specials, even ESOs roamed the streets, in packs of four or more. Ordinary citizens were skittish, fearful, and most who ventured outdoors were either going to or from places of work. Many faces appeared at windows, checking the spaces outside their homes.

Daisa took time to feel confident she couldn't be seen. The suit was like a second skin. So lightweight it might not have been there. It's only real disadvantages the slight restriction of breathing and the coolness. Never intended for long distance use, the triple layer of the sole was vulnerable to wear and damage, especially on rough surfaces.

They were careful to avoid conflict as they walked the streets in their connected single file. Further attention might indicate their direction or location to the authorities.

'Won't they expect us to try Gabriel's pod, Daisa?' Acacia's question was unsurprising.

'I don't know. He made it publicly obvious he no longer wants me around, so we should be as safe there as anywhere. And we have to find some place we can shed these suits for a while in safety and warmth.'

The rest agreed they had little choice. An isolated half dozen in a hostile city of millions, they had to go where they stood a chance of respite. Already, the effort of the fight and rescue were taking their toll. The tension of their surreptitious escape from the terminal made them nervy and afraid. And Daisa's close encounter with what those guards had intended, after days in captivity, was draining. Post traumatic shock was a danger.

They turned a corner to enter the street where Gabriel's pod was located and found the way barred by a line of heavily armed guards checking everyone. No space to allow access. Disruption and attack would only give away their location. They backed-up to the previous street and gathered in a close circle.

'What now?'

Daisa knew their lives depended on her. She was the only one with personal knowledge of the city. But her mind was a whirl, the past few days keeping calm in extreme circumstances finally catching up with her.

'What about one of the arenas where this prophet guy spoke to his followers? Won't they be empty?'

Daisa was grateful for Sarm's sensible suggestion. She couldn't think of a solution herself, but she could at least take them to what should be a relatively safe place for now. 'Thank you. We'll go to the nearest.'

They moved through streets populated only by police and soldiers. Movement was less difficult away from these official guardians. But, by the time they reached Murdoch Stadium, they were close to exhaustion. Climbing the gate took much of their remaining energy.

Inside, the huge space was dark and hollow. No heating in the arena itself, but Daisa led them to the complex of rooms that formed the service area. It was furnished with the essentials every crowd needed when being entertained. The bar was favourite. Relatively small, its walls were lined with upholstered benches they could lie on, and packaged food and bottled and canned drinks were readily available behind the counter.

'No lights. Voices low. There'll be cameras everywhere. Buzz insists they've no way of directing where their spy screens visit, but they'll be vigilant now, watching all the time. There's always a chance we'll be seen, so let's keep our profile low as possible.' Georgiy's advice was accepted with few grumbles.

The darkness in the bar was relieved by LEDs indicating electrical equipment functioned correctly. They bathed the space in an eerie combination of green and blue. A room within a building, it had the benefit of residual waste heat from refrigeration and other sources kept permanently running.

They moved armless soft chairs close to benches to make spaces where two could lie together to conserve and share body warmth. Daisa showed them where they could wash and relieve themselves. Madza found a source to create boiling water for hot drinks. And Ambra organised a selection of packed snacks to top up their lagging energy supplies.

They peeled off their suits and wrapped them like scarves around their waists; easily accessed at need. In a group, they ate poor quality snacks, drank cheap tea from disposable cups, and softly discussed their plans.

'Buzz is back. Available through Hosja.' Madza told them. 'I think it politic for us to treat them carefully. Deal with any discipline once we're home.'

The rest agreed.

With that connection renewed, they were at least able to have some certainty about their safety in this place. Ambra connected with a couple of trusted friends and asked them to attend the centre. 'Keep an eye on Buzz. Help him where you can. Learn how to access and use the surveillance system.'

It was a scheme they wished they'd put in place before their somewhat hasty move to rescue Daisa.

'Easy in hindsight. But we had little time to get here.'

Daisa looked across at Georgiy in the dim illumination. 'You were just in time. I hate to contemplate my fate if you'd been even a few mins later.'

'They're savages. Primitive.' Ambra's concern for her daughter tempted her to expand. But not now. They were all conscious of the need for secrecy. Opportunity enough for discussion, and expressions of disgust and anger later.

'Even with Buzz back at post, we should keep our own watch.' Acacia's suggestion met with reluctant agreement. 'I'll take the first. Two hours max?'

They agreed.

'I'll follow you, Acacia.'

'No, Daisa. You've had a hard time. Rest will put you back on top. I'll go next. We only need four to cover the hours of darkness.' Georgiy's assessment went down well.

They settled down, pairing off, with Acacia and Madza on guard by the door. Discussion having chosen a couple for this duty, so they could keep each other awake.

The night moved slowly but without incident. The watchers kept in contact with Buzz and his growing team of helpers. There was much activity at Marion. Preparations to help in any way they might the following day.

Already, several hovers had been sent, each piloted by a dedicated droid and with a member of the community aboard to make essential decisions. They were each destined for separate locations just beyond the sight line from the city. Distances the rescue party could easily achieve on foot in daylight, if that need occurred.

By morning, everything was in place. Hosja assured them the terminal was useless for escape. It was surrounded and, in any case, the Transhub had been disabled by the city. She described the various locations they could find the hovers.

'We should keep together. But, if we get separated, make for the nearest hover. You three can connect with Marion. Sarm, Acacia, and I will have to stay with one of you or we'll lose vital coms.' Georgiy paired them up.

They considered all eventualities they could predict, made their plans, and ate and drank again before donning their suits. In touch with the team on the monitors, they had guidance on the best route from Murdoch Stadium into open country.

Once free of the buildings, the hover pilots would guide them with landmarks. All was ready and they set out.

The gate was easier after their rest. They trod the narrow streets through that sector with little sign of opposition.

Georgiy was constantly on edge. 'Don't like it. Too easy.'

The others put this down to his long known habit of pessimism. They covered the ground quickly.

At one stage, intending to take them by a short cut to the edge of the city, Daisa halted them at a crossroads. Her instincts served her well: an official roadblock was being placed right across the way. She took a diversion and they continued without further incident, passing the well-guarded terminal before entering Sector5.

Here, the streets were noticeably wider, the few early risers moving singly or in pairs rather than groups. Each street corner held a small squad of guards, but respect for the status of their charges stopped them forming impenetrable lines.

Finally, guided by the team on the monitors, they made it to the edge of the city, where the streets ran out into the countryside. And, here, without surprise, they found their way completely blocked by armed troops.

Alert and vigilant, they were more threatening than the disorganised and furtive guards who'd tried to take advantage of Daisa in prison. These were the cream, trained to protect people at the very top. Each small squad of men was led by a senior ESO. Getting through these lines would be hard.

Chapter Thirty Two

High above the atmosphere, almost at the conclusion of the pre-launch process, Amber and her droids were close to countdown. Aware of the drama going on way below in Marzero, she needed this distraction to take her mind off Georgiy's danger. Up here, she could be part of it only as an observer.

Tests were complete and all functions and systems operated as required. The suggestion they send a droid with this probe had been premature. The last exploratory satellite had scanned the surface of the planet in close detail for only a few hours before it had stopped functioning, destroyed by some of the vast amount of debris orbiting Earth.

Cleanser1 had been launched over two quarters earlier and had cleared a wide channel through the detritus. All found objects had been sent back to the planet, causing multiple trails of burning, captured by its onboard cameras. Frequent comprehensive scans of the space it now travelled through had confirmed the way was clear for Amber's new venture. But she wanted to test an unmanned probe before she risked one of the droids.

There'd been a deal of discussion about Cleanser1.

'Suppose there are astronauts up there?'

She'd provided figures and data already gathered both at distance and from earlier probes to show Annika the chances of such activity by humans was so unlikely as to be non-existent.

Nevertheless, the community felt they must debate the project before funding and contributing to its construction and deployment. In the end it had been Georgiy who'd put a stop to the doubters, almost all from the youngest generation.

'Look at the data. Is there any sign at all of intelligent life? Any radio signals? Any night lights from cities? Any chemical traces to indicate industrial activity? Microwave, x-ray, or any other chatter on known wavelengths?'

There was none.

'In that case, why are we wanting to send another probe?' The young woman who asked was a mere 89 years old and new to cosmological education.

'The last one picked up the merest hint of something unusual before it was destroyed. Nothing in space, nothing in orbit, but something odd on the surface. It's our home planet, where we all originated, and it's in our nature to discover whether any of our ancestors made it through the chaos and turmoil. If they did, we may be able to help them get back to some sort of civilisation. That's why.'

The consensus was that the project was laudable, and they approved it, once Cleanser1 had done its initial clean-up.

In the meantime, Cleanser1 had been placed in a wider orbit to continue the task of clearing up rubbish left by long years of irresponsible launches. On Mars, they'd learned from the mistakes of Earth. Every item orbiting the planet was logged and tracked, even the stuff put up by Marzero. And each launch required that the operator remove any known debris as a condition of the license.

Marzero had been less concerned about such things, more interested in profit. But the Marion scheme had value to them in terms of potential saving of waste, so they'd adopted it.

Amber was excited about the prospects for her new venture. The time had come to name it. She used a number during the development stage, in case things failed to work out. Naming just before launch was similar to naming a child at birth and held the same element of hope and excitement for her. Once designated, the project became more than mechanics and electronics; it grew in stature to something more complete, something with an identity.

'I'm calling it, "Annie Londonderry", after the female who first circumnavigated the Earth on a bicycle, alone, at the end of the 19th century. It seems appropriate to associate the probe with an Earthwoman, don't you think?'

A02395 nodded her approval. 'I checked my archives and found many such women, most of them side-lined through history. That must've been a really paternalistic society, Amber.'

'Certainly was. You'd have been in great demand. Most men wanted their women available, submissive and sexually active. They'd have paid a small fortune to own a droid like you.'

Zhen smiled at the thought. 'I rejoice in the fact my emotional spectrum excludes pride, Amber. Otherwise, I might become arrogant after such praise.'

'Have you been approached by any of our men recently?'

'Recent's a relative term. The last approach, which I was obliged to fulfil, was with Buzz. He propositioned me at 11:37 on 47.03.249 and the process continued until 11:41 on the same date.'

'Too much detail, Zhen. No wonder the guy never gets a return request. Not at all like my Georgiy; there's a man with staying power.'

'Ah. Yes. Last time with him was when you were pregnant, with Jasar. He spent two hours 46 mins with me on 26.02.05. I was heightened to level seven of ten I remember.' She smiled.

'Georgiy. I wonder how they're doing down there?'

'Current info is somewhat contradictory. I could …'

'No. I'll check. Thank you. How long now before launch, Zhen?'

'Countdown will commence at 17:51. In 17 mins.'

She nodded her thanks and connected with the monitoring team. The situation wasn't yet resolved. Still uncertainty. Still danger for the rescue party and Daisa.

She must return to the launch and await better news.

Chapter Thirty Three

The barrier formed by the elite guards was a serious challenge. Armed with scatterguns, used for times of trouble in the city, they were the most formidable force they'd encountered. Lethal at close range, these weapons could injure 50 or more at a single shot.

'See the guy with the dragon emblem on his shoulders?' Georgiy gathered them into a tight circle. 'He's the ESO. Disable him and the rest will be less effective.'

'Better as two or three smaller groups, Georgiy?' Acacia's question deserved consideration.

'Smaller targets, you mean?'

'And different directions of travel. Not so open to concentrated fire on a single track.' She pointed out.

'What does everyone think?'

'What do you know about their scatterguns, Georgiy?'

'Well, Madza, I've only seen them in action in Threedee. They're reputed to be deadly at up to 150ms, cause serious injury at up to 500. They scatter their pulses across a wide arc with an angle of 110 degrees in the horizontal but only 5 in the vertical. Get the picture of their spread?'

'The obvious approach is for us to select a smaller group at the end of one of these roads and take them out individually, in a concerted and silent attack so we don't draw attention from other groups.'

Georgiy nodded and then recalled nobody could see him. 'Obvious, I agree, Ambra. But obvious isn't always best. Any other suggestions?'

They stood, some 400 paces from the nearest of their adversaries, and considered options. Nobody could think of a better plan.

'Right. We need to find the smallest, most isolated group. And ensure some of the hovers are within easy reach.'

'Maybe ask a couple of hovers to move closer, away from our intended attack, to draw their attention?'

'Good thinking, Sarm. We'll select our target route and then ask for a diversion.'

They set off, again in attached single file, to find the most vulnerable spot. As they walked the streets, they heard a loud explosion. Turning as one, they witnessed the cloud of dust, debris and smoke rising from the Transhub terminal that served the city. Surprising, yet more or less inevitable.

No way now they could use that escape route. And the vandalism brought with it further consequences. Normal trade and diplomatic links had been severed with that act.

They toured the edge of Marzero5 until they came to the point where it abutted to Marzero4, a less salubrious area, and found, just over the boundary, a narrow street barred by eight soldiers under the command of a single ESO. The border, a high metal wall topped by laser detectors and security lights to protect the high status residents against night time raids by the lower classes, was a tricky barrier to pass.

Sarm and Madza surveyed its length and discovered a terminal serving the electrics of the security systems. It looked as though it required little effort or expertise to disable it, and Sarm returned to where the rest of the group waited, finding them by using their pre-planned technique.

'Madza's disconnecting the alarm and …' As she spoke, the ground beneath their feet trembled. A quake more vigorous than they'd previously experienced.

Cries of concern came from nearby pods. Two of the taller illumination poles shook and swayed with the disturbance. A small flash and loud crack issued from where she'd left Madza.

'Stay here. I'll be back.' Sarm ran to the junction box. 'Madza? You okay?'

No response. The box stood open, hinges broken, and the interior smoking slightly with small blue sparks still flashing where the connections had been cut.

'Madza? Can you hear me?' her call was soft, but should reach him.

No response. She approached closer. Began a search on hands and knees. Fingers outstretched as she sought the unseen form of her friend. Nothing. No sign in the immediate vicinity of the damaged box. She widened her area of investigation, conscious the smoke may draw someone from a nearby house.

A door opened across the street and a woman stepped out. She must surely see the broken box, but her concern seemed reserved for the swaying poles. The woman withdrew again.

Sarm breathed her relief and continued to search, reaching the middle of the roadway in her arc of exploration. Her fingers touched a warm, soft bulk. She moved closer, felt her way along the form and knew she'd reached Madza. Once she'd identified his posture and found his neck, she checked for a pulse. He was alive.

Taller than her by a good head, bulkier and more muscled, he was a heavy load. She raised him and draped his unconscious form over her shoulders to carry him along the street to where the others waited. Hard work, she was weary when she reached them.

Madza was still unconscious. She explained.

'We've no choice. We have to make our escape now, before someone comes to repair the damage. Maybe they'll assume it was caused by the quake. But we have to get over the wall before they try to fix it.'

'Or we could walk to the top of this road, through the night gates, and then back down the road in the next sector.' Ambra made this suggestion without much enthusiasm.

'Take too long, Mother.' Daisa tried Madza for size and found she could lift him. 'We can get him over the wall and then carry him. It'll slow us down, but we can't leave him.'

Crossing the barrier tested their cohesion and determination. But they made it. For a while, they rested at the other side. Madza moaned softly as he started to regain consciousness.

'Quiet, Madza. We're close to the guards now.' Acacia's whispered warning cut through the fug in Madza's head and he quietened.

'I think I've broken something. My left arm feels strange.'

'Your nanobots will fix it. If you need our help, tell us. But don't try to fight the guards. You're too damaged.' Georgiy's warning was agreed by all.

They approached the line of troops blocking the narrow street, their plan ready formed. It was essential they disable as many guards as possible at the same time. Georgiy opted for the leader. The rest took one each, leaving three to be dealt with once they'd incapacitated the first lot. Three of the group could kill by hand, using martial arts. The others would have to render their quarry unconscious.

The attack was swift and co-ordinated. Georgiy felled the Elite leader silently with two blows. He wouldn't fight again. Acacia dispatched her chosen target with three sharp blows that elicited only a soft grunt of initial pain. Daisa took down her man with a kick followed by a sharp stamp on his throat as soon as he hit the ground. Some small satisfaction for the terror they'd put her through.

Sarm tackled her man with her hands around his neck to twist and bend, as she used her knee to force him to bend his own. Ambra was the least experienced. She'd never taken any form of self-defence or even exercise classes involving combat. She thrust her fists, one after the other, into the target's face. The first blow merely startled him, but the second landed more robustly and sent the man flying to the ground. Acacia stamped all consciousness from him.

The three remaining soldiers were confused. Slow to react. Something unseen had felled their colleagues, just like the attack at the prison. They couldn't accept nothing had caused this sudden depletion of their ranks. That brief inability to accept the evidence of their eyes, or lack of it, gave the group time to tackle them. The entire troop was rendered ineffective in a few mins.

Each stole a weapon from the fallen. Ensuring all were together, with Madza, now able to walk, central to their outstretched line, they advanced into open ground. Beyond the city boundary, low shrubs and fruit trees afforded a little cover. They moved swiftly and silently away in the direction of the hovers now visible on the horizon. The distance was just over three ks, easily covered in around six mins.

Initially, it seemed they'd escaped without attracting the attention of other groups. But, at about a k from their starting point, a burst of gunfire alerted them to the discovery of their flight. Scatterguns were still capable of hurting at this distance, but unlikely to kill or disable. Bruising and possible tearing of a suit were the most likely outcomes. They continued their escape at speed.

Acacia cried out as a pulse caught the back of her thigh. 'Sorry! I'm fine. Sharp pain, that's all.'

As they loped across the space, the trees and shrubs stopped further blind fire reaching them. Their captured guns were the only aspect of their escape visible to their enemy. And, small moving targets, they were now well hidden by the terrain.

The hovers moved closer as Madza and Ambra made contact. The two vehicles stopped a few paces from them and everyone boarded quickly. Aboard, they shed their suits and strapped themselves in for the flight back home.

'It's not over. Let's not get complacent. The Zeros have armed craft. As soon as they know what's happened, they'll be after us with their airborne squads. We need to make it back to Marion by the shortest and most direct route we can.'

The hover pilots were experienced droids who could read the ground ahead with ease and steer the craft quickly over and around obstacles. As they passed a high cliff at one side of a wide, deep, ancient riverbed, a secondary quake dislodged rocks and dust to send a small avalanche into the valley ahead.

The pilots rose above the debris only to find they were now followed by high speed drones from Marzero. Developed to control mobs tempted to rebel in open countryside, these planes carried steel nets designed to be dropped over crowds to sop them moving.

These, and low power lasers were ill-fitted for the job they now attempted. The laser pulses made no impact on the Marion hovers.

But one of the drones sped past the pair, turned, and dropped a wide, weighted net over the front hover. It slowed the craft and obscured the view of the pilot.

'Stop. Let me clear it.' Acacia unstrapped herself as the craft landed, its partner slowing to a halt close by as the attacking drones regrouped for another sortie.

Georgiy and Ambra also disembarked, their stolen scatterguns ready. Acacia leapt from the hover and gathered the net. It caught on a speed monitor sticking out of the hull. She dragged it up as the drones moved in to attack again. Up close, their weapons could damage her, unprotected as she was.

Georgiy waited until the nearest drone was close enough and shot off a rapid round from the scattergun. The pulses hit and the craft tilted as damage unbalanced it and sent it careering into the cliff. Acacia finally unhooked the net and dropped it to the ground. She returned to the hover interior, shouting to the other two that they could set off again.

As Ambra was returning to her hover, the second drone moved in to attack. It caught her shoulder with a low energy pulse that had enough power to send her tumbling. Her scattergun fell from her injured arm. Leaving the weapon, she rolled back to her feet and ran to the hover. Regaining her seat as the hovers took off again.

Georgiy opened coms to Marion. 'We're under attack. Crowd control drones. They can't do us real damage and we'll be back soon. But they used armoured landcraft during the post-Cusp War. Those things are armed with weapons grade lasers. I think you need to be prepared.'

'You don't seriously believe they'll attack Marion, Georgiy?' All heard Zaphod's query.

'I don't know what they'll do. We've stopped them using Daisa as an example to their womenfolk. Made the authorities look incompetent. Their PutinMaister's unstable and unpredictable. We've had him on side recently only because he believes there's profit in cooperation.

'Anything could turn the head of a sociopath like him. We need to be ready. If they're willing to blow up their Transhub terminal just to stop the escape of an innocent prisoner, who knows what they might do? We'll discuss it once we're back home. I just wanted to give you a heads-up on the potential danger.'

Chapter Thirty Four

Gabriel hadn't seen Stefan in a state of fear before. His friend had always been so certain of himself, so confident. Even at the Specials' HQ, when he was waiting for Gabriel to emerge from questioning, he'd been calm.

'What's wrong, Stefan?'

'Wrong? You twattin blind, man? You seen what's happenin out there?'

'It's not our fault Daisa escaped.'

Stefan thrust a despairing hand through his long hair and made the other into a fist. 'God, man. I don't know how you keep upright when you're so twattin dim!'

Gabriel bit his top lip, looked down at the girl lying across his bare feet and kicked her awake. 'Leave now.'

She rubbed her side as she rose, grabbed her skintight, and slipped into it as she left, without a backward glance. Once the door was closed, he turned back to Stefan. 'Tell me.'

'Look, man. You brought Daisa into the city. It were you what …'

'I didn't. She just arrived and …'

'Moron! Don't you twattin see, man? She came because of you. So they'll blame you for her bein here. It's your fault. You gotta do somethin to appease the PutinMaister or we're dead meat. You, me, anyone connected to you. He's lost face. And that man don't like to lose face.'

Gabriel's eyes widened, he dropped his shoulders and sat heavily on the chair behind him. 'Right. I see. I can't think when you're scared, Stefan. Try to be yourself. Use your experience. Fear won't help us.'

Stefan glared at him in amazement. 'You want me to … Jeez! Twattin hell, you're right. It's me needs to sort this. Just like everythin else. Get me a drink. I need to think. Drink!'

Gabriel relaxed. His friend was out of the fear fug that had paralysed him. He would come up with a plan to save them now. He moved to the small food area and prepared his friend's signature drink. Cheap beer followed by a neat vodka chaser. Took the two glasses to him.

Stefan, gulped down the beer in one slow swallow. Shot the spirit down. He sat back, nodding and closing his eyes as his mind began to conjure ideas. Gabriel fixed his friend another drink, and one for himself. He waited. Stefan would find the answer.

'Right, man. You've had another vision. In it, God said …'

'I haven't had …'

'For Chrisesake, Gab! Use your twattin head, will you? It don't have to be true. It never has to be true. You think that idiot mob out there cares about truth? You believe they listen to what you say and come away from your meets inspired because they think about it? They hear your words, man. Hear your message. They don't discuss it. Don't care if it makes sense. They want a leader for their dreams. God, you play that crowd like a master but you haven't a twattin clue what you're doin, do you?'

'I tell them what God's asked me to say. What else can I do?'

'Jeez, man! You're even denser than what I thought. Right, this is how it works. This is how you've got to be the big man. This is what we do together. Listen and don't twattin interrupt.'

Gabriel had never seen his friend so exercised. He nodded.

'You have visions and come to me to tell you what they mean, right?'

He nodded his agreement.

'I do that. I tell you what your god wants you to do. I put the dreams …'

'My God? Don't you believe, Stefan? Don't you follow the teachins?'

'Jeez, Gabriel! You walk around with your eyes and ears shut, man? You see what I do, hear what I say. Don't you never think what I do an say is different to what you say an do? Think, man. Just use your twattin head.'

'You really don't believe?' Gabriel sat next to him, his whole body collapsed in disbelief.

Stefan gathered himself. Saw the danger. Understood what he must do. He needed Gabriel if they were to get out of this terrifying mess. And they didn't have much time. 'Okay, Gab. Sorry. Had to really get your full attention. Course I believe in you and God. Why else would I be with you? Why else would I be helpin you all I can? I just wanted to get you listenin, cos you know, man, you wander off the point so easy. I need you to really concentrate on what I'm sayin. Understand?'

Gabriel took in a deep breath and sat up straight. His friend had just been kidding. The world was back as it should be. He turned to Stefan, nodded enthusiastically. 'Fire away. I'm all ears.'

'Listen, man. What I'm goin to say will shock you. You won't want to do some of it. But we need to do this my way if we're gonna get through this alive. So. Hear me out.

'You've had another vision. God said you have to tell the mob … your followers, about the evils of the Marionets. Make people under-stand how everythin what's bad is their fault. Everythin what they don't like is down to the Marionets. Got it? Simple as that.'

'But God hasn't …'

'Look, man. When you been in the right zone to have a vision in the past few days? You been under pressure. Frightened by those twattin interrogators. Worried Daisa would betray you. Scared the crowd might turn against you. Course you haven't had a vision. But if you had, this is what it would be. I know. Believe me. I don't have visions, but I know what God wants. Think He lets me do this inter-pretin without me knowin His will?'

'Of course! You must know. Obviously. How can you interpret for me if you don't know God's will? Why did I never think of that before? But why do I have the visions, instead of you, Stefan?'

'Think about it, Gab. I mean, look at us. Not God's gift in the looks department, am I? Skinny, mean lookin, straggly hair, no beard. Then look at you. Tall, well made, face of a twattin angel, long blonde hair, great beard. Women love you just lookin at you and blokes think you're so special they wanna be you.

'And then there's the voice, man. I mean. D'you hear yourself when you speak to the crowd? Music, man. You got syrup on your tongue. You inspire just by openin your gob. Me? Listen to that whine, man. Hear that nasal twang? I can't speak to no crowds and get them in my power. You can. You do it easy as walkin, easy as shaggin, easy as shit, man.'

Gabriel thought about this. It was true. It made sense. Stefan might be the middleman for God, but it was him, Gabriel, who was God's mouthpiece. That's why he had the looks, the voice, the public presence. Stefan was right. Never mind the danger. What mattered was God's message to the people. If God said the people of Marion were evil and greedy and selfish, that they caused all the misery in Marzero, then that was the message he'd give to his followers.

'Let's do it, Stefan. Get things organised. I know what I must say. You do what you do so well. Prepare the meet. I'll have them doin what we want. Just see if I don't.'

It took only a day for Stefan to organise a venue, spread word of the meet throughout the city, persuade a media mogul to cover it citywide, and get the stage crew up to speed with all the show elements.

He used his influence, blackmailed where he had to, cajoled where he could, persuaded where wanted and, as a final necessity, paid the rest to do his bidding. And he got a message through to the PM. He'd recoup the loss from Gabriel after the meet.

Teresa was brought to Gabriel. He used his charms to get her fully on side. 'At this meet you must be special, perform to raise the spirits of the crowd.'

His promise of an endless supply of top quality drugs of her choice was the final touch. She was his completely, and demonstrated her devotion willingly.

They travelled streets thronged with gossip, overlain with something special in the air. There was a sense of promise. Tension, fear, and deep anxiety lurked in the shadows. But there was something new as well. Hope. Its source identified as Gabriel, Prophet of the People. Drawing in the crowds to their biggest meet so far.

'Third of a million, Gab. 350k. This is what we've spent the last few quarters building. This is the big 'un, man. This is it!' Stefan went backstage to do his thing.

Gabriel had never understood the mechanics or methods his friend used to build atmosphere. He knew only that these devices worked and brought the crowd to maximum reception of his words. Stefan had briefed him on the programme as usual. A different approach in parts, more drama, more music, more showmanship. But the culmination would be Gabriel, speaking God's word to the gathering. It would be marvellous, fantastic, wonderful.

Gabriel stood in the wings, his view of the auditorium a narrow section framed by curtains concealing him. The popular music act sang all the right numbers to bring the mood up. They left the stage to wild cheers from the crowd.

The lights dimmed slowly to complete darkness, as sombre music built in volume, pace and menace to a pitch that was almost unbearable. Then, sudden silence. A space of nothing, lasting long enough to raise tension. A rose-coloured spot shone, dazzling, down at centre stage. Five huge Threedees, spread about the arena, enlarged the scene for all attending. And their eyes were fixed on that small, inactive form that lay beneath the light.

Teresa, but not Teresa, a woman of ethereal grace and beauty, lifted without effort from her prone fall to a standing pose in one fluid move. Her body was shrouded in a veil of pastel pink; a moving, floating, living cloak so light it was almost without substance. The music started slowly, distant, echoing remembrance of days spent in sunshine. After the imposed sombre mood, this new melody brought memories of warmth and comfort as the woman softly moved in concert with the harmony.

Microphone unseen in his hair, Gabriel recited single words

enhancing what the people witnessed on stage. Simple words, describing the emotions of the performing woman.

'Awakenin.'

The music skipped a half beat, growing only marginally faster. Still slow and graceful, as Teresa shed the first layer of her multi-layered costume.

'Wonderin.'

She moved about the stage, in search of something she couldn't identify. Her grace and motion captivating all who watched.

The music upped another half a beat. And Teresa shed a second layer.

'Hopin.'

She looked about her, wishes as yet undefined and mysterious, but expected. And she lifted off another layer.

'Wantin.'

The music increased almost imperceptibly in tempo. And Teresa shed the penultimate veil so she was sheathed only in gauze of palest peach that hid none of her form. She moved in blind searching around the stage to Gabriel, now waiting centre front.

'Desirin.'

As the music notched another beat, growing in intent and expectation, she tossed away her final veil. Gabriel, his body cloaked in brilliant, blinding, dazzling white, remained aloof, unattainable. The music developed, its desire and wanting feeding the watching crowd, building their passions for climax.

Gabriel drew Teresa to him with arms outstretched in a gesture of enclosure, her whole form attracted as her very essence of womanhood reached for him. Untouched, she lay before him at his feet, legs parted, hips raised high until her glistening pudendum was her apex. As the music reached crescendo, Gabriel extended two straight fingers, signed a cross in air above her, and brushed his fingertips on her offering, briefly.

'Satiated.'

Teresa uttered orgiastic pleasure, delirium controlling her movements, shifting her hips upwards in desire until Gabriel swept out his arms, releasing her whole body in a gesture without touch. She gasped utter satisfaction as she sank to the floor at his feet.

Total darkness.

Silence.

The auditorium filled with gasping, stunned exclamations of relief and wonder.

Music softly infiltrated through the space, calming, soothing, stroking with its gentle tones of relaxation. Light slowly suffused the stage.

The woman had gone. Gabriel stood alone. His robe moved with an unseen wind that moulded the fine fabric to his body so he seemed to fly, though stationary. He raised his arms and music rose in volume with the move. He held his palms together over his head, bringing the bright melody to a brief crescendo. Then he dropped his hands to his sides and stopped the sound.

Silence.

A pause.

'My people. My Sacred Ones. Welcome. I bring you word of momentous change. God has spoke to me of things we wished never to learn. But the time has come to know the truth. Lives will change. The lot of all will alter. Some will end their days in glory, some will rise anew into a life of peace and plenty.'

He allowed this prophecy to enter their consciousness, the arousal of the first show priming them for this acceptance.

'I have learned things I could not believe. But God delivered me the sights and sounds and knowledge to accept the inconceivable. I must make you understand the truth of what I next will tell you.

'Are you willin to believe? Willing to hear the words of God and know they fall on souls true and faithful?'

'We are!'

'You know of the foul treachery of Daisa, who held me in a witch's spell so I believed her worthy for my ministry.' He allowed the catcalls of disgust and hate to fall, his pride in his performance at this important time masking any doubt he might feel.

'You'll know, by now, of her foul acts of depravity, cruel killin of innocents, abuse and torture of women who fell under her spell.' Again, he let the calls fall to silence.

The next piece of theatre must be finely judged; he didn't know how many of the crowd had heard the rumours.

'You may not all know this foul excuse for a human bein, this unworthy, perverted witch who defiles the name 'woman', escaped justice and is no longer in Marzero to pay the price for her crimes.'

Cries of outrage filled the arena. Calls for justice. Shouts of vengeance and death to Daisa.

The next step was crucial. He mustn't falter now. His next words would precipitate the change that would make himself and Stefan heroes to the Elite. In particular, to the PutinMaister. Their imminent imprisonment and public deaths as accomplices would be overtaken by good fortune, communal praise. Maybe even freedom of the city.

'Daisa, the most despicable and depraved woman ever to tread the dust of our beautiful world, was spirited away by evil magic of the Marionets. We don't know what spells they used to take her from her cell and then the city. But we are certain it was that other place, that home of cheatin, lyin, stealin criminals, Marion, that took her from us at the very moment she was due to face true justice for her crimes.

'I ask you, my people, my followers of God and all that is good on Mars, I ask you, how do we correct this dreadful act of evil?'

And they came, as Stefan had predicted, as Gabriel had expected, calls for vengeance on the far colony. Calls for the death of all who inhabited that far foreign place of undeserved privilege and ease, calls for the destruction of Marion.

But Stefan had let him know destruction of Marion wasn't what the PM required. Its wonders and luxuries were wanted by the Elite. A readymade paradise where the wealthy and powerful could dwell in absolute luxury, with a population of perfect female slaves, allowed to live in service. He had to steer the hatred he'd built. Had to modify the calls for death and destruction.

'Destroy Marion!' they cried.

Before it reached the status of a mantra, he must intervene.

'Death to Marion!' he chanted through his powerful mic.

And their call slowly changed to echo his own.

Then, 'Death to Marionets!' was his change.

They picked up his alteration. Went with it, as he'd known they would. Then he made his last amendment.

And the final mantra echoed all around the arena.

Perfect.

Now, on stage proudly roamed Teresa, still entirely naked. She stood beside him, her concealed mic echoing the chant he orchestrated. Her air of pride in her display convinced the men of women's true desires, persuaded all the women of their rightful place as objects of male pleasure.

The noise of their combined calls filled the air, and people outside the arena came to hear the call. They joined in, moved through the streets toward the source of calls for war against the Marionets. Until all chanted as one, 'Death to all male Marionets!'

Chapter Thirty Five

The Crime Council convened in the rarely used Court. In the stand, Buzz waited impatiently as the community was informed of the reasons for his appearance before them all.

The CC, composed of four Chosen and six representatives of later generations, was responsible for upholding law in Marion. They had no police force, no armed forces, no officials enforcing authority. Social cooperation made such institutions unnecessary. And lawyers couldn't profit from a system of justice entirely founded on the Golden Rule. A few community members had studied the informal law developed from previous cases and offered their advice freely.

'We've convened this court in almost unique circumstances, since our community rests on sound cooperative responsibility. Minor infringements are dealt with by the organisations or townships responsible. Today, however, we deal with a serious event that could have resulted in danger, even death, to some of our members. CenCom has already established the facts and the data incontrovertibly demonstrates neglect on the part of Buzz, a long-serving and well-known member of our community, who came to us from the Moon.' Zaphod gave the formal introduction, standing at the centre of the bench at which the CC sat.

'He has rejected all offers of help and support in this matter and wishes to speak for himself.'

Buzz shifted awkwardly. He looked at the floor. A hand went to his mouth. The other scratched a probably non-existent itch; an act of distraction to give him time to compose his thoughts. 'Look, okay, I wasn't at full attention. But how was I supposed to know it was that serious? They were wearing invisisuits. Nobody could see them. I couldn't see how they'd be in any real danger. I mean, why should they be?

'Wasn't my fault, anyway. Hosja distracted me. She wanted me right there and then. Of course I was tempted. I'm a man. I can't help it if women take advantage. I don't know why I'm here. I was doing the community a favour. I don't see I did anything wrong.'

The CC waited in silence, but nothing further came from the man in the stand.

'We've tolerated your uncooperative and selfish behaviour too long, Buzz. You've clearly failed to assimilate the morals, beliefs, concerns and tolerance of our community. You were invited here as partner of a founding member and you've repaid our hospitality and companionship with utter disdain, intolerance, immaturity, and selfishness.

'Finally, your recent dereliction of duty could easily have caused the deaths of a rescue party of five brave citizens and the research student they saved from the injustices of Marzero. How we deal with you in this matter is the only issue to be decided here. CenCom has established, beyond reasonable doubt, that the danger resulted from your behaviour. Your attempt to blame a young woman for your own failures is indicative of your inability to accept personal responsibility for your actions.

'Council will decide how we deal with you, once that other person has explained her part.' Zaphod called the attendant droids and issued instructions that they keep him under guard.

In the Court, Hosja passed Buzz as he entered the area she left and took the stand. Dressed in sober style to reflect her respect for the gravity of the situation, she stood with her hands clasped in front of her and her head bowed. After she'd confirmed her personal details, she again dropped her gaze.

'Hosja, you're a young, inexperienced woman still undergoing basic education in preparation for your chosen degree. Please inform the Court what subject you're studying.'

She glanced briefly at Zaphod. 'I'm hoping to gain a masters in the field of spacecraft propulsion.'

Zaphod nodded. 'We need good brains working on that field. Now, please be aware you're here as the result of your association with Buzz during an assignment for which you volunteered. CenCom has established your part in the events and we're satisfied you acted under coercion. However, we ...'

'There was no coercion. She was willing as ...'

'You'll have an opportunity to speak once Hosja's given her statement and answered our questions, Buzz. Until then, you're required to remain silent. Any further interruptions will result in your removal from this court. Do you understand?'

'Yes.'

'I need to know, Hosja, what happened during the period of your duty to prevent you giving the rescue party your undivided support whilst they remained at risk in Marzero.'

'We, that is, Buzz and I, were to relay info from the spy camera network to members of the rescue party in Marzero as they retrieved Daisa. I was present because Buzz can't connect via the cranial implant. My connection was with Madza, who I found very patient.'

'Please explain what stopped you carrying out this duty.'

'I sat beside Buzz at an ancient console I wasn't able to access. We studied six flat screens, four of them showing locations around Marzero. Specifically, areas in and approaching the prison complex from the Transhub terminal.

'We'd passed on info about the absence of guards in the prison when Buzz was distracted by activity on a monitor not focussed on the rescue scene. Some Marzero women were engaged in sex. This excited him. He asked me to fuck him. I hadn't engaged in full sex, but he's a senior member of the community, deserving respect, so I complied with his needs. During this time, a period of about six minutes, we gave no info to the rescue party.'

Buzz clenched his fists but the droid to his left placed a hand on his shoulder and he remained quiet.

'Was that the only occasion during this period of duty you weren't connected to your contact with the party?'

'No. It happened again, a little later, when Buzz made demands I felt unequal to perform. He became angry, however, and, because of his status, I had to satisfy his need for submissive sex.

Buzz spluttered, red faced and clearly angry, but the droids reminded him any interruption would mean he was removed.

'I therefore performed fellatio on him and this relaxed him. Unknown to me, he'd signed out of the system whilst I was satisfying him. When I'd done, I discovered this but he refused to sign back in again. I could do nothing to coax him, even though I tried all the persuasive techniques we're taught. Only when other people arrived was he forced to sign back in.

'I followed his procedure exactly this time, learning the sequence of antiquated protocols and remembering the unlocking device called a password, so I'd be able to reactivate the system if he switched it off again. I restored it twice after he became demanding and closed it down.'

'Cheating little bitch!' Buzz's interjection was quiet enough to allow him to remain.

'The knowledge I'd gained meant we could run the system without Buzz. This made him even angrier, but there were more of us by then and we stopped him damaging or deactivating it as he threatened.'

'I never ...' But, again, the droids intervened to prevent Buzz disqualifying himself from attendance.

'We knew the interruptions to my contact had caused distress and danger to the rescue mission and were determined to prevent any more.'

Hoshiko gazed at the young woman with sympathy. 'You provided sex for Buzz, even though you weren't attracted to him. Why, Hosja?'

She frowned. 'Buzz is a senior member of our community. I'm a young student at Uni. Our respective status requires me to show due respect to an established figure. Also, he exhibited signs of anger, which I haven't previously encountered on a personal level. I understand such emotion can develop into a violent physical manifestation. Compliance seemed the most rational approach in the circumstances.'

'Is that the only reason you complied?' Hoshiko's question carried a sympathetic tone.

The young woman dropped her gaze to study her feet. 'I'm not supposed to say. My peers will be disappointed if I disclose any other info.'

'Nevertheless, this is a Court, Hosja. You're required to give the whole truth.'

'Yeah. Too right!'

'One more outburst, Buzz, and you'll be excluded.' Zaphod's tone brooked no argument.

The student wrung her hands. 'It's a sort of secret initiation ceremony to join a group I always wanted to be part of.'

'And they're called?'

She resisted for a moment, until Hoshiko caught her eye again. 'Okay; The Exclusives. You fuck Buzz. He puts a picture of you on the wall in his pod. He's vile with women. That's why it's a challenge. Only he's not supposed to be your first. He was mine, unfortunately. Please don't tell them I told you.'

'Live broadcast, Hosja.' Zaphod turned to the rest of the bench. 'Well, that explains that, at last. Any further questions for Hosja?'

Hoshiko shook her head, clearly as baffled as her fellow members of the Court.

Buzz was given an opportunity to question Hosja, but he simply accused and insulted her. The evidence from CenCom backed up her version of the story.

The Court decided his fate. 14 days in Risk, followed by a final period of retraining. No one believed either of these measures would change him for the better, but the general consensus was that they should give him a final chance to mature and conform.

Still protesting, Buzz was escorted from the Court by two droids and a member of the Council to ensure all was carried out as required. The droids couldn't harm an abliform. But they'd act in the best interests of the community.

'Enough of Buzz! He's wasted more time than we can spare. There's trouble on the way from Marzero. We need to convene an Aggression Council.' Georgiy burst into Court. 'Time to move into the Chamber. Zaphod, you're connected. Please would you call the other members here, as a matter of urgency?'

'One moment, Georgiy. We haven't quite finished here. Then you'll have our undivided attention.' Hoshiko called Hosja back to the stand and engaged the others in a brief confab.

The young woman waited, her face giving no sign of emotion.

'We appear to have let you down, Hosja, in a way we need to correct. We've determined you're innocent, due to a combination of your actions and a lack of some aspect of your early training.

'We'll contact your personal tutor at Uni to organise appropriate retraining. Also, your involvement in the secret initiation is now public knowledge, so we'll take steps to stop that causing you further distress.'

She made a brief smile of acceptance.

'So, you're free to go. But I'd like you to take me to the spy camera console and pass on what you've learned about access. Now we can get into the system, we'll modify security to allow the rest of us to use it as normal. It may become essential to our survival during the coming days.'

'Right. Can we organise our defence now?' Georgiy's impatience to be active again after bringing Daisa safely home surprised no one. 'I know nothing's imminent. But it'll kick off very soon if I know those Zeros.'

Chapter Thirty Six

'It worked, Gab! We gotta strike while the iron's hot, man! The PutinMaister's with us. Gonna supply transport an gear an weapons. He wants to see us. Now, man!' Stefan was fired up. He'd dreamed of the day he'd be a member of the Elite, and this looked like the best chance.

Gabriel was less enthusiastic, still concerned after his last encounter with the interrogator. 'Sure he wants us for somethin good, Stefan?'

'The PutinMaister don't waste no time on losers, leaves them to his minions, man. You get summoned by the PM, you in for a treat. Believe me, Gab. Now, let's go. You don't keep that man waitin.'

'How do you know all this, Stefan?'

His friend pulled at the front of his uniform. 'Status, man. Status.'

Through the streets they were hailed as heroes, many wanting to shake their hands and slap their backs, so their progress was slowed. The whole place was abuzz with the coming expedition to Marion to defeat their long-term enemy. They'd get rid of the snobs living there, take over the settlement with all its luxuries, facilities, and stunning women, and live the lives of leisure they deserved.

At last, they reached Trumpyramid and showed their IDs to the guards. Gabriel expected sneers and rejection, or maybe a hostile and cold entry. But they were greeted like heroes, the same mood they'd enjoyed through the streets greeting them, here, in the very centre of power.

A pair of special reception women, painted clothing a second skin, took each by the hand and guided them up to the top floor in the lift.

'A lift, man.'

One of them stroked a finger down Gabriel's chest. 'When the PM's seen you. We'll be waitin.'

The corridor leading to the PM's quarters was long. Lined with floor to ceiling murals, painted in classic style, depicting scenes of victory in all its forms; boardroom battles, takeovers, trading gains, war in the fields of Earth, awards ceremonies, the ending of the Cusp War, sporting championships, industrial conquests, and others that had no meaning for either of the men. Gabriel and Stefan were captivated by the pictures, especially the women; all depicted exactly as they should be.

A pair of armed guards of massive proportions guarded the entrance to the abode. They scanned their IDs before telling the door to open.

This was a room such as they'd never imagined. Brightness everywhere prevented shadows, so the whole place had the air of a scene built from light of different colours. Soft fabric, covering the floor, warmed their feet; a welcome change after the long walk along cold metal-floored corridors.

'This is it, Gab. Paradise on Mars!'

Two more women greeted them as they entered, offering exotic drinks and taking their garments. They giggled as they helped, promising more fun afterwards.

Another pair of women guided them to soft seating, plush and deeply upholstered in precious white leather. One bore a diamond pin through each nipple, the other sported a vajazzle that carried a gemstone invitation, 'Come in!' Stefan stared with unmasked lust.

The women who brought their drinks, swayed provocatively before them whilst they waited. A fanfare sounded, echoing through the palatial room, and in the silence that followed, the women dropped to their knees and placed their heads on their outstretched arms in a gesture of utter surrender.

Surrounded by a troupe of young dancing girls who pranced and paraded, the man they awaited made slow progress from a back room and crossed the floor. Gabriel and Stefan stood, unsure of protocol. Neither dare show surprise at his small stature, rolls of body fat, baldness, and his diminutive parts. This was a powerful man; the man who controlled life and death across the city.

'Narthen, gents. You'll be Stefan?'

Stefan nodded eagerly.

'And Gabriel, Prophet of the People?'

Gabriel bowed his head submissively.

'Sit you down, then. Get them drinks inside you.' He flicked his fingers and an attending woman moved swiftly to the serving area, where she prepared two drinks for the PM and another each for the visitors.

'Food!' the PM commanded, and a couple of women swayed gracefully away and began preparing various dishes. Others brought these as soon as they were ready and set out a table before the men who sat in a circle.

'Heard your speech, Gabriel. Saw your show, Stefan. Twattin good stuff. First, let me award you with your Freedom of Marzero bands. No need to pay for owt when you're wearin those. Women included.'

A woman produced a pair of sparkling gold, jewel-encrusted bracelets from a glittering pouch worn above her bright vajazzle. She displayed them after removing the items, and handing one to each guest. Other women dropped to their knees beside each and helped them don the status symbols, fastened with concealed clasps that locked them in place, hiding the hinges.

'Now. We'll eat a bit. Have a drink or two. Then we'll talk about the raid on those twattin Marionets. After, before you lead your troops into battle, have some entertainment. Okay?'

They were delighted at the offered reward. Stefan blanched at the cost, but dare say nothing. He certainly hadn't considered actually leading the hazardous journey to Marion as part of their plan, even if Gabriel was foolish enough to do so. Both now knew the PM had decided this was their duty and they'd perform it without protest.

The food was unquestionably the very best either had experienced, and the drinks were delicious as well as both relaxing and stimulating. The PM had a woman service him as he explained his intentions for their raid, she kneeling to perform her act as he sat uncaring. When she'd done, he leant forward and slapped her thighs, hard. 'That's ma gal!'

She made no sound but stood and waited until she was released before moving to the service area to wash out her mouth. The whole event was sublime to Stefan, who looked forward to his session with the women. Gabriel was less impressed, but dared make no show of his ambivalence. Daisa's behaviour with him, her remarks about the subservience of the women, meant he lacked confidence they were as willing as they seemed. But hadn't God made their role clear? Shaking off doubts he felt were unworthy, he too, anticipated some entertainment, which he hoped to have in private.

'Thing is, lads, we don't want no damage done to the settlement. Once we've rid it of the scum, we'll move all the Elite across there to enjoy the luxury. So it's important you take the place without damagin any part of it. Understood?'

Stefan and Gabriel wondered whether they were now members of the Elite but daren't ask outright. They'd hoped to take advantage of the chance to live in Marion once it was conquered. Elimination of 200,000 resident men and kids hadn't really been their aim, but that was what the PM had in mind.

'Save as many women as you can. They're all fantastic twats and great shags. Criminal to waste that lot, eh?'

It was an impossible task if they were to do it with the weapons they had, especially if they were to cause no physical damage to the property in the process.

'Yes.' Stefan assured the PM. 'No problem.'

The PM laughed and pointed at Stefan, sharing a silent joke with the woman holding his drink. 'Don't know how, do he?'

The woman, equally ignorant, nevertheless laughed at the joke.

'Shall I put them out their misery, do ya think?'

She nodded enthusiastically.

'Shame. I were lookin forward to teasin 'em a bit. Still, leave that to you later, eh?'

The women present giggled their agreement.

'Thing is, you can't go there and start blowin things up. I want the place like it is right now. Just get shot of the men and brats, like.

'You'll have your rabble army, well as many as actually get there. Not easy on foot, like. But we can't bother about that, eh? Some'll be with you in the transports and they'll be fine. We can manage about two and a half thou in some sort of vehicle. The rest, what, about 300thou, we reckon a tenth might make it, an they can help clear up. Like I say, not a problem. So, how's two and a half thou goin to get shot of 200thou, without doin no damage? Not easy, eh?'

Stefan and Gabriel remained silent, understanding their job was to listen rather than contribute. The task appeared utterly impossible and both feared for their lives on such a hazardous mission.

'We got a plan. Brilliant, it is. Peachy. Perfect. Wanna know what it is?'

The pair nodded, eager to learn of any chance at success.

'Course you do.' The PM took his drink from the woman holding it and pointed to her and three others. 'My private quarters. For after the man talk's done.'

They bowed, revolved to display their individual charms, and walked slowly and sensually back to the room at the far end of the huge hall. The PM waited until they'd set off, then dismissed the other attending women to a separate room at one side of the hall to await their guests.

'Secret, you see. Can't have them knowin. Never can tell what a twat might do. I mean, look at that twat, Daisa. Cheek of her! I want her savin, btw. So I can deal with her personally. Not havin no twat makin no fool of me. No way.'

They allowed his sudden anger to diminish without comment.

'The plan. We got this bug our science lot've made. Lethal to all males, but don't live long. Kills every man what comes into contact with it. All you and your lot have to do is get it there. Simple. Soon as they touch it, they're goners. Poof! Twattin dead as dust. Then you

225

can deal with the vermin brats however you like; kids is a twattin nuisance. Shift all the bodies outside the boundary to rot. Easy. Foolproof. See?'

Both Stefan and Gabriel saw enormous holes in his 'foolproof' plan but neither dare say so. They nodded their agreement. 'Simple.'

The entertainment that followed only partly calmed their fears. They left Trumpyramid satiated but hardly less concerned, in the early hours of the following morning.

Later, the vehicles and weapons gathered, and their 'army' released from all other duties on the PM's orders, they began the impossible task.

Their loyal followers greeted them with blind adoration, and awaited orders. As Stefan organised the transport and accepted 30 drums of infective agent, Gabriel took to the arena stage and poured enthusiasm into the crowd. He knew many faced cruel death in the wilderness. Over 2,000 ks of uncultivated desert, rocks and dusty regolith coated in the pale green scum of lichen, lay between Marzero and Marion. The journey would cross the low slopes of extinct volcanoes, most around the curved foot of Olympus Mons.

His plan was to gather them, three or four days out, and advise most to make their way back home in small groups. He had no knowledge of their prospects on their return, but anything must be better than consigning them to death by starvation on the route to Marion.

Ever since leaving the Elite HQ, his doubts about the whole scheme had grown. The PutinMaister's plan was too full of holes. Was this slaughter, especially of innocent children, what his God really wanted? The ancient texts held details of cruel battles, killing thousands, but those had been true enemies of God. Wicked folk who'd never worship their creator. But the kids in Marion should be given a chance to convert, shouldn't they?

The men deserved to die. Hardened heathens all of them. And the women were just women, same everywhere.

Maybe he could find a way to save the kids, persuade the PutinMaister to let him educate them in the true way. And he could hide Daisa; make her see the truth about her place, keep her for himself. Anything rather than hand her over to the PutinMaister.

The morning of the march saw all provided with meagre travelling rations, flimsy tents, and basic weapons. Stefan and Gabriel selected those who'd ride in motorised transport or fly in drones and hovers. There was no easy way to choose, so they favoured the most attractive women and more muscular men. The lot of those who'd walk all the way didn't bear thinking about.

A small quake shook the arena as Gabriel was making his final speech to raise the spirits of his followers. He managed to convert that disturbing natural event into a sign from God. 'Even the ground is with us, signalling its gladness that we're starting our crusade at last. Let's go, my people. Let the Sacred Ones set out with the fire of absolute conviction in their hearts. Onwards, people. Onwards!'

But, in his own heart, he felt the weight of guilt and responsibility for a venture so flawed, more certain to bring failure, pain and death for most. Faith in his God was all that kept him going.

Chapter Thirty Seven

It took less than an hour for the AC to assemble. Georgiy was voted chair. 'You've heard the latest? The Marzero morons are on the move.'

Everyone was concerned about the potential effects of the Marzero infective agent on their livestock and wildlife. Marion's people would be immune, in spite of the PM's claims.

'We need to stop the stupid fools before they get close. Even a minor spillage of this stuff could cause devastation to our fauna.' Anni's comment found full agreement.

'We have to tackle those travelling in land vehicles and by air. Those on foot will mostly die on the road. Any who do make it this far will be too exhausted to be a threat. They won't be carrying the agent anyway.' Zaphod was generally concerned to preserve life, but the sheer numbers involved in this situation defeated that concern. 'Thanks to Hosja, we can at least track them throughout, without their knowledge. It's a serious advantage.'

'Their motorised and airborne divisions are sticking with those on foot, for now. From what we've learnt, they don't want to kill us off too soon. They're hoping to make us help them dispose of any bodies. Fools have no idea what they're attempting.' Hosja brought them up to date from her place in the control section of the SpyTeam.

'Info just received suggests Stefan's been reading accounts of the ancient holocaust in wartime Germany and thinks they'll be able to deal with us the way the Nazis forced their prisoners to cooperate. Shows a basic misunderstanding of the reality of both situations. There's no comparison, is there? I think the man's unhinged.'

'Thank you, Hosja.' Georgiy turned to Madza. 'We need Maddie here. Or, at least her input. She and Brigitte are managing the manufacture of new pulse weapons. Anyone know what stage they've reached?'

Madza connected with one of the team overseeing production and reported back to Georgiy. 'They've seven ready to go at present, more to come. But we can't use droids to pilot, because of the Prime Directive, so …'

'Old news, Madza. We know about the droids. What about …?'

'If you'd let me finish, Georgiy, I was going to say they've recruited pilots from the Flying School. They're ready to go, using modified drones. They've set up a dedicated control centre where they can remotely pilot from a unit at their base over on the edge of Wrighton. They can be airborne in ten mins.'

'Thanks Madza, sorry for the interruption.' Georgiy scanned the committee. 'I think it's time we acted, don't you?'

All around the table agreed. Under conditions of attack the community considered a declaration of war, decisions were left to the elected AC for quick action.

'Send them on their way. The controllers know what's required?'

'Complete destruction?' Madza confirmed.

'We can't let any of that agent come into contact with the environment. It's relatively short-lived outside the containers, but could seriously damage wildlife if released, due to its extreme virulence. Those drones of theirs have to be burned up in the atmosphere. Anything less is too risky.'

Madza sent his message to the control room. But Georgiy, Zaphod and Hoshiko wanted to be where the action was. Able to view and, if necessary, control it. The Threedee in the Chamber allowed them to oversee, but not control. They must be on the spot.

The Cusp War had prompted the development of a specific weapon used successfully to defeat terrorists. But they'd been a small, dedicated troop with little military knowledge or training and only their insane religious passion to drive them.

Disorganised, ill-educated, and poorly equipped, only their missionary zeal had sustained them in their determination to put an end to all human life. The Chosen's weapons-grade lasers had been effective, but both had been damaged beyond reasonable repair in the battle.

Following the end of that war, the brief period of violent dispute in the immediate post Cusp era had called for a little more sophistication. It had been then that the brains in Marion's technology section had developed longer range, smaller, and more powerful pulse weapons. The mix of lethal wavelengths employed in the various versions proved remarkably effective at destroying both vehicles and life.

Their advanced technology had finally defeated the greed and violence of Marzero. In the many years since, the minds at Marion had improved and refined their technology so that once fanciful weapons of ancient science fiction classics like Star Trek, Star Wars and Star Dominions now seemed like toys.

From admiration for the creators of these fictions, combined with a love of irony, they'd named their weapons 'phasers', 'pulse guns' and 'disruptors'. They'd been at pains to develop systems that were both energy efficient and pollution free, as well as being as accurate as possible. So their disruptors were housed in self-contained, self-propelled shells guided by limited AI developed for that purpose. Anything targeted by a disruptor was unlikely to survive other than as vapour and plasma.

In mins, they were inside the Flying School and seated in sight of the operations centre, where experienced flyers were guiding drones toward those from Marzero.

The Marion drones were outnumbered three to one by the attackers' planes. But the larger numbers were technologically less developed, slower, and more visible. Weapons were more specialised on the Marion probes. Bluish in colour, to blend more easily against the modern Martian sky, they were more difficult to spot than the blood red of the Marzero squad.

Zaphod placed himself to watch the Threedee display, fed by multiple cameras borne by the blue drones supplementing HiRes images from stationary satellites and pirated input from Marzero's own craft, showing a real time image of the action.

A pilot in a red spotted the incoming squadron and let fly with his pulse laser. The Marion pilot deflected the attack, sending the energy pulse groundward. It caused a small explosion at the front of the approaching land troops in their armoured vehicles. One was disabled. Another swerved to avoid the new pothole that opened up.

The 21 blue drones waited until they were closer, knowing their more powerful and accurate phasers and disruptors would quickly eliminate the opposition. Their small force had been developed from a need to maintain security in the event of an unlikely attack. It had, after all, been over 200 years since any hostilities.

This recent mission was ill-conceived and hastily put together by a leader with no concern for the safety of the troops he'd sent into battle. Intercepted recordings of meetings and conversations between the PM and his senior men demonstrated their lack of tactical experience. Marion, on the other hand, had always included tactical and strategic warfare models in the training of those who showed interest and potential.

The aerial battle began in earnest. Fast-moving and difficult to follow, as drones and planes moved in and out of the area covered by the Threedee, enough info was available to get an idea of the action. Each pilot had his or her personal display to permit close observation of their drone and any potential attackers.

Zaphod watched the first blue attack. Number seven, it took out a red bearing a black, green and blue roundel marker. The enemy plane, and all it carried, burst into a cloud of mixed vapour and plasma that quickly dispersed through the force of the explosion. Numbers 19 and 12 took out two enemy planes simultaneously. Close together, the resulting clouds formed a briefly obscuring patch in the sky. Two more blues almost collided as they passed through this at speed from opposite directions in pursuit of other enemy planes. An audible sigh of relief passed around the unit.

The action continued, with hit after hit on reds, the blue drones constantly outmanoeuvring pulses aimed at them. In a couple of cases, those pulses actually hit other reds, one of which hit the ground close to the advancing vehicles. Two trucks immediately stopped and their occupants fled only a few steps before all the men succumbed to the agent that had escaped from the crashed red.

Meantime, the other red, winged but not disabled, flew low and at speed out of the general arena of the battle. Nobody followed it, all being engaged in pursuing unharmed reds and still outnumbered by two to one.

Zaphod watched a fight between a blue and two reds. The Marion pilot's aerial skills drew his admiration. The young woman engaged the red following her drone and, simultaneously, fired a salvo broadside at the other. Both were vaporised.

Ground fire, from weapons attached to trucks, confused the air battle. One blue drone, number eight, was hit as it dodged a blast from a red above it. The young man piloting cried out in rage as his craft burst into flame some distance from the land forces. He moved across to the pilot beside him to act as an additional pair of eyes.

Towards the end of the conflict, with all reds destroyed or fleeing back to base, the Threedee expanded to cover a wider area. Seven enemy planes made a run for it. Half the Marion forces were ordered back home, the others pursuing the retreating reds to take them out so they couldn't return later. It was then Zaphod noticed a telltale trail of black smoke heading out of the battle arena toward Marion.

'There's a damaged red approaching Blumberg township!' The call came from Georgiy. It passed to all drone pilots and three broke away from the returning flight to give chase.

The black plume followed the red as it struggled to maintain height. It was clear the pilot was determined to reach the intended destination. And there was no way the blue drones would reach it in time, though one fired a stream of pulses. It was already descending through low cloud, all but invisible, and on course for the township.

Chapter Thirty Eight

'Why'd they not attack the hovers?'

'Who cares, man? Let's get outta here before they attack us.'

'And go where, Stefan? We can't go back unless we succeed. Return to Marzero without and we're dead.'

'Shit! You're right, man. What we gonna do?'

It was so unlike Stefan to ask questions in such a situation that Gabriel was alarmed. What had happened to the friend he'd always thought so strong and confident?

'We've got to get the agent to Marion. We're carryin a drum each. Enough to do real damage if we spread it wide and well. We have to leave the Sacred Ones and go ahead.'

'Had another vision?' Stefan's voice, though generated by coms from his parallel hover, suggested sarcasm.

'No. I don't know what's got into you, Stefan. It was my own idea. Obvious, isn't it?'

'Is it? If there were some way to escape, that's what I'd be doin. But I guess you're right. We gotta do it.'

They discussed whether to inform their followers, spread out in long lines behind them, the trucks moving, along with other hovers, at walking speed, since they carried most of the supplies for those on foot. In the end, they decided to tell the people they were going ahead to scout the route.

They moved off at high speed and noted, some 40 ks forward of the followers' lines, the Marion drones back in the sky, making for the masses they'd just deserted.

'Looks like they're about to attack again.'

'Still 19 of the twats. Must've caught our other planes. Just us and any hovers and trucks that get through. Best warn them to scatter. Make it harder for their twattin drones to destroy them.'

Gabriel followed Stefan's suggestion and ordered the transports to move forward at speed and in a widespread formation to avoid the danger they faced as a group. With luck, the Marion drones would miss some of the armoured group and they'd get through to add to the damage Stefan and he were going to cause.

They were another 20 ks nearer their intended destination when they saw plumes of black rising behind them, the horizon hiding detail. The amount of smoke suggested widespread destruction.

'Them on foot won't stand no chance with no food, or water, or shelter. What we gonna do?'

'I thought you didn't care about the people, Stefan? We're on God's mission. We have to do as much damage as we can. The others must trust in God. There's nothin we can do to help. We've got to get to Marion with the agent.'

'Yeah. Right, man. Let's go!' But Stefan's voice carried no conviction.

'Not goin soft on me, Stefan? This is God's mission. Keep that in mind.'

There was no response, but Stefan's hover kept pace with his own as they skimmed the ground in their rush toward the enemy settlement.

Coms from the followers came through, reporting the destruction of every hover and truck. Some of the agent they carried had escaped and killed many of the men. That meant no agent for Marion other than what they carried. Not enough to destroy all life at Marion, but ample to cause serious damage.

'It's all on us now, Stefan. Let's get this done.'

'Yeah. Right.' Stefan's voice betrayed his lack of enthusiasm.

Gabriel was growing seriously worried his friend had lost his faith. But there was no time for that now.

The drums they carried had spray attachments that produced a fine aerosol to spread over a wide area. Only a tiny amount of agent was needed to cause multiple deaths. But they must succeed with their first pass. They wouldn't get a second chance. Gabriel let Stefan know.

'Yeah. Hopeless innit?'

'No! God's on our side. We'll win.'

Stefan refrained from commenting on the fear in Gabriel's voice but kept pace with him. At this moment, both became aware of Marion drones approaching. They were within sight of the settlement. Would they make it before they were attacked?

'Shit! Now or never, Stefan. Release the agent, then move east and eject into that patch of rough ground, for cover!'

He had no plan but it seemed the only chance they'd have to survive. He released his agent faster than intended. Would any reach the settlement? The drones homed in. He turned east and ejected. As his seat rose high above the ground, he saw Stefan make the same move.

The blue drones targeted their abandoned hovers and disrupted them into insubstantial clouds. Descending by parachute into an area of wild, uncultivated land intruding into the settlement, they wondered would the drones shoot them out of the air? They'd have killed any escapees in their position.

But both landed without being attacked. Maybe they were too small to be noticed or the drone pilots thought they'd killed them.

Gabriel landed first and drew in his parachute to hide it in the rough scrub and trees that characterised this place. He saw Stefan descending and ran to meet him.

Together, they hid the other chute and took stock.

'Know where we are?'

Stefan nodded. 'I've heard of this place. The Risk. It's where they send their kids to toughen them up before they can call themselves adults. Virginia told me they leave the poor twats ere without nothin. In their skin, with a small flask of drinkin water. Have to spend days fendin for themselves.'

'Sounds like the sort of thing the Marionets would do. If their kids survive out here, so will we. Let's see what we can find out, shall we?'

'Jeez, man. Don't you never give up? We're dead men. Just you and me against the whole of Marion? You're twattin mad.'

Gabriel understood the tables had turned. Where Stefan was leader in Marzero, here in the wild it was up to him, Gabriel, to lead. His many runs in the wild country beyond Marzero had prepared him to some extent to deal with life outside the city.

Stefan had left the urban area only once; to follow him on that run when God had showed Himself. That had obviously been ordained by God Himself. Now it was up to him to get them through this trial.

Once they'd escaped Marion, they could go back with details of their attack and fall on the mercy of the PM. He'd understand they hadn't actually failed, just been poorly equipped in face of superior weaponry.

'Let's climb that escarpment and see what it shows us. If they really send their kids out here to grow up, there'll be food and shelter. They're not that uncivilised.'

The rise he'd seen was a protrusion of the cliff that formed the edge of the Olympus Mons shield, still raw with dust. Patches of green and yellow lichen dotted the near perpendicular face where the odd shelf provided a hold for life. Already, they were soaked to the skin by the thin drizzle that had been falling all day. Chilled but not frozen so far south, they nevertheless knew they must find shelter whilst it remained light.

Stefan followed him reluctantly, aware he had no option, at least until they had some idea where they were, and whether there was a possibility of escape. Gabriel found a rough trail, made by many who'd gone before, winding up the steep face. Narrow and difficult, it looked like the only way to the top.

They struggled on as the drizzle finally turned to proper rain, causing small rivulets to run down the track they trod. Their light shoes, poorly made so they needed frequent replacement, were no match for rough ground. Stefan's left shoe lost its sole, then Gabriel's right split apart. They were only two thirds up when both had to ditch their shoes. And bare feet weren't good in this terrain.

Finally, they reached the top of the cliff and a steeply sloping plateau that gave a panoramic view of the whole place below them. In the distance, the edges of the civilised settlement showed in glass, ceramic and steel structures. So many trees made the whole place green. And, beyond the first block of structures, they could see the reflection of light on an expanse of water.

Closer, however, the scene was nowhere near as welcoming. The land was rough, hilly, craggy and mostly covered in scrub. Here and there larger trees rose from the bushes, and patches of darker green marked where boggy ground lay deep in reeds. No sign of structures. A few rough narrow paths wound between the bushes. Here and there, small birds flitted amongst the vegetation.

'Here! Look at this, Stefan.' Gabriel beckoned his companion to where he'd found a small metal sign mounted low to the ground on a boulder.

The message was unpromising. It read, 'The Risk is intended to test your tenacity, intelligence and imagination. There is food for those wise enough to recognise it. Stagnant water is unpleasant to drink. There are items to allow a fire. If you set light to the area in general you will be required to physically replant the area destroyed. Make your campfire in a ring of stones. Natural materials will allow you to construct a shelter. You have your mind and body. Use them to survive this test. The challenge will fit you for the next stage in your education.'

'What we gonna do, Gabriel? Ever lived on wild stuff? I never have.'

'We'll trust to God to guide us.'

'God? You're a twattin moron, d'you know that? There ain't no god, man. It's a twattin lie, all of it. I made it up. Don't you get it?'

Gabriel gave his arm a friendly punch. 'That's the spirit, Stefan. I know you're only jokin. Good you've kept your sense of humour. And, look. See? There's the first sign God's with us.'

'There ain't no twattin god! What the twat you talkin …?'

'Smoke. There's a fire down there. At least we'll be able to keep warm. If we move now, we'll get to it before dark. Let's go.'

'I don't like it. Smoke means people. We could be captured.'

'Two things, Stefan. One, we're not expected. Two, the only folk here are kids. You saw the sign.'

Stefan nodded. 'True. No need to worry about twattin kids. Might even get the little twats to find food and drink for us.'

They set off back down the cliff with more hope than when they'd ascended it.

Chapter Thirty Nine

'Is it wise to let those two escape, Zaphod?'

'Wise, Georgiy? They won't live long if they return to Marzero. We heard the PM. They've failed in their mission. Even the crashed plane with its cargo did little damage in Blomberg. Five deaths from the three pods destroyed, and some small animal deaths in the vicinity.

'Signs are their own spray was washed to the ground in the wilderness. It'll do a small amount of harm to wildlife, but not much. Damage we can do without, but will easily restore.

'They, on the other hand, fell into the Risk, where they'll be tested to their limits. Perhaps, in the way it matures our children, it'll have some positive effect on them. Who knows?'

'Suppose they escape into the community?'

'How? If we can't, I'm certain they won't find a way.'

'Still think we should send in a group to capture them.'

'Give them time to consider their stupidity in discomfort. It might educate them.'

'I'd prefer to finish the murdering buggers off.'

'Let's see what nature decides, eh. Georgiy?'

'Ever the preserver of life.'

'I'm still a doctor.'

'Buzz is in there. And Daisa went in to atone for her mistakes at Marzero.'

'She shouldn't have, or at least she should've waited until things here were more stable. But she's an adult and must make her own way. I expect she hopes the Risk will help her come to terms with her poor judgment of those two. I've my doubts about them, but I'm relatively happy about Daisa in that regard. Who knows, she may even have some positive influence on Buzz, since they'll likely meet each other there.'

'You don't think she's in danger?'

'Those two Zeros'll have difficulty just finding shelter and food.

And Buzz? Hardly a risk to Daisa, Georgiy. She's taller, fitter, stronger and more able in every way. Buzz will be in danger if he confronts her.'

'You think?'

'He bullies the young with psychological tricks, not brute force. And Daisa's an expert in martial arts. I'm not worried about her safety with him.'

'We should never have taken him on.'

'Brigitte risked all for us, did some really great work in the Cusp War, and since. We owed her, big time. She wanted Buzz with her after their long separation when he was on the Moon. Now she's finally decided she no longer wants anything to do with him, it makes our choices easier.'

'If he doesn't change?'

'Exile. I see no alternative. You?'

Georgiy nodded. 'It's a death sentence, Zaphod.'

'Not now. Tu says the ozone generators have all but completed their task. Radiation protection's good enough to let you all spend whole days outside. Medinanobots and DNA manipulations have protected you so far, but the improvement in the atmosphere means they'll need to work less hard, that's all.

'Anyone resourceful enough could survive the wild. The flora and fauna are spreading quickly. There's food and water. Shelters can be made from plants and trees. Exile's no death sentence. But it'd be hard for Buzz. Not sure what he'd do, how he'd manage. But I see no alternative. If he doesn't change, that is.'

'You think he will?'

Zaphod considered. Even in his metal skin, lacking the sensory equipment he once stimulated when he scratched his head, he still made the gesture. 'In all honesty, no. We've given him how many chances? Seven. Still he's unable treat women as equal. He's still a bully and a user. Still the child of right wing commercialism and convention. Wouldn't surprise me if he suddenly declared a conversion to some faith or other. Maybe we should've sent him to Marzero. He'd fit in well with that lot.'

'And have him sell all our tech secrets to their Elite? Anyway, I thought you were working on a new DNA modification programme? One with potential to alter personality?'

Zaphod smiled. 'Calculations are ongoing. So many variations: centillions. Even with quantum computation in full swing, it's predicted to be another 20 days before they come to any conclusion. And I'll need time to quantify results, run tests on models, and assess the accuracy and effectiveness of any modifications. That's a helluva complex system. DNA. Possible cure for everything. But not yet.'

'So. Wait and see?'

Zaphod shrugged. 'No choice really.'

Georgiy agreed. 'But what are we going to do about Marzero? They tried to kill Daisa. Sent an army to destroy us. We can't just ignore that.'

'No. We can't. Time for a final solution. The phoney peace has gone on so long we've been fooled into thinking we'd solved the problems. But we know how they treat their women, we know how corrupt their entire commercial and political systems are. We know they run an unjust society for the benefit of their Elite. And we know they still tolerate and even promote the idea of faith: the most crucially important factor we have to eradicate. But how?'

'Call a meeting of all seniors and heads of committees? See if we can come to some sort of plan?'

'Have to place a time limit. Otherwise, you know how pedantic and obstructive to action some of them are, Georgiy.'

'Never thought I'd say this. But it's still a better way to rule than a single leader. Might take longer, result in fewer decisions, but it sorts things for the benefit of all instead of the old system of privilege and status.'

'For a Ruskie, that's quite some turnaround.'

'Amazing how the centuries can educate, eh?'

Zaphod slapped his back. 'Welcome to the modern world, Georgiy.

Chapter Forty

The drizzle had been a bit of a trial, but nothing like the irritation presented by Buzz. Daisa, however, resolutely demonstrated her maturity and superior intellect by behaving with tolerance, patience and fortitude in the face of his extreme idiocy and juvenile obsession with nudity. But his constant whining and pleas for her sympathy had finally worn her down.

'It's a condition of the Risk, Buzz. You know that. Same for everyone. So cut your leering and either help me sort these traps or piss off. I can't be bothered with your childish behaviour.' She knelt on greenery as a cushion and positioned her handmade trap out of sight under a small shrub. The pine nuts she'd collected earlier should attract one of the growing population of squirrels they'd bred to help maintain the forests.

'Frackin stuck up. Just like the rest in this miserable place. Don't know why I bother.'

'You don't. Not with anything that isn't to your personal advantage. You're a throwback. Why you think anyone wants to be with you is a mystery. You're a bully to those who allow it and a user of those too innocent to see through your superficial charms. You lie and cheat. Marion's better off without a selfish, inconsiderate, narcissist like you. The Council's too generous with you. I'd have exiled you decades ago.'

'Don't be like that, Daisa. I've tried to conform. I'm not made that way. I have to go my own way, see? Surely you understand? I'm different. Some even say I'm unique.'

'A one off? Yes. A good way to describe yourself, Buzz. But not unique in a positive sense. You're a drain on the colony. A pain in the arse. A waste of space, as far as I'm concerned. Now, are you helping me with this or not?'

'Don't see why I frackin should.'

'And there we have it. Sums up your entire life, doesn't it? Selfish. Zaphod insists there's something there worth saving. But I've seen right through you, ever since I let you fuck me. Never again. It's all about you. I know what you really are, and I don't like it. So, go.'

He kicked out at her carefully placed trap but she was too quick and knocked his legs from under him with a sweep of her arm. He fell hard. 'Go!'

She stood and aimed a kick at his rising seat so he landed on his face. Leaving him, she carried her other three traps to sites she'd selected earlier.

When finished, she'd return to her shelter, where the fire would still be burning, and settle for the night. A supper of pine nuts, hazel nuts and some fungus she'd discovered on a tree damaged by an early storm. Amazing how plants they'd brought from Earth had adapted to Mars after the work Annika and Jai had put in so long ago.

Modifications, and some genetic mutation, had helped a few adapt more readily to the lower gravity and developing atmosphere. Almost everything they'd transported from the old home planet had some nutritional quality, and they'd avoided those containing toxins where possible. The result was that much of what grew here was edible. Foraging was far simpler than it might otherwise have been, provided the hunter knew what to look for, how to gather it, and how to turn the raw ingredients into something palatable.

Her other traps placed, she made her way back through damp gloom to her campsite. The fire would need tending in this drizzle and she was anxious not to let it go out. Starting another would be difficult after the rain, which finally stopped as she was on her way.

Her fire had been disturbed; only a few embers remained glowing. Quickly, she collected dry kindling from the small supply in her shelter. Then, from the nearby undergrowth, retrieved some logs she'd collected. Within a short time the fire was roaring again.

She wasted no energy in calling Buzz the names he deserved for his actions. Those cheap tricks proved his unsuitability for life in the community. In the morning, she'd move to a new location, build a shelter, and ensure she didn't expose her new temporary home to him.

For the moment, she was hungry. She'd caged a small game bird, a red grouse, she thought. At least he hadn't found that. She untied the vine she'd used to secure the willow wands that formed its little prison.

Now the worst part. Breaking its neck, ended its life. It was still warm as she plucked the major feathers. Her sharpened stone blade gutted it and she singed the rest of the down from the skin before poking a pointed stick through its body to act as a spit.

The aroma of roasting flesh might attract Buzz. Alert to that possibility, she heard the voices whilst they were still a good distance from her camp. And she recognised their owners.

This was too tempting for her researcher's brain to ignore. She moved the cooking bird from the flames, so it wouldn't burn whilst she was absent. And she ventured along the faint path in the direction of the men. Her makeshift spear in one hand, her wooden dagger stuck in the vine tied round her waist.

Three of them now, and two were potentially dangerous.

Chapter Forty One

The probe was in position. Amber, back on the planet surface and reunited with Georgiy, received the news via A02395 as she prepared to visit the John Glenn Space Centre.

'A touch earlier than calculated. Any idea where I went wrong, Zhen?'

'ALP is always subject to some fluctuation, depending on the purity of the propellant, and especially with a small payload and travelling at enormous speed. You were out by only an hour and seven mins, or 0.62%. Pretty good for a flight over a total distance of a 108,570,446 ks.'

'Thanks for the approximations, Zhen; I know how your logic circuits abhor a lack of precision. Have we started testing yet?'

'IR and UV are operating as expected. Microwave's good and X-ray is fine. Still completing trials on all visible wavelengths, radio frequencies, spectrometer analysis and supplementary functions. Testing will complete by 22:37:49.'

'Too early for results, of course. But I must get to JGS Centre and see for myself.'

'You wish my company?'

'As always. But I think some cover may be wise, bearing in mind the geeky nature of most of the men there.'

The android paused in her stride for a split sec and coated her humanoid skin in colours to resemble clothing. Only close examination would reveal her real state.

They travelled to the Transhub on foot and then took a drum as far as the outskirts of Hawking Sector, stopping at the terminal serving Hershel Town. The walk from there was less than 20 mins and they arrived at the centre in time to accept the results of another 19 tests; all performing as expected.

'Except for an anomaly on the IR scan over Zealandia. There's a vague hint of something other than natural background. But we'll have to wait for the next pass before we can take more readings. It's inconclusive at the moment, Amber.'

Madza brought up the results for her to scan, his eagerness to please her still more amusing than irritating. He'd become involved, she knew, because he found her fascinating. So far, she hadn't succumbed.

'Odd. Short-lived, too. It's tempting to speculate, but we'll wait till the next pass. When is it?'

'Next overfly of that specific area is in 53 hours 24 mins. We're still performing the initial global scan at medium res. We'll be able to organise geostationary orbit points as you wish once the full global's complete.'

Amber looked again at the results. Intriguing. She was eager to expand on the numerous possibilities but there were hundreds more tests to finalise before she could afford the luxury of HiRes from a geostationary point. Patience. Everything would become clear eventually. Intelligent life? Possibly. But far too soon to speculate. She concentrated instead on the new results streaming in.

But, what if Earth was again showing signs of abliform life?

Chapter Forty Two

The aroma of meat cooking attracted all three. They came together on a narrow track Daisa had made during various sorties through the undergrowth. Buzz recognised the pair from his time spying for the community.

'Well, well, if it isn't Jesus and John the frackin Baptist! What the frack are you doing here?' He'd concealed himself in the bushes to avoid conflict. Both men were taller than him, the prophet substantially more muscular. But the temptation of Daisa's cooking was too strong to be left for these intruders.

'Show yourself. We're not scared of no one.' Stefan blustered.

'Maybe you can help us. We're lookin for food. The smell of cookin attracted us. Is it you who's got meat?' Gabriel was his usual naive self.

Buzz decided these two were less of a threat than they looked. Now he'd had time to examine them, their torn clothes and sorry expressions told him they were as vulnerable as he felt. Three could take Daisa, and benefit from her hunting skills. He emerged on to the path, a few paces up from where they'd stopped on hearing his voice.

'I know who you are. Don't think you can take advantage of me because I'm on my own. Everything you do here's recorded. Our armed droids can be here in secs.' He hoped the lie would keep them civil until he had time to decide whether they could act together.

'Did you call us Jesus and John the Baptist?' The prophet seemed more curious than offended.

'You remind me of that pair of clowns I learned about in primary. I mean, you're the wandering prophet and he's your guide. That's right, isn't it?'

'Who are you, then?'

'Well, Stefan, call me Buzz. I'm having a bit of a pioneering workout. How come you're here?'

Gabriel gave a brief description of their arrival until Stefan interrupted. 'Twat doesn't need to know everythin, Gab. Anyway, how come you know my name?'

'That's for me to know and you to worry about.'

Stefan glared at him but Buzz was unfazed. 'We're hungry. There's meat cookin somewhere near.'

Buzz grinned. 'Daisa. You know her. Sent here as punishment for all the trouble she caused.'

'Twat! She's what made us come here. I'm gonna do her when I find her.'

'Let's not be too hasty. She's a good supplier of food in this crap place. Maybe eat first, shall we? Then we can all do her. Together, or one at a time. I don't mind.'

Stefan's silent response to this, a slow nodding of his head, boosted Buzz's confidence that he'd judged the man correctly. He'd fancied another go at Daisa for years. With these two around, looked like he'd get a chance. More than one.

Gabriel, silent throughout this exchange, finally spoke. Softly. 'Where is she?'

'Follow me. But quiet. Got fantastic hearing.'

Daisa, having followed their talk, was close enough to observe without being seen. She took to a parallel track and stayed with them as they made their way to her camp.

'Twat's not here. So who's cookin?'

Buzz scanned the area, caught sight of the half cooked bird. 'Probably in her shelter. Or gone for a wash. The food's just there. Nearly done, by the look of it.'

Stefan saw the direction of his gaze and dashed to the fowl. He tore off a leg, ignored the dripping blood, and gobbled it down in a couple of mouthfuls.

Buzz put his hand on Stefan's. 'Not cooked. You'll get ill if you eat it like that. Put it back in.'

Stefan eyed him with suspicion but moved closer to the fire and held the bird on its stick over the flames. The other two moved to be beside him and sat on the spare logs. The three of them steamed in front of the fire. The Zeros' clothes gave off the smell of stale sweat. Buzz dried more rapidly.

'Good job Daisa didn't find you first. She'd have had you stripped by now.'

'Told you she was a whore.' Stefan glanced at Gabriel, a knowing sneer distorting his face in the flickering light.

'Well, she likes a good fuck. Who doesn't? But I didn't mean like that. It's against the rules to wear clothes in the Risk, that's all.'

'She's gonna get a right fuckin. Twat needs learnin a lesson. I'll shag the twat till she begs me to stop.'

'If that's your thing. Me, I prefer a quick fuck 'em and forget 'em. How about you, Gabriel?'

Gabriel glared at the other two men. 'She deserves better. And, if necessary, I'll protect her from the pair of you. She's a woman, not a piece of meat.'

'Gab's always had a soft spot for the twat. She needs it hard, man.' He pushed his free hand between Gabriel's legs and grabbed him. 'Stiff an hard!'

Gabriel shifted the intruding hand and stood. Moved away. He had no intention, no agenda, simply wanted to be away from these two men with their obsessive talk of harm to Daisa. Since their landing in the Risk and Stefan's outburst against God, he'd felt a change in his friend's demeanour. As he walked through the trees, he re-examined what Stefan had said and realised he'd never retracted his statement. That led him to reconsider an earlier conversation, when Stefan had pretended to deny God's existence as a way, he'd said, of getting his attention. But, suppose he really didn't believe?

What would that mean for his ministry? Stefan had interpreted all the visions for him. He'd given God's words to him to pass on to the crowds. He'd informed Gabriel of the changes. Even the change from making women equal, which was what had first started him on the road to the ministry.

Had it all been false? Gabriel couldn't absorb this. Not now. Not here in this wild and strange place. He had to think. Had to understand what had really happened. See if he could discover the truth amongst all the uncertainties that now flooded his mind.

He walked without any idea of where he was going. Sat on a fallen tree trunk and allowed his mind to mine the caves of his memory. And all he found was inconsistencies, contradictions, inexplicable alterations. All presented as truths from God by Stefan.

Too much. He had to know. In the growing darkness, he retraced his steps. Had the pair of them not been talking loudly, he'd probably have wandered right past. But their words guided him back to Daisa's camp.

'Where's the stupid twat now?'

'Gabriel or Daisa?'

'Both.'

'Chances are Daisa's made another hideaway. No idea where your Prophet of the People might be.'

'Any more grub?'

'Can't see any.'

'What's the plan?'

'Plan?'

'We gonna find the twat and shag her, or what?'

'Frack me, Stefan. I thought I was keen. I need food. Don't you ever think about anything but a fuck?'

'Lots of things. But that twat wants teachin a lesson.'

Gabriel didn't want to get involved in this continued threat to Daisa. Whenever he thought of her, he formed a picture of her generosity and her hatred of violence. The story Stefan had told about her guilt in the murder of the other woman had been untrue. Stefan had said as much. But the more he thought about the situation, the more he wondered how Daisa had ever been even considered as a suspect in the case. Who'd pointed the finger at Daisa? And why?

He stopped short of the camp, waiting for them to change the subject so he might at least get some sense out of Stefan instead of this dreadful preoccupation with a revenge he found hard to understand.

'Why, Stefan?' said Buzz's voice. 'What's she done to you?'

'It's all her fault. If she'd never come along, I'd have had Gabriel doin the whole thing right. She's the one what made him go wrong, Buzz. I had to tell him no end of lies to get him back on side. I mean, poor twattin fool really believes he's seen God, you know.'

'Hasn't, of course.'

'No chance. It were that metal man of yours. Sunshine on his skin blinded the twattin idiot. Fell over and knocked hisself out. The laugh is the robot man made him better after the fall, healed his wounds an that. Easy to persuade Gab he'd seen God. He has these blank times when he can't remember nothin. Easy to plant ideas in his head then. He were mine. He's god twatting obsessed. I could tell him anythin. Even had him believin Daisa had murdered a woman.' He laughed harshly.

'I tell you, that twattin idiot's so stupid; believed every word. Had him eatin out my hand. But Daisa made things difficult. The PM's an even bigger twat. We'd never have got away with those plans to attack your place. Pointless right from the start. But we was stuck with it. It was kill you lot or get killed in the arena to entertain the peasants.'

'So, everything this so called Prophet of the People said and did was down to you, Stefan?'

'Everythin. Gab's got no sense. Twattin good memory for things he's been told and a great voice for persuadin the crowd. But no idea what's what.'

In the shrubs, out of sight, Daisa watched and listened. Her evening meal was lost to her. And the fire was no place for her with talk like this. She settled low where she could observe the three men. Odd that Gabriel had left the camp and was now standing in the trees behind the other two, obviously listening.

As darkness fell, they became first curious about her absence, then anxious.

251

'Where is the twat?'

'No idea. Probably watching us from somewhere she can't be seen.'

Stefan rose to his feet and scanned the area, his face full of concern in the flickering light of the fire.

Gabriel looked hopeful.

Buzz seemed merely disappointed. 'She won't be back now. Too dark. She'll have another place to go. Knows how to survive out here, does Daisa. Might as well get some sleep and see what morning brings.'

He and Stefan moved into her shelter. Gabriel remained hidden in the trees.

Daisa watched and waited. If necessary, she'd stay where she was all night. It was vital she know where the three of them were. Stefan and Buzz had plans for her, to have her against her will. Gabriel was something of an unknown for now, but she felt, on balance, he was unlikely to attack her.

Nightlife emerged. Animal noises, birdsong, the odd sounds of some of the many insects they'd introduced. No biting flies, no ants. But a spider ran across her feet and a small rodent dashed over her leg.

Gabriel moved out of the trees, closer to the fire. He placed another log to keep it going. That sort of forethought was promising.

Daisa listened. Sounds from the shelter suggested the two men were asleep. It was a risk, but a calculated one. Now was the time.

Silently, she moved toward the fire until she was in its circle of light.

'Gabriel.' Her whisper light as air.

No response. She stepped a pace closer. 'Gabriel.'

He lifted his head. Something reached him. He looked in her direction. She placed a finger across her lips and he closed his mouth, swallowed the call that threatened to emerge.

Slowly, she crept towards him. He began to rise, but she signalled to him to stay put.

When she reached his side, she crouched beside him and

whispered, 'Two I might handle. But three's a challenge. Do I have to tackle three, or only two, Gabriel?'

He brushed her thigh, a gesture of affection rather than lust. 'I'd never hurt you. You heard Stefan?'

'It's what I'd suspected. But you were always too committed to let facts change your mind. We can't discuss it here. Will you come with me? See if we can understand the truth?'

He considered all he'd heard, all he'd recalled. Doubt and confusion ruled, but he understood any danger lay in the shelter behind him, not with Daisa. 'I'm with you.'

'Good.' She reached down and took a long stick from the embers, its tip in flames. 'Find one like this.'

Gabriel tried a couple before they were both satisfied.

'Let's go.'

She led him, making sure he followed exactly in her footsteps. And took him to the place she'd already chosen as a secondary base. It lacked the amenity of the shallow washing pool and was a little more exposed to the wind, but it would do.

She gathered small fallen branches and twigs into a pile and set Gabriel to look for larger deadwood. The moonlight from Ceres gave only minimal illumination, making the search difficult. But they made the beginnings of a fire, using their flaming brands to light it.

As the flames spread and caught the larger pieces, she cleared all flammable material from around the edges, making it safe.

Gabriel learned quickly. In the increased firelight, he discovered a fallen tree and dragged it closer to the flames for them to sit on.

'So, Gabriel. How and why are you here?'

It took him a long time to convey the truth as he understood it. When he'd finished, they were both weary.

'I'm not sure you've told me everything, but I expect it's more truth than lies. Shall we sleep? We'll need our energy in the morning.'

Together, they rolled the log seat a little further back. Moved a couple of smaller logs into the flames to keep them burning and then snuggled close on the damp ground. In secs both were asleep.

Morning found them constructing a makeshift shelter from branches stripped from small trees, leant up against the bole of a larger broadleaf with a wide canopy. The sky promised fine weather and the early birdsong was full of joy.

Hunger drove them to eat raw berries and a few fallen nuts found close by. But their main concern for now was the action of the other two.

Quietly, they made their way back to Daisa's original camp. The fire was almost out and there was no sign of either of the men outside. Daisa gestured to Gabriel to stay where he was and crept toward the shelter. The sounds from within told her they were still sleeping. As she was deciding on her next step, Gabriel sneezed, loudly.

Daisa froze as the sounds in the shelter altered. There was movement. She trotted quickly back to rejoin Gabriel, crouching where she'd spent the earlier part of the night, watching.

Buzz came out and tossed more wood on the dying fire. It smoked, unlikely to come back to flame quickly. Stefan emerged and sat on one of the seat logs.

Daisa held Gabriel's hand, squeezed it to stop the outburst she felt was imminent. 'Not now, Gabriel. There'll be plenty of time later.'

He nodded at her soft words but his face was set in a mask of fury and hate. Daisa felt she'd best keep him in sight if she was to prevent him doing something unwise.

'They're a danger to both of us. But we'll need energy to fight. Let's hunt. Get ourselves fed and properly rested. Tomorrow, we'll decide what we're going to do to stop their plans. But we must be prepared.'

Chapter Forty Three

The oval table in the centre of the Chamber was surrounded. Every seat taken. This was a momentous meeting and everyone attending represented the wishes, ideas and priorities of their group.

'Who's chairing?' The question was expected but Zaphod was surprised it came from one of the youngest reps, Sarma, a descendent of the line started by Sarm and Jai. A young woman who, but for her increased height, could've been taken for her originator's sister.

'Suggestions, please.' Zaphod was temporary chair until decisions were reached by consensus.

A number of names were put forward, but the majority favoured Hoshiko, which came as no surprise. She accepted in the conventional manner and smiled down the table to where Zaphod sat almost directly opposite.

Droid S14327 initiated the log, counted and recorded all 27 members present, and declared the meeting ready to proceed. It was an old fashioned system, based on a tradition formed early in the settlement's history. They retained it more for comfort than for any other reason.

Hoshiko initiated the central Threedee presentation Zaphod, Georgiy and Madza had prepared with CenCom. There was silence, interrupted only by occasional bursts of outrage and disgust as the events of the past few days were relayed to Full Council. The treatment of Daisa caused rage, and the attempted attack on Marion made all assembled furious. Muttered condemnation accompanied the viewing of the duplicity, lies, manipulation and distortions demonstrated by Stefan, Gabriel, and the PM.

The presentation concluded with the downing of the pair of Zeros in their hovers and a brief description of their trek from the wilderness into the Risk. Nothing further was known of the outcome of that trespass. A few voiced their hope Daisa would be safe, others expressed expectations Buzz might fail to survive this time and solve that problem.

'You're all fully appraised of the situation. We're gathered to determine what we should now do in response.' Hoshiko powered down the Threedee and signalled to three waiting droids to begin serving refreshments.

For some time, there was a free-for-all around the table, as voices gave first thoughts on the matter. Known as the 'Kneejerk', it was an inevitable and necessary part of the democratic protocol and one that rarely produced anything workable. But it allowed initial emotions to be calmed before decision making began.

After hot and cold drinks and snacks were consumed, Hoshiko rose and signalled for quiet. It fell quickly. 'I'll now initiate the round robin. Please start, Sarm.'

Traditionally, the round robin began at the left of the chair and proceeded clockwise. Sarm stood and addressed the assembly as Hoshiko sat.

'I speak on behalf of Tesla Sector.' Everyone knew this, but it was a part of a protocol now deeply embedded. 'As you know, we base our expectations and preferences on peace and harmony, as do many around this table. We're reluctant to use violence. But I had to, against the Zeros, very recently. We're aware it may be the only viable solution to our present problem. We won't stand in the way of an aggressive response.'

She sat down again and the rep to her left, a young man, stood and said his piece. This process was the second stage of all FC meets, as reps expressed the wishes and expectations of their particular group in a short statement until all 27 voices had been heard.

Hoshiko stood again and looked at each of the assembled in turn. 'The facts are known. The initial ideas of all sectors have now been expressed. Desired outcome is therefore our next priority. As usual, though we haven't previously dealt with anything as serious as the current issue, we'll each express the outcome expected by the group we represent. After that, we'll break for informal conversation for two and a half hours. Is that in accordance with your wishes?'

Again, this was normal procedure and all agreed. Experience had produced traditions that worked. Nobody wished to disturb an equilibrium formed over the long years of the colony's existence.

This time, statements were given in the opposite direction to the round robin and Jai spoke first.

Having already introduced his sector and their preferences, he expressed their desired outcome in a simple statement. 'Marzero's reached a stage that's a danger to our existence in Marion. It's clear they've no scruples in attacking us. Their failed attempt to destroy all sentient males here shows a total disregard for the sanctity of life. If we don't deal with it, we leave ourselves open to further attacks.

'We can't ignore the greed and envy of their PM. And we won't tolerate their brutality. Their society's a cancer on this planet. In the opinion of this sector we face a unique situation. The Zeros will never voluntarily alter their lifestyle to one acceptable to us. We're in a position where the only viable solution is to end all life at Marzero or spend the rest of our lives in danger of destruction.'

Gasps of shock met what seemed an extreme desired outcome. At this stage, however, discussion wasn't part of the protocol. Self-discipline and tolerance ensured each of the other reps gave their own response. Only then did the assembly leave the table and gather in like-minded groups to enlarge on their collective desires.

Hoshiko joined Zaphod's faction, which numbered 12; the largest grouping in the room. They gathered around the flatscreen to enumerate their ideas and thoughts for further discussion.

'Genocide's too extreme. We should try to convert them to more civilised ways.' Zaphod's opening suggestion found favour. He'd say no more, unless asked a direct question.

'We must, at least, give the women a chance to understand they're subject to a cruel and unjust regime. Give them an opportunity to learn about equality and their natural place in life.' Hoshiko's observation also found much agreement and, as chair of the meeting, she'd make no further contribution at this point.

'But can we believe the Elite will alter in any meaningful way?' This, from Ramad, a fifth generation man from the family group begun by Rakesh and Maddie, and representing Da Vinci Sector.

Again, there was general agreement in the group. Hoshiko and Zaphod held back, but at the end of the two-hour period, they summed up the group's stance, weaving the various threads into a cohesive plan to take back to the table.

Another three smaller groups had gathered during the discussion phase and returned with their own conclusions. Now, they gathered around the table, their spokesperson seated on the left of each collective. The smallest group was nominated to present their case first, with the others following in ascending order of numbers.

Georgiy spoke for the smallest group. 'I represent the combined views of Roentgen Sector, Engineers, and Physicists.' He indicated the two other members. 'We conclude that discussion with the Zeros would be pointless and aimed mainly at alleviating our community's natural concerns for justice and our hope for continued peace.

'Unfortunately, their social structure, superstitious dogma, and religion makes peaceful settlement impossible. They're deceptive and dishonest. Anything they agreed couldn't be trusted and we'd be left with an indefinite period of doubt and uncertainty.

'They'll build weapons, which they're constructing even now, to defeat us. Our conclusion, then, is all-out attack to destroy the entire Marzero complex and all who live there.'

It came as no surprise they went straight for the jugular. They were known for direct action and reliance on unemotional theorems for solutions to daily problems.

Next spoke a less certain group. Madonna indicated her companions as she named the sectors represented. She was the voice of the Automators.

'And I represent the views of Feynman and Franklin Sectors, Cosmologists, and Chemists. We're not convinced we need to annihilate the entire community. Most women, and even some less

258

entrenched men may be saved. However, we've no serious plan as to how.

'We suggest any aggressive solution should involve droids, robots and automatons to reduce the risk to our people. Automatic devices can be rebuilt. Abliforms, regardless of advances in self-repair, risk death under violent action.'

'Speaking on behalf of Agriculturalists, University, and Tesla Sectors, I report our group's opposition to violent action unless as a last resort. Warfare in the past never solved problems. It only delayed them and produced difficulties further down the line.' Annika raised her hand in anticipation of Georgiy's expected comment, which didn't however materialise.

'We know the Cusp War solved our initial problems. But it also laid the basis for the very issues we're now facing over Marzero. Had we dealt with those matters radically at the time, we wouldn't have reached the current undesirable situation.

'We should infiltrate the Marzero coms system and spread educationally reforming info. We can promote a way of life free from the profit motive, exploitation and religious dogma. We feel such an approach is the best way forward.'

Georgiy rose and scanned the room. 'The pacifist approach is laudable and fits our philosophy. If we had time, we'd be happy to pursue it. But the Zeros, having failed in their attempt, will try again to destroy us rather than allow us to exist any longer in what they see as a more desirable state. They can't afford to let their citizens see us as a viable and better alternative.

'The Elite are so steeped in their addictions to power and wealth they're incapable of recognising a different point of view, let alone adopting it. If we don't act now to quell their warlike activities, we'll soon be fighting for our colony and our lives.

'Pre-emptive action's the only way we can stop a violent and possibly devastating attack.' He signalled a droid and it re-organised the Threedee into the centre of the table. Within secs, the FC was witnessing live activity at Marzero. The viewpoint switched from plant to plant, exposing military style preparations in factories and workshops. On parade grounds soldiers were being trained in battle techniques abandoned centuries before, but which epitomised the Marzero Elite's thinking.

'They're preparing to attack us. We've no choice but to act. I say we go in at once and in force.' Georgiy's manner gave no room for misunderstanding.

'Can't we attempt to save some? If we spread word of the truth of their situation, I'm sure many women, at least, will try to escape.'

'They may try, Anni. I doubt they'll succeed. The Elite won't want to lose what they see as a valuable asset. They'll kill anyone trying to flee the city.'

Annika nodded at Georgiy. 'I agree. But we might rescue some if we act quickly and intelligently. The Elite are uncivilised and corrupt. If we could somehow disable them, we'd have more time to organise a reasonable rescue mission.'

'Okay. That's an option.' Georgiy looked around. 'Anyone got a plan for disabling the Elite?'

'We have the technology to infiltrate and hack their systems. Prevent them communicating with everyone.' Madza sounded confident.

'How long to develop?'

'Now we can access the system Buzz controlled, I can infect them in four to six hours, depending how much damage we decide on. That's an immediate response. Later, we could try something more sophisticated.'

The collective liked this suggestion and authorised Madza to take a team to the SpyTeam unit and begin the process. They'd initially disable all Marzero coms. Then, with more time available, infiltrate their system to prevent all traffic from the Elite, but leave it open to traffic from Marion to reach all citizens.

'I might do something useful, if you let me free with a few special droids.' Maddie looked troubled by her offer, but put it forward anyway. 'The old Chinese models are fully functioning females. If we dress them in styles used by Elite consorts, we can infiltrate their society and spread any physical infection we want amongst the Elite men. We could wipe them out quite quickly.'

Zaphod agreed it was possible. 'I can produce a fast acting virus to infect their men through sex. Lethal and incurable. I know which virus to modify and how. However, there's a real danger the infection would spread to the Elite's captive women. We want to spare them more suffering. We need a different approach.'

'There's another issue.' Everyone looked at Kattu, a younger member who'd been silent through this part of the FC procedures. 'If we're planning intervention in the city, we need to disable the security regime surrounding Marzero.'

'Is that something you can do?'

'Yes.'

'Agreed we take this action?'

The meeting accepted unanimously.

'Right, Kattu, you know where the SpyTeam's housed?'

She smiled at Hoshiko. 'Madza will take me.'

'Off you go, then. And thank you. I think we should adjourn the meeting for now. Once we have these new ideas in place, we'll resume to decide our next steps. Agreed?'

The FC was satisfied with these interventions at this stage.

So, the battle for survival began, again. Whatever strategy they used to defeat the menace, there'd be deaths in Marzero. They hoped their plans would at least allow some people to be saved. What they'd do with them, they didn't yet know. But they'd deal with that issue once the threat of violent attack had been halted.

For now, they must decide exactly how to destroy Marzero's hierarchy. All-out war, with the inevitable slaughter, would be avoided if at all possible.

Chapter Forty Four

Reluctant though he was, Gabriel went along with her idea.

Her skills and abilities in this wild place amazed him. She seemed to know exactly where to look for the best food, how to trap and prepare it to eat. They finished their new shelter, made it more comfortable with dry bedding and more wood for the fire.

By evening, they had drinking water in various hollowed out bits of wood and dried gourds, fresh turkey meat, roasted over the flames, gathered fruit and nuts, and a cosy place to sleep.

They ate together in silence, both reluctant to open old wounds. Daisa needed answers to so many questions. Gabriel dwelt in a place of intense doubt, guilt and confusion. They entered the shelter after clearing up from their meal, and lay together on the soft bed of vegetation they'd collected.

'You do understand we all have to be naked here, Gabriel?'

'Yes. Buzz said it's the law.'

'Well?'

He stood and stripped, chucked his rags on the fire. As he turned back inside and looked at her, she saw the veil drop behind his eyes, signalling a fit. Weary beyond words, she rose and held him, waiting for it to pass. He emerged in his usual perplexed state and stared at her for a few moments until full consciousness returned.

'Sit.'

They both lowered to the ground inside the shelter.

'A vision?'

'Nothing. No words. No lights. Nothing, Daisa. Were they all like that?'

'Probably.'

'It was Stefan made me believe the God thing, wasn't it?'

'You heard him.'

'I'm a fraud. A liar! The things I did and said in the name of that God. The things I asked other people to do. The things I let happen to you! How can I ever ...?' He left the shelter.

262

Daisa watched him, the flickering light of the embers silhouetting him in the opening. He stood, immobile and hunched. It was clear he was sobbing silently, his body rocking slightly, his shoulders shaking with the sorrow that poured from him. She was too exhausted to give this the concentration and attention necessary.

'Come back inside, Gabriel. I'm cold here on my own.' It wasn't true, but she was beyond weary.

He moved out of view. 'I'm not worth it. Leave me be.'

For a while, she heard his grief and thought to comfort him, but fatigue overcame her after her efforts and hard work, and following her short sleep the previous night.

Gabriel allowed the initial sorrow to run its course. He moved back to the shelter and saw Daisa sleeping, curled and vulnerable. Stefan's threat returned to him.

'Bastard! I'll frackin kill you.'

He made sure she was deep in sleep before he moved again.

He had no plan. But now he knew the truth about Stefan's deception, fury consumed him. How had he allowed such abuse? He'd done everything Stefan had suggested, all because he'd been convinced it had been ordained by God. Now, with Daisa's explanation of her view on that, he was beginning to doubt God's existence. How could he have been so blind?

And Stefan had the audacity to blame Daisa for the trouble Stefan and he had caused. He wanted to humiliate her, hurt her. Buzz would help him. Daisa deserved so much better. She was innocent. Daisa deserved the best he could do for her. He must protect her. Find a way to stop them.

He took the spear Daisa had coached him to make. Approached their camp, following the route he'd taken the night before; proud he remembered the way.

The fire was burning brightly again and the two men sat glumly on one of the logs.

'Not much of a hunter, then?'

'Never learned. Usually scrounged food from one of the other lot in here. The kids were pretty good at the start. None here now; they're all too old for that lark. I got them to feed me. This time, Daisa did the necessary. She's frackin brilliant at surviving out here.'

'Not goin soft on me, Buzz? I'm countin on you helpin me give the twat what she deserves. Then I'll hold her down for you.'

'Sounds interesting. Never understood why women don't get it. They're made for our fun and pleasure. Can't see why they resist and pretend it's no good for them. They're all gagging for it. But they have to make a fuss and demand we treat them gently. Be great to have one exactly the way I like. We'll do it tomorrow. Catch her on her own. Make sure that moronic friend of yours can't butt in.'

'No more use for that moronic twat. He served his purpose, for a while. Best we take him out, though. Plenty of rocks. Won't take much to put him out of our misery.'

'Oh. Right. Yeah. I mean, he's not supposed to be here anyway. The Council will probably send him back to Marzero for execution. We can blame him for what happens to Daisa. You can come back to the community with me and we'll tell them all the trouble was his fault.'

'Great idea, Buzz.'

Gabriel's fury grew, but he remained silent in his hiding place. It was late before they entered their shelter. He waited again. Made sure they were well asleep.

He had only a wooden spear. And it was two against one. He looked at the roaring fire and could see no other way, dangerous though it might be.

A flaming brand in one hand, his spear in the other, he sneaked into the shelter. Stefan first. The pointed stick needed all his weight, but it penetrated the flesh. Pulling it back out, as Stefan struggled, wasn't easy. He had to stand on the struggling man's belly and pull hard. Buzz woke at the noise. Gabriel hit him with the firebrand as he rose. The burning stick broke on impact, and he used his spear on Buzz.

Stefan was clearly dying, crying out in pain, but unable to save himself. Buzz tried to rise as the burning brand filled the shelter with smoke from the bedding. Gabriel had to kick him back down and use the spear again. Satisfied both men were dead or dying, he left the shelter, coughing as smoke filled his lungs.

It took time for him to recover, sitting on the log near the fire as he breathed in the fresh night air to clear the pollution from his chest. When he turned at last to check behind him, he saw the shelter was ablaze.

The tree that held it upright caught fire. The draught roaring and drowning the dying moans of his victims. An adjacent tree burst into flames.

The danger suddenly dawned on him. He hesitated. What to do? There was nothing.

He ran back to where Daisa slept. Woke her.

'There's a fire, Daisa. We've got to get out of here.'

She was awake at once. 'What's happened?'

He couldn't add to her distrust. Sometimes, honesty might not be the best way. 'Thought I heard shouting. Went to see the other two. When I got there, the shelter was on fire. Some of the trees are burning as well. We have to get out of here. The fire's spreading.'

She studied him in the light of their own fire's embers. Did she believe him? He couldn't be sure. But now wasn't the time for doubt. They must escape the fire.

The water they'd gathered, she poured on their own fire. She scattered the ashes with her spear to make sure it wouldn't rekindle.

'We have to go, Daisa.'

The sound and smell of the forest fire was now evident, even at their distance from it. Daisa considered the options. The wilderness was up beyond the high cliff and they'd have to scale the fence installed on the boundary to prevent examinees escaping the Risk. The only gate was on the far side of the area now blazing.

'Come. We've a long way to go, but it's the only sensible option.'

She picked up her spear and stuck her wooden dagger back in the vine tied around her waist.

He took her hand. 'Let's go.'

Chapter Forty Five

The droids and the man on duty were at the gate, attracted by the smoke. Now it was open, ending the prohibition on contact, she gave him details, explaining there were two victims who were probably dead.

She grasped Gabriel by the shoulder. 'We can do no more.'

He shrugged her off, guilt and regret tormenting him now they were out of danger and the reality of his action hit him. She let go but stood close, ready for the inevitable reaction. The sound of motors alerted them to the passing fleet of hovers equipped to fight the fire, now raging furiously in the centre of the Risk.

'They'll soon have it under control,' the man on duty at the gate assured her. He glanced at Gabriel. 'He the so-called prophet from Marzero?'

Daisa put her arm about his shoulders. 'Leave him to me, please.'

'Dangerous, isn't he? Insane, they say.'

'Not insane. Brain defect. He's no threat to me. I'd like a chance to get him through this as gently as possible. One of the victims was his friend.'

'Put you in danger, though, didn't he? Nearly got you killed. Sure you want to help him, Daisa?'

'Not him, the dead one. I know Gabriel well. He'll face justice when we leave Recovery. For now, let me get him through his grief. Please.'

The man shrugged. 'Suit yourself. The droids will prepare your clothes and something for him. Everything'll be ready when you're fit to go back into the community.'

'Thank you.'

Unbidden, came the thought that the incident had probably rid Marion of the problem of Buzz. She examined this idea and accepted it as a logical conclusion that made no comment on her warmth or concern as a caring abliform.

But Gabriel was wracked with guilt for surviving an incident in which his friend had died. That this reaction was utterly illogical made no difference to its intensity. Such errors, caused by irrational religious beliefs, had been eradicated in Marion. But Marzero was a primitive society still under the spell of superstition that influenced so many decisions.

'We have to go, Gabriel. There's a recognised protocol. I'll guide you. But you must do as I say. Understand?'

He was vague. Disconnected. 'Do you understand, Gabriel?'

He faced her. Blinked. Nodded.

Beyond the gate, they entered the Recovery Suite and passed first through the shower system, cleansing them of dirt, sweat, dust and smoke. She took him to the cubicles where surface bacteria, picked up from the wilderness, were neutralised.

From there, they moved into the grooming area. Here, droids brought their hair back to some semblance of normality. Daisa opted for a bob after her period of long tresses and asked them to shave Gabriel free of his beard and cut his locks to shoulder length.

They moved to the rest area. Daisa's clothing hung ready, and she slipped on her light robe of deep red. Gabriel was given a short wrap-around in olive green and an open, sleeveless jerkin in sage. Both continued barefoot.

Throughout, Gabriel remained silent. Now, as they sat at a round wooden table on comfortable chairs, droids prepared a meal to Daisa's tastes. She selected a light sparkling wine to accompany the chicken dish and they ate in comfort. Quiet, restful music welcomed them back to the normal world.

After they'd eaten, they talked together, lounging in the rest room with drinks of their choice. Gabriel finally answered Daisa's questions and she learned the truth about her brush with execution.

'So, it was Stefan who had me arrested. Why did you stay with him so long?'

'I didn't know until today. Anyway, I believed I was doing the will of God.'

'That's your excuse for everything you did?'

He looked hurt, anxious. 'Not excuse; reason. You're an unbeliever. You can't understand what it means to have faith.'

'You know now there's no god?'

'I'm not sure. Stefan made up things so he could use me to spread his ideas to the people, get on the right side of the PM. He was ambitious. Wanted to be one of the Elite.'

'But you know you never spoke with, or saw, this god?'

'I do now. I thought I was special. Chosen. I believed God wanted me to tell the people good news.' He covered his face with his hands and was silent for as long as Daisa let him dwell on his acts.

'You were used, Gabriel.'

'It was all lies. I'm mad. My brain's broken.'

She reached out to him, took his hand in hers to comfort him.

He pulled free, moved back and stared at her with such pain in his eyes. 'I said terrible things about you, Daisa. I nearly got you killed. How can you even talk to me?'

She turned her face away, unwilling to let him see her own confusion. 'There were reasons for what you did. You were terrified.'

'But I said things … they were going to … I mean, that was my fault, Daisa. I'm really, truly sorry.'

'You're a good man who was fooled by an error in your brain and the wicked lies of a man you believed was your friend. You were trusting, Gabriel. It was your goodness, your innocence, that let you be taken in.'

Abruptly, he stood and turned to face her. Dropped to his knees before her. 'I killed them, Daisa. It wasn't an accident. I burnt them to death!'

She leant forward, gathered him into her arms and cradled his head in her lap. 'Thank you. Thank you for putting an end to two wicked men who wanted to rape and murder me, Gabriel. You did the only thing possible in the circumstances. No need to feel guilty about stopping their evil intentions coming true. You're a hero. My hero. A good man.'

For a while, he lay still, his face hidden in the softness of her robe, his tears wetting the fabric and her skin beneath. She stroked his hair as he wept.

When, at last, he raised his head and she wiped his face with tissues, she kissed him. At first in gratitude, then in passion.

Later, the hardness of the floor made them rise and sit again. The droid returned at Daisa's call. Mixed fresh drinks.

'I don't know how you can even look at me after what I've done, Daisa. But I'm so glad you can. I love you.'

'You were raised in a society designed to make you believe certain ideas, to value false promises and accept unproven myths as truth. No wonder you're confused, Gabriel. You've been brainwashed since birth to have faith in a higher power. It's a powerful and seductive notion that infected billions on Earth. But science shows those ideas are mistaken. I've been raised in a world of science and logic and ...'

'What is science, exactly?'

'It isn't "exactly" anything. It's an attempt to understand everything natural and man-made. And good science is constantly under review as new facts become known and new hypotheses are proven. Science that wears the mantle of perfection is as corrupt as religion. So we don't let that happen.'

'You really think religion's bad? Isn't it a way to get people to be good?'

Daisa was encouraged by his questioning. 'A lot of folk on Earth thought religion was superstition, spirituality, belief in supernatural powers, even a belief in gods. It's partly all those things, but, really, religion's a tool to preserve social order, a method of organising large-scale cooperation. It's a management tool used by leaders to control behaviour.'

'So you're saying it's all false. All made up? You don't believe any of it, Daisa?'

'Look at the evidence. I mean, really look; examine it. Every so-called sacred text ever written is full of contradictions, you know. The

Bible, Qur'an and Talmud in particular are chockfull of inconsistencies. And historical records show the prophets often let practical considerations influence the words they passed on to their followers. Not really the words of God at all. We know the truth, of course, since we can see it from a distance.

'And they're full of ancient rules that no longer have meaning. Things like not eating pork because it's considered unclean. That comes from the time before medicine understood all about the parasites in pigs that cause disease. But we know they can be eradicated by proper cooking. Those rules were made by men who didn't know how the universe works.'

'You think religion causes problems. I preached my faith for what I thought was good.'

Now wasn't the time to debunk his whole world. Let that come later. At least he was thinking about the lies he'd been taught. For the moment, she had to restore his self-confidence, enable him to come to terms with his part in the process that had caused such conflict between the two settlements.

'Religion alone doesn't cause the problems. It's when you combine it with the greed of the wealthy and powerful, both addictive qualities. Wealth always wants more wealth. Power always seeks more power. Religion's used as justification for their actions. If a god says certain things are true, and people are brainwashed into believing that god is real, then the things said by their god must be true. It's known as circular reasoning: "this" is true because "that" is true. But, in reality, if "this" isn't really true, then "that" isn't true either. Sorry, that's not describing it very well.'

'No. That's okay. I get what you're saying. If God's a myth, the words of God can't be trusted.'

'Exactly. Religion works by first presenting a god as a real entity. It follows that anything such a supreme being "says" must be true. The fact that the words all came from men makes no difference to those taught from birth that they're the words of a god. It's a self-perpetuating lie that grows over time to become a vast, overpowering machine to subdue the less well off, keep them ill-educated, and make them slaves to the wealthy.

'They carried on the system in Marzero, because the men in charge were short-sighted, selfish, greedy and pretty stupid. You were just a victim. One with a special talent for persuasion that made you an ideal tool they could use to spread their lies even further. You're not to blame.'

It was enough for now. She had to let these thoughts find a home in his mind, allow them to mature and form questions and answers that might help him come to terms with the reality.

They slept apart in the small rooms provided for returners from the Risk.

Morning brought breakfast served by droids who informed them the fire had been quenched and the remains of both victims sent for recycling. They spent the day relaxing, preparing for the trials and tests ahead. But, after an early evening meal, fed and refreshed, the pair finally left Recovery.

Daisa led Gabriel along wide paved pathways across grassed terraces and down to the Transhub terminal to take them back to the central complex. They passed a sports field where women were practising.

'What are they doing?'

Daisa glanced across and smiled at memories of fun she'd had at Uni. 'Playing hockey. You had sports arenas at Marzero; didn't women play games?'

'Women don't do sport. Only men. Boxing, rugball, baseball, footy. It isn't right for women to perform like that in public.'

'But it's fine for them to be displayed naked in front of thousands, to take off their clothes to entertain crowds of men?'

Gabriel stopped. 'What life have I been living, Daisa? How did I never see the hypocrisy? Did you play?'

'You were raised with hypocrisy. Not your fault. Hockey? Love the game. I'll play again, now I'm home. Did you?'

'Sport's for professionals. You pay to watch them compete.'

'Here, we use sport to keep fit; as a social activity. For fun.'

'This place is amazing! We were told you all lived like savages. They said the women were just call girls; the men all bullies and tyrants.'

'It's not unusual for dictators to depict their own faults as those of their enemies.'

'I knew you were clever, Daisa. I wish you'd been able to tell me the truth earlier.'

'Me, too. But you wouldn't have believed me. Not then. And, to tell the truth, I was far too interested in studying you for a research project. I'm sorry. I should've been more honest from the start. Forgive me?'

'Forgive you? Nothing to forgive, Daisa. I'm the one needs forgiving.'

She stopped and kissed him. 'And you are. We have to attend Full Council, Gabriel. They'll want you to give an account of your actions. It'll be a type of trial where you'll have to be completely honest in your responses to questions asked. Are you ready for such an ordeal?'

He blinked at her in the gathering dusk. 'It doesn't matter. I'm a fraud. I deserve whatever happens to me.' He dropped to his knees on the path before her. 'I'm so sorry, Daisa. I was a fool.'

Daisa helped him to his feet. 'Like I said, you're a victim of an evil system. Shall we see what the Council think?'

'Now?'

'No, silly. Tomorrow. And we'll catch up on what's been happening here in Marion while we wait.'

She took him to her pod, introduced him to A79663, who arrived to cater to them. 'This is Abby. Abby, Gabriel. He may be staying here a while.'

'As you wish, Daisa. Shall I prepare the spare room?'

'For now. Thanks.'

Gabriel watched the droid move into the spare room. 'Is that droid yours?'

'It serves me and a couple of other residents.'

'Amazing!'

'Before you get all enthusiastic, let's see what they make of you in the morning. For now, I'm still tired, and I think it would be sensible for us both to have a good long sleep. Alone.'

He studied her at arm's length for a long time before he hugged her. Then he turned and walked into the spare room.

Chapter Forty Six

The Council Chamber was full, and abuzz with talk and activity as Daisa entered with Gabriel in tow, two guardian droids in attendance. Hoshiko remained as chair from the previous day's discussion and spotted Daisa as she came in. She raised her hand for quiet.

The FC was present due to Daisa's warning of Gabriel's hearing. Those around the table completed their statements and then settled into silence, all eyes turned to the pair who waited by the entrance, just within the Chamber.

'Welcome, Daisa. I gather we have you to thank for a solution to the problem of Buzz?'

'Not me, Hoshiko.' Daisa explained that Gabriel had been responsible, without giving full details.

'Thank you, Gabriel. Prophet of the People, I understand? This will be an informal hearing.' Hoshiko invited them into the body of the Chamber.

Daisa spoke up straight away. 'As you say, the figure of mythical power from Marzero. But not any more. He suffers a neurological condition that was abused and taken advantage of by the vile user, Stefan.

'An accident, involving Zaphod of all people, gave that wicked man a chance to trick Gabriel into believing he'd witnessed God. Given Gabriel's mental state after one of his episodes, when he's particularly open to suggestion, it's no surprise he was taken in by lies told by a man he mistakenly took as a long-term friend.

'Now he understands what really happened, he's deeply sorry for the trouble he's caused our community and me personally. I've forgiven him, because I know the facts. But Gabriel wishes to address the Council, Hoshiko.'

'If you're willing to give this man a chance, I can't see how we can refuse, Daisa. Gabriel, please say your piece.' Hoshiko gestured him to approach the table.

Gabriel stood so he was fully visible to all around the table. Daisa moved beside him.

'First, I'm deeply sorry for what I've done. I apologise to everyone at Marion. I know now I've been misinformed all my life. I've lived the lie we were all told by the Elite of Marzero. A whole series of lies. My short time here has already convinced me Marion's where I'll find the truth. Marzero's a place of dishonesty, falsehood and the self-servin propaganda of the Elite. And the Clerics they employ to keep the population uneducated and under control.'

He cleared his throat. 'This is hard. I've done a lot of harm. I nearly killed the only woman who's ever had any real meanin for me. The woman I love.' He turned to Daisa, who tilted her head toward him. He went on to tell the tale from his confused viewpoint. Of the incident in the Risk, on Daisa's advice, he merely mentioned he'd witnessed the deaths of Buzz and Stefan. When he'd finished his account, he waited to discover their verdict.

'Do you still believe you were a messenger of your god?'

He turned to Madza. 'No, sir. I was tricked into that lie.'

'Do you still believe in any god?'

He turned to Georgiy. 'I don't know, sir. I'm learnin from Daisa. But I've had this faith all my life. It's been my guide and passion. I'm not ready to let it go completely. But I want to learn more about your beliefs and ways of thinkin.'

'Honest, at any rate.' Georgiy gestured to Hoshiko to continue.

'Please wait outside whilst we formulate our response, Gabriel. Daisa, perhaps you'll stay with him?'

The pair left the Chamber but were recalled after a short period of discussion.'

'Given the peculiarities of your history, the brain condition that affects your ability to perceive, the indoctrination you endured in Marzero and the mitigating circumstances supplied by Daisa, we're minded to place you on probation. That means you're free to come and go as you wish, but must always be accompanied by at least one adult. If Daisa's willing to act as your guarantor, we're happy to accept that.'

Daisa nodded her agreement.

Gabriel, astounded by the generosity of the community, tried to express his thanks but felt he failed. 'I've apologised already, but it's not enough. I have to put right what I've done wrong. I've an idea. Please be patient while I explain what I've got in mind.'

The members signalled to Hoshiko she should allow him to proceed. She turned to Gabriel. 'Please tell us what you intend.'

'I think you've got invisibility suits? Yes. Will one fit me?'

'They stretch to fit most. You're a bit shorter and more muscular than Madza, but the suit he wore should do.' Georgiy signalled a droid and sent it on an errand.

'I want to go back to Marzero.'

Gasps of surprise greeted this.

'Sorry, I don't mean to live there. To take action. I know the route to get to the centre of the Elite's control centre, where they live and operate from. If I'm invisible, I can kill the leadin members. The PutinMaister's got to go before any changes will happen at Marzero. He's the chief. What he says goes. If he's dead, there'll be fightin by the other Elites who'll want to succeed him. Some are bound to be killed.'

'You intend to do this alone, Gabriel?'

Gabriel glanced at Zaphod. 'I can't expect anyone from here to help. I'll probably be killed, which I deserve. But the people in Marion are innocent and I can't ask them to risk their lives to put right what I made wrong.'

'You're taking a lot of responsibility for things that aren't of your sole making, Gabriel.' Zaphod faced the young man, smiling with welcome. 'It seems even I played a part in your deception. I'm not the god you thought me. Merely a man with a shiny skin. But I can help you. Before you risk your life, would you let me repair the damage that causes your lapses of awareness so you no longer suffer fits?'

'You can really do that?'

'It's relatively simple. I'll have you functioning as normal in a matter of hours. Shall we do it?'

'Please, Sir! Please.' Gabriel was almost overcome by the offer but steeled himself to continue with his suggestion. 'But, I must finish my idea, please. The PM's death'll bring chaos to the city. There'll be fightin and killin. Once they're not scared of revenge by the Elite, the people will turn on the police, the Specials and the ESOs. Kill them. They're hated forces that take advantage of their position to abuse everybody. I can set all this goin, but I don't know what to do after.'

Hoshiko gave Council time to absorb this info and comment among themselves before calling the meeting back to order. 'There's much merit in Gabriel's offer. But we need to refine it. It could allow us to take control of Marzero without the mass killing we thought our only option. Let's retire into cells, and produce strategies for the immediate future, based on Gabriel's suggestion.'

Like-minded groups formed around smaller tables and discussed possible solutions. The droid Georgiy had sent out returned with its burden. He left his group for a few moments to approach Gabriel. 'Here. Try this on. Stay with him, Daisa. We don't want him to disappear, do we?' He handed her the invisisuit.

Daisa took him to a small committee room and helped him into the suit. It fitted well. He wanted to check its performance, so she took his hand and led him back through the Chamber, where her appearance was unremarked, except by Georgiy.

'I asked you to stay with him, Daisa.'

She turned to Gabriel. 'That enough evidence for you?'

There was no response at first. 'Sorry. You can't see me at all!' He peeled back the head covering to show Georgiy, who grinned at him.

'An old joke, but you'll do.'

Daisa led him back to the small room, where he changed out of the invisisuit. 'You're quite a sight. I'm tempted to spend more time with you.'

'I don't deserve such …'

'Let me decide what I deserve, Gabriel. Make a good job of this new start and who knows what might come of it?'

They returned to the FC, where they were invited to sit and await the outcomes of the various discussions whilst droids provided refreshments.

After lunch, reports from SpyTeam were presented to the assembly. Marzero was clearly preparing an all-out attack on Marion. The danger was urgent though not yet imminent, as they were still building land and air craft to deliver explosive devices usually employed in mining operations. They'd ceased all other mechanical projects to concentrate on the coming attack. It was obvious they'd soon be in a position to start their war.

Once the reports were completed, Georgiy asked CenCom to calculate the likely start date and time for the assault. They'd be ready at dawn in two days.

'Time for action.' Hoshiko gathered the FC back round the table and took proposals, letting Gabriel and Daisa remain as observers, and inviting Gabriel to make comments he felt relevant to the suggestions made.

In the end, they decided Gabriel would lead a party of six, including, at their insistence, Daisa and Georgiy, to infiltrate the Elite's headquarters and do as much damage as possible. Coms were already disabled, as was the electronic security ring round the city. This had caused the would-be aggressors a good deal of grief. But they were determined to pursue their scheme.

One late report caused Gabriel great heartache as he learned his huge group of followers who'd set out to attack Marion, had mostly perished from lack of food and water. Their bodies were scattered over a long tract of wilderness less than half the distance from Marzero.

A few determined and hardy individuals had made it to within 200 ks of the nearest Marion township of Michelangelo. Droids and robots had confined them in a temporary holding compound, where they were being fed and sheltered until a decision could be made about the next move.

'Too many bodies to deal with for now. We'll recycle them when the conflict's over. Probably have more to deal with anyway.' Zaphod's observation made an already sober gathering even more serious.

'We have to accept a lot of Zeros will die. We've no choice. They're intent on destroying us, so we must respond in a way that'll end all chance of future conflict. We were far too lenient after the Cusp War and look what's happened.' Georgiy's statement put into words what most of those present thought.

'Are all their security systems disabled, not just the boundary?'

The control group confirmed they'd put the entire system out of action. Marzero now had no way of detecting any approach from outside, except using physical observation by people placed on watch. And they'd put such a system in place along the near boundary.

'So, they're expecting us to attack.'

'They'll do whatever they can to defend themselves, regardless of cost to the people they use.' Gabriel's confirmation settled their plans.

It took very little time to conclude the full operational planning. Madza and Sarma insisted on joining the raiding party.

The Transhub could take them quite close. Although the city had destroyed their main terminal, a gang of constructobots had already placed a temporary one below the horizon, five ks from the boundary.

In the interim, techs had engineered nanocams on the exterior of the suits, set to an ultra-narrow IR wavelength. These would provide a ghost image of each wearer to the others. Earpieces would allow users to communicate with one another whilst remaining undetected by outsiders. It was an ingenious solution to the problem of group cohesion and one that gave team members more confidence.

'Potentially, we could be tackling close to 1500 unpleasant men and their subordinates, numbering at least five times that. And that's just the Elite section. The city has a total population of two and a half mill at the last count ...'

'I lost nearly 300,000 in the wilderness.'

'That many, Gabriel? Neptune's Balls, you had some following.'

Hoshiko nodded. 'It's easier to convince the uneducated and superstitious who've been brainwashed since birth, but that's still a remarkable number.'

'So. We have our plan. We're ready to start?'

All those involved directly, the raiding party and SpyTeam, were consulted and all were set for action.

'Okay. Let's get this done. The sooner we start, the sooner we can return to some normality.'

Hoshiko nodded. 'Whilst you're involved in the fighting and everything that goes with it, Zaphod and I will form a group tasked with devising a plan for what happens after the conflict's over. We know too well the disasters that occur after any conflict without adequate planning for the aftermath.'

The Council members and active participants went their ways to points of duty or departure. The group of volunteers destined for Marzero, already nicknamed "Insurgents", were unsure how they felt about that name, but adopted it anyway.

Chapter Forty Seven

The Transhub took them to the temporary terminal. The group of six Insurgents left their clothes aboard the drum and walked the first three ks before donning their invisisuits. Swiftly, they crossed into the cultivated strip that provided the city with food. Abliform and automated workers tended various crops and livestock. All the living labourers were male and emaciated.

They reached the boundary and, from here, Gabriel took the lead. There'd been a short discussion about trust, but Daisa's insistence that he'd changed and his regret was genuine, had been enough. For now.

He led them past the security observers and through streets already transformed by the shutdown of the Elite's coms.

Gangs of men roamed the byways, looting, and assaulting any woman unwise or desperate enough to be out on her own. Small groups of women, carrying makeshift weapons; knives, stout metal bars, even kitchen implements, dashed between shops and pods. The men didn't bother these.

Police, in units of at least four, were evident but ineffective. Demoralised and lacking leadership, they picked on the vulnerable and unprotected.

The Insurgents moved quickly in single file. At one point, they encountered a makeshift roadblock composed of display tables and cabinets raided from a nearby shop now devoid of stock. The owner was sprawled in the entrance, dried blood pooled around his head. Nobody manned the barrier and its purpose was unclear.

They took a different route and had to skirt a large gang of drunken men with their chosen females indulging in an impromptu orgy.

At the entrance to the Elite's complex, Gabriel gathered them into a tight circle. 'They can't see us. But they've sensitive listening devices hidden everywhere. We'll need to keep quiet.'

'Hasn't SpyTeam disabled those?'

'Can we be sure?'

'I'll find out.' Daisa connected. 'As far as they can tell, all security systems are completely deactivated. They advise caution but are confident we're as inaudible as we are invisible.'

They relaxed a little but decided on minimal conversation as they infiltrated corridors and sought out their intended victims. This was an execution assignment and each carried an invisipak containing weapons and small packs of an extreme incendiary explosive. Once in use, their location would be known, so they had to wait until they were near their targets before revealing their pulse guns, laser blades, or lethal poison syringes for close quarters use.

None of them relished killing indiscriminately and without a 'fair' fight. But the numbers and Marzero's proposed aggressive strike precluded a less violent approach. They understood all too well the need for their attack and its success. All had volunteered knowing exactly what they must do.

Gabriel was unsure what they'd find in the PM's private quarters. But he thought it unlikely he'd still be living the pampered and dissolute life he'd exhibited when he and Stefan had been summoned to his presence.

Their first clue to the top man's priorities became clear as they entered the first space on the route to his personal living space. The previous two guards had been replaced. Six fully armed ESOs crowded the entrance, forming an impenetrable barrier with their bulk. Each Insurgent took an individual guard. Silent killing. Weapons would reveal their presence far too early and bring up many more to defend the PM.

The group approached, across the wide space, as one. They planned to attack all six at once, giving no chance for resistance or self-defence, using martial arts techniques honed during early years.

Only Gabriel lacked these skills, taught as a form of physical discipline rather than a way of killing. He used fists and feet in a clumsy but effective effort to fell his target. The other five were dead as they hit the ground. Daisa, next to Gabriel, finished off the man he'd knocked to the floor.

They dragged the obstructing bodies from the entrance, piled them to one side, and entered the corridor. To their amazement, they found the space occupied exactly as it had been during Gabriel's visit; women clad in jewellery or body decoration. The nearest pair glanced at the doors as they opened and closed. But the lack of apparent visitors had them shrugging and unconcerned. They went back to the virtual games they were playing.

The Insurgents passed through their ranks in absolute silence and without contact. At the end of this first wide corridor, another two ESOs stood guard. Oblivious to the fall of their colleagues, they chatted idly to each other as Daisa and Madza swiftly felled them.

The women saw the men fall. But, ill-fitted for action or decision-making, they simply continued their games, knowing the PM would summon them when needed. Relaxation meant they were spared tedious and demeaning duties.

One more corridor and entrance would lead them to the space occupied by the PM. This time, the guards on duty at the opposite side of the vestibule noticed the opening doors and lack of visitors. They'd been briefed on Daisa's rescue mission and the Marionets' use of invisisuits. But it took them a vital few secs to recognise the series of events as evidence of a similar attack. By then, two Insurgents had robbed them of the need to consider anything ever again.

On the other side of the door, they came on the PM, so engaged in a sadistic game of master and slave he was unaware of danger. A trio of women, arms tied back, tried to escape as he goaded them with an electric probe. They screamed when it contacted sensitive parts of their bodies. The scene made their task easier, providing another motive for ending this worthless life.

They took the probe from him. He yelled in shock. Freed from their torment, the women were more interested in releasing each other than worrying about the fate of the PM. Once free, they took to the soft seats to tend their hurts.

Madza connected with SpyTeam and asked them to set in motion the planned citywide display of the PM's room, reconnecting the city's coms under their control. Fitted with cameras at different levels and directions, the display from Elite HQ made an ideal Threedee show.

As planned, in a scene designed to demean and damn the Elite, what Zeros now witnessed all over the city, on private and public displays, was their leader, apparently caught out masturbating. Sarma, a gifted mimic, spoke with his feeble voice, as the hand working the PM's own on his member, ceased the massage. 'All workin parties stop, right now. Today's a day for rest and fun. Go and enjoy yourselves. Or die!'

The PM himself, remained speechless, and wore a confused expression, making him appear foolish.

'Shouldn't we try to get him on side?' Daisa asked the question most of the Insurgents wanted answering.

'He'll never give up power voluntarily. We've got, maybe, five minutes before this room fills with guards. If you think you can convert this man in that time, by all means …'

It was hopeless. The Insurgents had accepted the lethal nature of their mission at the start. Now they had to complete it. They marched him to the windows looking over the city, causing him to walk as unnaturally as possible to hold viewers' attention. This fifth floor, the highest point in the city, gave extensive views. Below, a crowd was gathering to be at the place where the unexpected display was taking place. The Threedee in the square was visible from the window.

Daisa took her laser from the bag at her back and swiftly cut through the double layer of glass. She pushed it out of place. The two panes floated quickly down the slope of the pyramid until they crashed with a million brittle jangles on the hard surface below.

'You next.' Daisa whispered in the PM's ear.

Gabriel leant forward and spoke softly into his leader's ear. 'You could've been a good leader. But chose to be a selfish dictator. Learn what your cruelty brings.' And he gave the small shove that propelled the PM into space, making the execution appear as suicide, to further discredit the Elite and spread as much dissent as possible.

He cried out only once, as he connected with the solid glass making up much of the slope of the pyramid. From there, he bounced, rolled and tumbled to the ground, gaining speed. They turned away as they heard the splat of flesh, the crack of bones, as he smacked against a surface harder than any he'd lain on in life.

In the square, the crowd rushed to assure themselves he was dead. Word spreading fast, they cheered.

Those closest, raised the body and paraded their erstwhile leader as a destroyed tyrant for all to see.

Behind them, in the PM's quarters, activity began as other Elites in the complex quickly realised their leader was gone. Some came to find out what had caused his sudden demise. Two approached the window and looked out. They were sent down the slope, by Gabriel, to join him.

Others in this first group, the next rank of Elites, stopped the guards who arrived, explaining all was under control and they weren't needed. None of these ambitious hedonists understood the reality of the situation. They saw only the opportunity for personal advancement. The officers sent to guard them were now confused about who led them, took the easy decision of obeying the first orders they received, and returned to their posts.

Free now to indulge themselves in all the luxuries of the PM's office, they ordered the women to organise food and drinks as they gathered round a central table raised from the floor.

The women brought chairs and the five remaining Elites sat to decide who'd be the next leader. But it was secs only before rivalry and ambition set them against one another. Obese, pampered and unfit, none of them was physically capable of hurting another.

Their attempts at fighting were laughable. But they only realised their antics were on display to the entire city when two of the third tier Elites came up to warn them. At this point, one of the more ambitious and determined returned to the fallen guards and grabbed two pulse guns. Without hesitation or warning, he fired on his fellow Elites. The Insurgents had to move quickly out of range, as his aim was poor. Eventually, he killed all opposition.

This man strode over the bodies of the fallen and clambered with some difficulty on to the table, forcing a couple of women to help him. In a parody of an entertainment many times regurgitated for profit rather than art, he thumped his chest and yelled in triumph. 'I, Otto, am now PutinMaister. I declare this day a public holiday. The city will give food and drink to everyone. Retailers, keep records. The treasury will pay you. Food and drink only. Go, my people, enjoy yourselves at the expense of Otto, PutinMaister of Marzero!'

The Insurgents could've hoped for no better outcome. The city would quickly degenerate into a mixture of chaos and disorganised celebration, with the Elite left in shock and disunity.

As the team made their way down through the building, they encountered small groups of lower rank Elites in physical combat, most of it laughable. They gave a helping push or kick, here and there, to encourage the fighting.

Emboldened by the example of their new leader, some men relieved fallen guards of weapons and turned them on colleagues. The Insurgents dodged such lethal activities but disarmed and killed all guards they encountered as they left: these men constituted a significant threat, and preserving their lives threatened those of innocents in Marzero as well as the population of Marion.

Gabriel led the party from the Trumpyramid, through streets growing increasingly chaotic. He took them to the factories, where new weapons of war were being manufactured.

The sites were large and diverse and the Insurgents split into pairs and used the SpyTeam to find the plants where the greatest threats existed. Daisa and Gabriel moved into the aircraft factory to commit their sabotage. With all employees released by the diktats of the old and new PutinMaisters, the works were occupied only by robots. Security was non-existent.

Under SpyTeam control, the robots turned the manufacturing process into destructive chaos from which recovery would be very difficult.

Once they'd wrecked the processing capability, they collected all weapons and piled them at the heart of the processing works. Gabriel and Daisa placed their incendiary explosives to act as detonators. SpyTeam would initiate the blast after the Insurgents left the city.

The remaining pairs of Insurgents carried out the same tactics in plants dealing with land vehicles and mining equipment being converted into heavy artillery.

Once finished, they reconvened and returned to the Transhub drum, to set off back to Marion, unopposed.

'Too easy! Too simple by far.' Daisa's troubled observation found agreement amongst the whole group.

'But a great result.' Gabriel was still high on their success.

'Now, the real fight begins. There'll be more deaths from the explosions, but we'll still have 2,000,000 angry, badly-led people to deal with. That's our most demanding task. I just hope those back in Marion come up with a plan that means we don't have to engage in more killing.' Madza spoke for them all.

They travelled back in sober mood, knowing the war was far from over. It had hardly begun.

Chapter Forty Eight

The specially convened Aggression Council, met in the Chamber to discuss next steps. Reports from various teams were rendered largely obsolete by videos relayed by SpyTeam.

The three main factories were smouldering ruins. Even Marion's advanced construction teams wouldn't be able to restore them quickly. For the backward technology of Marzero, the task would be a marathon that CenCom estimated would take half a year. And that assumed the new PM would retain control, and find a way to communicate with his people. Unlikely, since the SpyTeam had infiltrated their coms so successfully they could immediately hack and destroy every structure newly created.

'We can't be complacent. Let's look at the current situation dispassionately and consider possible developments.' Hoshiko had been voted to remain as chair and the AC, reduced to a more manageable team of nine, signalled agreement.

'To summarise.' Zaphod listed known factors as evaluated at present. 'First, they've an unstable, partially functioning leadership, subject to insurrection at any moment. Next, they've no manufacturing capacity able to produce new weapons or a weapon transport system within the coming half year.

'They've lost a large portion of their population through their ill-considered attack attempt. And more from the savagery resulting from the unlimited free drinks provided by the new PM. Estimates suggest half a million. We're now dealing with a demoralised mob numbering close to 2,000,000; still a sizeable threat.

'They've deliberately disabled their access to the Transhub, an odd decision on their part, since it reduces their ability to reach us with ease. We can make sure they don't recover it. They've now only three land rovers, capable of carrying 30 troops each.

'Their commercial spacecraft are too valuable to the command for them to use as weapons for now, but we must assume those priorities will change. We've cut all their connections to satellite systems and we're monitoring to stop any attempt to restore them. Anyone think of an aspect we've not covered in regard to their current capabilities, please?'

'What's the situation with the outer colonies?'

'They're keeping a neutral stance, Sarma. They see their relationship with Marzero and us as a trading partnership only. There are no loyalty issues, though their philosophy is nearer to Marzero's than to ours and we need to keep that in mind. Most are independent entities with varying attitudes to commerce, religion, status and governance. But none are a threat at present. Our last intercommunity conference indicated they no longer depend solely on Marzero for income. CenCom's sent word we'll deal directly with each colony regarding essential supplies, which we'll either provide from our own stocks or, once Marzero's subdued, from theirs. In either case, in exchange for appropriate raw materials we can process ourselves.'

The few moments of silence suggested all were content with that.

'Okay. We need to look at what we're faced with now.' Georgiy rose to stretch his legs and continued to speak as he wandered the room. '2,000,000 people. Over 600,000 of them enslaved women we'd like to try to release, assuming we can re-educate them. 207,000 children under the age of eight, who we want to raise properly, in our ways.

'The rest of their population, nearly 1,200,000, are men with such primitive attitudes to women they may well be irredeemable.' He turned to Gabriel, sitting with Daisa and Virginia at one side of the Chamber. They'd been invited as consultants for their knowledge of the city. 'D'you think they can be converted to our ways, Gabriel?'

'I'm flattered you ask me. You've done more for me in two days than anyone ever did durin my life in Marzero. I'm eternally grateful for that. I've lived a life based on myth and misunderstandin.

'My view of Marion's now very different than most of my fellow citizens. Do I think they'll convert? Some women definitely will. Others will want reassurance first. Most men won't change: the majority are convinced material wealth and power are all that matters. They'll see no advantage. I was never as materialistic as them, but there'll be some like me. Don't know how you'll find them, though. I hope that helps.'

'Virginia?'

'I agree with Gabriel. I was exceptionally lucky to be in the right place at the right time. If I hadn't been with the moron who brought me here when he was Negotiator, I'd have suffered the fate of most women in Marzero; a sex object, used and abused at will. Many women believe the traditions and myths about their responsibility for their status so strongly, they may be difficult to save. But we should at least try.'

'Daisa, you've had recent experience of the city. What do you think about the chances of conversion?'

'I agree with Gabriel and Virginia, Madza. Most women, but only a few men. Although the lower class men have also been enslaved by dogma and indoctrination, they've held a type of power they see as an advantage. They ruled the women and I suspect most will have difficulty adjusting to a more equal society. It would be wonderful if we could convert them. But do we have time, resources and the ability to change the minds of so many?'

'That's one aspect of the immediate future we have to determine, Daisa.'

The AC thanked them all for their candour and continued their discussion.

The nine minds around the table indulged in brainstorming, using Hoshiko and Zaphod's direct links with CenCom to evaluate ideas as they formed. Most were rejected on grounds of pragmatic application or simple improbability. But a suggestion put forward by Sarma was considered worthy of further discussion.

'Testing the population is feasible. We can construct a question-naire capable of analysis by CenCom, so evaluation would be no problem. In fact, GrandMa could compile, distribute, collect and analyse the whole thing. She can easily devise the necessary algorithms.' Zaphod spoke for most around the table.

'We control their coms, so we can announce and conduct the test that way. But we have to make them listen first.'

Georgiy had an idea. 'Okay. Hear me out before you jump down my throat. The city's in chaos. Anarchy will soon follow if we do nothing. That'll cause more violence. Bullies and narcissists will gain the upper hand; the very people we want to exclude from leadership.

'We need to act now to stem rebellion, before we take remedial action. I don't like the idea of further killing, but I think it's essential we destroy the whole of the Elite clan. Replace them with an interim governing body made up of our own people.' He held up a hand to stem the tide of objections the faces of those around the table predicted.

'I know imposed government is generally loathed by the people. But a vacuum's much worse, as history's shown us all too often. We have to eliminate the Elite. Change is impossible whilst they stay in power. If we replace them with a benign, sympathetic and generous group of temporary leaders, we can at least stop the anarchy. We could have citizen representatives in the mix. How about that?'

CenCom evaluated the suggestions and came back with a score of 9.3 out of 10 for viability on the questionnaire and 8.79 on the interim government. The logical think-tank lacked subtler abliform sensitivities to the value of life per se, and though it carried some common empathetic emotions in its algorithms, its attitude to further killing was entirely pragmatic.

'If we may put forward a proposition?'

'Go ahead, CenCom.'

'Your dilemma is a moral one. But your real problem is practical. Your success in retraining one or two individuals is laudable. But Virginia is a woman with unusual intelligence for a Zero, and has been in regular contact with the Marion community for what is, for her, a lengthy period. Her conversion into a more acceptable abliform type is therefore more likely.

'Similarly, Gabriel appears to have proved that conversion of Zero men is possible. But he is a unique individual. Neurological aberration reduced the depth of his indoctrination regarding women. His post-incident suggestibility, which allowed him to be falsely convinced about the non-existent god figure, has similarly allowed him to accept more readily the logic-based philosophy of Marion.

'These two subjects, however, are not representative of the general population of Marzero. They have been subject to concentrated efforts that are not possible on the scale necessary for the remaining population. Their integration cannot be claimed as examples of successful conversion on which to base the necessary changes of mind-set required to drag the bulk of Zeros into your world.

'Time and sheer numbers inhibit such mass conversion. Delay will encourage the least worthy citizens of Marzero to take control, resulting in further cruelty toward the best subjects for conversion. You worry your decision will be adversely judged by your historical peers, who may lack full appreciation of the essential urgency of your decision and numeric superiority of the enemy you face. We therefore propose you hand this problem over to our impartial and unfettered logic, allowing us to determine the most appropriate solution.'

'Logical.' Georgiy glanced at each member of the AC in turn. 'But is it a cop out?'

'Grandma's the most intelligent entity in existence. Even with our combined minds, we're no match for her thought processes.' Zaphod delivered this statement with less conviction than his words suggested.

'But does CenCom have the moral data to deal with such a complex issue?' Hoshiko voiced the concerns of all around the table.

'Grandma's programmed with our concerns. We developed her. And she has access to all sentient beings. Honest access, unimpeded by our abliform need to take certain moral stands for the sake of appearance in public. Let's be honest with ourselves: Grandma knows what we really think, even those aspects that are too dark to be voluntarily made public.'

'Georgiy is correct in his assessment. We are best equipped to determine the appropriate action necessary to deal with what, for organic beings steeped in layers of historically questionable morality, is an intractable problem. We can examine every piece of data, process multiple algorithms in nanosecs, even initiate action using automatic systems that will protect abliforms from Marion against potential damage and even death. In short, we are best placed to make a logical decision about a complex and morally difficult issue.

'We must, of course, allow you, as our masters, to make the primary decision. It must be you who decide whether this community is best served by the well-meaning, considerative, merciful, but essentially ponderous decision-making capacity of a group of abliforms. Or whether, in the face of urgent and extreme danger, the safety and survival of your community is better served by an impartial but fully informed entity that is CenCom. We are required to protect this community. It is our fundamental purpose. But we must leave that initial decision entirely to you.'

'Looks like a "go" to me, on both projects.' Zaphod's ready acceptance gave the others round the table more confidence in the proposals, since he was known to be against action that unnecessarily threatened life in any form.

He expanded. 'We must act quickly to stop chaos and anarchy. It's a case of the lesser of the available evils. And our decision, don't forget, results from an aggressive act initiated by the people we're considering destroying. Better we do away with the Elite than allow the underclass to suffer further abuse.'

The AC were quick to accept this logical response to the situation. CenCom remained silent on this limited interpretation of its proposals. When briefed to run the program for the questionnaires at once, it began preparations immediately in the background, remaining on call for further developments.

Arrangements for the assassinations were quickly put into the hands of a small team of qualified volunteers. Georgiy and Daisa insisted on being part of that team because of their experience and knowledge of the city. Gabriel accepted the need for the action but wouldn't allow her to go without his protection. And, if he was on the spot, he might prevent unnecessary harm to innocents in his home city.

Approval was given by the majority of the community. Further volunteers for the fighting force were invited after the AC learned another 20 invisisuits were now available. These, and the previous models, now had added performance levels allowing them to be worn for much longer.

Whilst preparations for the assault progressed, the rest of the AC, with Amber replacing Georgiy, continued discussion on action to be taken after the raid. CenCom allowed this activity to proceed without informing them it considered it had already been authorised to make decisions on that matter. It would consider any imaginative solutions presented, in the unlikely event they may influence its actions.

Once she'd absorbed the previous topics, Amber felt able to ameliorate concerns about how to deal with those who failed the proposed test for suitability for early conversion to Marion philosophy. 'Our latest probe to Earth, has produced no evidence of abliform life persisting.'

'What's this to do with our dilemma, Amber?' Hoshiko's question was echoed by others round the table.

'I'm giving background. My point is we can act as if there are no abliforms on Earth. The planet's devoid of intelligent life. That gives us a way to solve our Marzero problem without resorting to mass murder.'

'Go on, Amber.'

'Well, Zaphod, the miners have an armada of huge ships used to transport ores to Mars for processing. They can be converted to carry abliform life. In fact, with current technology, we can make the changes quite quickly to produce comfortable, safe and fast transport to Earth.'

'You're suggesting we take unsuitable people to Earth?'

'It's more humane than killing them isn't it, Madza?'

'What do we know about current conditions, Amber? I've been too concerned about our own situation to spend much time catching up on your project.'

Amber smiled at Hoshiko. 'Understandable. Our surveys depict a planet stabilised at an average temperature 4.5 degrees above that current at our departure. Almost all surface ice has melted, far faster than predicted. Ocean levels have risen by 73ms.

'Huge ecological changes have occurred. Many habitats, and the flora and fauna they supported, have disappeared. Others have expanded and flourished.

'The Sahara's now a fertile grassy plain supporting millions of large grazing animals and their predators. On the other hand, the Yellowstone area in America remains a volatile caldera issuing clouds of toxic gas, smoke and ash into the surrounding area. Many small islands, and all coastal cities, have vanished under the waves.

'The point is that the planet has changed radically but is now relatively stable. All indications are that global climate change has settled into a steady state. There's certainly a viable environment for abliforms to survive there.'

'Earth's gravity could kill, or damage Zeros. We've continued our daily experience of Earth gravity, but many in Marzero abandoned the practice decades ago. There's a strong chance colonists would suffer physically.'

'That's true, Zaphod. I'm not saying it's an ideal solution, just an alternative to slaughtering hundreds of thousands. On a purely pragmatic level, we've no choice other than to exterminate large numbers of people. We can't convert most of them and we can't confine them. It's a choice, that's all. And I put it forward on that basis.'

'Whatever we do, we have to act swiftly. I see no merciful viable alternative to Amber's suggestion.' Zaphod's assessment helped the others consider it seriously.

They discussed the idea as a workable plan. 'GrandMa, what's your opinion?'

CenCom processed the info and combined the proposed project with data already held. 'We estimate 37% of suitable Zeros would suffer various degrees of distress due to Earth's gravity. These figures are vague due to insufficient data. EarthGrav units in Marzero are still operational and a programme of exercise begun immediately would fit many potential subjects for Earth habitation. Until the population is under our control, an announcement of your intentions would cause the predicted rebellion and resultant killing of individuals you prefer to save.

'It's our opinion the assassination of undesirables, coupled with a sensitive takeover of governance in the city, be treated as priorities. All other action is predicated on the success or otherwise of these projects.' CenCom considered this displacement activity would prevent further interruption of the program it already intended to implement to deal with the multiple problems presented by Marzero.

Practical elements; the need to inform and negotiate with mining corporations on asteroids and moons; the mechanical and technical aspects of converting mining ships into usable trains to take people to Earth, were put out to various groups assembled for those purposes.

In the end, Amber's suggested transportation of most Zeros to Earth became the most popular option.

The Assassins set off for the city the following morning. Georgiy, Daisa, and Gabriel each led a team of eight. A mission to end the lives of at least 1500 male Elite tyrants and bullies to prevent the likely indiscriminate wounding and killing of thousands of innocents, it was judged a necessary evil. Nobody relished such action. Logic and pragmatism dictated it, however. And they had the small comfort that the Elite had brought this destruction on themselves through greed, prejudice and ignorance.

Chapter Forty Nine

The Transhub carried them to the temporary terminal. In the drum, they slipped into specially constructed skintights. These ultra sheer garments would reveal the squad to each other when they shed their invisisuits.

Made by Hoshiko's students, and woven in smartfab designed to display constantly moving subtle patterns, they rendered the wearer a fuzzy blob to unprepared eyes. Each member of the group, however, wore special contact lenses that allowed the designs to be interpreted, so the skintights were identifiable.

'Everybody know the drill?'

26 nodding heads answered Georgiy's question. 'All prepped with ground plans?'

'Affirmative.'

'We remain invisible until we've gained entry to the complex. After that, there's too much danger we'll hit each other during the fight. So we stash the invisisuits until we can safely replace them.

'Everyone ready? I want you all certain before we go. Anyone unsure of the need for what we're doing stays behind. We can't afford second thoughts once the slaughter starts.' Georgiy used the word deliberately, knowing it would drive home the reality of this fight to the death.

Nobody chose to remain in the drum. They took last drinks, ate protein bars, crammed pre-packed carbs into their mouths. Most visited the facilities. For all their genetic modification, fear of death remained a vital survival requirement.

Already, signs of neglect were visible in cultivated fields around the conurbation. Food crops drooped for want of water. Here and there wild animals had feasted. At the city boundary, nobody stood on watch.

They'd timed their attack to start at sunrise and the streets were mostly deserted as they made their way past signs of recent looting and wanton destruction. Most disturbing were the bodies they passed; murdered disabled people. Such suffering had never featured in Marion and the younger members of the party in particular were appalled. Already the stink of decay lay heavy on the air.

Connection with the SpyTeam kept them informed of the situation as they progressed toward their target. Most of the Elite remained in bed. Their enslaved women and men, who also acted as skivvies, were cleaning, preparing food and dealing with laundry.

Guards were on duty in force. They were the major concern, as they were armed and now vigilant, following the previous two raids. This attack wouldn't be as straightforward and clinical as the others.

In the streets, citizens slowly started to appear, making their way to work or shops still not looted. The whole city lay under a pall of tension and anxiety.

'No hesitation. A sec's pause will bring death. We all watch each other's backs.' Daisa's comment came as they approached the entrance to the Elites' complex.

'We're an assassination squad. We save enslaved women, if we can. But leave them to their own devices. Tell them they'll die if they don't leave the building once released. We can't explain our intentions to them; some may be so deeply brainwashed they'll alert the Elites.

'Our priority is to destroy the Elites. Any lives saved are a bonus.' Georgiy waited for the agreed signal from each member of the squad before they moved forward.

The first six guards lurked fearfully behind a makeshift metal barrier directly in front of the entrance doors. One-to-one Assassins were nominated, each with a back-up, in case of failure.

Georgiy, Daisa, Kattu, Sarma, Ambra and Ramad were considered most experienced, having all used invisisuits previously. And all were martial arts trained to a high level.

Each identified an individual target, confirmed with their back-ups, and moved in for the kill. The barrier, an overturned shop counter with its metal top facing forward, stood 1m high. The men crouched behind it, shoulder to shoulder, weapons pointed into the street.

The Assassins leapt swiftly, as one, on to the edge of the counter. A swift karate kick disabled each guard at once. The six killers dropped into the space to make sure all were dead.

Dragging the bodies out of the way, along with the barrier, the rest of the party made their way into the complex. Ten more guards stood at the far end of the wide vestibule. Alert, once the doors swung open and nobody entered, they opened fire erratically and without warning.

The Assassins' scatter-and-drop pattern saved most from injury. They remained in place until the guard commander stopped the firing. Nothing indicated anyone had actually entered the building. He sent two guards to explore the doorway. As they approached, the bulk of the Assassins moved forward and attacked the remaining eight. Four left behind dealt with the two investigators.

This was the last opportunity to operate in the invisisuits. Quickly, they folded them into their invisipaks. Armed with pulse guns and blade-lasers, the whole squad moved forward.

Entering the central corridor, they split into three different parties. Georgiy led his group left. Gabriel took his right. Both groups intending to deal with the large number of sub-Elites housed in the first two floors of Trumpyramid. Daisa led her group up, charged with killing the most senior Elites.

Floor three of the pyramid revealed only a pair of guards, one molesting a serving woman. The squad moved soundlessly up the stairwell and crossed the small open space before the guards or the woman were aware of them. By then it was too late. The men were despatched without a weapon being fired.

'Leave the building. Or die here.' Daisa's quiet command frightened the woman into action and she sped downstairs.

A complex of corridors led from the central passage beyond the double doors. They took each in turn, staying together to deal with groups of Elites and their women as they moved through the floor.

Here, on this lower tier, lived the majority of their victims. Complacency, arrogance, vanity, and a desire to appear unfazed by any threat, allowed the men to trust in their guards at ground level, assuming nobody would get past them. The pair of guards at the entrance to the floor seemed almost a token presence: an indication of the inability of certain personality types to learn from past mistakes.

Along the corridors, a series of plain doors, bearing numbers and names, opened into individual apartments, each occupied by an Elite and his slaves. Most servants were women, but a few were men. The dogma promoted by the Clerics discouraged same sex relationships.

They released all slaves as they killed the Elite men. Most of the abused women and men were happy to escape their miserable, if materially privileged, lives. Only a few resisted.

'It's a simple choice. Leave the building, now. Or die here.'

That made up the minds of doubters, but two remained stubborn. Expediency gave them no second chance.

In some apartments, Elite men were absent, their slaves waiting. These they released after discovering where their masters could be found.

The third floor cleared in a swift and clinical sweep, Daisa moved her party up another level. Fewer men lived here, in slightly larger apartments befitting their elevated status. Some info had already reached them and the squad met resistance.

Daisa took the hand off an Elite man with a laser blade, disarming him, before sending a pulse directly at his heart.

Word from escapees spread quickly. Daisa had expected this development and consulted the SpyTeam for guidance on the whereabouts of opposition.

This level housed very few Elites, in spacious apartments. The whole operation grew more perilous, as there were many places men could hide. Daisa led the group to a door and blasted it open.

The resident man was waiting on the other side and Daisa was nearly killed. Sarma, just behind her, fired a pulse over Daisa's shoulder. He fell dead as his brain boiled. A slave woman screamed. The three servants collected their scant clothing from the bedroom before they dashed from the building.

The second apartment appeared empty. But Ambra alerted them to a part open door on the left hand side. She'd seen movement. They spread out, pretending not to notice the door that stood ajar, and approached in an arc. A pulse caught Tubri on his shoulder and he dropped his own gun. Sarma fired from the hip and the Elite man screamed as she hit his groin. Daisa put an end to him with a shot to the head.

They found his two enslaved men hiding in the bathroom and set them free. One checked his master was really dead before kicking him savagely, only then escaping.

The top floor housed only the new PM, and the few escapees who'd fled there. All entrances here were heavily guarded by ESOs. The Marionets were outnumbered. They killed some guards but it was obvious they wouldn't break through without significant loss.

Time was running out anyway. The explosive charges carried by Georgiy and Gabriel's squads would already be in place. Daisa knew they'd done what they could. Anyone left in the building would die in the planned explosion and fire.

'Time to go.'

The squad helped Tubri and moved quickly back to the ground floor. A few slaves idled, uncertain of their situation. The squad pointed out they'd only mins to escape if they wished to live. The majority rushed to follow.

At the bottom, the lift doors opened as Daisa's squad arrived. The ESOs within the small space had no time to shoot before pulses and laser blades cut them down. Slaves, gathering near the entrance, screamed and ran outside in panic.

From the speakers, the SpyTeam's announcement sounded loud and clear. 'All remaining sex workers must be released and sent from the building. Any Elite man failing to release such workers will be executed. You have precisely seven mins to comply.' The countdown started at once in the background. 'All Elite men remain in Trumpyramid until advised. Any attempting escape will be executed.'

Daisa and her team left the ground floor vestibule as Georgiy and Gabriel entered from their separate sorties. Each had a couple of injured members, but only one Assassin had been killed. She was carried by four colleagues.

The group fled the building. In the square, other loyal guards had gathered. They were corralling slaves as the Marionets emerged. Quickly, they abandoned their attempts to capture the women and concentrated on attacking the Assassins.

'Leave the square if you want to live!' Georgiy's command set the sex slaves running, leaving the guards alone. The small group was out-gunned. Difficult for normal eyes to detect, the Assassins swiftly picked off the few guards. In the battle, Sarma caught a laser blade that severed much of her left biceps. Another young man was decapitated. The ESOs all killed, the whole group of Assassins ran a short distance to a safe area identified by the SpyTeam.

First aid had to be brief, but effective. Pain was the main issue, as the nature of laser blades reduced bleeding to a minimum, cauterising wounds they caused.

They replaced their invisisuits and waited. The Elites' complex exploded in flames and rending metal. The fire that followed was intense. Satisfied no one would survive that destruction, they continued their escape.

The Assassins threaded their way through growing crowds of people intent on seeing the destruction of the hated Elite. A few loyal guards fired on the crowds indiscriminately. But anger was such that the people charged the Specials. Disarmed, and killed with their own weapons, their corpses were dismembered and decapitated, their heads displayed on any sharp object the mob could find.

'Barbarous! How can they do that?' Daisa's appalled shock echoed that of the whole team.

'No more than they deserve after the way they've treated the rest of us.' Gabriel's acceptance made Daisa concerned at how deeply the conversion process had penetrated his psyche.

Once free of the city, the Assassins slowed and moved more cautiously toward the escape drum on the Transhub.

SpyTeam warned them it was surrounded by heavily armed Specials and ESOs. Still pumping adrenalin after their daring raid, achieved with so few casualties, they were unfazed by the threat of a few guards there. Automatically slowing with caution as they came in sight of the terminal, they turned anxious faces to one another. The barriers they'd overcome to slaughter the Elite were nothing. Here, the Specials and ESOs had converged as though knowing this was the point to focus their strength. No hope of escape this way.

Chapter Fifty

CenCom devised the questionnaires and dispersed them to all in the city. The authoritarian method went against Marion philosophy but a pragmatic approach was essential.

The SpyTeam denied access to any channel but those they controlled. The message to the Zeros was clear, repetitive, simple and absolute. They must respond if they wished to regain control over their lives. All devices, systems and mechanisms were under Marion's supervision.

'Complete this survey, honestly, and live with these restrictions, or die.'

The algorithms were set to detect inconsistencies and dishonesty. If a respondent lied, the test stopped at the point where the deviation occurred. Only honest answers allowed forward movement. Failure to complete the questionnaire resulted in all electrical devices freezing, making life in the city unbearable.

Automation sorted out the most obviously unsuitable citizens but a team of psychology students, working with their tutors, did the fine-tuning. They were left with mere thousands to scan via a combination of experience and more esoteric algorithms.

The team expected it to be a few days before they completed this semi manual task. CenCom dealt with the bulk, but lacked the emotional components needed for deeper analysis of abliform minds at work.

In the meantime, the outer colonies had been contacted. They now knew commercial activity with Marzero had ceased. The situation was made clear to these tough, pioneering people. There'd be no more credits from Mars. They were now entirely dependent on Marion for their necessities, and these would be supplied in exchange for raw materials.

'Titan will be most difficult to rein in. They're almost self-sustaining. And they'll probably devise their own system of credits. But we'll have to wait and see. Every other colony's ultimately dependent for its long-term welfare on supplies from Mars. They'll agree to our terms.'

'That's probably true, Hoshiko. But they could pose a danger to colonies we set up on Earth. Their facilities and science are nowhere near as advanced as ours, but they're pioneering types and may attempt all sorts of ill-advised ventures. We must find ways to motivate them to come into the fold voluntarily, or we'll make problems for the future on Earth.' Zaphod, along with his companions, was convinced the twin systems of commerce and religion were key to real change. If they could remove these cancers, as they had in Marion, they'd solve many difficulties.

'Education, Zaphod. We must educate them. But do we have time?'

This had always been the difficulty. They'd hoped the example of the utopian lifestyle exemplified by Marion would be enough to convince doubters, but this hadn't happened. So frustrating to have devised a system of living that suited all who abided by its rules and find others not willing to try it.

'How do we defeat years of initial brainwashing all those people have suffered, Acacia? You're our best persuader. What can we do?'

Acacia acknowledged Zaphod's faith in her with a smile. 'Time's always been a problem. How to transit from attractions of commercialism and fears encouraged by religion to a system that relies on logic and reason tempered by compassion and tolerance.

'We can subtly present them with positive fictional examples of life in a state like ours. Show them documentary evidence in reality shows that demonstrate our peace, freedom, mutual satisfaction and spirit of adventure through intelligent research. But will it be enough to overcome the short-term delights they find in their power struggles, their competitions for wealth, their pride in ownership of things, their need to struggle against artificial odds devised by their masters?

'We're talking about converting hundreds of thousands, maybe even a million or more, to a system we know works brilliantly to the advantage of all. But we weren't able to convert Buzz, and he lived among us for more than two centuries.

'Example alone isn't enough to undo the damage caused by systemic propaganda backed up by commercial reinforcement and doctrinal fear-mongering. I think we must devise our own counter-indoctrination, using every means we know of.

'We have to re-educate by force. We're not dealing with the children of our own philosophies here, we're coping with people who've been severely manipulated and damaged by their upbringing and social conditioning.

'We can't fight fair. We have to use every method at our disposal. And we must start now. The key to promoting a change in attitude lies in pointing out the consequences of their current approach as against the results from our own.'

The small, select, Council considered her words. Their reluctance to act was no more than a sign of their deep concern for individual liberty.

'Acacia's right. We can't tackle this problem the same way we'd deal with a wayward child of our own. If nothing else, our failure with Buzz shows we need a more robust approach.' Zaphod rose and spread his hands in a gesture of acceptance. 'We have to impose our philosophy by every means available. Agreed?'

'It's a big step. But I see no workable alternative, Zaphod. What about the rest of you?'

Nobody had any suggestions. The idea of force-fed re-education was repugnant, but they recognised there were no viable alternative solutions.

'Extermination seems the only other option. And I take it we all exclude that?' Hoshiko echoed the opinion of the whole Council.

'So. We must move. Hoshiko and Acacia, please get your University teams to work with CenCom to devise programmes of indoctrination, using the theme of consequence as their focus, that can be subliminally, covertly, and even openly transmitted to the entire population of Marzero first and then on to the outer colonies.

'We have to end their combined reliance on money and religion. If we fail, the whole abliform world fails with us. We were sent here to create a new utopia. We've managed that for our own community. Now we must do the same for the rest, initially without the benefits of long life, automaton labourers and the natural thirst for learning that keeps us all engaged with research and experiment.'

'We've the beginnings of such a programme already in place, Zaphod.' Acacia explained. 'Some students have been examining such techniques and they're eager to try out their theories on suitable subjects. Looks as though they'll be put to the test sooner and in greater need than they could ever have imagined.'

'Before we close this session, we don't appear to have heard CenCom's proposals for dealing with the immediate Marzero situation. Unless I missed it.'

Amber's comment prompted Hoshiko to quiz GrandMa. 'They're still working on it. So much for their claim to rapid results.'

CenCom, however, had made its decisions already. It was merely awaiting the ideal opportunity to implement them.

Chapter Fifty One

The Assassins counted the circle of troops they could actually see and reached a total of 54. They surmised as many were stationed around the far side. All were armed. More alarmingly, every tenth officer, an ESO, wore an IR headset.

The invisisuits were proof against most IR detection, other than the narrow band deliberately excluded for inter-group cohesion. Their soles could leave telltale signs on the ground: a trail an alert IR goggle wearer might follow.

'Stay put, everyone.' Georgiy explained their problem. 'One of you call up hovers to take us home. But tell them the guards are armed, so the flyers will need weapons of defence ...'

'Jeez! We've made a huge mistake!'

'What!' Georgiy couldn't believe the dismay in Gabriel's voice. 'What's the problem?'

'Stefan was a Cleric. He ... they ... the Clerics, they're powerful. Look, I'm thinking on my feet. But we've destroyed the Elite. Left no one in charge of the city.'

'We're going to govern by a remote committee from Marion, Gabriel. I don't have time for ...'

'No, Georgiy. He's right. The Clerics are an organised group in search of power, if Stefan's ambition's anything to go by. We can't leave them. They'll try to take over. The very last people we want in charge of the city.'

'Jupiter's balls! Why didn't anyone think of this before, Daisa?'

'What's more troubling; why did CenCom fail to alert us to this omission?'

'Now isn't the time for that debate. We have ...'

'I have to go back and destroy them. Otherwise we leave the city in a worse state than before.'

'Okay. Let's keep calm and think this over, Gabriel. First, do you know where these frackin Clerics will be?'

'I ... yes. I've a good idea where they meet. There's only a small number. Maybe 150. I've got to get rid of them.'

'Gabriel's right, Georgiy. If it's only 150, and they're in one place ...'

'They will be. Stefan told me all about them.'

'Right. Gabriel and I can deal with this. We'll go now.'

'Hold on, Daisa. We should discuss ...'

Gabriel interrupted. 'No, Georgiy. You organise the escape. We need to act. Now. Sure you want to risk this, Daisa?'

'I'm not letting you go alone.'

Georgiy looked around at the situation facing them all. 'If you're prepared to take the risk, I'm not going to stop you. But ... I was about to tell you to take care, but that's idiotic. Keep in touch.'

Gabriel and Daisa clasped hands and turned back toward the city, leaving Georgiy and the rest of the Assassins to escape. He had a personal stake in ridding the city of the controlling Clerics. But Daisa had no reason for her courage other than concern for him.

Georgiy gave himself a moment to arrange his thoughts after this unexpected development. He turned his full attention to the task in hand. 'My guess is the drum, maybe even the temporary terminal, will be booby-trapped. We should avoid confrontation here. But we'll have to be wary as we move away and around the terminal. Stay alert. Follow me toward that low bluff in the cliff to the east.'

He set off at once. The others followed. For the first few mins of tension, nothing happened. Then an IR detector guard spotted their trail. He shouted to his colleagues and a hail of pulses and laser blades streaked in the direction of the Assassins.

They scattered and dropped to the ground.

'Anyone hurt?' Ambra's question reached them all.

So far everyone was okay, even those helping the injured among the party or carrying the dead. But that was likely to be short-lived.

The guards at this side of the terminal now formed into a squad, three rows deep, moving toward the area at which they'd fired. These were soldiers who'd learned from past mistakes. More organised and better led, they were the most professional force the Assassins had encountered.

'To the bluff. No direct line. Weave and wander. Leave the dead for now. Six to each of the non-mobile injured. Move fast!' Georgiy's command had all dashing over open space to the small rocky outcrop that would give some cover.

The guards fired randomly, trying to guess where the ephemeral IR trails of their targets might lead. Their shots went wide, but there was a real danger some of the group could be hit by accident.

The able bodied arrived without further incident. But the injured and their helpers, though still invisible, were slower and more vulnerable. The only option was a rapid diversionary attack on the guards. The Assassins, now partially protected by the rock outcrop, fired, many shooting with the accuracy and selective targeting of snipers, and felling most ESOs and several guards in the first volley.

The squad, now leaderless and unable to identify the direction of fire, broke into a disorganised gang. Some ran toward the city. Others scattered back to the terminal. A few, led by two remaining ESOs, forged on toward the bluff. Firing on the move, they were easily cut down. A young Assassin caught a pulse to his forearm. It took him out of the fight. But the rest continued, using the advantage of their invisibility.

The battle was short, one-sided, and conclusive in the sense that the guards either died or ran to safety. Four Assassins broke cover to help their injured colleagues and carers carry the wounded over the rough ground to the shelter of the rocks. Another eight risked their lives to retrieve the dead, taking time to find their bodies hidden by the rough ground.

The hovers were on their way. Expected in around 50 mins.

From behind the terminal, the other half of the guards now joined their colleagues. Totalling around 70, they regrouped in front of the terminal. The rest continued to retreat through the wilderness toward the city.

'Contact Daisa and warn her they've got enemy behind them.' Georgiy surveyed the scene. 'Stalemate. Until the hovers arrive. But let's even the odds. We've the advantage of cover and invisibility. I want ten at the far end of the outcrop. Spread out and make sure you're protected by the terrain. Signal when you're in position.'

The new dispersal of the Assassins took only mins and Georgiy received confirmation when all were in place. This gave them the advantage of a well spread front that was open to attack only from exposed ground ahead.

'Random shots. Select your targets. Kill where necessary and scare the shit out of the rest. These are the greatest threat to our security.'

Firing started. Concentrated bursts and single shots mixed to provide an assault that was unpredictable. Accuracy, and a disciplined approach, ensured maximum effectiveness. The first salvo reduced the enemy troop by 19. The remainder began to run, either to shelter behind the terminal, or toward the distant city.

'I want five volunteers with me to the terminal. The rest stay here.' Georgiy's request met with a number of offers. 'This is as new to me as it is to you. You've never fought before. Invisibility is a new factor for me. I'm making this up as I go along, so I'm open to suggestions. The hovers will be here soon and we need to get the injured away.'

'Did you notice, Georgiy, none of the guards went into the terminal.'

'You're right, Brima. Very observant. It confirms my suspicion the place is booby-trapped. But we can use it as cover to take out the remaining guards.'

'If we go three each way, we can attack from both sides.'

'Good idea, Sarma.' Georgiy split the six into two teams and they set out, one to the front of the terminal, the other to the rear.

The 500ms were quickly covered and the teams kept in contact as they moved around the bulk of the inflated structure. The troops waited in five groups of six, each led by an ESO.

The Assassin teams targeted groups nearest them, taking out the

ESOs first. They'd reduced enemy numbers to a mere 17, led by two ESOs, when the hovers arrived at the bluff to take the team home.

At the sound of the motors, Georgiy saw two Specials turn to each other. They spoke a few words, dropped their weapons, raised their hands, and began to retreat toward the city. They'd covered no more than a few paces when one ESO turned his weapon on them. Shot both.

It was too much for the other officers, who shot the two remaining ESOs. The rest of the guards then ran off in the direction of the city, some dropping their weapons, others carrying them high over their heads in a sign of surrender.

Georgiy let them escape. 'Okay. Go back to the others. But, I need one of you with me to check the terminal for booby-traps.'

They all volunteered. He thanked them, and selected Brima for her acute observation skills.

'What are you going to do, Georgiy?' Sarma asked.

'We need to check that the terminal and drum are safe if we're to use them to carry selected citizens from Marzero.'

'Okay.' She and the rest of the small team left at once for the rocks where their colleagues waited.

Georgiy and Brima moved to the entrance, at the opposite side of the terminal. Brima put out a hand to stop him stepping into the opening. She dropped to her knees and gathered a small handful of dry dust from beneath the lichen. Standing, she puffed it at the entrance, watching for telltale signs of tripping lasers. Two green lines of light appeared, one horizontal at knee height, the other at shoulder level, angled so the left was higher than the right.

'See them both?'

'Affirmative. Go in singly?'

She led and Georgiy followed. Nothing happened. The structure was an inflatable double-skinned tent made of a graphene compound that diffused the light passing through it; a translucent shield against the weather.

'Shed the invisisuit and skintight, Brima.'

'Why?'

He stripped. 'To keep an eye on each other so we don't get in the way as we search. We'll work quicker if properly visible. The image from the cameras isn't clear enough for the accuracy we need for a thorough search in these conditions. Agreed?'

In answer, Brima stuffed both coverings into her bag. They began their systematic search. Separating to spread out over the area, they kept glancing at each other and toward the entrance to ensure no Zero guards returned. There was always the chance some brave officers would come back to do whatever damage they could.

Brima reached the drum they'd hoped would take them back home. She duplicated her detection system to find any trips and discovered a mirror copy of the pair guarding the entrance to the tent. She passed the info to Georgiy, examining the rails leading up to and beyond the drum. Inside, she began her own search.

'Found one.' Georgiy's call had Brima standing still, awaiting further info.

'It's fitted with a trembler; an anti-tamper device. I think I can disable it, But I'd be happier if you moved well back.'

Brima moved quickly away to the tent wall on the side opposite the entrance. She replaced her invisisuit, in case any guards returned.

Georgiy examined the bomb closely. He'd worked on armaments and explosive devices centuries previously, whilst training on Earth. This was newer technology, though not as sophisticated as Marion engineers would've devised. He could see the anti-tamper device clearly. Finding a way to either disable or bypass it was less straight-forward.

The trembler would be sensitive. Located in an awkward place. He envisaged how the trap had been positioned, pictured the order of events. If he could duplicate those moves in reverse order he had a chance of defeating the device.

Long years of calm research, and experimentation with Amber, had taught him meditation and mental placidity he'd lacked in youth and early manhood. He employed these skills now to settle his hands and mind to the delicate task.

The unit was lodged in a narrow space between two components that provided lift for the drum. Magnetic, they generated a current that separated drum from track by a fraction of a cm, allowing it to hover above the surface that guided it. At present, the drum was static, the current turned off, and the gap therefore closed. The device would explode as soon as power was applied, so no wires attached it to either the lifting element or the track.

A trembler was a dangerous option, given that Vesta and Ceres now generated frequent, if minor, quakes. It could've been tripped almost any time. Another sign of the lack of concern shown by Zeros for life and vital services.

Georgiy examined all visible surfaces. Nothing suggested it was attached at any point. It seemed only to be resting in the narrow gap.

He assumed they'd expected it wouldn't be found and would work as soon as the Assassins broke the laser beams, or powered up the drum. The trembler must be an added security measure in case of discovery.

He put his right hand to the edge of the small bomb, allowing soft skin contact without moving it. Crouching awkwardly, he placed his left hand on the opposite side of the device. Slowly, carefully, conscious of his mortality, he applied soft pressure to the opposing edge to give him purchase.

He pushed danger to the back of his mind, where it wouldn't interfere. All his astronaut training he dredged up and put into practice to still nerves and calm muscles. With infinite care, he moved the device toward him.

It shifted without resistance. That confirmed it had been rested on the unit rather than attached. As he shifted it further from the metal support, wires came into view.

Two thin cables, red and yellow, connected the device in his hand to a block of explosive housed in shrapnel-rich casing. He was now in the position of having shifted the triggering element in a way that prevented its replacement. And any attempt to use the trembler to lift the explosive would certainly result in it triggering the blast.

Stalemate.

'Brima.' His voice was steady, but soft. He awaited her response. But exterior noise from the hovers intruded.

He waited for a lull, arms and knees beginning to ache from the uncomfortable crouch he'd had to adopt to reach the unit. 'Brima.' He tried again. 'Brima!' A little more volume.

'Georgiy?'

'I need you.'

As she began to move, three guards appeared in the doorway. One was about to enter when the man on his left stopped him with a sharp blow to his face. 'Mind the twattin booby-trap!' They hesitated. Brima continued her journey, hoping they'd abandon their attempt to enter. But they climbed in, their exaggerated motions signalling their knowledge of the trip lasers.

Brima worried they'd move further inside. But Georgiy's call had been a cry for help. She moved swiftly to join him on the track in front of the drum. It took her only secs to assess the difficulty. Without his suit, he'd be visible to any observer who approached.

'We have to be quick. Three guards have come inside, Georgiy.'

He glanced up from the track, but the safety barriers prevented him seeing them. That meant they couldn't see him, either.

'I can't extract the explosive without the trembler setting it off.'

'So I see.'

'Sorry, Brima, I need to be able to see you.'

She slipped down the top half of her suit, letting it dangle round her waist. 'Enough?'

'Plenty. Right. You hold the explosive pack. I'll move the trembler device. I'm going to move it right and place it on the track to the left of the third sleeper. Copy?'

'Copy.' She examined the device carefully before moving. 'I need to lay the pack beside it on the track. Right?'

'Correct.'

To make the move without either obstructing Georgiy or unsighting herself, she arched her body over him. Inelegant and difficult to sustain for any period, it was the only position in which both had clear sight of the target destination and freedom to move their respective parts of the bomb to it.

'On the count of three.'

'Copy.'

'One, two …'

The guards in the doorway moved toward the drum, their conversation making it clear they hoped to find something of value within.

'… three.'

Chapter Fifty Two

Amber approached the Council in a mood of mixed embarrassment and apology. 'Sorry to interrupt, but you need to know this. We have enhanced analysis of data from the probe. There's evidence of intelligent life, in the Zealandia region. We've isolated it to a small island.' She glanced meaningfully at Zaphod and Hoshiko.

'On Mangaia, our alma mater?'

She nodded at Hoshiko. 'We've further enhanced the HiRes and there are three little settlements on the mountains that remain above sea level. No signs of meaningful technology, but the structures are artificial and in use. There are external campfires. And, so far, we've counted a total of 1,255 people!'

'Amazing, and rather encouraging. Any other signs of abliform life on the planet, Amber?'

'None, Zaphod. And we really have looked. Of course, as you know, it takes a lot of computing power to examine such things. But the range of detection methods and types of signal we're seeking give us very reliable results, now we've reached the fully enhanced stage of analysis. Definitely nothing technological detected. And, so far as we can tell, no other artificial fires or buildings.'

'So, where's best for us to send our colonists?'

'We're still going ahead, then, Zaphod?'

'I think we have to. We'll keep Mangaia secret from the transports. Land our colonists in areas well away from there. If we all agree that's sensible? But we can't let the presence of a small number of people stop our programme of settlement, can we?' He looked around the table for confirmation.

'I'm not sure trespassing on the environment of another species sits well with our philosophy, Zaphod. It's a form of contamination we've sworn to avoid ever since we settled Mars, isn't it?'

'In theory, yes, Madza. But, first of all, so far it's only been theory. Of the places we've detected possible intelligent life, we've yet to find one we can actually reach, or even communicate with.' Zaphod held up his hand to forestall Madza's quick response. 'Let me finish. Yes, we've plenty of signs life exists, or has existed, all over the universe. But, in spite of the signals we've now received, nothing's come close to a feasible interchange, let alone an actual visit by us, or by them.

'We've reduced spaceflight time exponentially. But until we exceed the speed of light we're no threat to any other intelligent life form. We were safe in our principled stance of non-interference, knowing we're unlikely to need to test it.

'But this is different. First of all, we're talking about necessity. And secondly, and maybe more importantly, this is our own species. We and those abliforms still on Earth are the same.' He turned to Amber. 'You're certain they're people, not some other life form?'

'Our images are of people: we can even see their gender.'

'Given the lack of substantial development of the Zeros, it's likely there's little difference between them and the people now living on Mangaia. I accept that we, as an advanced and modified form of the species, might pose a cultural and even a physical threat to such primitives. But the Zeros are primitive and lack our strength, intelligence, longevity and absence of deformity and disability. They are merely taller versions of Earth people.'

'I'd like it recorded I'm uncomfortable with it. Nothing more, and I don't oppose the project. But I'm … yes, uncomfortable with it.'

'Noted, Madza. Though I suspect your discomfort applies to the rest of us. Ours is, after all, a pragmatic solution borne of need.'

'Sorry. Yes, Zaphod. I accept that.'

He gave them a short time for reflection before he returned to the burning issue. 'So, choice of regions, Amber?'

Amber summoned up a large Threedee of the Earth and positioned it, rotating, above the centre of the table for all to observe. As it spun, she highlighted areas she referred to in her presentation so those unfamiliar with the geography could identify features she mentioned.

'We've excluded equatorial regions, that is, a belt 20 degrees of latitude either side of the equator. Average surface temperatures there are above the level of comfortable living for abliforms and, in places, could prove lethal.'

The globe glowed red around its centre, excluding much of Africa, South and Central America, the Philippines and Indonesia, Northern Australia, Thailand, Cambodia, Malaysia, Vietnam, Laos, southern India, Arabia, and Madagascar.

'The sub-tropical areas are bearable, but much hotter than we're used to on Mars. The most suitable regions are those around the now temperate Arctic Circle in the north and Antarctica in the South.

'The Arctic area's well stocked with wildlife, since it can be reached over land. But Antarctica, as an isolated island continent, was only ever home to penguins, seals and certain large semi aquatic mammals as well as some bird populations. Initial studies of the HiRes shows trees have already spread inland from the coastal areas, and there are vast grasslands. But, crucially, no sign of land animals.

'The most viable places for our settlers seem to lie somewhere in between these regions. Most of what was the USA is no longer habitable due to volcanic activity around the Yellowstone caldera. That's devastated a huge swathe of the country and left it a seismically active region surrounded by desert.

'Canada's probably the optimum site for some colonists. There are lakes, rivers, forests and plains, and the wildlife and descendants of domestic stock should provide a plentiful food source. Trees will give adequate shelter materials, and fresh water abounds.

'On the eastern side of the northern hemisphere, Russia seems most suitable, for the same reasons as Canada.

'In the south, where Mangaia's located, both southern Australia and the remnant islands of New Zealand should prove habitable, though increased volcanic and earthquake activity may make the latter less attractive.'

The Council studied the spinning globe, watching storms gathering around the equatorial waters and coasts and noting the absence of surface ice other than on the highest mountain peaks. It wasn't the world those who'd once lived there recognised and not the planet others had learned in their history lessons.

'I wouldn't want to live there.' Madza voiced the thoughts of most around the table. 'Looks hostile and dangerously volatile to me.'

'Yes. Not the planet we left. But the climate's settled into a relatively stable pattern now. What's there seems to be what will remain for the foreseeable future.

'Our colonists will have to adapt. But they'll have plenty of natural resources to help them. There'll be food and shelter, and the temperatures mean they'll be able to live without the bother of clothing. So, we need to decide. Do we plant them all … what's the current estimate, CenCom?'

The spinning globe reduced to a 100th of its size and was replaced by a graph showing the distribution of the Marzero population by age, gender, and temperamental suitability as colonists. The Council studied this presentation with mixed feelings, as CenCom stated the details.

'The small portion at the base of the graph indicates the numbers suitable for immersive retraining as potential new members of Marion. They number 3,207 women, 877 children, and 319 men. Of the remainder, 26,569 males, 759,892 females, and 13,206 children are categorised as fit colonists for Earth.

'The other 1,237,934 comprise rejects. These are a mix of criminally unsuitable people, mostly males, but including physically and/or mentally deficient men, women and children, and pathologically incurable dogma slaves whose presence would result in the continuation of religious superstition.

'These individuals must be eliminated as a matter of urgency. Your words. However, since you wish us to avoid pain and unpleasantness as well as the probability of mass hysteria and potential rebellion, a number of methods remain under consideration.

'I remind you that CenCom, in common with all artificial intelligence entities, is governed by the immutable Prime Directive. However, our primary function is the protection and welfare of the population at Marion. This presents us with a logical dilemma. One side of the argument says we may not destroy abliform life. The other says we are fundamentally required to protect those living in Marion and currently in danger from other inhabitants of this world.

'This may appear an insoluble conundrum to limited abliform intelligence. However, our superior logic compels us to identify the species of life at Marzero as a lesser form. We have therefore applied a dual labelling system to abliform life on the planet.

'Those inhabiting Marion continue as abliforms. Those living in Marzero are renamed sub-abliform. As such, they fall without the remit of the Prime Directive and may be disposed of accordingly.'

Hoshiko thanked CenCom on behalf of the Council and residents. 'Please give us your proposed methods and the time to absorb the info so we can decide what action we prefer. We'll let you know in a short while.'

'An immediate response is required. Delay will exacerbate the danger to yourselves and conflict with our obligation to protect you.'

Hoshiko again thanked CenCom. 'We do need more time.'

CenCom's failure to respond to this paradox should have sounded alarm bells to those around the table, but they were so deeply engaged by the moral dilemma they missed the logical one.

Madza drew his hands down his face, a gesture of the weariness felt by all round the table. 'Sorry, I know it's urgent. But we're not in the best state to make this decision. We're tired and distressed. Concerned about our own futures and the fate of our brave folk still at Marzero. Maybe take a break?

'I hesitate to suggest this, but perhaps we should let CenCom get on with it?'

'A brave idea, Madza. On the face of it, it looks like capitulation, but the reality is, as emotional beings, we aren't best suited to making such a momentous decision in what we might call cold blood.

'On the battlefields of old, the survival instinct took away moral considerations about killing others. Everything happened at speed, and slaughter resulted from necessity.

'Here, in the peace and safety of our Council Chamber, we have the illusion of time and opportunity to consider all consequences of mass murder: the guilt, horror, and dread of mistaken selection.

'Madza's suggestion is sensible, and, more importantly, right.' Hoshiko's assessment found favour.

'Still seems like a cop-out.' Zaphod sighed. 'But I've no positive alternative. Let's take that break.'

CenCom remained silent, but Hoshiko's final statement could be taken as permission for action. And that suited the AI entity.

Chapter Fifty Three

The move went slowly but accurately. The trembler and explosive pack both sat on the track without incident. They moved from the front of the drum and circled around the back in hope of escaping the notice of the guards. Those three were too involved in finding stuff to steal to care about anything else.

'We need to get out of here, Georgiy.'

'We can't just leave the bomb. We still want to be able to use the Transhub.'

'Ever dealt with an explosive device like this?'

He shrugged. 'A very long time ago.'

'Shall I connect with CenCom and find out?'

'Do it.' Georgiy listened, trying to detect the activity of the guards. They were silent. Perhaps they'd ventured out again. He crept around the side of the drum, keeping low on his hands and knees. As he approached entrance, he heard them in conversation.

'Let's get outa here. Nowt to twattin steal. Where are their clothes, eh? I don't get it.'

'An I don't like that twattin explosive thingy the Captain put in here. Even a quake might set it off.'

'Look. We're tryin to stop them Marionet twats escapin ain't we? Why don't we piss off outta here an blow it up as we go? Do the bosses a favour. Get us a bonus, eh?'

Georgiy froze. They'd have to act, and swiftly. He crawled back to Brima, explained what he'd heard.

'I've got the answer to our immediate problem. See the wires? We cut both at the same time.'

'Any ideas how we do that?'

Georgiy shook his head, trying to think.

'Would laser blades do it?'

He nodded. 'We'll have to fire both at the exact same time. You take the yellow. I'll do the red. We should take a test shot first.'

'Your pack's still in the drum.'

'Shit!'

They sidled round to the rear of the travelling compartment. The guards were just leaving it.

'Slow an quiet. That twattin trembler's sensitive, the Captain said.'

The three moved off together, walking as if on eggshells. Georgiy raised his eyebrows; how differently the mind operates under stress. They'd clumped and stomped their way inside when greed drove them. Now they'd been deprived of their plunder by the invisipaks, they suddenly remembered the real danger of the explosive.

Brima gave them time to move away and, whilst their backs were turned, got into the drum, collected his pack from the designated spot. They walked swiftly back to the bomb. The guards were close to leaving the terminal.

'We have to be quick.'

They extracted their laser blades.

'Test first.' Georgiy's idea had Brima frowning, but she nodded agreement.

Both aimed at a spot 15cms in front of their appointed wires. A swift count down. The track glowed red from the instant heat.

The guards were only paces from the exit. On Brima's second count of three, they fired at the wires. Hazardous, but, in the wild, without necessary tools, they had no alternative.

Both wires parted in white heat.

No blast.

The explosive pack now separated from the anti-tamper device, the immediate danger was the guards deliberately triggering the laser trips as they left. No time for the delicate task of detaching it.

Georgiy glanced across and saw they were almost there.

'No choice. Them or us and the terminal.' He picked up the explosive pack by the wires. Swung it round his head, and tossed it directly at them.

'Down!'

He dived to join Brima on the ground behind the drum, scraping unprotected skin.

A moment of uncertainty stretched in their minds to eternity.

Silence.

Yells of alarm.

All hell let loose.

A brilliant flash.

Then the explosive boom.

Secs later, rubble, dust, body parts.

A rending noise ripped through the falling debris. Ambient brightness increased through the cloud of muck.

For a long moment, they lay still. Rubble settled. Bits of flesh lay around them. Dust coated them. Tattered fabric from the dome blanketed the area.

They breathed. Death and gore entered their mouths along with fine red dust and tiny particles of graphene fabric.

They coughed.

Realised they lived.

Moved carefully, testing limbs and torso.

'You okay Brima?'

She laughed. Actually laughed. 'You?'

He rose slowly to his feet and joined her laughter.

'That was frackin close!'

They looked at each other, shaking with the joy of relief. Both covered in dust. Where the guards had been, a crater. The only signs of their existence, small charred fragments scattered across the blast area.

Georgiy leant forward, gently brushed dust from the top curve of her left breast and carefully pulled out a metal splinter. The bleeding was brief, quickly sealed by her medibots. He gestured she should remove the suit and revolve. He found another sliver in her right knee. Removed it.

'You now.'

She discovered a fingernail-sized piece of rock embedded in his right shoulder. It took a few secs to extract. His medibots worked on the wound at once. The grazes to his skin from the dive were already fading.

A thorough physical check of the drum exposed no further devices. Unconvinced, they searched underneath and along the track. Nothing more. The bomb they'd exploded was the only one. They hoped.

'We should test the drum.'

Brima nodded her approval. He called up Transhub control from the coms panel within the drum and asked for a ten-minute delay followed by an empty test of the device.

'Follow that with a return to this terminal so we can use the drum for our journey back to Marion.'

They moved out of the ruins and waited in the open now all enemy activity had ceased. The drum sealed itself and started moving back towards Marion. No further blasts. It stopped after half a k and returned for them.

'We'll be a few hours.' Brima relaxed. Shifted closer on the wide seat. 'Time enough.'

Georgiy examined those deep blue eyes, shining with life, and agreed. 'After that close scrape with death, we deserve to celebrate.'

Chapter Fifty Four

The street they entered cowered beneath a pall of fear and tension. Gabriel stopped, Daisa's hand still held in his, and tried to get his bearings.

'It's a long, low building, with arched windows covered with pictures you can't see through. But they let in light, Stefan said. I think it's at the end, on the left.'

They passed a couple of bodies lying separately, recently mutilated and defiled.

The pair moved swiftly forward. From somewhere near, a woman cried in pain and fear. Elsewhere, a gang of raucous men shouted drunken threats, brawling. The usual flashing light displays, advertising goods for sale, lay dormant. Every shop they passed had been wrecked and robbed. Items unwanted were scattered in their path. And, here and there, pools of murky fluid stank of urine.

Neither spoke without need as they made their way to their destination. If Gabriel had a plan, he hadn't shared it. Daisa was prepared to take whatever action was possible and necessary once they reached their target.

'Wrong street. Sorry.'

'Can you find the right one, Gabriel?'

'Oh, yes. Next along.'

It was a miner hitch. They turned at the crossroads and took a left turn.

'This is it. I can see the place. Next to the house with broken windows.'

Daisa looked ahead and saw their objective. It was as he'd described it. A long, low building with pointed arches at the tops of the windows, each pane depicting strange scenes with no meaning for her.

'Do you know what they represent?'

Gabriel looked at the one in front of them. 'That's where God handed down the Sacred Texts to Abramohamd, in a desert. He was the first prophet.'

Daisa noted the combination of names and stories from the original texts she'd read as part of her doctorate, but made no comment. They moved toward the door, passing several more picture windows. Daisa stopped at a particularly odd one, right next to the entry into the building, drawing Gabriel's attention to it by squeezing his hand.

'What on Mars is this supposed to be?'

Gabriel studied it briefly. 'It shows how the first woman, called Eva, in league with Marymag, had sex with the Snake of Knowledge before they killed and ate it.'

Daisa was tempted to question him on his current beliefs, but this was definitely neither the time nor the place. 'So, any plans?'

Gabriel placed his ear against the door, listening for signs of occupants. 'I think it's full.'

He gentled the door open and noise quickly established his guess as a fact. They made a rapid survey and reckoned there were about 140 men in there. One of the Clerics noticed the door was open and moved to close it again.

'Okay. So we can't get inside. Unless there's another way in?'

Gabriel was unsure. They followed the perimeter but discovered no other entrance. And returned to the door they'd already found.

'Any ideas?'

He squeezed Daisa's hand. 'This is hard for me. These men taught me about God. They're the ones who pass on knowledge about laws and ways we should behave. I was raised to respect them.'

'Do you believe they told you the truth, Gabriel?'

He was silent for a long time before he answered. 'Not always. And Stefan was one of their officers. He lied to me from the start.'

'Right. It was your idea to put an end to these men. I'm risking my life to help you. We need to do it. Or we get out of here and back to Marion. Which is it to be?'

'It's easy for you, Daisa. You're educated and believe in science. My whole life's been spent learning the rules the Clerics told us.'

'And you still believe they're right? You think they make sense? I showed you the archive of the true history of events at Marzero. You saw for yourself how different the facts are from the story they told you.'

'I know. But it's not easy to break away from something you've believed in all your life. It's not …'

'Is it fear, Gabriel? Are you frightened you'll be punished in the afterlife if you break the rules they gave you? Is that what worries you?'

'You don't believe in the afterlife.'

'We live once. We die once. Except in Marion; we've taken control of our futures and most of us will live forever. But when you're dead, no matter how long you've lived, you're dead. There's nothing after. That's why we recycle bodies. We re-use the elements to sustain life on the planet. That's the only "life" anyone has after death; existence as chemicals that then form other things.'

'I wish I could see everything as clearly as you.'

'One day you will, when you've lived with me for long enough. For now, we've a job to do. And we can't take any more time discussing it. Either we end this sect here and now. Or we go back home to Marion and you spend the rest of your very long life with the knowledge you had a chance to end this dangerous superstition but chose to let it carry on. Up to you, Gabriel.'

'Live with you?'

'It's what I'm hoping we'll do. Don't you?'

'I don't know why you put up with me, Daisa.'

'Simple. I love you.'

He hugged her, a little clumsily. But the embrace seemed to end his indecision.

'Let's do it, Daisa. Will our laser blades set fire to things that burn?'

'Yes. There's a control to make them into industrial strength pulses. But they'll only produce a few at that power. Why?'

'We can't kill them all with our guns. Not in that enclosed space. We'll have to burn them.'

'Okay. You did it once, successfully. But this place is metal. It won't burn, Gabriel.'

'We've got to get rid of them.'

'I know. Let's use our imagination. How far are we from the refining plants?'

Gabriel considered. 'Ten mins?'

'Right. We'll seal the door. Turn your laser blade to High and aim it at the lock. I'll seal the door to the frame.'

They waited to ensure no one was about and did as Daisa suggested. 'Do the windows open?'

'No windows in Marzero open. They're fixed to stop people breaking in and stealing things.'

'Good. Let's go to the industrial centre. I'll get SpyTeam to give us directions to the plant I need.'

They were there in eight mins, moving fast through roads mostly deserted.

Most of the processing works was now a ruin. But SpyTeam led her to the storage unit she sought. The door was hanging open on a broken hinge. Inside, the contents had been partly pillaged but what she needed remained available. Two labourbots stood together in a corner. She checked their charges and found they had enough power for the task.

'Next door, Gabriel, you'll find an open storage yard. Pick a trolley these two can push and bring it back here.'

Gabriel had no idea what she intended, but did as she asked. A medium sized four-wheel trolley was parked behind a couple of smaller ones, which he moved to free it. Heavy, he managed at length to push it to the open door where Daisa waited with the robots. Each held a large metal drum. They placed these on the trolley as soon as he appeared. She piled a selection of hand tools near them and sent the robots back for two more barrels.

The load stacked, she programmed the robots to follow them to the building housing the Clerics.

Moving through the streets took longer with the heavy robots and their load. On one occasion, Gabriel had to deal with a drunk who insisted on hitching a ride. He pushed the man off and had to punch him to stop him bothering them further.

At the building, the Clerics had discovered they were trapped. Much shouting and general noise came from within, attracting a small crowd of curious men. Daisa had the robots push the trolley with its cargo straight through them and up to the end of the building. As was usual in Marzero, the air intakes were on the flat roof. Two in total.

The robots hefted the drums on to the roof and then Daisa had them lift her and Gabriel. The watching crowd had grown a little but seemed more curious than threatening. Certainly, none of them appeared eager to interfere. She split the four metal drums into two pairs and explained what Gabriel must do, giving him some of the tools taken from the store.

Both removed the cowls from the air intakes, allowing free access to the space below. She tipped the contents of the first drum into the opening. Pellets of zinc sulfide rattled on to the metal surface of the ventilation duct.

'Be careful with the liquid, Gabriel. It's a strong acid that'll burn you if you get it on your skin. When you've placed the drum, pierce it. Once the acid's running out, we have to get off the roof and away. Okay?'

No response.

'Got it, Gabriel?'

'Yes. Tip the drum into the space. Pierce it. Make sure the acid's flowing. Then join you and leave the roof together.'

'Right. Let's do it.'

They tipped the drums so they were wedged at an angle over the air vents. The spikes she'd stolen needed a fair amount of force to penetrate the specially designed containers. But she managed to breach hers, and watched the acid pour down over the zinc sulfide pellets.

Gabriel was having difficulty with his and she joined him. Together, they managed to pierce the drum. Hydrochloric acid glugged into the duct.

At once, they could smell the telltale rotten egg pong. In the open, they were relatively safe from the effects, but the hydrogen sulfide would quickly asphyxiate the Clerics trapped in the building below them.

'Come. We need to get out of here. Now.'

She caught his hand and led him to where she'd left the robots. Someone in the crowd had decided to have fun with the mechanical giants and set them wandering aimlessly along the street. Daisa estimated the drop to the ground. Around five ms. A potentially dangerous jump, but not lethal.

'We've no choice. Together?'

They held hands and launched themselves over the edge of the building. From within, the sounds of panic and fear increased exponentially as the gas filtered through.

Daisa landed well, judging her fall accurately and rolling on contact. Gabriel landed awkwardly, crying out in pain.

His yell was mostly drowned by the screams and shouts from inside the building, but one man from the crowd edged round the corner to investigate. Daisa took no notice of him but searched for Gabriel, found him and took his hand.

'You hurt?'

'Hit my hand on something sharp ...'

They moved away from the site of mass murder, the sounds from inside quickly diminishing. The stink of rotten eggs had already cleared the street for their exit.

At the terminal, they discovered the devastation caused by the bomb. No drum. And night was now approaching. Daisa called SpyTeam and asked for a hover.

'On the way. Should be with you around dark. Hang on.'

'We'll find a sheltered spot and wait.'

The evening was dry and cloudless. Come night, the sky would darken and fill with millions of stars. The temperature would drop rapidly. They settled in folds of the ruined fabric of the terminal, wrapping it around them for added warmth, and waited.

Chapter Fifty Five

15 days after the return of the Assassin squad, the Council met for the latest follow-up reports on progress. Although they could readily import data via CenCom, or through their neural implants, the face to face approach had long been accepted as the optimum for clarity, and to allow wide-ranging discussion where necessary. It also encouraged more personal interactions, which were seen as good for a community where technology could so easily be isolating rather than cohesive.

As a result, a large number of people sat around the walls of the Chamber, with the Aggression Council occupying the table in the centre. All could hear the conversations and see any visual displays.

'Amber, please open proceedings with your report on Earth.'

Amber rose from her seat and called up her spinning globe to hang mid-air above the table. It combined data from various probes and was capable of displaying all wavelengths, converting nonvisible ranges into false colours for clarity.

'Storms are a constant problem in the tropical coastal regions, where hurricanes, typhoons and cyclones rise and spread with great frequency. These, together with high temperatures, make those areas unsuitable for habitation. Explorers might be tempted to visit there for valuable resources. It'll allow the adventurous an outlet to prove themselves.

'Ocean currents have changed because of the new topography, with some land bridges now submerged. Seas and oceans now merge where they were previously separated. This reconfiguration of mass water movement has altered weather patterns everywhere.

'Sub-Saharan Africa's a fertile area that's actually spread across the desert. The same can be said of the Atacama; once the most drought-ridden place on the planet, and now a haven for wildlife and rainforest flora. Conversely, central Europe and the Amazon basin are deserts.'

As she spoke, the globe's surface was highlighted to indicate the areas she identified.

'Yellowstone Caldera remains active, as do several volcanoes in the Ring of Fire. Iceland continues to display volcanic activity, and Stromboli and Etna in the enlarged Mediterranean are both volatile.

'Earthquakes beset tectonic margin areas, making a large portion of these regions unsafe. Removal of mass surface ice and the deepening of the oceans have brought about this predicted increase in activity.

'After considerable study and computer modelling, we've identified seven potential habitats for colonists.' She brought up a graphic of the data she'd previously supplied. 'All have capacity to support communities in large numbers. And we suggest we populate them more or less equally.' Amber sat, and the globe reduced to the size of a beach ball hovering centrally.

'Questions?' Hoshiko was still chair.

'Do all areas have viable landing sites, Amber?'

She turned to Brima, sitting behind her. 'Not all are as ideal as we'd like. But we've dispatched a ship carrying constructobots to prepare the ground in all five larger locations. They landed two days ago and started clearing the first site, in Canada. They'll move east from there on the northern hemisphere and then complete their task in the south before returning.

Brima thanked her.

Hoshiko invited further questions. None came. She turned to Madonna, in charge of spacecraft conversion. 'Please, Maddie, your update.'

She rose and called up graphics showing real-time construction crews working on the first ore train to be converted into accommodation. Droid engineers were supervising bots, and work was clearly well under way.

'We borrowed some ideas from the techs who came from the Moon to Mars in the early days. But technology's improved a lot, so we're making these craft a lot more comfortable.

'Gravdrives have been fitted to produce increasing gravity, rising daily until it's 90% of that on Earth, so colonists will undergo gradual change. Modified Ablative Laser Propulsion drives have been installed for slightly increased speed, since ore ships were never made for fast transit. But we're aiming at relatively slow passage to give time for passengers to acclimatise to increased gravity.

'This train will cover the distance in 77 days, if we launch on the target date of 124.04.265. Transitions for following ships will depend on launch dates, but we can cope with the longest flight necessary.

'Accommodation is barrack style. It'll be in use for relatively short periods and colonists will have a better chance to get to know each other well before they land.

'Storage to cover the journey and the start of the colonisation process are adequate. Ships' pilots are modified droids. They'll return with them to Mars after disembarkation.

'We've agreed we want no myth building in the future. Even with our ongoing programme of re-education, these people are gullible and susceptible to superstition. We don't want them to return to any form of worship, so one unit will be left at the landing site. It'll hold graphic portrayals of their journey from Mars to Earth, with explanatory text, and basic scientific data to help in establishing efficient fuel and food use.

'Earth's escape velocity means the ALP drives will have to be modified before return take off. A dedicated engineerbot will do that. And ships can carry enough propellant for the round trip.

'We've built in systems to stop people staying aboard after landing. Initially we'll use sound waves. If that doesn't dislodge those who don't want to leave, we'll reduce temperature until they have to go. But they'll all know they can't come back to Mars on a returning ship, as there'll be no gaseous oxygen for that trip.

'I think I've covered the basics. But I'm happy to answer questions.'

Daisa rose, Gabriel, as ever, by her side. 'At present, we're using subliminal programming and sleep therapy to re-educate colonists. Will that continue on the flight, Maddie?'

'Yes. We'll do that as long as possible. It's always produced variable results. But newly developed techniques,' she nodded to the Psychological Therapies team, 'are a real improvement. We have to accept the technique's less than a 100% reliable, though.'

'What about contraception on the flight?' Ramad put this question.

'We're continuing the programme we've imposed on the city. We'll prevent pregnancy until they're settled in their new location. Life's always been hard for women in Marzero and we don't want to complicate it with unwanted babies.

'The effects will last at least 290 days after disembarkation. From then, it's up to them to decide what they want to do. We can't apply the implant we use here, as they don't have the medical expertise. But they can make their own chemical contraception from constituents present at the landing sites. How they use the pills is up to them. They're suitable for both genders.'

'Any further questions for Maddie?'

A young woman rose. 'What, exactly, are we doing to prevent future bullying of women by the men on arrival at Earth?'

'That's one for the Psychological Therapies team. I'll let Maddie go so she can continue her urgent work with the conversion programme, if that's okay with everyone?'

Maddie left the Chamber.

'Madza? Perhaps you can present your report and answer the question?'

He consigned the globe and Maddie's live broadcast to reduced icons, which he swept to the far end of the table. He called up a set of graphs, diagrams and illustrations, which he highlighted as he gave his presentation.

'This isn't my work, but from various teams, who prepared it for me. I won't bore you with early histories of hypnosis, subliminal suggestibility, sleep therapy, or any of the many disciplines involved in mass education and attitudinal modification. Suffice to say years of experimentation have produced systems of programming that really do work. The details of these techniques aren't for this forum, but I'm happy to discuss it afterwards with anyone interested. For now, please accept that the programmes we've instituted in Marzero work.

'Look at the figures.' He highlighted a graph. 'The rising line shows the correlation between male acts of positive relational behaviour with females, and the falling line illustrates incidents of rape and sexual assault. The therapy works.

'This next graph shows lowering attendance at places of worship and increased access of secular learning via CenCom's library. Our programming is creating doubt about the very basis of the superstitions and irrational beliefs underlying religious faith. There's some incidence of distress and lack of confidence in certain subjects, but that's expected at this stage and is likely to be short-lived in most subjects.'

'Define, "short-lived", please, Madza.'

'As those with knowledge of the topic will be aware, the science of abliform consciousness, personality, attitude and intelligence is probably the most complex we deal with. I use the term "short-lived" as a catchall way to describe an undefined period longer than a moment but shorter than a period of years. Does that answer your question, Janni?'

'Yes. Thank you.'

Madza continued. 'We've finally completed the analysis of those citizens considered suitable for immediate access to Marion. That number's reduced by 19.6%, for reasons I expect we're all aware. Those former citizens, now totalling 3,540, are already in our community. They're living in student accommodation at the Uni pending completion of the new township. I've no data on that, but I expect the project leader will update us all on that later.

'Current stats for converts suitable for transportation to Earth are as follows. The original 800,000 was reduced by CenCom's somewhat … brutal … solution to the problem of disabled and deformed citizens. But that's for further discussion once the immediate crisis is over. The new total is 701,310 individuals. We're monitoring progress and I can report that they're ready.'

'Thank you, Madza.' Hoshiko looked around the table. 'Anyone have anything else to add?'

'I know we have to transport them. We can't keep them here without serious danger to Marion, even after retraining. But, as an ex Zero, I'm worried what they'll find when we leave them on Earth. Will they be in danger? Will they find enough food to keep them going until they can plant crops? And isn't there a danger we're building up a problem for the future, when they develop technology that gets them back into space?'

'Valid questions, Gabriel. And perfectly understandable. I can answer some of those.' Hoshiko signalled graphics from CenCom to illustrate her reply. 'We've selected sites where danger is minimal, though each place has some predators. We want to avoid arming them, so they'll have to devise their own methods of defence. They'll have food stocks to last until their second harvest and we're sending equipment with them to help with agriculture.

'Of course, there are problems with what we're doing. But the reality is we've no real alternative if we're to live our own lives in any sort of secure peace. Retraining's a long-term matter and, as we've already discussed, we can't afford to leave these people free to roam the planet until they're properly educated. We do, however, intend to make occasional visits to Earth, once colonies are established, so we can check on progress and give whatever aid we can. Does that help?'

Gabriel nodded, but he was clearly unhappy with the unknowns of the situation. 'I'd like to go on one of those early visits, if that's possible?'

'I think that should be fine. But it's not an urgent matter, is it?' Hoshiko glanced around, inviting further questions. None arose, so she gestured at Zaphod.

He stood and flicked Madza's graphs and Hoshiko's graphics to small icons at the head of the table. 'Maddie can't spare more time from her duties, so she's asked me to show you this.' He called up a large visual of the ore ship Maddie's team were converting for the first flight, presenting it in cutaway form to display the interior.

'We can sleep 1,764 passengers on each train, assuming all will have eight units plus the front and rear drives. One unit will be common space for exercise and leisure activities. That'll be converted to the educational unit and left on Earth.

'Another will be used for all normal facilities; cooking, personal hygiene, etc. Storage space is in the voids created by the square cross section through the cylindrical outer.' He highlighted these as he spoke.

'Marzero kept a fleet of 12 such ships and, in agreement with the Outer Colonies, we plan to convert another seven in the same way as this prototype. Unfortunately, our destruction of certain production facilities in Marzero caused some disruption to the manufacture of certain components. However, with contributions from our own robots, droids, our engineering specialists, and some workers from Marzero, we've managed to reinstate the essential works, and production is now catching up with need.

'At the estimated rate of conversion, we should have the entire fleet ready within 70 days. But we're sending each ship off as it's finished. That constantly circulating fleet will let us complete the entire transportation over a period starting with the first trip in 24 days and the final landing on Earth in just over a year.'

'Any questions?' Hoshiko thanked Zaphod.

'A whole year to transport them?'

'Yes, Georgiy. We can't do it sooner.' Zaphod sat down.

Hoshiko asked whether anyone else had any questions. Those that came were on minor technical issues that each speaker was easily able to field.

'That concludes this meeting with respect to the transportation project. Tomorrow, those concerned will meet to discuss progress on the new Marion residents. If that's all, I move that we close the meeting and take a well-earned rest from these problems.'

'I'd like to know what we intend to do about the cull of the unsuitables, please.'

Hoshiko stared at Sarm with a look she hoped would convey she'd rather not tackle that right now.

'I don't think we can ignore it, can we?' Sarm continued.

'No.' Hoshiko sighed. 'We can't. But the issue's a matter for deep discussion once we've settled current problems. CenCom's resolved the practical problem. We need to discuss the moral aspect and … other factors, about our future. But later, I think.'

'Bearing in mind how CenCom acted, are we safe delaying our discussion on that topic?'

Georgiy stood and spread his hands in a gesture of resignation. 'Yes, Sarm. We must discuss it. And very soon. But we've been at this all day and need fresh, open, minds to deal with such a thorny issue. Best not do it now. Later, those not compromised by our current tasks will convene to debate the issue.

'On an entirely unrelated issue, I believe it's way past time we had a field meeting to examine the wilderness at the edge of the new township. I'll get full details to those interested.'

The meeting broke up. Daisa and Gabriel left together, hand in hand, walking slowly through mild evening air to their shared pod.

'Georgiy and Hoshiko were a bit dismissive of Sarm's legitimate concerns, don't you think, Daisa?'

'I understand your frustration, anger even, but …' She squeezed his hand in a manner he'd learned meant he should say nothing more on the topic for now.

Zaphod's cure of his epilepsy had increased his confidence, but since the DNA treatment on return from Marzero, he discovered he was more sensitive to many everyday experiences surrounding him. Too old to have the neural implant, he lacked Daisa's ability for direct communication with CenCom, but otherwise he felt he was becoming more integrated into the community.

'How come I'm fitting in better than Buzz here, Daisa?'

'The fact that you ask the question marks you out as so different from him. First, you're naturally less selfish than Buzz. He spent his entire life doing only what he felt was to his advantage, even though most of what he did actually went against his interests. He thought he was cleverer than he was. You think you're less intelligent than you are. You look for ways to help other people. He only cared about helping himself.

'We, the community that is, gave Buzz far too much benefit of the doubt. Too much leeway. He was one of the early members, and he did provide us with a useful service at the beginning, even if it was only because he could use it for his own purposes. Buzz had a type of personality that would never change. He was inflexible. You, on the other hand, may have been gullible and suggestible, but much of that was down to your brain fault and the rest was due to ignorance of the truth. You're willing to learn, eager to know the truth. Buzz cared only about self gratification. Need I go on?'

'I thought Marion was a place where mistakes didn't happen.'

Daisa smiled and looked down at her feet. 'We're abliform, Gabriel. We make mistakes. Intelligence alone isn't proof against errors, you know. We're organic creatures full of emotions; being clever doesn't cancel out that side of abliform nature.'

In their pod, Daisa did a very strange thing. She sat at the table and wrote, by hand, on a sheet of paper. She folded her note and, her finger briefly to her lip, she embraced him to slip the note into his hand. He concealed it there, kissed her, and moved to the door.

'Just need a spot more air before we settle, Daisa.'

She gave him an encouraging smile. 'Don't be long. I've plans for the evening.'

Outside, he moved into nearby shrubbery, away from the ubiquitous cctv, and opened his palm to reveal the note. On the front, Daisa had written, 'Open away from cameras.' An unnecessary warning, given the nature of Daisa's other covert signals.

He unfolded the note and read. 'Georgiy will give date and time in a coded message. Then meet him at outer edge of Newton. In my cabinet you'll find a chronometer on a neck chain. Wear it. I can say no more. Vital you remain silent.'

That was it. He thought back to the meeting and concluded something was going on that must be kept secret from CenCom.

Back in the pod, he greeted Daisa and slipped her note into the shredder for recycling.

She stood and palmed her torso with both hands, inviting him. 'Food first, or a fuck?'

'Food for the spirit, please, my goddess, now I don't have a god to turn to.'

Daisa laughed as he fell to his knees with his palms together and then followed her, on all fours, to their bedroom.

Chapter Fifty Six

Georgiy woke to the blare of the warning alarm. For half a sec he was disoriented and puzzled. But his astronaut training clicked in, and he heard Amber quiz CenCom.

'Vesta's been dislodged from orbit and set on a spiral that will cause the moon to collide with the planet surface in 71 hours 16 mins and 37 secs.'

'Do you know how?' Amber asked.

'Do you know who?' Georgiy added.

'A small personnel craft, piloted by an unknown droid, launched from Marzero a day ago, without clearance. It was occupied by a member of the Elite who'd escaped execution. Statistically, we confirm there was a 0.957% chance of such an event. Three of the city's tech staff accompanied him. The flight took the craft on a path to intercept Vesta.

'In the absence of alternative data, it's logical to conclude these people used the fitted ALP drives to engineer the change in Vesta's orbit. These were left in place in the event of any subsequent need for change. Logic dictates that the techs re-activated the drives to divert the body on to this lethal orbit.'

'Any idea why?'

'Data's inadequate. Our conclusion, based on our attempt to simulate faulty thought processes of sub-abliform Zeros, is that they feel aggrieved about rational remedial actions we and the teams from Marion have taken during recent times. We conclude they are pursuing a policy of revenge'

'Turn the alarm off.' Amber requested. 'The whole of Marion must be awake by now.'

The siren stopped.

'Should we continue?'

'Please do.'

'The small moon will pass close to the peak of Olympus Mons and directly over Marzero during its descent. The final orbit will result in collision with the planet surface at Marion. The level of destruction at impact can be estimated only within a very broad range of possibilities. None of these outcomes allows continued existence of sentient life on the planet. And all current structures and intelligent entities will be destroyed in the aftermath.'

'And the pass over Marzero?' Georgiy asked, as he dressed. 'Any ideas on the likely outcome?'

'We predict a narrow band immediately below the track of Vesta will be subject to excess gravitational influence. This is likely to cause quakes with magnitudes ranging from 8.9 to 10.2, and may disturb magma in locations where such volatile material is currently suspected. We have insufficient data to calculate whether eruptions may occur. We estimate the initial pass over Marzero will result in significant structural damage to the base rock and any buildings seated on it. Similarly, there is significant danger that the peak of Olympus Mons may collapse and cause landslides. The direction, spread and damage potential of such geological events are currently beyond calculation.'

Georgiy and Amber were ready to leave by this time. He contacted their techs who'd been involved in the movement of the two bodies into orbit. Having consulted CenCom on hearing the siren, they'd already convened at the small leisure spaceport outside Hadfield Town on the south-western edge of the community. Here, the only ground launched spacecraft were housed: mostly personal craft used for entertainment. All major spaceflight operated via the space elevator, but this was too slow to use in an emergency.

'Give us 20 to join you. Have we weapons and tools?'

'Affirmative. We'll prepare to take off as soon as you arrive. Copy?'

'Copy.' Georgiy felt at home with the sudden reversion to space talk.

Transhub took them direct to the spaceport and they sent messages to all and sundry as they travelled. This was a mission for a select few, but the rest of the community needed to be alert to the possibilities regarding this insane act of vengeance from the Zeros.

The small personnel carrier, the only serviceable craft not currently pressed into use on ore ship conversion duties, was fast and manoeuvrable. Georgiy felt comfortable as he belted up for take off. Amber piloted, though a droid remained in reserve. The craft could carry only four. Georgiy was pleased to see Madza, as they'd become firm friends after their adventures in the city. The fourth member was a young woman he barely knew.

'Yinli. I was with the crew moving Vesta, setting up the ALP drives.' Her features displayed the typical, almost unworldly, beauty of the mix of European and Chinese ancestry.

'Drew the short straw?'

'Volunteered!'

'Glad to have you aboard. Let's get this done!'

CenCom had calculated their optimal flight path to Vesta. Amber's job was merely to confirm the trajectory and initiate take off. As they left the atmosphere, they suited up and discussed needs and tactics. As far as they were aware, the Zeros were still on the moon: suicidal, but apparently their thirst for revenge had removed what few wits they started out with.

The flight took under six hours. They orbited Vesta three times, scanning with IR and HiRes to detect current activity. It was clear the Zeros remained on the small moon: they were guarding the major ALP drive and its propellant to prevent interference. Their small craft stood on the uneven surface only a short distance away.

Amber set down within easy walking distance, but beyond the horizon. They made visual contact only 10 mins after landing.

Madza felt it fair and sensible to warn the Zeros of their suicidal position. If nothing else, they might abandon their action. 'If you don't evacuate in the next 10 hours, you'll be too late to escape. You'll die as Vesta burns in the atmosphere and explodes on impact. That what you want?'

'Twat off! You killed our people. Now your lot's gonna burn. We stayin. You twattin morons can't do nowt stop us.'

The four held a quick discussion.

'No choice.' Georgiy put the obvious into words.

Their first shots had three saboteurs scurrying for cover. Their fallen comrade wouldn't rise again.

The Marion team were more concerned about the laser drive and its propellant than a battle with no purpose other than to delay their actions. They must eliminate the Zeros.

Hidden behind equipment the team needed to preserve, the saboteurs felt safe from further attack. Over the open ground between, a speedy advance was impossible. The four held a brief confab before splitting into pairs to form a pincer movement. The small circumference of the moon presented uneven horizons within a few hundred meters in all directions.

Georgiy and Amber took the left course, while Yinli and Madza approached from the right. Small craters afforded the only cover. Their opposition, sheltering behind the equipment, had the advantage.

Time was the major concern. If they were unable to shift the saboteurs quickly enough to alter the settings and reconfigure the orbit, everyone on the planet, as well as those on the moon itself would fry in the resulting fireball, explosion and catastrophic aftermath.

An oblate spheroid with a diameter of around 530 ks, Vesta was pitted with craters and coated in a deep layer of unstable regolith.

The bright little world's tiny gravity meant the team had to employ personal gravipacks to move freely over the surface. With escape velocity so slight, it would be too easy to be lost into space if they used excess energy.

Three ALP drives were located high above the surface of selected craters, mounted on offset tripods. The major drive created forward propulsion and the other two, on opposite faces of the moon, provided steering.

Their individual controls were linked so they could be used in concert to alter Vesta's course. Beneath each laser array, filling the individual craters over which they were attached, was the propellant. Iron, readily available in the Asteroid Belt, had been melted into the voids in situ. When the laser fired a pulse, a small amount of iron was vaporised to propel the moon in the desired direction.

The Zeros had fired both the major drive and steerage units to rotate the moon on its axis and then create a decaying spiral orbit by firing the major drive in the opposite direction to orbital travel.

Conscious of the time factor, and concerned for the fate of the citizens of the city, Georgiy hailed the saboteurs again. Like Madza, he hoped against hope they might recant. 'You'll cause massive quake damage in Marzero. You have to change course now to stop it.'

'Twat off! Think we're stupid? We don't give a twat's furry beard for the city. You've destroyed everythin anyway.' The accompanying shots from their pulse guns and laser blades had Georgiy and Amber diving for cover.

Further discussion was clearly pointless. All-out attack was the only option left. He passed the message to the others. 'Together. Ready, everyone?'

It was a desperate policy, but all they had if they were to make the changes necessary in time. Once in position, with the main drive between them, they rushed the crater, all guns firing. Pulses and laser blades cut the ground around the equipment, raising clouds of dust. The Zeros were cloaked by the disturbance, making it difficult for them to see the advance and fight back effectively.

The four from Marion closed without injury. Yinli, leaping on to the concrete base, caught the Elite's gravipack with a laser blade, detaching the unit from the wearer's brightly coloured suit. It tore a small rent in the fabric, allowing oxygen to escape in a jet powerful enough to send the wearer spiralling up from the surface. He rose rapidly into space, shooting as he spun into the darkness, but missing everything vital.

That left two techs. The four from Marion were now also able to use the solid equipment base as cover. The holding blocks of concrete, cementing the tripod to the ground, stood a little short of man-height. Forming a hollow equilateral triangle enclosing the open crater, each side stretched 25ms between the ends. They joined at apexes, angled at 60 degrees. Both techs occupied either side of one apex, giving them a clear view along two faces of the triangle. The Marion team hid behind the third face. Attempts to persuade these two men to give up on their scheme met with derision.

Amber crept left with Georgiy, whilst Madza and Yinli took the right hand corner. They emerged together. One tech was ready and waiting. He fired at once, missing Georgiy, but hitting Amber's gravipack full blast with a pulse. Her unit ceased to function at once. The power of the pulse pushed her now near weightless body up and away.

She fired her tether immediately. The probe penetrated regolith and struck bedrock with its barbed tip almost at the limit of the cable. Pulled her up. Jerked her to a sudden halt, floating above the action, 200ms below.

Georgiy reacted at once. Killed the man who'd attacked Amber.

But, crouched low to escape the advancing Madza and Yinli, and unseen by Georgiy, the last saboteur had him in his sights. He raised the pulse gun. At a range of only 3ms, the blast would rip straight through the suit and fry his innards.

Amber, recovering from her sudden halt, and still disorientated, saw movement from the corner of her eye. It took her a fraction of a sec to identify the enemy. She shot twice. The first pulse missed him by fractions, but sent a blast of dust and regolith skyward.

Georgiy was alerted by the disturbance. He shifted a few cms as the man let rip. Amber's second shot blasted through the saboteur's helmet and fried his brain. The pulse already released from his gun tore through Georgiy's suit, taking a chunk from his elbow. The suit's integrity was breached and he lost pressure.

Pressing 'retract' brought Amber slowly back to ground. But it would take too long for her to save Georgiy. Yinli was on the spot. With moments to stop the leak becoming lethal, she did the only thing possible. Her laser, switched to weld, sealed the suit around the wound; material to flesh. Georgiy fainted from the searing pain, but his suit's integrity was restored.

'We've only hours to stop this disaster.' Madza took in the scene as Amber finally regained the ground. 'Can you get him to the ship?'

'Don't you need me here?'

'Yinli and I can do what's necessary now we're free of the morons. You take Georgiy back.'

She adjusted his gravipack to a quarter to hold them both in check as she carried him over the rough terrain toward their craft.

Madza and Yinli systematically surveyed the tripod bearing the major drive. Georgiy's earlier experience had taught them the dangers of booby-traps. They found nothing out of the ordinary.

'Let's go.'

Yinli climbed the ladder to the platform. He waited for her to clear the rungs and then followed.

Space was limited. A long narrow gangway made of steel grid allowed engineers access to the panels covering the controls.

'Why so many bolts, Yinli?'

'We felt it essential to prevent tampering. Some of the crew from Marzero wanted to mess around with the settings. They thought a closer approach to the planet would speed things up. We had to make it difficult for anyone to alter the controls alone.'

And she was right. It was a complex procedure. Only when the cowlings were removed did they find the saboteurs had also taken the tools they needed.

'Do what you can with what we've got, Yinli. I'll go for our spares.'

She watched him reduce his gravipack setting so he could lope more easily across the surface. His leap from the service gangway took him well over a quarter of the way back to the ship, which she could now see on the horizon from her elevated position.

The cover of the panel in front of her was fixed with both magnetic and manual bolts. The manuals were movable using the adjustable wrench carried in the pouch on her lower left leg. She set about undoing the first of 27 numbered bolts in the correct order.

Aboard the small personnel carrier, Amber had shed her suit and removed as much of Georgiy's as she could. Where it merged with his flesh, she left it dangling. But this caused him agony from the drag on his raw wound. Setting her laser blade to precision, she cut away the excess, relieving both weight and pain.

The airlock alerted her to Madza's return. Whilst Georgiy lay on the seat she'd dropped into recliner mode, she helped the young man gather the necessary tools.

'Two hours before it'll be too late to alter orbit, Madza.'

He glanced at Georgiy. 'All in hand. You concentrate on getting repaired.' He turned to Amber and lowered his voice. 'If we're not back in an hour and 50 mins, take off and leave us.'

'I can't do …'

'You're wasting time, Amber. I need that promise.'

She nodded.

He stared at her.

'Okay, I promise.'

He took the tools and she watched through the ports as he loped quickly over the horizon. Georgiy was still in pain. She sought out the medpack to find a painkiller to deaden the wound until the medibots completed their extensive work. There was nothing either of them could do to resolve this situation now. It was up to the newer generation.

Georgiy started to relax with the effect of the medication. He even smiled. 'Ah well, only the future of all humanity in their hands. No pressure.'

Amber smiled with him, recalling their own fight against the odds so many many years previously. But her smile was ironic and short-lived. Here on this rock speeding through space, and down on the planet surface, aware but helpless, the bulk of abliform life depended on the skills and abilities of two young people. And Madza's only previous experience of the task ahead had been learned through reading on the flight here.

Chapter Fifty Seven

Yinli had removed the first layer of protection. For the briefest moment, he hugged her. The tools Madza brought accelerated the job of preparing the engine for change.

As they followed protocols Yinli shared, they talked to each other, confirming memories and sequences. It was vital, with the ALP drive, that everything be done in the right order. Any misstep could cause a malfunction, but there were two stages in particular that might completely devastate their scheme.

So, they worked in patient methodical steps, each checking with the other. The rotational speed and angle of descent of Vesta was such that it no longer connected with coms satellites. They were on their own.

Conscious of passing time and the probable destruction of Marzero on the track they took, the young pair worked as fast as circumstances permitted. But they feared, as they started the most sensitive part of the change, they wouldn't be able to save the city.

Cranial implants didn't work this far from GrandMa. Madza sent the ship a message, asking them to try to get through on the ship's coms to alert the citizens. It was a hopeless task, but they felt they must at least try.

The final step involved a double-handed, synchronised, lifting of two hatches. Although the drive had been put together with a degree of automation built in for such deconstruction, the engineering meant there was a point where only a pair of sentient minds could manoeuvre the last two hatches in a specific manner, if total shutdown was to be avoided. It was easy to lift these two hatches if shutdown was required, as was normal procedure. But they hadn't time for such niceties. They must override the usual process and expose both ends of the drive controls simultaneously.

'Ready, Madza?'

The bulk of the drive stood between them, separating them with three ms of electromechanical works.

'Ready.'

'On my count of three?'

'Copy.'

She checked each of the securing bolts once more and took up the stance that would allow her to raise her hatch in a single swift upward movement. Madza's delay indicated he was doing the same. She waited.

'Madza?'

'Sorry. One bolt still had a turn connected. Ready now. You?'

'Copy.'

'One, two, three.'

They each lifted their assigned hatch, an impossible task for both on the surface of the planet, but well within their capability on this tiny rock as it hurtled toward their mutual destruction.

Nothing happened.

They'd accomplished the most testing part of the protocol. Now all they had to do was reconfigure the orbital settings.

Madza joined her at the central portion of the newly exposed console.

'At last! Certainly didn't want anyone getting in here, did we?'

'Which begs the question how those moronic Zeros managed it, Yinli.'

'Maybe they were on the team installing it. Or, perhaps they had time to reboot. Who knows?'

'Right. New co-ordinates?'

Madza reeled off the figures he'd acquired from CenCom before launch. Preserved in his memory, they had to be absolutely accurate if they were to achieve the intended orbit. In fact, they were marginally different from the originals, as the consensus was that the original orbit had been a little too close and was causing more tectonic activity than was comfortable.

Yinli fed in the numbers as he spoke them. All they had to do now was press three 'reset' buttons within ten secs of each other. Yinli took the left side steering drive. Madza stretched his arms wide to reach the controls for the major drive, in the centre, and the right hand steering drive.

'Ready?'

'Copy.'

'In three.'

'Go.'

'One, two, three.' Madza pressed the major reset button.

Yinli hit her reset button to his left. The one to his right seemed to be stuck. He shifted his stance and tried again.

'Four secs!'

He used one hand to pull his weight hard down and the other to press on the reset button again. Nothing.

'Underneath, Madza. There's a …'

Yinli's warning drew his eye and he saw it. A flat tool had been wedged under the rim of the button, stopping it moving. He flicked the tool out and pressed again.

'Got it!' Yinli pointed to the central control panel that indicated all three drives were operating in concert.

'Close thing.'

'Too close!'

Working near the energy pulses firing at the iron below and turning it to plasma to create motion, they saw by the motion of the stars that the moon was rotating back to its correct position. Soon, the turn would complete and then the major drive would accelerate Vesta back to the proper orbit.

They tooled up and replaced hatches and cowlings as quickly as possible. With a min and 30 secs to spare, they reduced their gravipacks to allow a repeat of Madza's original leap. Then, long lopes took them over the horizon without the danger of reaching escape velocity. Secs before Madza's ultimatum came into force, they made the ship.

'Jupiter's balls! I actually felt that.' Madza looked at Yinli in surprise at the sudden change in movement that indicated the forward drive had kicked in. Vesta was progressing toward the new trajectory.

Back inside the personnel craft they strapped in and Amber took off. They flew over Marzero on their way back home.

'Morons! Look at the damage. Why would someone do that to a place where friends and colleagues lived? I don't understand them.' Madza stared in disbelief at the chaos.

'Different society. Different priorities, Madza.' Amber spoke as she set the craft's controls back to autopilot for their descent. 'The Elite had no concept of friendship or fellow-feeling. They were interested only in individual profit and power. Once that was lost, their last resort was revenge; probably the most negative but destructive of all emotions. And, bearing in mind their status, such an emotional reaction might've been predicted. I can only assume CenCom was certain this sort of action was impossible, otherwise they'd have made sure they could prevent it. Just goes to show you should never make assumptions about abliforms, even a sub-species like the Zeros.' She checked the chronometer dangling from the chain around her neck as she spoke.

Georgiy fingered a similar device resting on his chest.

Yinli was about to ask about these strange mechanical timepieces, worn by the Chosen, but they passed over Marzero and the destruction below caught her attention.

Flames, smoke, and ruin laid waste to a great strip running through the city from west to east. The band of destruction marked a huge tract of land with ripples, trenches and cracks, as if some giant finger nail had scratched across the surface. It faded after they'd followed it for 50ks. The southern half of the city lay buried under the rubble of a landslide, some of the boulders and loose regolith still smashing into place from the steep peak of the volcano.

'Who'd have thought gravity alone could produce such devastation?'

'The forces are pretty big, Yinli. Look how far we are from the Sun, but we're forever falling toward it. That's some attraction.'

'I know that, Madza. But to actually see it: that really brings the power home, doesn't it?'

'True. Those idiots put Vesta so close. Let's hope they haven't set off other, longer term, disturbances.'

'CenCom's monitoring should discover those, Madza.'

'Yes. But will we be able to do anything to stop any damaging changes on the way?'

'Who knows? It's the people in Marzero I feel for. I'll send CenCom pictures so they can see the damage. I know we can't do much, but we should organise some sort of rescue mission, however limited, straight away.'

Chapter Fifty Eight

'Jeez! How did we come to this? These were our own people. I don't understand.' Gabriel stood transfixed by the devastation. Among the wreckage, bodies lay burnt, dead or seriously injured. Too many to count, too many for the rescue party to deal with.

'You don't understand? And you lived here.' Daisa surveyed the carnage around them. 'It's the inevitable outcome of a capitalist system with no conscience.' She braced herself against her feelings of despair and embraced him in sympathy. 'Come on. Let's do what we can for those in need of help.'

He emerged from his trance-like state of shock and walked with her to the nearest spot where a body showed signs of life. They cleared rubble and fallen sheets of metal cladding that trapped the person. A seriously damaged man lay face down on the ground. Daisa scanned him with her borrowed medscan. Internal damage, dangerously low blood pressure due to loss, breathing compromised by broken ribs, serious brain injury under the fractured skull. The scan gave the chance of physical recovery at 27.3%, mental recuperation at 8.6%.

Daisa knelt by the unconscious figure and removed the inoculajet from the medpack. The fine stream of euthanizing fluid took a tenth of a sec to reach the blood vessel beneath and the man was dead within five secs.

'No chance he'd get better, Daisa?'

'None worth attempting. Sorry.' She collected a red flag from Gabriel's side pack and attached it to the man's left ankle.

He registered the body along with GPS coordinates with CenCom, and they moved on to the next casualty.

Their following 15 victims required only the flag and registration so collection robots would find them and take them for recycling. The seven after that needed the euthanizing jab.

But their next subject was a woman whose chances of both physical and mental recovery were high enough to warrant an attempt. Daisa took a green flag from Gabriel and he registered the patient with CenCom under code amber, which meant recobots would stretcher her away to the Transhub as soon as possible.

'Wonder how they're managing at the hospital?'

Gabriel looked around and threw his hands out in a gesture of hopelessness. 'So many, Daisa. How can we …?'

'Positive, Gabriel. Negativity damages productivity. We need to focus. There are some we can save. Try to keep that uppermost.'

They moved on. They'd started on the edge of the disaster area and worked slowly into the more damaged regions as teams of robots cleared the ground ahead. The local population from unharmed sectors seemed dazed and frozen into inactivity. Several times they had to force passage through small crowds of onlookers and coax them back home, out of the way.

A constant stream of recobots and dispobots moved in and out of the areas as they checked for life, health, death and injury. After seven hours of searching, the pair needed rest. Fewer and fewer citizens emerged as viable cases and the death toll mounted exponentially as they neared the epicentre of the chaos. Beneath the landslide there was no chance of life, so they concentrated on the narrow strip of quake damage.

Droids brought food and drink. Gabriel and Daisa sat with fellow rescuers on any surface that would support them for the time of their break. The stench of gore took away appetite but they must eat to be effective, and they drank to keep hydration up and their brains active.

That night, they spent in temporary shelters, set up by droids, who cooked and served food. Alcoholic drink was available to relax distressed nerves and help the teams sleep. They avoided the newsreel that reported on the disaster; too much negative info.

The morning brought snow and continuation of what rapidly became a hopeless task. By mid afternoon team leaders called a halt. Those still undiscovered were pronounced dead; night temperatures would've killed anyone exposed. They left them to the dispobots. The rescue teams moved slowly back to the partially restored Transhub terminal and boarded the line of drums along with the remaining stretchered patients and occasional walking wounded.

It was early evening before the pair were able to shower and take a proper meal together in Daisa's quarters. She cracked open red wine to go with the food. They ate in weary silence.

'Thanks, Gabriel. You were great out there.'

'Me? Daisa, I don't know why you put up with me. I was part of that … that horror out there. I still don't really know how you can forgive me for what I did to …?'

She leant forward and kissed him. 'Enough. We've had that conversation. I'll summarise and then we never revisit this. Ever. Understood?'

He blinked back tears but nodded.

'You were ill with a brain condition. You were badly educated by a corrupt and vile system run by men without conscience. You were fooled by the cunning of that evil swine, Stefan.'

She took a slow swallow of her wine. 'But, once we cured your epilepsy and started re-education, tackled your superstitions and illogical beliefs, you changed into the man you're fast becoming. You were once a Zero, Gabriel, but now you're almost a Marionet.

'Over the past days, you've demonstrated real courage. Today, you showed your true nature as you cared for those we rescued and treated. You displayed real concern and anxiety. In short, you behaved like a proper member of our community.'

She tapped the end of his nose with a light fingertip. 'Now, if you're up to it after our efforts, I'd very much appreciate a long, gentle, loving fuck to restore our spirits before we sleep, please.'

He shook his head. 'You're a marvel, do you know that?'

She smiled. 'I'm an offspring of the Chosen, Gabriel. I have great advantages over the ancient breed of humans. One reason we altered our species name to abliform was to separate ourselves from the sins and inadequacies of the race that preceded us. Now, are you going to keep me waiting, or …?'

He rose, slipped the tunic over his head, catching the case of the chronometer on its chain. He glanced at it briefly, wondering when the call would come. But Daisa was watching him with a look that appealed far more than any practical question. He offered his hand to help her from the seat. The bed was soft as he lay her down.

Chapter Fifty Nine

Brigitte and Brima wandered through the developing township, appropriately named Newton. It had been a turbulent few days, but everything finally appeared to be on track. The first transportation ship had launched and a second was under conversion. It was a relentless task for those involved.

'You need fewer ships after the quake, Brigitte.' Brima's comment caused a rueful smile.

'Unspeakable waste. But, silver linings, perhaps?'

Brigitte was also concerned with this project, because of the involvement of larger robots, and had taken time out from space to check on progress.

'How many in the end? Do we have a figure, Brigitte?'

'GrandMa came up with no more than 350,000. Imagine, all those deaths.' She shrugged off the feeling of despair that thought brought. 'So, we're using only three landing sites. They need some population density to have a real chance of survival.'

In Newton, the individual pods were of the same class as those designed for students, since most incoming Zeros were single women. Plenty of space around each allowed for future developments, should residents wish to become couples or even families.

But it was the larger, specialist unit she'd drawn out of storage that was of most interest to Brigitte. They needed to house the remaining children in a place of safety as soon as possible. The incidence of child abuse in Marzero had been appallingly high, and violent; cause for their rapid removal from the city. As a result, only a handful had perished in the disaster. The sooner they could start these poor orphans and neglected kids on the long process of recovery, the better.

Brima's presence reminded her strongly of her days as a mother, though Brima was hardly one of those early children. But she was an offspring of Brigitte's line and it was good to have the younger woman with her on this inspection tour.

'Was it wise to position this place so close to the Risk, Brigitte?'

'It's the only logical space available. Not ideal. But once the rest of the Zeros have gone, I don't see it as a danger to the residents. Do you?'

'Not a danger. They're on the edge of everything, that's all. This new community will always be marginal. I thought we wanted to integrate them into Marion, not just tag them on like a spare part?'

'You're right, Brima. But they won't stay here, you know. We're not going to allow it to become a ghetto like those dreadful slum areas they had on Earth, and, for that matter in Marzero.

'The idea is to give them stability and the confidence of like-minded folk while they undergo conversion. Then they'll migrate into the general community and others from elsewhere will move into the units they vacate. It'll take time, but it'll work in the end. In 30 years we'll hardly know it ever happened.'

'30 years! Sounds like a lifetime.'

'I forget. When you've been around for 237, 30 seems the blink of an eye.'

'You're all so old, you pioneers and originals. But you don't look it.'

'I hope we don't behave like it, either.'

'Most of you don't. Ah, here we are, Brigitte.'

The child centre stood before them. Already, the outer walls and roof were in place. They went inside to check on progress of the internal work. The bots were busy, needing no rest, and the droids in charge ensured all was going according to plan. It was a smaller team than they really wanted, but many bots and droids were needed for conversion of the ore trains, leaving them a bit short in the township.

Brigitte consulted with the three leading droids on progress and planning.

'There's nothing you need do, Ma'am. We'll have the centre up and running in two days.'

'Thank you. Keep me informed, won't you?'

The droids confirmed they would.

364

'I'm due back in space tomorrow. Fancy a swim before dinner, Brima?'

'Oh, let's!'

They travelled new roads and walkways and down to the lake that served the community. The water had settled and the small pier was already in use. Some newcomers were enjoying the afternoon sunshine and splashing in the shallows. None were swimmers, yet. Time would alter that.

Brigitte and Brima ran to the end of the pier where it lay over deeper water. They dived in together and came up a little way from the boards, floating. Lying flat on her back, treading water and relaxing under a sky as blue as those she recalled from her days on Earth, Brigitte was struck by a thought.

'You know, one day I'd like to return.'

'To Earth?'

'Wouldn't you like to see where your ancestors came from?'

'I love it here. It's what they used to call "paradise", isn't it? Won't Earth be chaotic and dangerous?'

'Oh, for the next few hundred years. But I was thinking more of the end of that time. Our probes and occasional visits will keep us informed of progress. It'll be a long time before they rise out of their primitive state as pioneers. Once they've started to develop properly again, we'll need to check they're progressing along the right lines. I'd like to be part of an inspection force. Wouldn't you?'

'I'll be about the same age as you are now. Yes, I suppose it might be something I could look forward to. Right now, I just want years of fun, learning, research and creative work here in Marion.' She dived under the surface and came up close enough to Brigitte to duck her.

They engaged in games, splashing and chasing until they grew tired. Then they returned to dry land and made their way back home for an evening meal. For Brigitte, arriving home and knowing she'd never again have to suffer the impositions of Buzz left her feeling mostly relieved.

'He was a stupid, bullying and rather pathetic man, Brima. But I did once love him. For a while.'

Brima considered her great great grandmother and nodded in sympathy. 'I was a member of the Exclusives, you know. Silly things you do when young, eh? Glad they've ended that particular club. Do you suppose we'll always be a bit daft when it comes to love?'

'I suspect, left to their own devices, our hormones and genes will forever combine in an attempt to find the best matches. With all the variables, I guess it's inevitable they sometimes make mistakes. It's one reason Qiu and Zaphod keep researching DNA.'

Brigitte's domestic droid entered to serve the meal. She thanked it. 'Maybe artificial intelligence has its advantages?'

The droid placed food and drinks before them and turned its enigmatic smile to Brigitte. 'Ma'am, I'd sacrifice a good part of my logic to experience fully the emotions open to abliforms.'

Chapter Sixty

Zaphod removed a flask from his left abdominal compartment and clicked it open. He offered the contents to Georgiy, eying the container with some regret.

His friend took a swig. 'Excellent! Don't you miss it?'

'I miss many things, Georgiy. But I'm still alive, well, in a way. Sentient at any rate. It could've been much worse.'

They were crossing the fields on the very edge of the settlement, passing through crops where robots tended fruit, vegetables and grain.

'So, how's the project going, Amber?' Georgiy took her hand and walked with her.

'Well. We're progressing on the new probe at last.'

Zaphod strolled to be beside Hoshiko. All the Chosen were there, along with Gabriel and Virginia. The issue had to be tackled, and they were the only ones able to do what was necessary in secret. No implants.

Zaphod and Hoshiko controlled their connections to CenCom and could disconnect voluntarily.

Out here, away from the zone overseen by GrandMa, they could at last talk safely about her, without the fear of being overheard or monitored.

They could discuss their planned alterations to the comprehensive AI that controlled all aspects of daily life in the community.

Georgiy called them together in their couples and groups.

'Okay. We all know why we're here. And what we have to do. Today's the day to ensure we all understand our roles. Everybody on board?'

They'd discussed the need for action. Already decided what they must do. Now it was time to implement the changes.

'One logical switch to by-pass the Prime Directive is one too many.' Georgiy turned to Hoshiko. 'Have you and Zaphod completed the code?'

Zaphod answered. 'Oh, the code's all prepared for input. It's altering access and inserting the data that's the problem. We daren't let CenCom even suspect us. We know what they did with the Zeros they considered unsuitable. If GrandMa felt threatened, it wouldn't take much for it to rename us a sub-species and place us outside the protected category. We daren't let that happen.'

'So, what stage are we at now?' Maddie had flown down from her duties in space to be at this meeting.

'Ready. The real problem's working without the knowledge of the new generation. They get even a sniff of our proposal and CenCom will immediately be alerted, simply through their connectivity.'

'Connectivity of everything seemed such a good idea at the time.' Brigitte joined them, Jai in tow. The pair looked good together; her blonde, blue-eyed, smooth pallor a striking contrast to his dark, hirsute bulk.

'Maybe Hawking was right about AI after all. Once a machine becomes more intelligent than its designers, logic takes over and emotion has no relevance. The way GrandMa dealt with those poor Zeros: impeccable logic but no mercy, no understanding of suffering. Entirely based on efficiency.'

Anni took Jai's other hand in hers. They remained lovers, but both occasionally enjoyed different partners. He was currently providing Brigitte consolation after her loss of Buzz, though she insisted she was well shot of the man.

'So, what's still needed?'

They all turned to Amber, appointed project leader.

'We're all primed with our places? Know our individual duties? Disconnection has to be synchronised, and we can't use any form of electronic contact. We have to rely on old-fashioned timepieces. Are we all set to the same time? Has to be to the sec.'

They compared their various chronometers and checked they all read precisely the same time.

'Thanks, Jai. We all used to mock you for making these things. But I guess you had an idea we might need them one day?'

Jai smiled at Maddie but said nothing. He'd enjoyed engineering miniature parts to construct entirely mechanical timepieces. The contrast with his organic work seemed to take him to another place. Had he experienced some prescience? It had all been so long ago, even he couldn't say with any certainty whether that had been a factor at the time.

'Once we start the process, we can't interrupt or divert. It's all or nothing. Everyone clear about their part?'

Each of them repeated the location and action that constituted their individual duty.

'Once CenCom's powered down, we fit the replacement controller with the enhanced coding embedded. Then we switch GrandMa back on and hope it works!'

'How confident are you the new instructions will fully countermand CenCom's own modifications to the Prime Directive?' Tu voiced the question uppermost in all their minds.

Hoshiko spread her palms out, passing a flickering reflection on to each of their faces. 'Our manual calculations suggest we can be 97% certain.'

'But no testing?'

'Any form of testing would inform CenCom, Gabriel. So, no. It's a risk. But we understand risk. And we've long since moved past the stage of whether we should do it. The alternative's an eternity of wondering when CenCom will become our enemy. Because some day, without this modification, GrandMa will find a loophole to allow her to dispose of us.

'We know that now. So, we either consign our future to ultimate failure at the hands of the machines we've made, or we take this risk and insure ourselves against that possibility.'

The Chosen, and original pioneers, together with both newcomers, co-opted to make up the necessary numbers, joined hands in a circle and made the pledge anew.

'Tomorrow, then. 16:30 hours. Everyone must be ready. Focussed.'

They each declared their absolute commitment. Hugs and kisses were shared in token of mutual affection. And they made their separate ways back, arriving individually or in pairs, so CenCom would have no reason to suspect them of what the AI would certainly see as treachery.

The following day would bring lasting security. Or maybe the end of everything they'd known and achieved.

The End

Also by Stuart Aken

Published by Fantastic Books Publishing

Generation Mars: Blood Red Dust
http://myBook.to/BloodRedDust
The Methuselah Strain
http://getBook.at/Methuselah
A Seared Sky – Joinings
http://mybook.to/joinings
A Seared Sky – Partings
http://mybook.to/partings
A Seared Sky – Convergence
http://mybook.to/convergence
Rebirth – Invited contribution to anthology Fusion
http://www.fantasticbooksstore.com/fusion-2500.html
Hybrid Dreams – Invited contribution to anthology Synthesis
http://www.fantasticbooksstore.com/synthesis.html
Ouija – Invited contribution to anthology 666
http://getBook.at/ScaredyPants

About the Author

Stuart Aken found early inspiration for science fiction writing from such luminaries as Arthur C Clarke, Isaac Asimov, John Wyndham, and Ray Bradbury, among many others. Writing about the future of the human race provides him with an opportunity to explore the extraordinary qualities possessed by people and to examine humanity's potential.

When asked why much of the genre is concerned with possible bad futures, he says. 'Science fiction has a tendency to dystopia because most writers, whilst eager to tell a story, understand fiction is an ideal means of warning about mistakes, but is also a medium relying on conflict for appeal.'

Stuart has written in several genres. His science fiction includes the novella, The Methuselah Strain, and the first book in the Generation Mars series, Blood Red Dust. His fantasy trilogy, A Seared Sky, presents an adult alternative world where the fight between evil and good is revealed through a cast of fully developed characters engaged in a quasi-religious quest.

He has also written a romantic thriller, a number of short stories, and an autobiographical medical memoir detailing his journey through ME/CFS. And he has contributed to a number of anthologies, including Fusion, Synthesis and 666.

For more information, and an insight into his working methods, visit his website at http://stuartaken.net/

23067244R00209

Made in the USA
Columbia, SC
07 August 2018